Single All the Way

Also by Elaine Spires

What's Eating Me

'A truly enjoyable read. Entertaining…
at times hilariously funny' *****

'One of the best books I've read this year.' *****

Sweet Lady

'I couldn't put it down.' *****

'Ms Spires is a master of the unexpected.' *****

'Without doubt, one of the best new writers
out there today.' *****

Holiday Reads

'A wonderful, feel-good, summer read.' *****

'Brilliant for dipping into whilst on the beach
or by the pool.' *****

Singles' Holiday

'Real characters that show all our human foibles.' *****

'Brilliant read. She had me at the first page.' *****

Singles and Spice

'Loved the characters. Loved the setting. Loved the
storyline.' *****

'Made me want to ring up the holiday company and book
straight away!' *****

Single All the Way

Elaine Spires

Printed and bound in UK by Publish Point from KnowledgePoint, Reading.
ISBN: 978-0-9928672-1-8
Print Edition
Published by Elaine Spires October 2014
Second Edition 2019

For Paul.

Thanks for the support and faith in my writing you've always shown, little bruv.

Author's Note

Single All the Way is the third book in the Singles' Trilogy. It includes some characters you've already met in the first two books of the series, Singles' Holiday and Singles and Spice, plus one from Holiday Reads. I hope you will enjoy meeting them again as well as some new friends for the first time. Our setting, the village of Tolleshunt D'Arcy is real, but the Golden Goose and the Blue Boar Inn do not exist. I have also taken liberties with the layout and geography of the village and surrounding areas. All the characters are fictitious and any resemblance to any person living or dead is purely co-incidental. Writing this book, about a snowy, Essex Christmas, while I was in the midst of a hot and steamy Caribbean summer was no easy task, but I make no complaints. I am also delighted to announce that Singles' Holiday is now a stage-play. It was first performed at the Brentwood Theatre by Melabeau Productions on 11th October 2014.

I would like to thank Kim Nash, not only for editorial input but for her review and blog-tour organisation and for her continued support. She makes me believe I really am a writer. Thanks also go to Lisa Morena at Vanilla Gecko for turning my vague description into a great cover. And as always to my beautiful daughter Melanie, who supports everything I do unconditionally.

And, of course, to you, my readers, for your continued faith in me and for asking for a third Singles' book. It means so much that you enjoyed the first two.

Elaine

DAY ONE

✦

J ADE FUMBLED WITH the heavy key, cursing as she dropped it and then her handbag with it. Given the weight and size of it she was glad it had missed her foot. As she knelt to pick up her phone, purse, pen and tampon that had spilled onto the carpet hot tears splashed onto her dress and the backs of her hands.

Bollocks!

She stuffed the things back into the black evening bag, bought with such hope and illusion just six days earlier, angry with herself for crying before she'd got into the privacy of her room. She stood up and fought to insert the key in the keyhole. Wiggling and manipulating it she finally heard the dull, metallic click allowing her to push down on the ornate handle, stumble into the room and collapse onto the bed and sob her heart out. She cried for half an hour non-stop, until, exhausted, she hiccoughed, pulled herself to a sitting position and cradled her knees to her chest.

What the fuck am I doing here?

Nothing had been as she'd imagined it would as she'd during her fantasies of the last three weeks when Christmas and Twixmas in Essex had been confirmed. She'd envisaged herself moving around the room at pre-dinner drinks;

flitting from group to group, like a rather splendid Red Admiral in her black and red velvet and lace dress, dropping a witticism here, an insightful observation there, before sitting down to a delicious meal where the conversation would be as sparkling as the Cava. Then, there would be dancing and she would partner all the men in turn, twirling and tripping across the floor, all eyes on the two of them, showing off her newly-acquired skills, learned on a crash course at Wilma and Frank's Dance Studios, Lincoln.

Pre-dinner drinks had been torture. She'd got to the bar early and made a beeline for two men, Vince and Don, who were standing together, pints in hand, only to be frozen out as they talked football. She'd moved onto three women who came in next, who'd introduced themselves as 'The Three Sues: Blonde Sue, Tall Sue and Slim Sue,' and who seemed to be sharing some kind of private joke, which hadn't included her. They'd moved into the foyer to listen to a local women's choir singing carols for a while, but some of the group started grumbling about being hungry and had gone through to the restaurant, rather rudely, Jade had thought. The singers had been left to finish their repertoire alone.

At dinner she found herself with Olivia on her right and John on her left. Frances, who had met Olivia on a Travel Together tennis holiday in Turkey that summer, was sitting on Olivia's right. They were keen to catch up and were talking ten to the dozen about their holiday and someone called Polly who Jade gathered had been the tour manager, and someone else called Umit that one of the women had had a fling with. She thought it had been Olivia, but as she managed to overhear more and more of their conversation, it became obvious that it had been Frances who'd had the fling.

Good God! She was middle-aged!

Turning to her left Jade tried to get into conversation

with John, who was part of a group of four friends that included Vince and Don and another man, Mick. Like a group of little boys they had all insisted on sitting next to each other instead of spreading out which was what usually happened at dinner and would have made it more sociable for everyone. Jade's attempts at conversation fell on deaf ears as all four were already drunk and their language and demeanour had deteriorated rapidly as the meal had gone on.

When the music had finally started, the deejay arriving twenty minutes late, shouting out 'Traffic!' by way of an apology, theThree Sues ran onto the dance-floor dragging Geoff, an accountant from the Wirral whom they knew from a series of Travel Together black-tie balls with them and formed a tight circle, excluding everyone else. Frances and Olivia had stayed at the table talking; two of the women, Kim and Janet, had gone off to bed; the four drunken friends got even drunker and started singing loud, coarse lyrics to the Christmas music the deejay was playing and the others just stood around in the bar making polite conversation. By half past ten she'd had enough and excused herself.

There's no way I can stay here for another four days!

✦   ✦   ✦

BACK IN THE bar Frances had managed to stop Olivia's long maudlin reminiscence about her love rat David, whose infidelity she'd found out about while on the tennis holiday in Turkey. Frances liked Olivia; they'd got on well on that holiday in spite of their age difference and Frances had been pleased when Olivia had said she would join her in Essex for Christmas. But she didn't want to spend the whole Christmas holidays going over old ground. If Olivia was really and truly over David, as she claimed to be, then what was the point in keeping on talking about him? Besides, she'd noticed a cute-looking barman earlier! She giggled to herself; she was getting a real penchant for toy-boys on these Travel Together holidays. Her hand went automatically into her handbag and pulled out her phone for the tenth time in as many minutes. She looked down at it but saw the screen was empty; no missed calls, no texts or messages.

'Am I boring you?' Olivia said, looking at the phone in Frances' hand.

'Not at all! I just don't think you should keep on talking about David all the time. Not if he really is yesterday's man as you claim.'

'I don't mean David, although I'm sorry if I keep going on about him. It's you.'

'Me?'

'Yes. You seem a bit distracted. You keep looking at your phone.'

'Do I?'

'Yes, you do. You keep taking it out of your bag and checking it, as if you're waiting for a call from someone.'

'No! I'm not! I just happened to notice that the signal wasn't that good, earlier, and so I was just having a look to see if it'd come back.'

'Well I've got full signal,' Olivia said, taking her phone out and looking at it.

'Don't let's worry about phones! Come on! Let's be sociable!'

Frances jumped up and went and joined the blonde, friendly Geordie girl with the smiling face at the bar, bringing Olivia up in tow.

'Sorry, I didn't catch your name earlier.'

'Penny. And you're Frances and Olive, aren't you?'

'Olivia,' Olivia corrected her.

'And Dave, Geoff, Pete and Colin and the Three Sues,'

Penny said, pointing at each of the men and then the three women who were sitting in a large semi-circle. Angela had joined the four men at the bar and the five of them were singing carols loudly and off-key.

Frances deliberately pulled a chair up between Dave, who she knew from her holiday in Antigua three years earlier, and Pete, forcing Olivia to sit on the other side of the circle.

I'm doing her a favour, she needs to mix!

Dave emptied his glass and looked round the group.

'Anuvva drink, anyone?'

'I'll get them with you,' Pete said. 'You got the last round in.'

'S'alright. S'only money, innit?' Dave said before taking orders.

'Want a hand?' Frances said, jumping up and following Pete and Dave to the bar, intent on getting a closer look at the barman, whose badge said he was *Beniamin* and whose mannerisms and bearing made her realise, immediately, that if she was to have a Christmas toy-boy, then it wouldn't be him. When they got back to the table the deejay, seeing that it was almost midnight turned up the volume and played Slade's Christmas anthem.

'Ehh, come on!' Penny said, jumping to her feet. 'It's nearly Christmas!'

There was a joint-squeal from the Three Sues as they all stood up and ran behind Penny onto the dance-floor.

'Oh, God, not this! It's like bloody Butlins! I'm off to bed!' Angela said, downing the rest of her drink and striding off.

'Well, if you can't beat 'em...' Pete said, as all the others followed him to shake their best moves.

Only the Four Friends stayed in the bar. They put their arms around each other and started their own drunken, out-of-time, knees-up to the music. And as the clock struck midnight and the bells from the church next-door rang out to announce the arrival of Christmas Day, the Travel, Together group kissed each other or shook hands and said, 'Merry Christmas!'

✦   ✦   ✦

JADE COULD HEAR the music coming up from the bar. Although the Blue Boar Inn was over three hundred years old, its walls were thin. She could hear the group singing but nothing would have persuaded her to go back downstairs. Wallowing in her misery, she thought she had never felt so lost and alone in her life. As her mind ran back over the sad events of the last two months, she laughed at her naivety in thinking that doing a singles' holiday would be the answer. If tonight, which had been a nightmare, was anything to go by she wanted none of it. How people went on them regularly she couldn't begin to imagine. Jade was abruptly brought out of her thoughts by the unexpected beep of her mobile.

> **I'm probably the last person you want to hear from, especially tonight, but I can't sleep for thinking of you and knowing I've made the biggest mistake of my life. I know I don't deserve it but would you talk to me and give me the chance to make it all up to you? I still love you. I know that now. How could I have been such a twat? Please give me a chance. Can I ring you tomorrow? Can I have the best Christmas present ever? PLEASE XXXXXXXXX**

Jade blinked away her tears and read the text over and

over. Mitch wanted her back! He wanted her back! There was no way she was going to wait until the following morning. She dialled his number, overjoyed to hear his somewhat nervous *'Hello!'* after just one ring, and they talked for an hour, after which she threw all her stuff back into her suitcase, left her key on the reception desk, strode outside into the cold night air, put her case in the boot, got into her car and with a huge smile on her face and not even a thought for the Travel Together group, put her foot down hard and roared off into the night.

It was 2am on Christmas Day.

DAY TWO

✦

JUST ONE MORE and then I'll put them away!
Eve's hand hovered over the box of Lindor chocolates. The ones in black wrappers were her favourites because they were dark chocolate, but she'd also developed a real liking for the coconut ones that were in this Christmas limited edition. Her hand swept into the box like a heron into a lake and pulled out two chocolates; one dark, one coconut. Eve grinned.

If in doubt, one of each!

She scolded herself for being worse than a child as she closed the lid on the box and placed it on the far side of the coffee table in the hope that if she couldn't quite get to it then temptation would also be out of reach. She snuggled back down under the duvet and turned the sound on the TV back up as one of her favourite films, *Whistle Down the Wind*, started. It was a film she'd seen at least six times and one she always cried at, especially the bit where the kitten died and today was no exception. Just over two hours and six chocolates later she wiped her eyes and blew her nose loudly as the credits went up. She stretched and threw the duvet off, padded across the carpet in bare feet past the gorgeous-smelling four-foot pine tree that was covered in lights and baubles, to put the kettle on, thinking that there was nothing like a weepy film, especially an old black and white one. As the kettle made its own weird sounds, Eve glanced at the clock.

One o'clock. Time to put the dinner in!

Opening the freezer she pulled out a frozen Christmas dinner for one and turned it over to look at the instructions, which showed that dinner would be served in fourteen and a half minutes including standing time. She popped the meal into the microwave and smiled as she poured herself a diet cola. She was spending Christmas alone for the first time in fourteen years.

Wonderful! Perhaps I should be drinking something stronger than this to celebrate?

She giggled to herself at the thought. Her usual tipple was always a joke among the groups she accompanied as most couldn't understand why someone who had a free bar everywhere she went wouldn't take full advantage of it. Eve never drank; through her job as a tour manager for Travel Together, a singles' tour specialist, she'd seen too many people make idiots of themselves because of it. And not just her Travel Together clients. She thought of her father and his love for the bottle and how unhappy it had made her mother over the years. She surprised herself; her father was someone she rarely thought of now and even in her irregular calls to her mother he was rarely mentioned. She sighed. It was Christmas Day and it hadn't crossed her mind to ring her family. She shrugged and decided to speak to them sometime later and to make up for it she would visit soon, once the charter flights started. And, as it would have been over by then, she could tell them all about the wedding. Perhaps show them some photos. Perhaps even take Michael and Natalie to meet them.

Perhaps not!

The time for telling the story had long passed, although, if Michael wanted to visit Corfu there was nothing she could do to stop him. He'd mentioned it several times over the last two years and she'd always put him off. He wouldn't be put off for ever and she could hardly blame him. He had a right to know about his Greek heritage, she just needed to buck up the courage to take him. She smiled to herself at the thought of a woman in her early fifties having to buck up the courage to introduce her illegitimate son that they'd known nothing about to his grandparents. But she knew for Michael's sake she had to do it while her parents were still alive. Putting all thoughts about Corfu and her family out of her head and clutching her glass, she made her way back to the sofa thinking how happy she was. Christmas Dinner for one; all the chocolates she wanted; pyjamas on all day; watching whatever she wanted on TV; nobody at all to look after or placate or talk to or pick up the pieces for. Christmas Day alone! She had requested Christmas off and after much tutting and eyebrow-raising because it was one of the busiest times of the year, Travel Together had finally agreed. They knew that for fourteen years she had done a sterling job, always going the extra mile and dealing with emergencies and problems with expertise and without fuss. She deserved to have one Christmas off. She was brought out of her thoughts by the ringing of her mobile phone. Seeing who the caller was brought an even bigger grin to her face.

'Merry Christmas, my darling!' she said.

'Merry Christmas, Eve! How are you?' asked her son.

'All the better for hearing your voice. I was just thinking about you, actually. Happy birthday for yesterday! Did you get my voicemail message?'

'Yes, I did! Thank you! And your card and voucher. I was going to ring you back but knew we'd be talking this morning. Hope you don't mind. It all got to be a bit of a blur. We went to the pub for lunch and it turned into a session. There were about fourteen of us in the end. Went for a Chinese about ten and rolled home in the early hours. I missed the midnight service so Mum wasn't really impressed. I had to force myself out of bed this morning to make up for it. Natalie's hung over as well. Anyway, thanks for taking the time to call.'

'That's okay. I thought you were probably out and about when you didn't pick up. And what about today? Are you having a nice time?'

'Great, thank you! It's trying to snow. There are some little flurries but nothing serious. We're drinking ginger beer and sorrel wine while we're waiting for our lunch to be ready. How about you?'

'Well, I've almost eaten my way through a box of chocolates watching an old film and now I'm drinking a diet cola waiting for my lunch to ping.'

'I wish you'd have changed your mind and come and spent it with us. We don't like to think of you being alone.'

'My darling, that was the whole point of not working, so that I could spend it alone. Some me time.' There was a moment's silence. 'Please don't take it wrong, Michael! I'm just a bit burnt out having done almost back to back trips for the last three months and after all we'll all be together for New Year's Eve and then, of course, the wedding.'

'I know. I just don't like the idea of you being on your own on such a special day, though. And neither do Mum and Dad. Or Natalie.'

'How are Alice and Bertram?'

'They're fine and they say 'thank you' for their presents. Oh, hang on, Mum wants to speak to you herself.'

Eve could hear lots of background noise; the Browns obviously had a house-full of people. And then, she heard the quiet, educated voice of Alice, the woman to whom she owed so much; the woman who had adopted Michael shortly after his birth on Christmas Eve thirty-four years ago and who had turned him into such a fine man.

'Merry Christmas, Eve!'

'Merry Christmas, Alice! It sounds like you're having a great time with a house-full of people.'

'Yes, my dear. We are blessed to have Bertram's brother and sister-in-law with us and his younger sister, Matilda and her son Jarred and his girl-friend Loretta, as well as Natalie, of course. And the sorrel wine is flowing!'

'Sounds wonderful! You must save me some. I've had it a couple of times when I did trips to the Caribbean at Christmas time.'

'Of course we will! I'll send some with Michael when he goes down to see you for New Year's Eve. We're sorry you aren't here with us, but I understand and respect your wishes. And thank you very much for our lovely gifts.'

'You're very welcome. And thank you for the hamper. I'm going to pig-out this afternoon and evening watching TV. I've already made great inroads into the chocolates.'

'Well, you have a wonderful day, my dear. We will be thinking of you and you will be in our prayers before the Christmas meal. And we will, of course, all see you at the wedding.'

'I can't wait to meet everyone,' Eve said. Michael's family had hired a coach to being them down to Hertford-shire and back.

'Hold on now, Natalie wants to speak to you. Goodbye, Eve and God bless you!'

'Bye.'

'Happy Christmas, Eve!' Natalie bellowed into Eve's ear. For someone who was hungover she was remarkably noisy. 'Thank you for my present! It's so lovely! Where did you buy it?'

'Bali. I saw it and knew immediately that it would suit you,' Eve said, imagining the delicate silver and gold bracelet around Natalie's slim wrist. 'And thank you for my sweater. The colour's gorgeous.'

'Well, I know you like green and I thought it was a really pretty shade and the cashmere's lovely and soft to touch.'

'I love it. I imagined you'd had more input than Michael in buying it,' Eve chuckled.

'No! He was the one who first spotted it in the shop,' Natalie said, immediately jumping to her beloved's defence. 'But tell me, are you really okay being on your own today? Are you sure you're all right?'

'Perfectly. I couldn't face Christmas with another group. I just want some time to myself.'

'Yes, I can understand that,' said Natalie, who having been on two very eventful singles' holidays herself knew how hard Eve worked and how tiring it must all be. 'I just don't like to think of you sitting eating Christmas dinner on your own,' she added, her voice, wobbling.

'I am fine. Really. And we'll all be together next week for New Year. And you're not with your parents today, are you?'

'No, but we're spending tomorrow with them. As we'll be living much nearer them than Michael's parents it seemed politic to spend Christmas Day here. And besides, they've got each other and my sister and her brood,' she added, smiling as she thought of her sister, Leanne, who had a lively three-year-old, Daisy and *totally-not-planned* twins, Violet and Rose, who had just celebrated their second birthday.

'And I'm sitting here like little Dolly No-Mates!' Eve laughed.

'No! Yes! Oh, well, you know what I mean! Just don't like to think of you on your own, unless you want to be, of course,' she added, laughing herself.

Just then Eve heard the microwave ping announcing that her Christmas meal would be ready after it had stood for two minutes.

'I've got to go, Natalie, because my dinner's ready. I'm having a full roast turkey dinner with all the trimmings but with none of the preparation or washing up after!' she announced.

'Well, you enjoy it, Eve. Merry Christmas! Ring us later! Love you!'

'Love you, too!'

Eve smiled to herself. She did love Natalie but she sometimes found her a little bit exhausting. She was a warm, kind, generous, beautiful girl who didn't suffer fools gladly, always wore her heart on her sleeve and spoke her mind. Eve hadn't been sure about her suitability for Michael at first and had been quite alarmed when Michael had confided in her that he was going to propose to Natalie less than a year after first meeting her on a singles' holiday that Eve had led to Antigua. Her anxiety arose from the fact that Natalie had called off her previous wedding with just a month to go and Eve didn't want her son to be put through the same upset and heartbreak as Natalie's ex. But now she couldn't have been more pleased. It was obvious to everyone who met them that Natalie and Michael were made for each other. His proposal, made on the back of an elephant that went down on one knee when he'd turned up at the Taj Mahal unannounced and unexpected while Natalie had been on a Travel Together holiday with Eve the previous year, had gone viral. And she couldn't wait to see them on New Year's Eve and to witness their marriage on 2nd January. Thinking of the wedding, which brought another big smile to her face, Eve went into the kitchen where the aroma of her ready-made Christmas dinner was rising in a tempting waft from the microwave.

✦   ✦   ✦

HALF AN HOUR later, Eve was back on the sofa, feet up, stomach full. It hadn't been the best Christmas dinner she'd ever eaten, but it certainly hadn't been the worst, either. That accolade went to an airline meal she'd had en route to Australia one year when she'd left Heathrow on Christmas Eve and arrived in Sydney on Boxing Day. Christmas Day had actually disappeared which might have explained why the airline had made no concession to Christmas whatsoever. Her Christmas dinner that year had been a tasteless beef stroganoff and the complaints by her group on arrival in Australia had been endless. Eve had also treated herself to a Christmas pudding but had decided to wait until she had room for it, which would probably be around tea-time. She stretched out on the sofa and hugged herself, she felt so good.

Nobody to take care of but me!

She switched the TV on again and flicked through the channels, seeing that the Queen would be on in twenty minutes or so before the usual blockbuster film. She turned the sound down thinking she'd have a quick power nap. She'd just gone into a surprisingly deep sleep when the phone rang again.

Melv!

Her heart skipped a beat at the sight of his name.

'Merry Christmas, Melv!'

'Merry Christmas, baby. What's up?'

'I'm fine. Here. Just finished eating Christmas dinner. You?'

'Well, just had some breakfast and I'm sitting in my office…'

'In your office? On Christmas Day?'

'Why are you surprised? You've never been in a resort at Christmas?'

'Of course I have, but most general managers delegate so that they can have Christmas Day to themselves.'

'Yes, but you know I'm not most general managers!' Eve loved the deep, growling laugh he gave as he spoke. 'I'll be eating with my kids later on and then they're going to their mom's for the rest of Christmas Day and I'll stay here for a while. We've got a big entertainment's programme on this evening. And besides, in just another few days I'm on vacation.'

'It doesn't seem possible, does it? You'll be here in just a short while and we're going together to our son's wedding? I can't believe it!'

'Well, you'd better believe it, Eve! I'm counting the days.'

'Do the kids… have you told them…?'

'About Michael's wedding?'

'Yes.'

'Yes I have. It's no big deal. I mean, the big deal was telling them about him in the first place, but since they met him this summer, they're cool with it all. Juliet wishes she was coming with me. I have to capture the whole wedding on my iPhone and send it through to her. I think she's been secretly harbouring the wish to be bridesmaid.' He laughed again.

Eve laughed with him, but inside she felt the usual wave of disappointment as she still had to be introduced to Radley and Juliet. When they had asked Melv about Michael's birth mother he'd simply told them that she was a Greek student he had met when he was studying in England. They weren't told that she was also the Travel Together tour manager that visited the Mango Tree Resort several times a year and who they had seen on several occasions but never spoken to.

'So, you missing me?' His question cut into her thoughts.

'Not really,' she teased. 'I'm sitting watching the Queen mime her way through her Christmas Speech, with my belly full and a box of chocolates that are calling me from across the coffee table waiting for James Bond to start.'

'Oh well, I'm certainly no match for James Bond, I'll give you that!' he chuckled. 'But I sure wish I was there with you today.'

'Well, as we said, just a few more days and you will be here.'

'And next year, I promise you on the grave of my mother, may she rest in peace, next year we will spend Christmas together. And every Christmas after that.'

'Well, we'll see,' she said, delighted by his words but damned if she was going to show him. She didn't understand herself sometimes. She'd never considered herself to be someone who played games yet where Melv was concerned it was almost as if she was afraid to let him know just what he meant to her and how much she really did love him.

'So, are you having a white Christmas?'

'Not here in Essex, but Michael said they've had a few flurries in Durham today.'

'I called him yesterday to wish him a happy birthday and he said snow had been forecast. I'm sort of torn between wanting to see snow yet not wanting to be cold!' Melv joked.

They chatted for a couple more minutes, talking about the wedding mostly and their plans for the ten days Melv was going to spend in England until she heard his office phone ringing in the background.

'Hold on, Eve. Hold on, babe, let me get this,' he said. She could hear him on the other line and from his tone it sounded as if something had just spoiled his day. 'Gotta go,

Eve. We've got a problem with a burst pipe in one of the suites. The whole room's under water and the folks aren't too happy about it.'

'Oh dear! Go! Speak to you soon.'

'I'll call you later. Love you.' And he hung up.

Seeing that the Queen had finished Eve turned the sound up in preparation for Daniel Craig. She leant across the coffee table and brought the box of Lindor closer, her hand slipping inside.

Hmm! Mr Craig and Lindor! A heavenly combination.

She was unwrapping her second chocolate and James was falling from a moving train having been taken out by one of his own when her mobile sprang into life.

Hmm, just call me Little Ms Popular!

When she saw the caller ID her hand recoiled as it would from a flame.

No! Please! Not today!

She toyed with the idea of not answering because she knew that if Travel Together's emergency contact number was calling her on Christmas Day it wasn't to wish her the compliments of the Season. Sighing, duty getting the better of her, she reached out and slid the green receiver icon.

'Hi, is that Eve?' It was a voice she didn't recognise. Probably one of the myriad of temps who took the job because they were looking for glamour and excitement in the travel industry and left after four months because they couldn't take any more of the irregular hours, demands of the MD, having to field questions from clients they couldn't answer because they were sitting in an office in London and didn't have a clue about any of the destinations, while trying to exist on minimum wage.

'It's Jamela. From Travel Together,' she added, when Eve didn't immediately know who she was. 'We need you to go to a hotel and take over a group.' There was a moment's silence as Eve waited to hear some more details.

"Is there nobody else?' she finally asked as Jamela seemed to have been struck dumb.

'No. All the tour managers are working except you and besides it's right near you.'

'Near me? We've got a hotel in Horndon?' Eve asked incredulously.

'It says it's near Maldon in the information, that's Essex, isn't it?'

'Yes, but that's not near me! And besides, it's Christmas Day, there are no trains so how am I supposed to get there?'

'Alan said to tell you to drive.'

'Alan?'

'Yes. I phoned him and he said to pass the job to you.'

'Did he now? Well, ring him back and tell him it's Christmas Day and if he wants me to work he'll have to ring and ask me himself!'

Eve hung up absolutely livid. Alan Dryden was the MD that Bill Wickes, the ex-owner of Travel Together and Eve's ex-partner, had brought in three and a half years earlier when he'd decided to take semi-retirement. Eve had disliked Alan from the very start; he was arrogant, sarcastic and unapproachable and the atmosphere within the company had changed from that moment. He held the tour managers in contempt, questioning whether they should even be paid, yet alone allowed to claim expenses as in his eyes, they were on a free holiday. Eve had been surprised that Bill, usually a shrewd businessman and a very good judge of character, had given him the job. Several experienced tour managers had left after crossing swords with him. And now, Alan had had the nerve to tell some office junior to ring her on Christmas Day and order her to go to work. She found herself shaking with anger, and the thought of him prompted her hand to dip into the box of Lindor again. She'd missed a great chunk of the film, too, talking to Jamela, although to be fair, poor girl, she probably hadn't chosen to work today and she definitely wasn't being paid anything like the going overtime rate. Five minutes later Eve's phone rang again.

'Eve! Merry Christmas!' This mellow-Alan was one Eve didn't recognise and one that had obviously been on the fortified wine. 'How are you?'

'I was fine until about five minutes ago when I was ordered to interrupt my Christmas Day and go to a hotel somewhere in Essex.'

'Well, you see, we had a tour manager who was doing her first job for us. Never done the job before and, well, it wasn't what she expected, I don't think. Anyway, to cut a long story short, she walked out leaving everyone high and dry. The hotel manager phoned our emergency number when nobody had seen her all morning and then after the chambermaid went into her room it became obvious she'd gone.'

'And what was it exactly that made her walk out? Are they the group from hell? Is the hotel absolute rubbish?'

'Well, I don't know. We haven't been able to contact her. Her phone's switched off. But I tell you this, she won't be working for Travel Together ever again!'

'Well, if she's walked out, she probably has no intention of working for you ever again!' Eve shook her head as he spectacularly missed the point.

'So you see, we've got a bit of a dilemma now: a group on holiday in Essex until 28th with no tour manager.'

We?

Eve decided she had nothing to say. She wasn't going to jump in and make it easier for him, so she rode the silence, imagining his round face, made even redder than usual by the drink, with its small, beady eyes and shaved head, probably perspiring.

'You still there, Eve?' Alan asked after a few seconds.

'I'm still here.'

'So, what do you say?'

'To what?'

'Well, you know…will you go and finish the job? I mean, it's only three more days,' he added quickly. 'A really short trip. It'll be over in no time. Not like the trips you're used to doing.' Eve was quiet again so he ploughed on, changing tactics. 'And there really is nobody else, Eve. All our tour managers are working except you.'

'What about someone from the office? Mandy? Or Andrea? They're both usually quite keen to jump on the tour managers' band wagon, aren't they?'

Mandy was the Customer Services Manager and Andrea Head of Marketing and it always annoyed Eve when they pulled rank and put themselves on one of the better trips a couple of times a year with the excuse that they needed to know the product. Why didn't they ever offer to work at Christmas? Or go on a trip that wasn't long-haul or exotic?

'Mandy's in her place in Tenerife and I can't get hold of Andrea. I have tried but she's not answering.'

Yes, I'll bet you have!

Alan and Andrea's affair was common knowledge within the company; common knowledge and one of life's little mysteries. Eve had often thought that if Andrea, thirty-nine, matronly and single, wanted regular sex then there had to be other men or even other ways, surely?

'You could always do it yourself,' she said, knowing she was playing Devil's Advocate.

'Well, I would, of course I would, but there's no trains and I've been drinking so I can't drive myself and of course, this being Christmas Day, there are no taxis to be had and even if there were it would cost the company a fortune to get me to Essex because I'm at the in-laws in Gloucestershire.'

Eve could have kicked herself for being known throughout the whole of Travel Together as the tour-manager-who-didn't-drink, because she would have had no qualms about saying she'd been drinking, too, and was, therefore, unable to drive either.

'It's right near you. It's Essex.'

'It's not right near me! It's bloody miles away, not round the corner. And besides, it doesn't matter where it is. I specifically asked not to work over Christmas. Today is Christmas Day and I'm not happy you'd just assume that I can drop everything and race to pick up the pieces dropped by someone who should probably never have been given the job in the first place.'

Alan chose to ignore her comment. He'd ruffled a lot of feathers with his policy of employing attractive thirty-something females with no experience of the job and very little common sense, erroneously thinking that clients wanted a tour manager who looked the part; whatever that was. Unsurprisingly, the turn-over of tour managers at Travel Together was high.

'What? Are you with people then?' Alan sounded surprised. He knew that Eve was divorced and, being ignorant of the existence of Michael, childless with her family at the other side of Europe in Corfu. It really wound Eve up that he automatically assumed she was friendless, too.

'I have a house-full of friends,' she lied as her eyes watched the action on the TV screen, angry that she was missing the film. 'We're just about to sit down to our meal.'

'Well, could you get there late tonight?'

Eve said nothing, determined not to make it any easier for him.

'Or tomorrow? Even early tomorrow morning would do…'

'Possibly. But so could you. Your alcohol level will have come back down again by then, won't it?'

'But if I left the in-laws and crossed the country to go to work on Boxing Day, Sandra would divorce me. You don't know what she's like. She could make things…difficult.'

Eve could feel herself weakening and not because she didn't want Alan to get into trouble with Sandra. On the contrary; she'd met Sandra twice and had quite liked her. But Eve was basically a good person and an excellent tour manager. She knew that in the age of the camera phone, the internet and social media that the whole world could know in no-time that the Travel Together tour manager had walked out; abandoning her group and leaving them on their own. At Christmas. Okay, it was in Essex not Outer-Mongolia, and most could probably get themselves along the A12 and up or down the M11 or round the M25 and back home but she felt uneasy, almost guilty. And she was annoyed with herself for letting slimy Alan Dryden get round her. Down the distance of the phone line he could sense her weakening.

'I'll make sure you're paid double-time,' he said.

'Tour managers always get paid double-time at Christmas,' Eve reminded him. 'It's the one perk you haven't got round to ending,'

'Triple-time, then!' he blurted out. 'Triple time and from now on I'll let the tour manager's department know that you get first pick of every single job. How does that sound?'

'Alan, I've been with Travel Together for fifteen years which makes me the longest-serving tour manager, so I practically get the pick of the jobs anyway. Unless Mandy or Andrea are muscling in,' she couldn't resist adding.

'Well, double-time for your next three trips as well! How about that?' Alan could hardly believe his own generosity. 'I'll get Jamela to email you the client list and tour details and then she can let the hotel know to expect you first thing in the morning. What do you say? Eh? Say *yes* and you can get back to your guests,' he said, laughing and suddenly full of bonhomie.

'Okay,' Eve heard herself say. She sighed and loathed herself for saying it.

✦   ✦   ✦

HALF AN HOUR later Eve was studying the paperwork for Christmas and Twixmas in Essex. James Bond had been abandoned, unfortunately. She'd just have to watch him on Catch-Up another time. She was extremely relieved to see that the trip ended after breakfast on 28th. That would give her a day before Melv arrived and more than two full days to prepare for New Year's Eve. But before then there were two walks, two quizzes, a formal dinner-dance and a disco to get through.

Bugger! Boots and a posh frock.

No chance of just taking a hold-all then. Her eyes scanned the client list, her lips smiling as she saw a couple of familiar names.

JOHN BAXTER	41	
JANET BENTON	64	
DONALD BRIGGS	37	
ANGELA CARLSON	44	vegetarian
FRANCES DAWSON	54	
SUSAN ELLIS	45	
OLIVIA FISHER	32	
SUSAN GIBBS	49	
MICHAEL HANRAHAN	42	
KIM MICHAELS	50	
VINCENT MIDDLETON	40	

Eve realised she needed to let the group and the hotel know when she would be arriving. She thought the phone was going to ring out when it was suddenly answered by a young woman with a faint foreign accent, who sounded very out of breath.

'Merry Christmas and thank you for calling the Blue Boar Inn and Hotel. Tania speaking. How may I help you?'

'Good evening. My name's Eve Mitchell and I'm the tour manager that's going to be joining the Travel Together group first thing tomorrow morning.'

'Ah, yes! We were hoping someone would come to replace Jade. The group members have been asking for you.'

'Is it possible to speak to someone in the group, please?' Eve thought it best to speak in person rather than send a message through the receptionist.

'They are in the bar and they are quite…er…happy,' Tania said.

'Well, there must be someone that's sober, isn't there?' Eve sincerely hoped that the whole seventeen weren't off their faces.

'I will go and see. Please hold the line,' Tania said and Eve heard her place the receiver down followed by her heels clacking across antique-wood flooring to a distant cacophony of music and voices. Three minutes passed until Eve's ear was assaulted by the grating sound of the receiver being snatched up and a loud, lively Geordie accent.

'Hello?'

'Hello. Who am I speaking to, please?'

'My name's Penny. Penny Pomphrett.'

'Hi, Penny. This is Eve Mitchell speaking, from Travel Together. I'm going to be joining the group first thing tomorrow morning as the tour manager.'

'Ehh! We'll be glad to see you. We've been wondering who's going to be looking after us since Jade disappeared like. She seemed a nice girl but she didn't have much idea and got herself into a state at dinner last night when the lads wanted to sit together like, but we never expected her to walk out on us!' Penny laughed and Eve joined in, pleased to hear that at least one person in the group was taking it all right.

'Well, we're really sorry about that, Penny. I've just spoken to our Managing Director who's asked me to apologise on the company's behalf. Behaviour like that is totally unacceptable and not something we would have expected from a Travel Together tour manager.'

'Things happen, pet. She was young and it was her first job so she said.'

Eve blanched on hearing that. *Never admit you've had no experience* was the First Rule of Tour Managers. You were supposed to be there to make the clients feel safe and secure and you couldn't do that by telling them you didn't have a clue. Unfortunately, she wasn't surprised. Perhaps Jade had thought she was going to a four-night Christmas party to enjoy herself.

'Well, could you let everyone know that I'll meet you all at breakfast in the morning. I'll be waiting for you all in the dining-room from 8 o'clock and we've got our walk starting at ten-thirty sharp.'

'Ehh, well, I hope they'll all be ready for that; they're putting them away this afternoon!'

'And rightly so! It's Christmas!' Eve said with a cheer

she wasn't feeling. 'How was Christmas lunch?' she asked, bracing herself for a complaint.

'It was fine. Far too much. There was about eight or nine other tables. Local people, like. But they've left now. We're the only ones staying in the hotel, although there's more booked in for tomorrow's lunch and the black-tie ball on the last night so the manager's been telling us.'

'Oh, that's good. What are you doing this afternoon and this evening?'

"Ehh, well, there was supposed to be board games after lunch and the hotel staff have brought Trivial Pursuits, Monopoly and Cluedo into the lounge. A couple of us are going to play once James Bond's finished. Three have gone out for a walk and like I say five or six are already the worse for wear.'

'And tonight? It's buffet supper, isn't it?' Eve grimaced.

'Yes, a buffet supper at seven followed by dancing in the bar to some CDs or TV or more games.'

At least something's organised!

Eve gave a sigh of relief. She was pleased the hotel staff seemed on the ball enough to carry on with the programme.

'Well, thanks for your help, Penny. Please give our apologies to everyone and I'll see you tomorrow.'

'See you then!' Penny said and hung up.

Eve hung up, too, and in spite of Penny's pleasant tone and reassurances, she couldn't help feeling her stomach sink. She laid her mobile on the coffee table and her hand automatically went into the box of Lindor and came out with the last one. Eve's fingers frantically swept through the box in the vain hope there might be another ten chocolates hiding in it. Disappointed that there weren't, she sighed. She thought she'd better go and pack her case before she lost the willingness to do so completely. Chomping on the last chocolate, she stood up and made her way across the room to the stairs trying to remember where her walking boots were.

Merry Christmas, Eve!

✦   ✦   ✦

PENNY MADE HER way from the reception area along the corridor and back into the bar and lounge area of the Blue Boar Inn. The Four Friends, as she and everyone else now thought of Vince, Mick, Don and John, had started doing shots and getting louder by the gulp and had been joined again by Angela. Penny always tried not to judge people on first appearances, but she'd disliked Angela from the moment they'd pulled up next to each other in the Blue Boar's car park yesterday afternoon, Penny in her five-year-old Peugeot 206 and Angela in her six-month-old Mercedes E-Class Cabriolet, spraying water from the heavy rain as she skidded to a halt. Not that she was jealous of the car, mind. There was just something in the way Angela had almost sneered at Penny who'd smiled and introduced herself as they both pulled cases from the boot of their cars.

'That was the new tour manager on the phone.' She raised her voice so that those watching the TV or chatting and the group in the bar could hear her. 'She sends her apologies on behalf of Travel Together and says she'll be here by eight in the morning to meet us all for breakfast and then she'll be coming on the walk with us at half ten.'

'Tell her to bugger off! We don't need looking after!' one of the Four Friends called out. Penny was unsure if it was Vince or Don as they both had dark hair that was going grey and she got them confused. Mick had red hair and a big beard, so there was no confusing him and John was bald. He also had Angela sitting on his lap and he was holding onto his drink with one hand and massaging her thigh with the other.

'Yes, we're not fucking kids!' Mick added, before burping very loudly. 'And I'm probably not going on the walk and she can't make me. I'm not here for the exercise.'

'Ehh! Well don't shoot the messenger,' Penny, annoyed at their attitude. 'I'm only telling you what she said.'

''Course you are, love. 'Ere, come and 'ave another glass of champagne.' Dave, another bald man, but a nice, friendly Londoner, that Penny liked for the way he tried to talk to everyone and include them, topped up her glass as she sat back in her place next to him on a deep, crimson, velvet sofa.

'Cheers!'

'Cheers! Anyone else for a top-up?' Dave asked, looking round. 'After all, Travel Togevva's paying.' The duty-manager had told the group that the company had invited them all to a bottle of champagne each as a goodwill gesture after Jade had walked out. Seventeen bottles had duly been put behind the bar for them.

'Me, please!' Frances waved her glass towards Dave, who got up and filled it, along with Olivia's and Colin's and then he went over to the Three Sues and Geoff, who were at a table playing cards in the far corner.

'There you go!' he said, smiling as he filled the glasses.

'Thank you!' the Three Sues chorused back at him.

'Do you remember the Dolly Sisters?' he lowered his voice to ask Frances, before he sat down again.

'Oh, Christ, yes! Always dressed the same. Did line-dancing.'

'One got pissed and fell over. Walked around wiv a plaster on 'er 'ooter for a few days. That was the only way we could tell 'em apart!'

'What were they called? Both their names began with D. Was it Dawn and Diane?'

'Nah. Dawn and Donna, weren't it?'

'You're right! It was!'

'Well, I fink we've got the triplet version over there,' he said, nodding his head towards the card table, where the Three Sues sat playing rummy, each wearing black slacks and red Christmas sweaters. Frances burst out laughing.

'I wonder what became of them.' she said as Dave took his seat again next to Penny. 'They were two teachers who were on our holiday in Antigua,' Frances explained to Olivia. 'They behaved like two thirteen-year-olds. Both dressed exactly the same. Honestly! If one had a pink checked bikini, the other one had a pink striped bikini. If one was wearing a light-blue t-shirt, the other one was wearing a sky-blue t-shirt. They liked all the same things, finished each other's sentences… I mean, there was no harm in them, they were quite nice really, but a bit strange and hard going.'

'Remember when they 'ad their 'air braided?' Dave called across to Frances. 'They looked like two bleeding blonde tarantulas!' He laughed loudly at his own observation, only to be drowned out by shouts from the Four Friends and a shrill scream from Angela who was now sitting on Mick's lap with her skirt revealing firm thighs and only just hiding her knickers. Frances caught Penny's eye and they both raised their eyebrows just as the big double-doors creaked open and Kim, Janet and Pete came back in from their walk; faces glowing and an air of cold about them.

'That bleedin' door's enough to give you the creeps,' Dave said.

'It adds atmosphere,' Frances said.

'Like something out of 'orror film. Friller or something.'

'Ehh, you look frozen,' Penny said to the newcomers.

'Not really,' Kim replied, taking off her coat and scarf and shaking her hair into some semblance of style. 'It's chilly, but it's perfect weather for a Christmas walk. As long as you avoid the puddles!'

'Yes, I feel as if I've walked off some of that pudding,' Janet said, smiling and crossing to sit in the armchair on the other side of Penny, near the huge log-fire that was burning in the grate. Penny liked the look of Janet, who'd told her over breakfast that she was a retired midwife. She had gorgeous shiny black hair in a short bob and dark, smiling eyes and Penny had taken to her warmth and charm.

'Well now I feel guilty, like. Perhaps I should have gone with you,' Penny said, not very convincingly.

'What can I get you, ladies?' Pete asked in his quiet, lyrical Ulster accent.

'There's free champagne compliments of Travel Togevva,' Dave told him.

'Is there now?'

'Yes. And our new tour manager will be here in the morning for breakfast,' Penny added. 'She phoned while you were out. Sounds nice.'

'Actually, I was thinking more along the lines of a hot chocolate with a brandy in it,' Kim said.

'And a Bailey's for me, please,' Janet said, smiling again and rubbing her hands together.

'Well, I think I'll join you in the chocolate and brandy, Kim,' Peter said going through to the bar, where Milos, the solitary barman who'd drawn the short-straw and had to work on Christmas Day, jumped to attention, pleased to have someone who wasn't drunk to serve.

'Sorry! Have we interrupted the film for you?' Kim said, nodding at the enormous wall-mounted TV set.

'Not really,' Penny said. 'We've been chatting in between watching it. And as you can see, Colin's really engrossed in it,' she said laughing as she pointed at Colin who was now snoring loudly, paper hat down over his forehead, oblivious to the laughs of the others.

✦   ✦   ✦

FRANCES WAS HAVING a ten-minute lie-down before getting into one of her Christmas dresses. She'd had her shower and put her make-up on and just wanted a little time to herself before going back down. She picked up her phone that was on the bedside table and checked it again; no missed calls, no texts or messages. She sighed with frustration and disappointment as she put the phone back down. She couldn't believe he'd carry out his threat of having nothing more to do with her. She couldn't even put his silence down to not knowing she wasn't at home for Christmas because she'd told him she was going away. And besides, he nearly always called her on her mobile. Her mind wandered back to their last conversation, just over a week ago and her stomach churned. It had all started off so well; she was at a loss really as to what she'd said that had upset him so. She thought about ringing him again, but her previous call, on Christmas Eve, just before she'd left home had been rejected. She couldn't face the awfulness of being rejected again, and there was no reason to think he'd accept her call today if he hadn't two days earlier.

Oh, fuckety, fuckety fuck!

There was little she could do. Well, other than wait for him to calm down and make the first move or try to call him again.

Perhaps I'll get Christmas and New Year over with first. It's all too emotional.

She couldn't really believe that he'd go through to New year without calling her. She thrust her hand into her toiletries bag and brought out a couple of indigestion tablets. Her stomach felt a bit queasy; it was always the first place she felt nerves or any upset. Chewing on the tablets she checked the phone one more time.

Stop it!

She shook her head and counted to three and leapt up from the bed. There was nothing for it but to have a bloody good Christmas drink and try and forget this horrible situation at least for Christmas Night.

✦   ✦   ✦

THE ATMOSPHERE AT the buffet supper was more relaxed than it had been at dinner the previous evening. The twelve group members helped themselves to a delicious spread, which consisted not only of cold turkey, beef and ham, but a wide selection of seafood, dips, pasta and potato salads, a variety of savoury tartlets, several types of sausages, samosas and spring rolls, Spanish omelette, a dozen or so different cheeses, and a naughty-but-nice dessert trolley, which offered Christmas pudding, chocolate mousse, winter-spice cheesecake, chocolate eclairs, Christmas cake and fresh-fruit salad.

'I never thought I 'ad enough room for any more food,' Dave said to Kim as they both piled food onto their plates.

'Neither did I! I was very pleasantly surprised by how good Christmas dinner was. And this looks fabulous, doesn't it?' she said. 'I never used to be very adventurous with food, but I'm glad I am now!'

'You tuck in, girl! It's Christmas!'

'It was my trip to India that made me start eating things I'd never even thought of trying before. And to my surprise, I found most of them delicious!'

'Well, that's travel for ya! They say it broadens the mind, don't it?'

'Ehh! I want to make sure I've left enough room for

pudding,' Penny said as she made her way back to the table. 'It's be a shame not to have a bit of everything on that sweet trolley. Can I sit next to you?' she asked Colin, who blushed and nodded his head without saying a word. Penny had noticed that he hadn't spoken much at all.

Perhaps he likes to just observe.

The Three Sues sat to the other side of Colin, with Slim Sue next to him. She had very little food on her plate; just some cold meat, a tomato and some leaves. Penny couldn't help looking.

Ehh! Imagine only eating that when there's a real banquet available!

Geoff sat at the head of the table, chatting to Blonde Sue, who was on his right; Janet was on his left, next to Dave, then Kim, then Pete, then Olivia with Frances taking the head seat next to Penny. Geoff and the Three Sues only really spoke to each other, which left Dave to chat to Kim, Pete to Olivia and Frances to Penny and Colin.

'Have you been on any Travel Together trips before, Penny?' Frances asked her.

'I have. I went to Paxos in July. I had such a good time. I was a bit wary, you know, about going on a singles' holiday; I thought it might not be for me, but my mate Mary who I usually go on holiday with met a lad and they made plans, so it was go on my own or not have a holiday at all!'

'I think we all felt like that the first time. I know I did. I went to Antigua and then this summer I went to Turkey. That was a tennis holiday, all a bit intense! How about you, Colin? Is it your first time?'

''Er, no, no. I usually go away every Christmas with Travel Together.'

Both women swivelled round and looked at him, neither having imagined he'd be anything other than a singles' holiday virgin.

'Do you not have any family?' Penny asked, a wave of sympathy for Colin engulfing her.

'Yes, I've got two sisters and a brother. But I prefer to spend time away from them. I don't mean that to sound awful, but we run a business, a family business and so I work with them all year round. And Christmas with the family can be quite stressful in my experience.'

'I know what you mean, pet. I wasn't upset when our Philip announced he was taking his wife and two kids to Florida, to Disneyland and our Jimmy said he'd booked to go to a chalet in the French Alps with a group of friends. I'd just wished I could have afforded it to go somewhere exotic, but I've just had a new kitchen and bathroom fitted.'

'We all seem to revert to childhood when we get together,' Colin observed. 'And I've no wish to get caught up in family politics, so about eleven or twelve years ago I booked my first Travel Together Christmas. To Edinburgh it was. And I've been doing the same ever since.'

'Always in this country? Do you never want to go abroad, like?'

'Yes, always in Britain. I can't take too much time and usually four or five nights is break enough for me.'

'Well, we don't need a tour manager coming tomorrow, do we? You must know more than any of them, Colin, with all the experience you've got,' Penny teased him.

''Erm, well, I'm not sure about that,' he said, colouring.

'What sort of business do you run?' Frances asked, putting down her fork to give her stomach some respite. The indigestion tablets had done their job but she didn't want to push her luck.

'It's a garden centre. Oh, just a smallish one. But the pre-Christmas season is very busy for us with trees and lights and decorations…'

'And mistletoe!' Penny said, laughing and digging him in

the ribs. He went scarlet.

"Er, yes. Mistletoe, of course, and holly and ivy and poinsettias. We close at lunchtime on 23rd December and by six o'clock, the centre is stripped clear of Christmas stock all ready for the staff to come in and restock on 30th and 31st December, ready for re-opening on 2nd January.' He sounded pleased with himself as he explained it all to the two women, losing his initial shyness as he warmed to his subject.

At the other end and side of the table Dave and Kim discussed music. Dave was impressed to hear that Kim was a music teacher and played the violin and the piano.

'I wish I was musical. I can't sing at all,' Dave said. 'I bet you're right good, ain't ya?'

'I can hold a tune, but I'm not a singer,' she said.

'Well, you can give us a turn it there's karaoke any night, can't ya?'

'I don't think so!' Kim laughed. 'I love music but I'm not a natural performer.'

'You could always give us a tune on the old Joanna then. I used to play a bit when I was younger. Used to fancy myself as the next Elton John. Except I'm straight, of course! What's your party piece?'

'I haven't got a party piece, I really only play for myself.'

'So, what do you play then? For yourself?'

'Usually Chopin. I love the Nocturnes. Opus Nine Number Two, of course, probably his most famous. But I'm particularly fond of Number Twenty in C-Sharp Minor, there's such an air of pathos and sadness about it. And I like his Prelude Number Four, too. How about you?'

'I'm more of a Chopsticks man myself!' Dave said as they both burst out laughing. 'Can't you play any Loofah?'

'Loofah? What kind of music do they play?' Frances called from the end of the table, repeating a question she'd put to him when they'd first met at the Mango Tree Resort.

'Ha! Ha! Ha!' Dave roared with laughter. ''Cos I ain't posh, she fought I was saying Loofah and they was a group, instead of Loofah. You know, Loofah Vandross,' he quickly explained when Kim also seemed a bit lost as to who Loofah might be. She and Frances laughed along with him.

'I loved that man. So tragic when he died,' Janet said, shaking her head at the thought as she popped a spicy prawn into her mouth.

'It was a sad day for the world,' Dave agreed. 'Nice to meet a fellow fan.'

'Oh, yes. There was something about him. And George Benson, Aretha Franklin, Randy Crawford and Teddy Prendergast, people like that are my favourites,' she added.

'Well, I take me 'at off to you, Janet! You've got good taste, girl! And what brings you to Essex for Christmas?'

'I like to get away. I have no close family, just a nephew who lives in Manchester and I never want him to feel obliged to have to invite me. I wanted to go to Trinidad but the flights were far too expensive because of the time of year so I'm going later in the year and I decided to book a short Christmas break in this country. You?'

'Much the same as you, really. I wanted to go abroad but couldn't get nuffink for the dates I wanted. I'm going to a wedding on January 2nd and so I thought I'd just book a short break.'

'Oh, who's getting married?' Kim asked.

'A couple I met on a Travel Togevva 'oliday. The one Frances and me was on togevva. She's going an' all. Nice couple, Michael and Natalie.'

'I know them!' Kim said, excitedly. 'I was on the trip to India with Natalie when Michael turned up and proposed! He did it on an elephant. Got the animal to go down on one knee. Oh, it was lovely. Right outside the Taj Mahal. Ever so romantic.'

'Small world, innit?' Dave said and the two women nodded in agreement.

Pete was talking about Northern Ireland with Olivia, who had just booked to go on a short-break with her sister at Easter.

'We're flying into Belfast and spending two days sight-seeing and then we're going to take a car,' Olivia explained.

'You'll be going north to the Giant's Causeway, I imagine?'

'Yes. We've been told there's a lot to see.'

'There's a list the length of your arm. Especially in County Antrim. Be sure you visit the Old Bushmills distillery. And Ballymena, of course, the first home of Saint Patrick in Ireland.'

'Where exactly do you live?'

'I live in Belfast, in a place called Andersontown, which was quite well-know for all the wrong reasons during the 70s and 80s.'

'The Troubles?' Olivia looked at him as if he'd just announced he lived on Mars.

'Indeed. But it's as good a place as any and it's what I'm used to, although I've been promising myself to move out now I've retired.'

Olivia looked at him surprised. With his piecing blue eyes and ready smile, his broad shoulders and his dark hair that had only just a touch of grey, she couldn't believe he was retired.

'What did you do? Before you retired?' she asked him.

'I was a fire-fighter.'

'Oh!' Olivia smiled. 'There's something about a fire-man!' she said.

'So I've heard say!' Pete said, modestly.

'And why did you come here for Christmas? Did you

want to get away from your family?

'Not exactly. It's the first Christmas without my wife.'

'Oh, Pete! I'm so sorry! I shouldn't have asked...'

'You're fine! How could you know? It's normal that people are going to ask each other why they're on a singles' Christmas break, so they are. I have two daughters but I just thought I'd rather be with people I don't know. Being all together we'd just notice her absence even more.'

Olivia nodded, taking in what he'd said. Before she could reply they were interrupted by Milos, who had been joined by Beniamin, topping up their glasses of wine.

'As soon as you have finished eating we will put on music for you,' Milos announced. 'Everybody must dancing! Because it is Christmas!' he added, smiling.

'I'll dance with you!' Frances heard a voice say and then realise it had been her. He looked at her with dark eyes, his hair flopping forward over them and smiled.

'It will be my pleasure,' he said.

There was a sudden burst of noise as Angela and three of the Four Friends stumbled into the restaurant.

'Where are we supposed to sit?' Angela shouted and slurred at Milos.

'You may sit at this table, madam,' he said, indicating a round table set for six next to the table the rest of the group were sitting at.

'Bring us some wine!' Mick said to Milos as he sat down, farting loudly as he did so, sending Don and Vince into loud laughter.

'Excuse my pig, he's a mate!' Vince shouted over to the others, not understanding why they weren't all falling about with laughter.

'Ignore them! They wouldn't know a good time if it bit them on the arse,' Angela said, standing up and going over to the buffet table. She came back a few minutes later, holding a plate of food at a precarious angle.

'When did you say the rep was getting here?' she asked Penny, butting straight into her conversation with Colin and Frances.

'Tomorrow morning.'

'Well, she'll hear a few things from me when she gets here! This place is the pits. The food's diabolical; disgusting.'

'We were all just saying how much we are enjoying it,' Frances said, giving her a sweet smile.

'Well, I don't know what you're used to eating, but this is muck! Muck! I'm a vegetarian! There's nothing for vegetarians!'

'Actually, I'm used to eating good-quality, nutritious food. In case you're interested, I always have. And I saw more than enough choice there for vegetarians. There's a whole section taking up half the table clearly marked, *Vegetarian*. Perhaps if you weren't so pissed you'd have seen it.' Frances smiled even more sweetly, to take the sting out of her words. The whole table held its breath; several of them were battling to hold in their laughter, while one or two looked somewhat alarmed at what might kick off. But Angela, somewhat taken aback by Frances' retort just tottered back to join the three men, muttering under her breath.

'Where's John?' Mick asked, pushing his chair back and standing up just as Beniamin leaned forward to pour his wine. Mick's shoulder collided with the bottle, knocking it from Beniamin's hand.

'Oi! Lookout!' he shouted, looking at the sleeve of his pale blue shirt where a dark red stain was snaking its way down his arm. 'That won't fucking come out!'

'I am so sorry, sir. I was not expecting you to stand up so suddenly.'

'Fucking foreign poofta!'

'I think you need to calm down a little bit,' Pete said, standing up and addressing Mick. 'It was as much your fault as his and there's no need for that kind of language.'

'What's it to you? You a poofta, too?'

'What I am is neither here nor there. I'd just ask you to quieten down and moderate your tone and attitude a bit. It's Christmas Day and we're all here to enjoy it in our own way.'

'I'm not fucking listening to this!' Mick marched to the double doors just as John was making his way in.

'Something's give me the right runs,' he said to Mick, who pushed right past him and through the doorway. 'Oi! What's up with him?' he asked the others as he walked over to their table.

'The stupid waiter just spilled wine all over him,' Angela said, knocking her own glass over. 'Oops!'

'I've got the right shits,' John said. 'Don't think I want any tea.'

'Oi! Do you mind? We're eatin' an' we don't want to 'ear nothing about you and the runs, mate!' Dave called across to him.

'Sorry, mate! No offence!' John said, before clutching his belly and running from the room just as Milos put a Christmas compilation CD into the deck and Mariah Carey's *All I Want For Christmas* started belting out. On the table of twelve, everyone looked at each other and smiled.

'Let's dance!' Frances said, standing up and waving her hands as the others and grabbing Milos, who just happened to be walking by.

✦　✦　✦

EVE WAS LANGUISHING in the bath. She'd googled the Blue Boar Inn, which, she had to admit, did look rather nice. It was a sixteenth century coaching inn that had undergone serious refurbishment several times and boasted that it was now 'restored to its original glory'. Although it had just thirty-three rooms it also had a ballroom and 'atmospheric' bar and lounge area and the dining-room was situated where the stables had once been. She looked at the map and worked out it would probably take her about an hour to get there; A128, A12, and then onto a B road she couldn't remember the number of. There shouldn't be much traffic that early on Boxing Day. The paperwork had shown that a local guide would be accompanying them on both walks; the quiz questions had been provided as had the list of twenty-three people who would be joining them for the black-tie ball, fifteen of whom would be staying the night at the Blue Boar Inn, four would be in a guest house half a mile away and four had no accommodation booked. She assumed they must live close by. It seemed strange to be doing a trip within the UK; she hadn't done one of those since a ballroom-dancing weekend in Wigan thirteen years earlier, and that had only been to help out. She much preferred her usual long-haul trips. It would be nice to see Frances and Dave again, although she had been expecting to see them at Michael's wedding as he and Natalie had invited several people from the Antigua holiday to come along and celebrate their marriage with them. She remembered Kim Michaels, too, from the Golden Triangle trip the previous year, when Michael had turned up quite unexpectedly and proposed to Natalie. She remembered a quiet, mousey woman, who had been suffering awfully from symptoms of the menopause during their trip. She shuddered as she suddenly felt the water turn cold. She wrapped her big toe around the plug chain and pulled it loose before standing up and enveloping herself in a thick bath sheet. The aromatherapy oils had done their job; she felt relaxed and ready for bed. Tonight she wouldn't even think about the Blue Boar Inn and the group that awaited her in Tolleshunt D'Arcy. She set her alarm clock for five-thirty and sank into bed. Her initial anger at Alan had subsided; she didn't even feel all that grieved about it really. Once she was there she'd do her best to give the group a good time and with things like the walks and quizzes the time would probably pass very quickly. And she firmly believed that if you did good turns, you got paid back in kind. And, after all, in three short days, what could possibly go wrong?

How much trouble can three days be?

DAY THREE

✦

FRANCES WAS BROUGHT up from the depths of a dream where she was a child wandering through Santa's Grotto but not liking anything she saw. Her mother, dressed in a bright red coat and hat identical to the one Frances was wearing was getting cross with her and was pulling her arm.

'Frances! Frances!' Her mother's voice was deep with a foreign accent.

She opened her eyes to find herself staring into Milos's dark ones, just inches from her face. Mindful of the amount of alcohol she'd downed the previous evening, she put her hand over her mouth and pulled back from him.

'I must to go and help in kitchen now. And nobody must to know I am here with you through the night or I will be sacked,' he said, kissing her nose and running his hand over her breasts, down her belly and giving her pubic hair a tug, before pushing the duvet away and leaping from the bed.

Frances had felt a jolt as he'd touched her. Like the other young lovers she'd taken in the last three years, Milos hadn't flinched from her scarred left breast. He'd stroked it, asked if it hurt her and when she replied that it didn't, he'd kissed it tenderly. Frances felt another jolt at the memory of the previous night and then another as she watched him come out of the bathroom and slip his slim, muscular body into his clothes. She didn't really know how they'd ended up here together, it had just sort of happened. He and Beniamin had joined in the dancing with the group, admittedly she'd thrown herself at him a bit and had danced with him more than anyone, and then as the music ended and everyone drank up and said their *'Goodnights'*, he'd come to collect her glass and had leaned towards her.

'You are in room six, no?'

'Yes.'

'Leave door unlocked. I come in fifteen minutes.'

And she had and so had he. She'd closed the door but hadn't turned the key. She'd gone through to the bathroom and had a shower and put on her sexy lace nighty, a Christmas present from her boss, Carolyn, a divorce solicitor who'd got Frances a good settlement when she'd divorced Malcolm, and who loved hearing about her little *liaisons*, as she called them.

'Doubtless it'll serve a purpose over Christmas,' she'd said to Frances, laughing as she'd handed her the gift. It was rose and gold silk and very low-backed, reminiscent of the dresses Ginger Rogers had worn in the old black and white films and it clung to Frances, who was a curvy size sixteen, in all the right places. She'd just cleaned her teeth and sprayed a bit of Chloe behind her ears and down her cleavage when the door creaked open and in he walked.

Christ! I hope he doesn't decide to ring me now!

Still, she was in no doubt, if he rang her she would, of course, pick up. Sexy, young Milos would have to go and wait in the bathroom!

The next couple of hours had passed in a blur of touches, sighs, kisses, squeals, nibbles, flesh and orgasms. Hmm! She'd enjoyed herself immensely. Sex was so much better in her fifties than it had ever been earlier in her life and Milos had appeared to have had a good time, too. He was now fully-dressed and came back to the bed and planted a kiss on her forehead while fastening his watch strap at the same time.

'You sleep again. Is very early,' he said. 'I see you later. Merry Christmas.'

As he quietly closed the bedroom door behind him, Frances couldn't help checking her phone again; still no missed calls, no texts or messages.

Try and let go of it! Make the most of today!

She glanced at the alarm clock and saw it wasn't even six o'clock. She gave a great big grin at the thought of a couple more hours sleep.

'Bliss!' she said to herself and she rolled into the middle of the bed, taking in the lingering scent of Milos's aftershave and pulled the duvet up over her shoulder. Within seconds she was back in a deep, satisfying sleep.

✦   ✦   ✦

JANET OPENED HER eyes and blinked for a second or two before realising exactly where she was. She looked around and took in the room and smiled to herself. Her hand went up and touched the little gold cross hanging from her neck.

I got through it! I got through Christmas Day! Thank you, Jesus!

As a child growing up in the West Indies she'd gone to church every Sunday morning, decked out in the finest outfit her family could afford. Every evening after supper her father would read to them from the Bible and he would tell them, warn them of the terrible things that would befall them if they ever turned away from God and His son, Jesus Christ. She and her five brothers and two sisters lived in fear and terror of ever upsetting this fierce, revengeful God who was capable of sending down fire or flood or plague and pestilence if they so much as even thought about straying from the Path of Righteousness. Once she had left Trinidad and gone to England to practise her midwifery, she'd used her able, intelligent brain to decide that religion, all religion, belonged in the realms of fairy stories. She believed in a power greater than herself; how could she not, witnessing the miracle of birth every day of her working-life? But this power was not an elderly, bearded, deity full of vengeance, malevolence and retribution, but rather a benign miracle-worker with a gentle hand; her own Higher Power was Mother Nature.

Yet over the last year, when she retired, and with the turn her life had taken, she had got to thinking about things again and she had turned back to the Church. She wasn't born-again and she wasn't evangelical. She just found a solace in sitting quietly inside a church, drinking in the atmosphere and feeling at one with her Maker. She was really looking forward to going into St Nicholas's in the village when they went on the walks. She clutched her cross tightly in her hand and started whispering her habitual morning prayer of gratitude.

✦   ✦   ✦

PENNY ROLLED OVER in the large, comfortable bed and gave a happy little sigh. She opened one eye and looked at her alarm clock, which was showing *6:30.*

She gave another, longer satisfied sigh at the thought that she didn't have to get up for at least an hour and a half, or perhaps even longer. They were leaving for the walk at half-past ten, so she could go down about half-past nine, have breakfast and then go straight on the walk. She found herself in a good mood and was pleased that she'd actually quite enjoyed herself on Christmas Night. The group had danced and chatted and drunk together, like old friends instead of a strangers that had been thrust together two days earlier. They'd even got Colin on the dance-floor, doing a great impression of your dad at a family wedding. She wasn't sure what she'd expected really; she just hadn't wanted to spend Christmas on her own or as a spare part at one of her friend's houses. She had good mates, she really did, but they were all married with kids, or in relationships, or going to spend it with their parents or families. Most of the time being single didn't bother her. She'd had two long relationships that hadn't worked out; the first because she hadn't felt ready at twenty-two to fall into the pattern of engaged-married-starting a family and the second because she'd fallen for someone with OCD, and try as she might, living with him had proved impossible for her. But with her love of kids and talent for making anywhere she might live a home, she had never really imagined that at forty-two she'd be single still. She had a good social life, in fact she was out almost every night, with her tap-dancing, dog training and hospital radio show where she was a volunteer. She wondered how Sam was getting on in the kennels.

Better not to think about him, it'll only upset you! He's probably fine!

She could have worked over Christmas, but she'd put in a lot of overtime in the last couple of months saving up for the trip of a lifetime to Australia and New Zealand with her friend Julie that they were planning for the following autumn. And, as she knew from experience, sometimes, working in the ambulance service at this festive time of year could be tragic and sad. No, when all was said and done, she'd made the right decision to come away. And she was looking forward to the remaining three days.

The only thing that had spoiled last night had been that

woman Angela and those awful men. Well, not really spoiled. There'd been the incidents at dinner, which Frances, Pete and then Dave had dealt with rather well, and then after that the five of them had disappeared back into the bar and hadn't joined in the dancing. She hadn't seen them for the rest of the evening, although, when she'd come back up to her room, she'd heard noises coming from behind a locked door on the far side of the room. At first it scared her, but then she realised that it was an intercommunicating door, which led to the room next door: Angela's room. She creaked across the wooden floor in her bare feet and put her ear to the door, giggling at what she could hear.

'Come on, big boy! Come on!' she'd heard Angela shouting, followed by what sounded like slaps. 'You can do it! You can do it!' Followed by more slaps and a few groans.

Penny had giggled silently again, not caring that she was eavesdropping, as she was absolutely unable to avoid overhearing the antics going on in room ten. She could hear the bed grinding and groaning and creaking in a frantic rhythm.

'Oh, yes! Oh, yes! That's it, yes, that's it! Keep going! I'm nearly there!' More groans followed then even louder creaks from the bed. And then the pace seemed to slow right down.

'What? What? Don't stop now! Don't stop! Oh for fuck's sake!'

'Sorry. Brewer's droop,' a male voice said.

One of the Four Friends?

'Well, finish me off by hand or mouth then!' Angela ordered.

'I can't I feel a bit sick,' came the reply.

'Oh, you filthy bastard! Don't throw up in my bed!'

Penny heard frantic movements and sounds she couldn't identify followed by a slam of the bathroom door.

Bastard!' she heard Angela shout again.

And then there was silence.

Penny had put her hand over her mouth, afraid she would laugh so loudly she would give herself away. Angela obviously had no idea she could be overheard. Penny thought if she brought anyone back they'd have to do it in silence. Not that that seemed to be on the cards, mind!

Ehh! I don't really fancy any of them. Well, Dave's a laugh. And Pete's a nice man: a gentleman.

No! She wasn't there to get off with anyone, just to enjoy a different Christmas. And it had certainly been different so far, especially after Angela's antics. She smiled to herself again; she was quite looking forward to meeting Eve, who'd sounded nice on the phone, and going on this morning's walk.

✦   ✦   ✦

PETE WOKE UP with a jolt, surprised to find that he had actually been asleep. He rolled onto his back, bent one arm over his head and looked up at the ceiling. He thought back over the night. The party, if you could call it that, had been pleasant enough. He'd had a couple of dances and a few beers and had surprised himself that he'd started to relax and enjoy it all. But once he had got back to his room, the sadness he'd been holding in all day, multiplied a hundred-fold because of the emotion of the season and aided and abetted by the amount of alcohol he'd drunk meant that he'd started to heave and sob as soon as he'd locked the door behind him. He'd thrown himself onto the bed and cried loudly and indulgently, his fists bashing the pillow beneath his face, trying to work the anger, upset, grief, regret, guilt, shame and loss from his system.

He had no idea how long he had cried for, perhaps an

hour, perhaps two. He had finally dragged himself into the bathroom and stood under the shower, hoping the cleansing, healing power of the water would work where all else had seemed to fail. Finally, he'd dried himself and had got into bed, but he hadn't been able to sleep. He'd tossed and turned, the events of the last two years going over and over in his head, like a tumble-dryer on a permanent cycle. He'd last looked at the clock at twenty-past four and had considered getting up to make himself a cup of tea. That must have been when he'd fallen asleep. He sighed and picked up the remote control for the room's TV set. There was probably nothing on of interest but anything would be better than the images inside his head.

✦   ✦   ✦

EVE WAS ABOUT three-quarters of the way to the Blue Boar Inn. She'd left the A12 and the A414 to take the B1022, trusting the satnav completely. She had the radio on and sang along with the seasonal songs it was putting out.

Surely by tomorrow we'll be back to normal music?

The road twisted and turned its way through the Essex countryside, exposing villages with quaint names that made her wonder what their roots had been or what the names had originally meant as she saw signs for Woodham Walter, Woodham Ferrers and Woodham Mortimer.

Perhaps Mr Woodham had been a very rich man with a Walter, a Ferrer and a Mortimer!

She smiled broadly when she read *Tom Tit Lane*, finding it amusing for some reason. High hedges, ornate railings and iron gates gave an occasional glimpse of beautiful houses, some with a tastefully-decorated Christmas tree standing at the top of the driveway, others rather ostentatiously over-the-top with lights all over the roof and down the front, with

Santa and his reindeer landing and taking off again. Sturdy farmhouses stood back from the road with welcoming lights in their windows, like curious eyes watching her drive past, wondering where she was going and what she was doing out and about and alone before seven o'clock on Boxing Day.

I could murder a cup of coffee!

Still, according to the satnav she would be arriving at her destination in twenty minutes time. She'd had a really good run and she smiled at the thought of an endless coffee-pot and a full-English breakfast. The reviews of the hotel had all agreed that the food had been excellent and if she concentrated she could imagine the welcoming aromas of freshly-brewed coffee and British bacon. That would set her up nicely for whatever the day might bring. She'd just have time to go to her room and drop her case before going down to the restaurant where she would wait for the group to turn up. She was wearing her walking boots, thinking she'd get her feet used to them whilst driving. She stared through the windscreen at the grey, East Anglian sky and wondered if the weather would hold today. The fields were very wet from the heavy rain that had fallen just before Christmas.

She'd checked the forecast for today, which fortunately wasn't for any more rain or for any snow, just heavy cloud and low temperatures. Good walking weather, really. Of course, it would have been better to have a clear sky, but that might happen later on in the day. It was still almost two and a half hours before the walk began. It was to be from the Blue Boar Inn down to the village of Tolleshunt D'Arcy with a stop for coffee or something stronger at one of the local pubs and a look at a famous house before setting back to the Inn by a different route in time for lunch at one-thirty. Then, at three-thirty there was to be a quiz followed by afternoon cream-tea and then dinner at eight with a disco afterwards.

All quite exhausting! Still, that way the day will pass quickly.

The B1022 had become the B1026 as she passed the Mill Beach caravan site and drove through Heybridge and then Goldhanger.

Nearly there!

✦   ✦   ✦

DAVE STRETCHED AND scratched as he made his way to the bathroom. He was pleasantly surprised by the warmth of his room. He'd packed pyjamas and a heavy dressing-gown that he'd bought especially for his Christmas away. He usually slept naked and when he was at home he'd slip into a pair of jogging bottoms and a t-shirt around the house and put a sweatshirt over them if he felt cold. Somehow he'd thought that because the Blue Boar Inn was old, it would be chilly and damp. He'd envisaged a tiny grate in the room and that the maid would knock discretely at six each morning to come in and get the fire going before he could venture out of bed. He laughed at his own naivety.

You're losing the plot, me old son! This ain't something out of Agatha Christie or bleeding Downton Abbey!

Even though the floors were wooden, made to look old – *distressed* Dave thought the term was – and polished to a beautiful sheen, they were warm, probably due to a sophisticated, twenty-first century, underfloor heating system. He pulled open the shower curtain, stepped into the bathtub and opened the tap. He let the abundant warm water fall onto his head and stream down over his body. He'd always loved the feel of water; he found it therapeutic. Not that he was in need of therapy! At least, he didn't think he was, but he wasn't sure. He sighed as he soaped himself and thought back over the last few months when he'd arrived at the very surprising conclusion that he was lonely. He had no parents, brothers or sisters, having been abandoned as a baby and brought up in a string of children's homes. In his twenties he'd fathered a child, Josh, who was now nearly twenty-six, but he'd had very little contact with him and his son considered his step-father to be his real dad. Dave had never wanted commitment; he'd had a string of affairs but had never met anyone he'd really wanted to settle down with. He liked being single and he liked the reputation he had of being a bit of a *Jack-the-Lad*. He'd always been happy to have a fling and walk away. In fact, although he wasn't proud to admit it, he'd been at his happiest while having affairs with married women. Oh, yes! You had to be discreet and you had to be careful, as he'd found out one night when he'd opened the door to his motel room thinking it was room service, only to be confronted by the knife-wielding husband of the woman who was lying naked in a state of semi-arousal on the bed. Fortunately, he'd learned to take care of himself physically from a very young age.

That had been a close shave, though!

But she'd still tried to keep the affair going and Dave had had to point out that as fond of her as he'd become, he'd grown even fonder of his kneecaps and eyeballs. Still, as long as you chose the right woman – one who had too much to lose by her husband finding out and who wasn't looking for anything long-term or permanent – then you were laughing. For two years he'd had a long-distance affair with a woman he'd met in Antigua, Geri. But he'd finally had to admit that she was neurotic. She'd phone him day and night; send him abusive texts if he hadn't replied to one of hers within five minutes; always ask to come and stay with him, which he didn't mind, but she never wanted to leave; kept on trying to get him to move in with her. How was he supposed to do that when his business was in St Alban's and she lived in Wiltshire? And there was no way he was giving up his business: *Mr Wright's Used Cars and Personalised Number Plates*. He'd worked too hard and too long to build it up. Moving it from East London to St Alban's had almost been like starting over again, but it had all been worth it eventually. No, there was no way he was moving to Wiltshire. And he hadn't wanted her to move in with him, either, and besides she couldn't because her two kids lived with their father ten miles from her. She was all mixed up, too, and liked the old sherbet a bit too much for his liking. Not that he didn't like a drink himself, but the secret was moderation. Like those silly sods last night. Why did people have to drink until they fell over? He'd never understand that. He hated being sick; to him it was the worse thing in the world and the thought of drinking and throwing up time after time was incomprehensible. And more and more often he'd had to stop filling her glass or even put Geri to bed because of the state she was in.

How can a bloke ever be attracted to a woman who drinks like a fish?

He didn't know the answer to that. In Antigua she'd had a few too many on several occasions and had thrown herself at a couple of the men and it had all gone a bit pear-shaped, but Dave had enjoyed her company and at first had been pleased to stay in touch with her, and had liked it even more when they'd gone to each others for weekends and their relationship had become intimate.

But sometimes he'd been glad he didn't have a pet rabbit.

He turned the shower off and grabbed a beautiful, thick, dark-blue bath sheet and his thoughts turned to the women in the group. Last night he'd had a good time just dancing, chatting and joking with them. He didn't really fancy any of them, but by the end of the night, Blonde Sue had finally broken ranks with the other two Sues and had had a slow-dance with him and then they'd had a bit of a snog by the lifts before she'd squealed and said she had to go. She wasn't really his type, but then again, he'd learned early in life never to look a gift horse in the mouth. He hadn't come away looking for a new partner, but if a bit of action happened, well, he wasn't going to say '*No!*'.

He finished drying himself and started to get dressed. He hadn't told any of his staff he was going away with a singles' group for Christmas; he didn't want them to pity him, or invite him to theirs, which they doubtless would have done. He didn't consider himself a loser spending Christmas with a group of strangers. It was better than sitting by yourself watching the telly with nobody to pull a cracker with. But, for possibly the first time ever, Dave wished he had a permanent partner in his life. And that surprised him. He pulled his sweater over his head and mentally shrugged as he pulled it on.

Silly old sod! Go and 'ave some breakfast!

✦   ✦   ✦

WHOEVER INVENTED THE satnav deserves a Nobel Prize! Perhaps they've already been given one?

Eve couldn't believe how easily she had found the Blue Boar Inn. Well, in reality, she hadn't found it; she'd been guided to it by her trusty satnav, the best £120 she'd ever spent! It wasn't an all-singing-all-dancing one because she didn't need that. It just got her from Point A to Point B and that was all she cared about. And today, Point B was the rather wonderful-looking Blue Boar Inn. It stood imposingly at the top of an in-and-out driveway, surrounded by beautiful gardens, which even in winter were full of colour and style. Two huge fir trees stood either side of the main door, both tastefully decorated yet understated, with very pale blue lights that were on, as it was still not quite daylight, giving the front of the building a wintry wash reminiscent of an ice palace. Classy. She drove to the side of the building and pulled into a space, sighing with relief as she switched off the engine. She shivered as she got out of the car and stretched her legs and then opened the boot and took out her suitcase and tour manager's shoulder bag, which held her clipboard and all her paperwork.

She dipped her hand into the side pocket and pulled out her Travel Together name-badge, which also bore the company's T2G logo, and fixed it to her sweater under her open coat. Straightening up and taking a deep breath, she crunched across the pebble drive onto the larger stones of the entrance and pushed open the ornate glass and wooden door.

'Ello Eve!' I never knew it was you coming to take over!'

Eve turned at the sound of Dave's voice, smiling in recognition. In two steps he'd come over to her and enveloped her in a great big hug.

'How lovely to see you again!' Eve exclaimed.

'Innit? Although, we'd've bin seein' each other at the wedding, wouldn't we? You're going, ain't ya?'

Dave, like the rest of the Travel Together group, was ignorant of the fact that Michael was Eve's son, and thought him to have been just one of her clients.

'Yes, I am! I can't wait. I'm sure Natalie will be the most beautiful bride. And how are you enjoying yourself here? What happened to Jade?'

'Well, we dunno. She was 'ere the first night. A bit uptight and nervy. Like she wanted everyone to do just what she said. Not laid-back like you,' he added, laughing. 'She didn't seem to know 'ow to 'andle people. There's a group of blokes 'ere, four of 'em, and they're right tosspots. Excuse the language. But she seemed to be frightened of 'em. And then she went off to bed early. LIke before all of us. Well that ain't on, is it? And we got up Christmas morning and she'd gone!'

'Oh dear! Well, I'll just have to try to make it up to everyone.'

'Oh we was okay. The 'otel manager looked after us and we 'ad a good Christmas dinner an' a nice buffet last night an' a bit of a dance an' that. Yeh, it weren't bad at all. But we'll all be alright now the cavalry's 'ere!'

'Right, well, I'm just going to check in and then I'll come through to the dining-room and find you.'

'Alright, love. It's just through there. I'm chuffed to bits to see ya!' Dave gave her another hug and then strolled through to the dining-room, while Eve walked over to the front desk, dragging her suitcase behind her and rang the bell. A tall man in his early-thirties, wearing a dark suit and maroon tie appeared through a doorway from behind the reception area.

'Good morning! Checking in?'

'Yes, please!'

'You must be Eve? I'm Chris. Chris Edwards, the duty-manager.'

'Oh, nice to meet you, Chris,' Eve said shaking his offered hand. 'Thank you so much for looking after my group after Jade's early exit.'

'Oh, please, don't thank me! That's what we're here for. I just hope that everyone enjoyed themselves. We tried to carry on according to the programme that we'd been sent. Fortunately, the walks are today and tomorrow so all we really had to do was feed them, give them the board games and play the music!'

Eve laughed as she signed the old-fashioned register he

held open for her.

'Goodness! It's a long time since I've seen one of those!' she said.

'We like to maintain everything in keeping with the history and age of the hotel. That's why we have these rather large, old-fashioned keys,' he turned from a board mounted on the wall and held a key out for her.

'It weighs a ton! You must see a lot of broken toes,' she quipped.

'From time to time,' Chris admitted. 'I'll let you get up to your room and have some breakfast and meet your group. Perhaps you could just catch up with me sometime later today, to sort out the champagne bill and a couple of other queries?'

'Yes, of course!'

Chris rang the bell twice and a young man appeared from the direction of the dining-room.

'Milos, this is Ms Mitchell, the Travel Together tour manager.'

'Eve, please! Not Ms Mitchell.'

'Can you show her to her room; it's number twelve.'

'Certainly!' Milos grabbed her case and walked towards the lift, which was in the far corner of the reception area, almost hidden from sight by a large, Christmas tree, ornately adorned with Victorian decoration and faux-candle lights.

'Thank you,' Eve said to Chris. 'I'll see you later.'

Milos had taken her to her room, shown her where everything was and she'd put the kettle on to make herself a coffee and was just unlocking her suitcase when the phone in the room rang.

Not problems already, surely?

'Hello.'

'Hello. Is that Jade?'

'No. It's Eve.'

'Oh, sorry, I must have been put through to the wrong room.'

'No, you haven't! Or rather I don't think you have.'

'Well, I obviously have, because I want to speak to Jade, the Travel Together rep. You're not her, are you?'

'I'm not Jade, but I am the Travel Together tour manager. Jade had to leave and I've been brought in.'

'Well! Nobody told me! I was expecting Jade.'

'Look, who is this?' Eve was hovering between amusement and annoyance at the caller's tone.

'I'm a walking guide.'

'Tony? Tony Harris?'

'Mr Harris, yes. I'm supposed to be meeting you for a walk at half past ten this morning.'

'Yes, indeed! We shall be in the reception area all ready and waiting for you.'

'I should hope so. I don't like being kept waiting. There's nothing I hate more than a group that's not punctual. It's rude and impolite.'

'Yes, of course it is. Which is why you won't be kept waiting. As I've just said, we'll be ready for you.'

'Yes, well, we leave at half past ten so tell them to be ready five or ten minutes before. There's always some silly woman who wants to go to the toilet just as we're leaving, or someone who's forgotten to bring their camera.'

'I'll make sure everyone's there, on time, fully-toiletted and carrying everything they may need.' Eve couldn't resist teasing him. Her humour fell on stony ground.

'And you have to sign my invoice so that I get paid. I know these companies like to hang onto your money for as long as possible, but I'm not having that. My invoices will be in the post as soon as tomorrow's walk's over so that they've got no excuse for not paying me.'

'Quite right, Mr Harris! See you at ten twenty-five!'

Eve put the receiver down and grimaced.

✦   ✦   ✦

TEN MINUTES LATER Eve went into the dining-room to find Dave sitting with an older black woman with a short, shiny bob and a shy-looking man in a pale-blue shirt and striped tank-top.

''Ere she is! I was just tellin' Janet and Colin about you an 'ow well you looked after us all before.'

'Thank you, Dave. Hello, Janet. Hello, Colin. Nice to meet you both.' Eve took a seat alongside Dave, opposite the other two. Milos, who seemed to be doubling as bell-hop and waiter, appeared beside her.

'Would you like tea or coffee, madam?'

'Coffee please.'

'You would like cooked breakfast?' he asked, offering Eve a menu. She flicked her eyes over it, smiling at what she saw.

'Full English please. With the eggs very well done. Thank you.'

'Please serve yourself to cereal, fruit, pastries or yo-ghurts.'

'I think I'll just have the full-English. That should set me up nicely for the walk.'

'Yes. I must say, I'm looking forward to it. I like walk-ing,' Janet said. 'Three of us went for a walk yesterday afternoon to try to work off the huge Christmas dinner they'd served us.'

'Did you go far?'

'Not really. Just twenty minutes or so. We didn't want to pre-empt anything we might be doing today or tomorrow. It was just a leg-stretch.'

'Well, today we're going into the village to see D'Arcy

House and have a coffee, then coming back to the hotel through the back roads or footpaths. I think it's a bit wet on some of the route, after the heavy rain they had here a couple of days ago.'

'Yes, it poured down on Christmas Eve. An' apparently they'd 'ad a fair bit of rain the previous few days,' Dave said.

'Well, no rain forecast for today, I'm pleased to say!' Eve said, smiling as Milos appeared with a pot and the aroma of freshly-brewed coffee reached her nostrils.

'Oi! Oi! 'Ere's some of the others!'

Three women came in, one short and blonde, one tall and one extremely thin and sat at the far end of the table. Eve stood up and went down to greet them, holding out her hand.

'Morning! I'm Eve, the replacement tour manager,' she said, smiling and shaking hands with each of them in turn.

'Nice to meet you. We don't know what happened to the other one,' the tall woman said.

'She didn't seem to have much idea,' the blonde one volunteered.

'Perhaps it was something we said!' the thin one added as they all laughed.

'Well, all I can do is apologise on behalf of the company. It's not usual to have a tour manager walk out after the first night, especially not at Christmas, and it's something I can't apologise enough for.'

'It's not your fault, is it?' the blonde one said. 'I feel a bit sorry for you having to come and face the music.'

'Why? Has something terrible happened that I don't know about?' Eve asked, genuinely concerned.

'No, not really. It's all gone on fine. In fact, we've hardly missed a tour manager,' the thin one said.

Well, thank you very much!

'But there's a vegetarian who's going to be gunning for

you. She reckons there was no choice for her at the buffet supper last night, but there was, wasn't there?' She turned to the other two for back-up.

'Plenty of stuff. Trouble was, she was too drunk to find it,' the tall one said. 'And so were the four blokes she's hanging around with.'

'Oh dear! Well, I won't keep you from your breakfast. Enjoy it! And I'll see you in a bit,' Eve said and went back to take her seat.

'They filled you in then, about the bunch o' drunks?' Dave asked.

'They mentioned something. They'll have sobered up by this morning,' she joked, crossing her fingers under the table where nobody could see them.

'Oh, that looks wonderful!' she said to Milos, who'd appeared bearing the best-looking full-English breakfast that Eve had seen in a long time. She couldn't wait to get stuck into it.

'Ehh! Well, you must be Eve! I'm Penny. The voice on the telephone.'

A pretty, blonde woman who looked to be in her late thirties came up to the table, hooked her bag over the back of the chair next to Eve's and sat down.

'By, it's good to see you, pet,' she said, smiling and squeezing Eve's arm. Eve put down her knife and fork and offered her hand, which Penny took and shook vigorously. 'Are you enjoying your breakfast?'

'I most certainly am! It all looks wonderful.'

'Did everyone sleep okay?' Penny asked, looking round the table, nodding as she did so. Eve couldn't help thinking she'd make a good tour manager. 'Oh, morning, Pete! Morning Geoff!,' she called to the two men who had filled the spaces between the Three Sues and the rest of them.

'This is Eve, our new tour manager,' Penny beamed,

nodding at Eve. Geoff and Pete shook hands with her.

'Are you new, too?' Geoff asked, looking somewhat amused.

'New? New? She's been with the company about twenty years, ain't you, Eve' Dave spluttered.

'Fifteen, actually.'

'Oh, well, that's a bit more reassuring.' Geoff said. 'Have I met you before?'

'Quite possibly. What holidays have you been on?'

'Oh, I haven't done any holidays as such. I just like to go to the black-tie balls. I've done about thirty of them. That's where I know the Three Sues from. We always meet up at the black-tie balls.'

'I haven't done a black-tie ball in years,' Eve said. 'I usually do long-haul trips.'

'So how come you were free to do this then?' Geoff asked, as if he disbelieved her.

'I'd especially asked not to work this Christmas. I wanted to have time to myself. But, they called me in as the only tour manager who wasn't working when Jade… left.' She had to search for the word.

'Yes, right little 'oudini,' Dave said, making the others laugh.

'Do you have any idea why she went?' Pete asked Eve, as he poured himself a cup of tea.

'None whatsoever. I don't think she's been contactable so I know nothing about her reasons for walking. My job is just to pick up the reins and hope we all enjoy our time left here,' she said, moving swiftly on, not wanting to get into a slagging-off-Jade session.

'So, is it like, you and the three of them at these black-tie balls?' Dave asked Geoff, thinking that it might be something he could look into in the New Year.

'What do you mean? There's nothing like that going on!'

Geoff looked indignant. 'We just met at one a couple of years ago and now we always book on the same ones. It's nice to meet up with friends.'

I'll bet it is!

'No offence meant, mate. Just thinkin' out loud.'

'Eve!'

'Eve!'

Hearing her name called out in stereo, Eve swivelled round to find Kim standing behind her and Frances thundering across the dining-room, arms wide open ready to envelop her in a huge hug. Eve stood up and gave Kim a hug and then found herself lost in a fog of Chloe and cashmere as Frances' arms went round her.

'How lovely to see you both!'

'What a small world! I can't believe it's you!' Kim said, smiling, remembering with genuine gratitude and fondness Eve's patience and kindness to her when she'd been a bit of a pain on a trip to India the previous year. 'I promise not to give you any grief this time,' she whispered, moving closer so that the others couldn't hear.

'How are you? Better now? You look well,' Eve said, taking in Kim's face and overall appearance, which were much happier and healthier than on the Golden Triangle Tour.

'I'm fine. Moved on with my life and menopause all got through!'

'Good, girl!' Eve was genuinely pleased to hear it.

'I can't believe it's you!' Frances said, taking a seat next to Janet. 'This is Eve! The tour manager I told you about. In Antigua!' she said to Olivia, who'd just walked in to join them.

'Oh, hello!' Olivia said. 'I've heard so much about you. I hope you're going to restore my faith in Travel Together tour managers. The two I've met so far have been a waste of space.'

'Yes we had a right div in Turkey. Tennis holiday. Oh, coffee please!' she said to Milos, blushing slightly and hoping she wasn't giving herself away.

'She thought she was on holiday herself. Always in the bar, always in the pool, always in your face,' Olivia said. And she wanted to dictate what the group should do all the time. Like, she got annoyed if you didn't want to turn up to a coaching session or take part in the tournament or walk down into Bar Street with the rest of the group, like a bloody school-trip.'

'Polly, her name was,' Frances interjected. 'Do you know her?'

Oh, I know her alright!

'I think I've heard of her,' Eve said, remembering how surprised she'd been at the once-a-year tour managers' meeting to find that the intense, bird-like creature who never stopped talking and who'd been her client on a trip to Mombassa, was now working for Travel Together.

'And then this one; Jade. Spends one evening with us, goes to bed early and leaves us to it and then we get up for breakfast on Christmas morning only to find she's gone!'

'Well, I'm here now and I hope you'll leave with a better opinion of us all by the end of your stay.'

'Course we will! You were the best rep anyone could wish for!' Frances said. 'I mean, look at all you dealt with in Antigua. That storm when all the resort got flooded. That bloke who had an accident. What was his name?'

'Deano, weren't it?' Dave said. 'Got off with the lady vicar.'

'And Michael finding his dad, and that bolshie Welsh-man getting lost in the storm on his bike. He was a right mouthy sod, he was. I didn't like him at all.'

'Huw?'

'Yes. Huw. That was it.'

As the conversation moved onto how people had slept and the day's upcoming events, Eve did a quick headcount and realised that five people hadn't come down to breakfast yet. She assumed they were the *Angry Vegetarian* and the *Four Drunken Men*. She looked at her watch. It was a quarter to ten. Still time for them to put in an appearance. She stood up, deciding to go back to her room to clean her teeth and grab her stuff.

'I'm just going up to my room. I'll be back in reception just after ten and we have to be ready to leave by twenty-five past. Our walking guide, Mr Harris, wants to leave punctually at ten-thirty. Okay?'

There was a chorus of *'Okay' 'Thank you, Eve.' 'See you then,'* as Eve left the table.

'Well, she's seems a bit more the ticket than Jade,' she heard Penny say as she walked away.

'We'll be alright with 'er,' Dave agreed.

As she was crossing reception, two men, who looked rather worse-for-wear, and somewhat like each other, in that they were both wiry, with greying short hair, got out of the lift and passed her heading for the dining-room.

'He said he wasn't going to make it when I knocked on his door just now,' one said. 'Said he felt like shit and didn't want any breakfast. Said he'd see us when we got back for lunch.'

'Excuse me! Are you with the Travel Together group?' Eve called after them. They both stopped, looked at each other and then at her.

'Yeah,' one said.

'I'm Eve Mitchell. The tour manager who's come to take over the group,' she explained.

'Oh, right! Hello.' one said as they both stood looking at her, seemingly unsure of what to do or say.

'And you are?' she prompted.

'I'm Don Briggs and he's Vince Middleton,' the slightly taller, slightly younger one said. 'There's two more of us, Mick Hanrahan and John Baxter. Mick's hungover and he won't be coming on the walk this morning. We're not sure about John. He didn't answer when I knocked on his door about ten minutes ago. Mind you, he might already be in having his breakfast.'

'No, I've just come from the dining-room and I didn't see him. Perhaps he was in the shower when you knocked.'

'Yeah, he might have been,' Vince said, grinning, as if he thought it unlikely. 'Or perhaps he got lucky last night!' he said, laughing as if he'd cracked a really funny joke.

'Well, as long as you're certain there's no need for alarm then I won't panic,' Eve said. 'Please be ready in reception at ten twenty-five, ready to leave at ten-thirty sharp. See you then.' She smiled at them and went over to the lift as they hurried into the dining-room.

'Better get a move on!' she heard Don say as the lift door slid open and she stepped inside.

✦   ✦   ✦

IN ROOM TEN Angela was wishing John would get a move on; a move on out of her bed and her room. She'd never seen anyone go into such a deep sleep before. In fact, if it wasn't for the fact that he snored at the decibel level of a jet engine, she'd have thought he was dead. She thought back over the events of the previous evening and shook her head.

What were you doing with him?

Not only had he not been able to maintain his erection – something that had never ever happened to any man before while he was in her bed – he hadn't even been capable of finishing her off.

Grrr!

She growled again with the frustration of the previous night's debacle flooding back over her. She had been terrified he was going to vomit in the bed or in the room. As soon as he'd said he felt sick, she'd shoved him off the bed hard and then run to open the bathroom door and put the light on and then jumped back out of the way as he'd staggered in, heaving as he went. She'd slammed the door after him, not wanting to hear the sounds he was making or experience the vile aroma filling the bathroom. After five minutes of listening to him throwing up, it had gone silent. She'd hammered on the bathroom door.

'Pull the chain and clear up!' she ordered him and she was grateful to hear the loo flush and the sound of water being splashed around, before the bathroom door opened and he lurched back out into the room, launching himself face-down on the bed, which is where he still remained. She'd gone into the bathroom to inspect it, holding her nose as she did so and threw some of her Shalimar around.

Seventy quid a bottle to use it as a fucking air-freshener!

And now, she'd showered and dressed and pulled on the thick leggings she sometimes used when out riding and a pair of knee-length boots over the top. She hadn't brought her walking boots, thinking that she didn't need them; after all, it was country lanes of Essex not the Lake District. She'd done her make-up and gathered her hair into a high plait and was ready to go down to breakfast. Yet the oaf from last night was still snoring happily in her bed. She'd shaken him a couple of times, but he'd barely stirred; just swallowed or missed a breath and then carried on as before. She had no qualms about leaving him for the maid to find but didn't really want to leave him alone in her room. The few valuables she'd brought with her – jewellery, credit and debit cards, driver's licence – were all in the wall-safe that the hotel provided, hidden discretely behind the painting of a Cavalier. But even so... She looked at her watch and saw it was 9:50. She wouldn't have time for breakfast at this rate, but there was no way she was going out without it. She crossed to the large, antique wardrobe standing next to the dressing-table and took out one of the five-inch stiletto-heel shoes she'd been wearing the previous evening. She crossed back to the bed and with a certain degree of malice brought the shoe down heavily on sleeping, snoring John's backside.

'What the fuck? Christ!' he jumped up clutching his buttocks.

Angela dropped the offending shoe and kicked it under the bed.

'Oh, you are awake then?'

'Fuck! Who wouldn't be? I thought you'd stabbed me. You haven't have you?' He swung round trying to see his own backside, then stepped forward to try to see it over his shoulder in the mirror.

'It was just a slap. And besides, you seemed to like slaps last night,' she said, deliberately trying to insinuate he'd been asking for it. 'Anyway, it's time for you to go back to your own room. Breakfast's nearly over and we've got a walk this morning.'

'Fuck that! I'm not going on a walk. You go and I'll stay here,' he said moving back towards her bed, rubbing his buttocks. She jumped into his path and put her hands on his chest.

'No! Not so fast!' she said. 'Pick up your clothes and go back to your own room. I don't want you staying in here.' Her tone invited no argument. Slowly and sulkily, John picked up his clothes. He slid into his pants and trousers and pulled his shirt over his head, the buttons still done up from the previous evening when he'd been in too much of a rush to undo them. He picked up his socks and shoes and padded barefoot towards the door.

'I'll see you later. Ready for Round Two,' he said.

'In your dreams!' Angela whispered under her breath as he closed the door behind him and was finally gone. She counted to twenty to give him time to get back to his own room, wherever that was, and then she opened the door and almost sprinted down the corridor, determined to make it to breakfast before they closed at ten o'clock.

✦   ✦   ✦

EVE WAS BACK in the reception area by ten past ten and she took a seat in one of the big, deep armchairs that were placed throughout it. She had few qualms about this job now that she'd met almost everyone and she smiled to herself at the thought that on the type of Travel Together trip she usually did she'd be on countdown for home with just three days to go and yet on this one she'd only just arrived. She unbuttoned the cardigan she'd put on, feeling the effects of the hotel's efficient central heating system. Her lined, waterproof jacket was draped across the back of the armchair. She sat back, crossed her legs, sighed deeply and waited for the others to arrive. Without realising it, she must have inadvertently closed her eyes and perhaps even started to drift into sleep as she was suddenly brought back to the moment by the sharp, rapid-fire sound of quick footsteps crossing the foyer.

'Are you from Travel Together?' a somewhat shrill woman's voice enquired.

Opening her eyes, Eve was faced with a well-groomed, well-made-up woman who looked to be a very well-preserved mid-forties, who wore her fair hair tied in a long plait, knee-high boots over black leggings and an expensive-looking pale grey sweater.

'I am. I'm Eve Mitchell, the replacement tour manager,' Eve said, offering her hand, which the woman ignored. 'And you must be Angela.'

'I want to talk to you about this dump.'

Eve looked around the reception area slowly and pointedly, taking in the exquisite floor, the expensive rugs, the opulent flower displays and Christmas tree, the general good taste of the place, before letting her eyes rest back on Angela.

'This dump?'

'Oh, I know it might look alright, but once you look beyond the gentrified, pseudo-Tudor facade, it's barely passable.'

'I am surprised! I've only been here a couple of hours but I've found everything to be of an extremely high standard,' Eve parried. 'What specifically have you found to be below par?'

'Mainly the food. I am a vegetarian.'

Quelle surprise!

Although she'd met some lovely ones over the years, Eve had also come across the militant, card-carrying veggies and vegans who chose to travel to far-flung corners of the world in developing countries and then demanded to have food to meet their lifestyle choices. But this was England; this was Essex. Surely everything for vegetarians would be on hand here?

'Last night I couldn't eat anything at all on that buffet. Nothing!'

Eve delved into her tour manager's bag that was sitting at her feet and pulled out the paperwork, which included the menus for the entire stay. She flicked over the page marked *December 24th* and came to *Christmas Day*. She ran her finger down the page, pausing at *Christmas Lunch*.

'Was lunch okay? You had spicy parsnip soup and then

a choice of nut roast or acorn squash stuffed with mush-room rice pilaff for main course?'

'Yes.'

Eve continued to peruse the menu, knowing what it said because being fore-warned, she'd already had a look.

'And then the evening buffet is showing a cheeseboard with a selection of British and Continental cheeses, broccoli and Cheddar tartlets, pasta and pesto salad, potato salad, quorn goujons, mushroom and Brie sausages, smokey aubergine and coriander dip, Spanish omelette and samosas with tamarind chutney as vegetarian dishes.'

'Well I didn't see half of that! Nothing like it! All the serving dishes were empty.'

'But surely the staff refilled them.'

'They didn't! All the vegetarian food had gone by the time I went into dinner.'

'And yet, you're the only vegetarian in the group.'

'Are you doubting my word?' Angela's tone took on an ugly turn.

'Not at all!' Eve looked back at her list and ran her finger down it, counting under her breath this time. 'It's just that there were, let me see; yes …three…five…six…seven…nine…eleven…twelve   non-vegetarian   dishes   for everyone else to choose from. That seems a lot of food choice for people to have eaten the vegetarian options.'

'Well, of course, if the Travel Together rep hadn't bug-gered off and left us to it I'd have had someone to tell me when to go into dinner, wouldn't I? As it was, those of us who were having a drink in the bar were left to find out for ourselves when dinner was being served, by which time, the other greedy lot had eaten it all!'

There was an awkward moment's silence before Angela realised that nine of the greedy lot were standing behind her listening to every word she said. Undaunted, and working on the principle that attack is the best form of defence, she ploughed on.

'And another thing! It's Christmas. Something that seems to have passed Travel Together by completely. I mean, not even a Christmas card from the company! Other tour operators give their clients gifts.'

Not even the tour managers get a Christmas card, love! Not since Alan took over.

'And then, this morning at breakfast! They advertise that they serve until ten o'clock. I went in before ten and they served me in a very half-hearted manner!'

'All I can do is apologise profusely for my colleague's lack of professionalism. I am very sorry, we the company are very sorry, that you were left to fend for yourself on Christmas Day. I will take up the lack of food and your other comments with the manager, Mr Edwards later today and I'll bring down a Comments Form for you to complete with your observations about what you consider to be a lack of service and standards and that will be sent to our head office and the Customer Services Manager herself will contact you. And I will also check with Mr Edwards and the chef that there is enough vegetarian food to meet your requirements.'

Oops! I nearly said 'demands'!

'Yes, well I should certainly hope so. But quite frankly, it's not good enough!' Angela turned on her heel and clacked her way across the floor then took the stairs two-at-a-time while the others watched her go, shaking their heads.

'I think she was at a different buffet from me, you know,' Janet said. 'There was food a-plenty. At half-past nine the waiters were coming round asking if we didn't want any more because it was a shame to clear away the platters with so much food still on them.'

'And her attitude just now in the dining-room was appalling,' Olivia said. 'It was almost five past ten when she waltzed in yet she dared the staff to refuse her. She said she only wanted a yoghurt and a cup of tea. She ate the yoghurt in two minutes flat and was gone.'

Eve smiled and put the menus back into her bag and then took it to the front desk where she asked Tania if she could leave it behind the desk.

'It is not valuable?' Tania asked.

'Just paperwork,' Eve said. She looked at her watch. It was twenty past ten.

No sign of Mr Pleasant and Punctual!

Just as she thought that, the main door swung open and a very tall, angular man, wearing a Regatta waterproof jacket and matching trousers, strode in. He stamped his feet on the large welcome-mat and pulled down his hood before marching over to Eve and the group.

'I was waiting for you outside. We always meet up outside, ready for the off. Not inside.' He made it sound like a hanging-offence.

'Good morning, Mr Harris! I'm Eve.' Eve started to hold out her hand and then, seeing his expression, thought better of it. Mr Harris looked at his watch.

'It's twenty-five past. Is everyone here?'

Eve looked round the group, doing a swift mental head-count as she went. There were twelve people waiting to go on the walk.

''Erm, we seem to be a couple short,' she said. 'But they were all told half past ten and it's not quite that yet, is it? And I think one, perhaps two aren't coming.'

'Well can you find out if they are or not? We can't waste time hanging around for people who have no intention of turning up!'

Smiling, Dave moved forward and took hold of Mr Harris's arm, guiding him around until they were face to face.

'Mr 'arris. We've all bin lookin' forward to comin' on this walk this morning, but let me point something out to you: we ain't kids and you ain't a schoolteacher. And Eve, she ain't used to being spoke to like that. So, you can get off your 'igh 'orse and speak to 'er properly, or you'll be finding yer doin' the walk on yer own. Alright?'

There was a moment's silence broken only by a couple of giggles and murmurs of agreement while Mr Harris let Dave's words sink in. Before he could reply the lift door slid open and Vince and Don came out.

'Sorry! You waiting for us?' Don said.

'Well, someone has to be last, don't they?' Vince added, grinning round the group. 'The other two are giving it a miss.'

'So, there's just Angela to come…' Eve looked towards the staircase that remained empty. 'We'll give her another minute or two and then if she's not coming we can set off, if that's okay by you, Mr Harris.'

'Fine! I'll be outside!'

He marched back through the main door, followed by Geoff and Slim Sue.

'We're just going to snatch a couple of quick puffs,' Geoff said, holding the door for Slim Sue. 'We'll be outside.'

'Well, he's a little ray of sunshine, isn't he?' Frances said, laughing.

'I don't understand why anyone would work in a service industry when they don't like people,' Pete said.

'Ehh, but I'm sure you had people in the Fire Service like that,' Penny said, shaking her head and laughing. 'I know I've got a couple of colleagues that wouldn't win *Laugh of the Month*. They act as if people have accidents on purpose.'

'You're right, so you are,' Pete said.

'Sorry if you think I muscled in, Eve,' Dave said. 'But I didn't like his attitude.'

'Well, we'd never have guessed, like!' Penny said, making everyone laugh.

At that moment Angela appeared at the top of the stairs wearing an exquisite Holland and Cooper wax jacket and matching fur headband. She paused just for a second or two, long enough to know that everyone had noticed her, and then she slowly descended the staircase.

'Christ! She looks like something outta 'orse an' 'ounds,' Dave said. Eve bit her lip to avoid bursting out laughing.

'She's a vegetarian. I'm assuming that's fake fur!' Frances said, looking innocent as those standing next to her laughed and Angela, who'd obviously heard, blinked furiously and looked away from them.

'Okay! We're all here! Let's go!' Eve said, heading for the door, with the rest of the group following her closely behind.

✦   ✦   ✦

AN HOUR AND three-quarters later they were finishing their drinks in the bar of the Golden Goose, in the centre of the village. It had been a pleasant, well-paced walk following a well-trodden footpath that cut across fields, followed behind hedges and went over the odd style or two from the Blue Boar Inn into Tolleshunt D'Arcy. Having considered himself well and truly slapped down and chastised by Dave, Mr Harris had mellowed somewhat as the walk began and had, in fact, proved an informative guide who certainly knew a lot about the village and surrounding areas.

'Now, I'll lead and if you can bring up the rear, please,' he'd called to Eve as the group gathered outside the door of the Blue Boar Inn. 'And the rest of you, make sure you stay between the two of us and that way nobody can wander off on their own or get lost. Not that it'll be easy to get lost; we've got a very straightforward walk this morning from here into the village. It should take us just over an hour. Then we'll have a look at the things to see on the northern side and go into the Golden Goose for some refreshments, which are not, I repeat, not, included in the walk. Once we are sufficiently refreshed we will return her via a different route, and our ETA, that's our expected time of arrival…'

'Estimated. It's estimated time of arrival, not expected,' Penny interrupted. 'Oh, sorry!' she added, seeing Mr Harris's face. Eve had to bite her lip for a second time.

'As I was saying, we are expected to arrive back here at half-past one. We can only do that if everyone keeps up. So, if there are no questions…'

Mr Harris looked around the group and then at Eve, daring anyone to ask him anything. Eve shook her head and smiled, in what she hoped would be taken as a friendly sign that she had no questions.

'I think that's all clear,' she said, also looking round at everyone else. Nobody had a question. Everything was clear.

'Right, well, let's be off, then! Follow me!' And Mr Harris marched down the drive towards the road. After ten minutes or so the group had fanned out so that they covered an area of about a hundred yards between Mr Harris and the leaders, who were Angela, Pete, Colin, Janet and Don, and the stragglers who were walking with Eve: Frances, Olivia and Kim. Everyone else was fanned out in the middle, with Penny and Dave in deep conversation about cars.

'Well, I've got my little Peugeot and it does me well enough, like, but sometimes I think I'd like something a bit… classier. Do you know what I mean?'

'Course, Doll! You want something that ain't gonna drink up the old petrol but that looks good. And that's important, cos after all your motor says a lot about you, dunnit?'

'You're right. I sometimes think I'd like a convertible, but then again, we don't always get the weather. Although this last summer was a cracker. Well, until the middle of August it was, like.'

'You don't 'ave to 'ave a soft top. You could go for something with 'ard top. Like a Focus. That's a good-looking car. And if you 'ave 'ard top it ain't so cold durin' the winter. Sometimes with a soft top you can freeze your bollocks off. Oh, not that you would!' he added with a laugh.

'I could freeze my tits off, though, and I wouldn't like that much, would I?' Penny laughed along with him.

'I'll give ya me card before we leave and give us a ring in the New Year an' I'll 'ave a look an' sort something out for ya,' Dave said, pleased with himself at finding a way of keeping in touch with Penny, who he'd suddenly taken a very big fancy to. He looked out of the corner of his eye at Blonde Sue, who was walking just slightly ahead of him talking to Vince, while the other two Sues were just behind him and Penny, talking, of course, to Geoff. He hoped Vince was doing him a favour and stepping in. Blonde Sue had seemed alright after an afternoon and evening of drinking free champagne and a half dozen or so beers, but she wasn't really his type.

And what is it with women coming on these things with their mates?

He couldn't understand it, really. The Dolly Sisters in Antigua, the Four Friends and the Three Sues here. Still, at least the blokes had split up a bit with two not coming on the walk and the others mixing with other people. That's what these gatherings were about; mixing with new people, not sitting talking to your friends.

'So, 'ow you liking Travel Togevva?' he asked Penny.

'Ehh! I think they're grand. I'd never thought I'd go away on my own, like. But you're not on your own really, are you?'

'Nah. You soon get talkin' to people, don't ya? And most of 'em are alrigh' to get on with. I mean, you get a few funny ones, but on the 'ole everyone's 'ere to enjoy it an' 'ave a good time, ain't they?'

'Well, I am! I enjoyed myself in Paxos. At first, I thought I'd made a mistake because it was a bit quiet, like. But the crowd were good and that's what made it really. It wasn't the best hotel in the world but what I liked was that I had company if I wanted it and I could be on my own and read my book if I wanted and there was always someone to eat your dinner with and have a bit chat to and a drink afterwards.'

'Yeah, that's what I found. Funny really, when we was in Antigua, if felt like you'd known the others for years after just a coupla days. Bit like this, really,' he added.

'Well, I'm glad I came,' Penny said, smiling at him. And he suddenly felt warm and fuzzy.

At the back of the line Kim, Frances and Olivia were filling Eve in as to what had gone on with the group on the first day and a half before she'd arrived. Eve had already heard some of it from Dave, but she listened politely. Frances was walking with one hand in her pocket, where her phone lay on *vibrate*. She hadn't wanted to have the ringer turned on, because it belted out the theme from Only Fools and Horses very loudly and if he did ring then she'd be drawing attention to herself. This way, she could feel it vibrate and then just signal to the others to walk on ahead while she had her long-awaited conversation. So far, her carefully thought-out strategy had been for nothing. Olivia had started talking about the tennis holiday in Turkey again.

'Give it a rest, Olivia, I'm Turkeyed out! Especially after yesterday!' Frances screamed with laughter at her own wit, Eve and Kim joining in. She could see, though, that Olivia looked a bit hurt.

That'll teach me to get stuck with a lame duck!

'I'd thoroughly recommend the hotel, though, it was brilliant,' she said, taking Olivia's arm as they walked to take the sting out of her previous comment. 'It's set on a hillside that leads down to the beach and they've left lots of the trees in place, so at times, for example, if you were having your lunch in the snack restaurant, it was like having a picnic in the woods.'

'But don't go unless you're an absolute tennis maniac,' Olivia warned, bearing Frances no grudge. 'Because you'll be expected to play morning, noon and night. I mean, it was supposed to be an improvers' week, yet you had to be almost at Sharapova's level to start with!'

Eve and Kim laughed at her exaggeration.

'It sounds like hell to me!' Kim said. 'I love watching tennis, but don't ask me to play. A holiday's supposed to be relaxing, not getting all hot and sweaty running around after a ball.'

'Well, I'd played in sixth form college and I'd thought I was quite good, but I was pathetic compared to the Fragrant Fiona and Felicity, the two stars of the holiday!'

'Can you go to the hotel without doing a tennis holiday?' Kim asked Eve.

'I think so. I seem to remember we do it as a normal summer holiday. It does sound great.'

'Oh, please ask Travel Together to let you do it and then I'll book,' Kim said.

'Well, you certainly don't want to be stuck with Polly as your tour manager!' Olivia said.

'The staff are lovely,' Frances added, with a wink. 'I

think you'd like the barman, Kim. If you go there, ask for Umit. And tell him Frances sends her love.'

Kim looked at Frances, her eyes slowly widening and her mouth dropping open. She shook her head slightly.

'You didn't… Did you?'

'Afraid so! He's damaged goods! But don't let that put you off a holiday fling, he comes highly recommended!'

Olivia, Kim and Eve burst out laughing at Frances' audacity. Eve suddenly remembered she'd had a fling with a young guy who she'd met on the catamaran trip they'd been on in Antigua. One of the Arawak Arrow crew. Handsome, virile young men were obviously becoming a holiday hazard for Frances.

Good for her!

Then Eve noticed that Olivia was limping.

'Are you okay, Olivia? We're not going too fast are we?'

'I think I've got a blister. These trainers are new. I needed a new pair and I didn't want to go to the expense of getting walking boots as well, just for a walk today and tomorrow. But I should have broken them in. There's an inner seam that's rubbing my big toe.'

'I've got a couple of plasters in my pocket,' Eve said.

'Blimey! Did you used to be a Girl Guide. Talk about *Be prepared!*' Frances chuckled.

'I grabbed them because I thought my own boots might rub because it's been a while since I've worn them. Here. sit down on that,' Eve said, indicating a large boulder at the side of the footpath. 'It'll only take you a minute and then you'll be comfortable and we can catch the others up.'

Olivia perched on the boulder and whipped her trainer and sock off. The blister looked a bit angry but fortunately, she'd caught it before it got to the weeping stage. She leant forward and placed the blister over it and then put her sock and trainer back on.

'Just make sure you clean it properly when we get back to the hotel. Have you got any disinfectant?'

'I've got some tea-tree oil. That's supposed to be good.'

'Yes. Put a few drops in the sink and make sure you soak your foot.'

'Will you be able to get your leg up there?' Frances teased her.

'Probably easier than getting it over!' Kim quipped and the four of them laughed raucously, causing some of the others to look back.

'Oops! Come on!' Eve offered her hand and helped Olivia to her feet. 'Let's make an effort to catch up with the others!'

At the front of the crocodile of walkers Mr Harris had been waxing lyrical about East Essex and the Blackwater Estuary Nature Reserve.

'I know that as a county we have a somewhat dubious reputation, but I have to say much of it is undeserved.'

'I have to admit, I've watched the odd episode of the Only Way is Essex, it's big in Ireland, you know, and yet I've been pleasantly surprised so far. Everyone's seemed quite normal and I haven't heard anyone say *'Shuut up!'* once!' Pete said.

'Probably because the majority of the people we've met since we've got here have been foreign,' Angela said, sneering. I mean the girl on the reception desk, Tamsin, is it?'

'Tania,' Pete corrected.

'Whatever! Well, she's not English, is she? The two men who work the bar are Eastern European, I'd say, from their appearance.'

'The manager's English,' Mr Harris volunteered. 'Mr Edwards. He is actually from Essex, too, but the other side, Harlow, near the border with Hertfordshire. And the chef and most of the maids are local women, usually looking to earn a living while the children are in school. But I think those of us you will meet later this morning, in the Golden Goose, you'll find have little in common with the cast of that awful programme. Although, I have to say, because of our proximity to Europe, we've always had a very … erm … continental outlook on life and a very mixed population in this part of Essex. Colchester, which was, of course, the Roman capital of Britain, is only fifteen miles away towards the north-east of us. That has a rather splendid Dutch Quarter which dates back to the mid-sixteenth century, when Flemish weavers fled to escape religious prosecution. And then, because of our famous jam industry at Tiptree, we've always had foreign students coming for the summer to pick fruit,' he concluded, smiling as if he himself were responsible for Essex's multiculturalism and racial and religious tolerance.

'Where are you from?' Don asked Angela.

'Berkshire. Bradfield. The next village to the Middletons actually. They live in Bucklesbury.'

'Ooo! I am supposed to be impressed?' he teased her. She looked at him coolly.

'I don't know? Are you?'

'Well, you're not that far from me.'

'Yes, I know, You told me yesterday that you're all four from Somerset.'

Don blushed at the reprimand. Janet caught Pete's eye and raised an eyebrow but they all carried on walking as if nothing had been said. A couple of hundred yards later the footpath ended near a t-junction, which led to a slightly wider road.

'Shall we wait for the others to catch us up?' Mr Harris suggested, stopping at the top of the footpath.

They slowed down and stopped and turned, looking

back while waiting for the rest of the group to join them, which took a couple of minutes, Olivia's plaster application having held up the stragglers longer than they'd thought. Once they were all together, Mr Harris addressed them.

'The road we're on now is Whitehouse Hill, or to give it its technical name, the B1026. In a short distance it will become Station Road, although the station itself closed in the early 1950s. Station Road leads into North Street, which is where we are heading. Now, I'd like to explain a few other things to you. The name Tolleshunt D'Arcy has Saxon roots. It was originally Toll's Funt, which was Saxon for Toll's spring or fountain.'

'Wouldn't like to try that after a coupla beers!' Dave joked, several of the group laughing, Mr Harris frowning.

'Toll was an Anglo-Saxon chieftain who set up several settlements in these parts in areas of forest where water was available. Then, after the Norman Conquest, a nobleman, Ralph Peverel, was given a very large area as a manor by William the Conqueror. On your way here you may have seen signs for the village of Hatfield Peverel. That also takes its name from the same Norman noble. However, there seemed to be more daughters than sons in the family through the generations and the family name changed several times until in the fifteenth century one of the daughters, who inherited the house, married into the D'Arcy family and so the local manor house became known as Tolleshunt D'Arcy Hall and the village took the same name.'

'That's disappointing. I was hoping it'd have something to do with Colin Firth's Mr Darcey. You know, in Pride and Prejudice.'

Mr Harris looked at Penny as if she'd taken leave of her senses.

'Funny ol' names, ain't they? When I was driving 'ere I saw a signpost I thought said *Great Totty*. But it was Great

Totham!' Dave burst out laughing and so did the group. Everyone except Angela and Mr Harris.

'On tomorrow's walk,' he continued, as if he hadn't been interrupted at all, 'we shall see the Hall, which is a wonderful example of early sixteenth century architecture. Today, we will, as I've said, enter the village from the north and walk southwards as far as D'Arcy House, which as you will see is a fine, well-proportioned Queen Anne house, and which, from 1864-1932 was the home of the diarist and horticulturalist Dr John Salter. He was also the vice-president of the Kennel Club and Provincial Grand Master of the Freemasons.'

'Goodness! Such grandeur!' Frances said, in such a tone that nobody could tell if she was being sarcastic or not, although her sly wink at Penny probably gave her away, causing Penny to stifle a giggle.

'Please keep to the right of the road so that we are facing on-coming traffic and as close to the hedge as you can for your own safety,' Mr Harris said.

They set off again, in single file this time, roughly in the same order as before, everyone more or less happy with their walking companions. Much to his chagrin, Angela and Don were now walking slightly ahead of Mr Harris, who was doing his best to catch up and overtake them. After all, he was the walking guide and as such should be right at the front, leading. Janet was glad of that as it meant she was now only alongside Pete, the most pleasant, polite man you could wish for, and Colin, a man of few words. The three of them walked at a fair pace, one behind the other, taking in the views of the countryside in companionable silence. She was a sociable woman and she liked the chatting that went on at mealtimes and in the bar and the lounge, but she loved the peace and quiet as they walked and was pleased that neither of the two men felt the need to make meaningless polite conversation. They could do that when they stopped for their refreshments at the Golden Goose.

Before long they were entering the northern border of the village and passing quaint, characterful houses boasting early and mid eighteenth century dates above the doors. They trudged on passing the Village Hall, where Mr Harris made another brief stop.

'We are extremely proud of our local community, especially our Village Hall.' He pointed to the modest-looking one-story building. 'As well as housing lots of clubs, like the bowls and the W. I. it doubles as our post office three days a week!' he said with pride, waiting for the group's reaction.

'Really?' Eve jumped in quickly when there was none.

'And in early December we had a most successful Christmas Market with craft and gift stalls offering local produce and goodies. We have bingo on the last Friday of the month, and, on New Year's Eve we will be holding a disco in there!'

'Wonderful!' Eve exclaimed, eyeballing the group in the hope they could raise a bit of enthusiastic excitement.

'Sounds like a good place to live, don't it? Lotsa community spirit.'

Thank God for Dave!

Mr Harris beamed at Dave.

'It is a good place to live,' he agreed.

They continued on a short distance and came to a bend in the road, which seemed to serve as the centre of the village, with a pub, The Queen's Head, on the left, a rather splendid old-fashioned red phone box outside it, and a maypole on the right.

'Ehh! I feel as if I'm in Midsomer Murders. John Nettles is going to come walking out the pub at any minute,' Penny joked.

Mr Harris walked them over to the maypole, which had

a wooden box-like structure around the bottom section.

'Our maypole is one of only a very few original may-poles left in the country and is a listed monument,' he said with pride.

Cameras flashed and phones clicked.

'I've always fancied myself dancing round a maypole holding a ribbon,' Penny said, doing a couple of little dance-steps on the spot.

'You can always pole dance, Penny,' Frances quipped, digging her in the ribs.

'Ehh, you! What are you like? Barely known me two days and you're insulting me!' Penny replied, her laughter taking any sting out of her words. 'Still, I could bolster my savings for my next holiday with a bit of pole-dancing, couldn't I? I'm saving up to go to Australia with my friend Julie.'

'Well, I'd chip in!' Dave said, winking at her and laughing.

'Right! Everyone finished taking photos?' Mr Harris asked, pleased to see they'd all been snapping away, posing for selfies or small-group photos in front of the maypole. Some had even strolled over to some of the old cottages to take their pictures, their souvenirs of the Boxing Day walk. Everyone rejoined him and they continued south for another hundred yards or so until they came to an imposing house, which gave right onto the street.

'So, this is D'Arcy House,' Mr Harris said, stopping on a small green opposite it, which led to a private cul-de-sac, so that they could see and appreciate it better. 'From 1935-1966 it was the home of the author Margery Allington.' He pointed to it. 'Those of you who knew you were coming here probably did your research and Googled her,' he said, knowingly. Several heads nodded.

'So you'll know that she wrote detective stories and

created the famous sleuth Albert Campion. And, of course, she really put our village on the map with her memoir, the Oaken Heart, which was about Tolleshunt D'Arcy during the Second World War.'

'I fought that bloke what killed his family put the village on the map,' Dave said. 'You know. It was in all the papers. Some farmer,' he added, looking round for the others to agree with him. Mr Harris was aghast that the group should know of such infamy and chose to ignore Dave's remark.

'Anyway, there, as you can see, is the blue plaque on the wall of the house,' he continued hurriedly. 'It is a private family home now and we are not allowed to go in. But, as it evident from the outside, it is rather splendid.'

The Three Sues gave their phones to Geoff who took a pic of them standing at the door. The others all queued to do the same. Janet took her pictures of the house from a distance. She wanted to get the whole building in.

'It's times like this make me realise I love 'istory,' Dave said, coming and standing beside her. 'I nevva liked it at school.'

'Well, perhaps you needed more field trips, to bring it alive for you,' Janet suggested.

'I think you're right. If I'd've seen old 'ouses and bin told about 'em I'd've bin more interested,' he agreed.

'Right! We'll now walk back towards the centre of the village and then into the Golden Goose for our refreshments, which I'll just remind you are not included in the walk.'

'It's wonderful to see monuments maintained, isn't it?' Janet remarked to Colin and Eve, who were standing next to her as they slowly started off again. 'This village is so quintessentially English.'

'It is,' Eve agreed.

'Yes,' Colin said. 'I enjoyed listening to the history of

the village and D'Arcy House. And I think the Blue Boar Inn is an interesting place to be staying.'

'I saw some pamphlets on the reception desk about the history of the hotel. I'm going to grab one when we get back,' Janet said.

'Good idea!' Eve said. 'It's certainly atmospheric. And although they've renovated it extensively they've managed to keep the feel of the place.'

'I wonder if it's haunted,' Colin mused.

'Oh don't! I'll be sleeping with the light on tonight!' Eve laughed.

'If people did you no harm in life, they'll do you no harm in death,' Janet observed, philosophically.

'Agreed! But if anyone's around I'd rather not know!' Eve said giving a little shudder.

Walking back past the maypole they turned up a side street and went into the Golden Goose to have some refreshments, *which were not included in the walk*. There was a fair mix among the group of those having hot chocolate or coffee and others having beer or a brandy in their coffee to warm them up. The Golden Goose was a cheerful-looking establishment, which seemed to be doing a roaring Boxing Day trade, considering the size of the village. All the bar stools were taken and more than a dozen people, many with dogs at their feet, stood chatting with those who were sitting. Most of the tables were taken, but the landlady, a Barbara Windsor look-alike, who obviously played on this, smiled and waved them through to the snug, at the rear of the pub.

'Plenty of room through there, ladies and gents! Come on through! You're all more than welcome! Merry Christmas to you!' she shouted as the group followed her instructions and went through or made their way to the rear of the main bar where the toilets were situated. A young lad appeared immediately behind the snug bar and started serving their drinks. Mr Harris turned to Eve with a beaming smile on his face.

'I think this morning's gone rather well so far, don't you?' he asked, his rhetoric obvious.

'So far, I would say it has!' Eve agreed. 'Thank you. You've been most informative.'

'Well, I won't have so much to say on the way back because we cut up this road that the pub's in, turn left at the top, and then go along the lane which bends round and brings us back to the Blue Boar Inn from the other side.' He looked at his watch. 'Should take us just under an hour, so they might want to be drinking up soon. Especially if some of the ladies have still got to use the facilities. That always takes a time.'

'Okay. We'll give them ten minutes more and then we can start making a move' Eve agreed, wondering why it was always *the ladies* who seemed to keep Mr Harris waiting.

She looked round the group, happy to see everyone smiling and chatting. They all seemed to be getting on well. Janet, Colin and Pete were standing at the bar talking quietly together; Dave was with Frances, Kim, Penny and Eve; Don and Vince were talking to two of the Sues. Geoff caught her eye and signalled that he and Slim Sue were slipping out for a cigarette. She smiled and nodded at him to show she'd understood. As they pushed the snug door to go back through the bar, Eve caught a glimpse of Angela in the bar, talking to two men. She was cupping a large brandy snifter in both hands and looking over the rim at the older of the two men, a silver-fox with a short goatee and a beautiful spaniel at his feet, in what Eve could only think of as a *girlie fashion*.

Hmm! Might have to keep an eye on her.

Frances shuffled past waving her phone in the air.

'Just going outside for a second. No signal in here!'

Vince approached her on his way to the gents.

'Sorry about Mick and John. You know, not coming this morning.'

'It's their Christmas break,' Eve said. 'Nothing's compulsory. They don't have to come if they don't want to.'

'They both had a bit of a skinful last night and Mick couldn't even open the door to us. John said he hadn't slept much and that he wasn't coming either. I think he probably got lucky,' he laughed, adding, 'Shame really, that he's missed it,' when he saw that Eve hadn't reacted.

'It really is no problem as far as I'm concerned,' Eve tried to reassure him. 'As long as I know where everyone is and that nobody's had an accident or some such, then I'm always happy for people to do their own thing.'

'Thanks,' He turned to pass her and then he stopped. 'And I know you've probably heard that we were a bit loud last night and the night before...' Eve said nothing, neither confirming or denying what she might have heard. 'But, we didn't mean to cause offence or nothing. You know what it's like. We all know each other from the rugby club and it all gets a bit wild sometimes.'

'I'm sure if any of you were offensive to anyone that you'll be man enough to apologise,' Eve said, smiling.

'Yeah. Yeah. Sure. I'll make sure they do,' he said, smiling at her and then continuing on his way to the toilet, almost bumping into Frances who was making her way back to the others to finish her drink. She'd managed to get a weak signal outside, but it was still no missed calls, no texts, no messages.

Eve, went round them all asking them to drink up as they had to move on to complete the walk in time for lunch. Penny screamed with laughter as a black and brown mongrel jumped up against her and sniffed all round.

'I think he can smell my Sammy,' she said to the apologetic owner, who was pulling the dog off.

'Well, there's not much I can say to that, is there, love?' the man said, giving her a wink and a huge grin. Penny screeched again.

'Ehh! Sammy's my dog, you cheeky thing!' she reprimanded him.

They all called their goodbyes to *Barbara Windsor* and the regulars in the bar.

'Make sure you come back and see us! We do lovely pub grub!' she shouted as they made their way through the bar and back outside.

'Is it me, or has it got colder in the last half hour?' Frances asked, shivering as she zipped up her jacket.

'It probably feels colder because it was lovely and warm in there,' Olivia said. 'I must say, I'm looking forward to our lunch and seeing that roaring fire in the lounge back at the hotel.'

'Me, too! I can't believe I'm peckish after the huge breakfast I ate,' Kim said. 'I think I must have worms!'

'No, course you haven't! We've just walked all the breakfast off by now,' Frances said. 'And I love Boxing Day lunch. I assume it'll be cold meats and pickles, won't it, Eve.'

'Off the top of my head, I think that's one of the choices,' Eve said. 'I left the menus with my paperwork back at the Blue Boar.'

'Of course! Why would you march around the countryside clutching a batch of menus?' Frances asked, giggling.

'You'd be surprised what we tour managers march around with!'

✦   ✦   ✦

THEY ARRIVED BACK at the Blue Boar Inn, chilly and

hungry at twenty-five past one.

'There you are! That's good timing for you!' Mr Harris beamed round the group as they walked up the driveway. He stopped and asked them to gather round him.

'Now, tomorrow morning, we leave slightly earlier at nine-forty-five, because our walk is somewhat longer and we still have to be back in time for lunch, which is going to be a bit later than today at two o'clock. We'll end up in the village, but we'll be approaching it from the south side and we'll get a good look at the church, St Nicholas's, and also D'Arcy Hall. Everyone clear?'

Everyone nodded and smiled at him.

'Thank you very much, Mr Harris. We've enjoyed this morning and we look forward to tomorrow,' Eve said, starting off a little round of applause, which rippled through the group. 'We'll see you here, outside, at nine-forty-five sharp.'

''Erm, and if you could please sign my invoice,' Mr Harris said to her as the group marched off into the hotel eager to get to their lunch. He unzipped his jacket and delved into an inside pocket, pulling out a sheet of A4 paper that had been folded into three. He opened it and presented it to Eve, flourishing a pen from a side pocket with his other hand. Eve signed the invoice and handed it and the pen back to Mr Harris.

'Well, thank you very much, Mr Harris. Enjoy your lunch and the rest of Boxing Day! Got any nice plans?' she asked, to show polite interest more than anything.

'I shall be eating a cold lunch at home. I live just a ten minute drive away; that's my car over there,' he said, pointing at a very dirty four-by-four. 'And then I shall be visiting my dear wife.'

'Oh!' Eve was unsure what he meant. Mr Harris sighed.

'She's in a nursing home. She's had dementia for a

number of years, since her late forties actually.'

'Late forties? Goodness me! That's young...' Eve was genuinely shocked.

'She doesn't recognise me, or anyone now. She doesn't know where she is or who she is. But I visit every day, because I'm certain that deep down inside, somewhere, is the Mary I love, married and spent twenty-seven very happy years with.'

He looked into the distance, almost lost in his own thoughts. Eve felt a lump come to her throat. She was annoyed with herself.

After all these years working with singles' groups, have you still not learned not to judge people by their appearance or on first impressions?

She gently placed a hand on his arm. No wonder he was sharp and a little strange.

'It must be very difficult for you...'

'It's harder for our daughter, Elizabeth. She's twenty-four and engaged to be married. It's the time of life she should have her mother with her, looking at wedding dresses, picking bridesmaids colours. She rarely goes to see her, because she can't bare to see the empty, ageing shell that her beautiful, strong, kind, compassionate mother has become. She can't even feed herself. Yet, she was such an amazing woman.'

'I'm sure she was,' Eve said, kindly. 'And I'm sure you're right that on some level she knows who you are and looks forward to your visits every day.'

'Well, I'd best be off!' Mr Harris said. 'See you tomorrow!'

He strode briskly over to his car and the lump in Eve's throat got bigger and tears flooded her eyes.

Poor man!

As she watched him drive away she wondered how she

would ever have coped if she'd had a husband who was ill like that. She couldn't imagine. She'd been married once, but it only lasted a very short time. She'd found marriage constrictive, like a jacket that was a size too small. She felt a huge relief when she'd divorced, although she'd then lived with Bill, who'd owned Travel Together, for six years. That had been less restrictive until he'd wanted them to marry. Fearful of more suffocation, she'd turned him down and they had parted amicably. He'd given her a payoff and then employed her as a tour manager. She had no complaints.

No! Marriage certainly isn't for everyone!

As she pushed open the door and walked into the hotel, it dawned on her that she hadn't called her mother the previous day. All the sudden change of plans with the new job had completely put the thought out of her head.

I'll ring as soon as I've had my lunch.

And she decided she'd also ask to speak to her father. It had been far too long since she had done that.

✦   ✦   ✦

THE CONVERSATION AT the tables was lively when Eve took her place. The Four Friends, Blonde Sue and Angela were sitting on the round table, the others on the long oblong one. A burly ginger guy with a beard raised a hand to her as she came in.

'Hi! I'm Mick,' he said. 'Sorry about this morning, I decided to have a lie-in.'

'No problem at all! Nice to finally meet you,'Eve said, smiling at him. She turned and addressed the bald man sitting next to him, who looked a bit sheepish.

'And you must be John,' she said.

'No shit, Sherlock! You're bright!' he said, laughing at his own wit.

'Sorry about him,' Vince said. 'Shut up John-boy and eat your dinner!'

'Is your choice of food okay, Angela?' Eve asked, having checked the vegetarian options on the menu before she'd come into the restaurant. 'Pear and asparagus risotto, feta and red-pepper flan and eggs Benedict with wilted spinach?'

'It'll do!' came the reply. Angela hadn't even looked at Eve; she seemed engrossed in her conversation with Don. In fact, she seemed to deliberately ignore John who directed a question at her.

'Are you sure you didn't stab me? I've got a right bruise and what looks like a cut on my arse,' he said.

Something going on there, but I don't want to know!

Angela didn't take her eyes off Don's face; she was doing a great job of being totally unaware of John's presence.

Eve was pleased she was going to be sitting on the oblong table and took the space between Olivia and Geoff.

'Ooh! This salmon's gorgeous! You can't beat a bitta salmon, can ya?' Dave said, sighing with pleasure. 'An' the cold buffet's beautiful, Eve. Great big slices of cold turkey. Loadsa pickles. Just like I like it! And nothin' like a bit of Branston, is there?'

'My foot's a bit sore. I'm going to bathe it as soon as I've finished lunch,' Olivia said. 'But thanks for the plaster. I'm so glad you had one on you. I'd never have thought of taking one, even though I've got a strip in my toiletries bag.'

'As you said earlier, I have to *'Be prepared'*. Eve hooked her fingers in the air to form inverted commas. 'Haven't you noticed that I wear a jacket with lots of pockets?'

'I have to say, in fact I probably said it to you in India, but I don't know how you do your job, I really don't,' Kim said, from across the other side of the table.

'I think it's rather a lovely job,' Olivia said. 'Staying in nice hotels, seeing the world…'

'Dealing with stroppy buggers like us!' Frances interrupted.

'Well, not all the time!' Olivia said. 'I mean, it must be a nice job or why would people apply to do it? That Polly in Turkey said they have dozens of applications every week.

'That's probably because people look at someone like Eve and think she's living the life and they want to do the same,' Penny said. 'I mean, I know this is only a short Christmas break, like, but you must do some fabulous trips, don't you, Eve?'

'I've been very fortunate in that I've been almost everywhere in the world I ever wanted to go. And all our trips are fabulous,' she said, towing the company line.

'So if it's not a great job, why have you done it for so long?' Olivia insisted, turning to Eve.

'Oh, it can be a great job, don't get me wrong. I love what I do, but when things go wrong they tend to go wrong with bells on. But it becomes a way of life, rather than a job, is, I think, the answer to your question. You get used to being away and then coming home for a week or so, catching up with people, picking up the threads of your life for a short time and then packing your case, checking your paperwork, writing your group's welcome-letters before you go off again, somewhere else.'

'I suppose it's never boring,' Kim said. 'Certainly not nine-to-five!'

'It's never dull! Although, there is always a certain routine to it, irrespective of where you are in the world. The job is the job whether you're in Essex or Egypt.'

''Ere! I've just thought. You're an Essex girl, ain't ya, Eve?'

'I am indeed! I live in Horndon-on-the-Hill, which is right by the Thames, on the south side of the county, but I wasn't born in Essex.'

'Where was you born?'

'Corfu.'

'You Greek? I don't think I knew that! Well, I'd nevva 'ave thought it.'

'I've been in England for years, since I was eighteen, so I've lost my Greek accent completely.'

'Well, I couldn't do your job. I'd lose patience with people who did stupid things after I'd warned them not to. Like the bloke broke his leg, in Antigua,' Frances added, warming to the drama of Eve's working life.

You didn't know the half of what I dealt with in Antigua!

'But you take it in your stride. It's part of the job. I mean some of you have stressful jobs, don't you? Pete aren't you a fire-fighter?' Eve asked wanting to move herself from the epicentre of the conversation.

'Oh, aye, I was. And I suppose I saw things and dealt with things that other people would have blanched at. But there was something about the job I loved. And when you're doing a job you love you take the rough and the smooth.'

'Yes, you're right, Pete,' Eve said.

'And Penny's an ambulance driver!' Dave volunteered. 'That must be a stressful job, specially if you're the first one on the scene of a motorway pile up or something.'

'It can be. Like Pete says, though, you deal with it. When you get to your job you just go into professional mode and get on with it. It's what you're trained to do.'

'Do you find you have an active social life to counter-balance work?' Olivia asked her.

'Sort of. I take Sam to dog-training classes and I volunteer at the hospital radio station, too. Just once a week, like. And I go tap-dancing,' she added with a giggle.

'Oh that sounds like fun,' Eve said.

'It is. I'm only a beginner like, but I've mastered my

time-steps and I'm doing an exam next year.'

'That's good, innit?' Dave said, looking at her with respect.

'But look at what you dealt with in India, Eve!' Kim said, bringing the conversation back to Eve and the trials and tribulations of her job.

'What happened in India?' Frances wanted to know.

'One of the group died. On the dance-floor. Just as we'd done the Hokey-Cokey,'

'No!' Frances said.

'Bloody 'ell!' Dave gasped.

'Poor man! How awful!' Janet whispered.

'Yes! A nice man, a real gentleman, he was. Jim! That was his name. He came from somewhere near the Lake District.' Kim filled everyone in with the details. Eve felt a wave of sadness sweep over her at the memory of Jim and his death. He had been an extremely nice man, as Kim had said. But one with a couple of dark secrets that Eve had found out while sorting through his personal effects after his death. It had upset her that she'd discovered them. It had soured her memory of him.

Ignorance is bliss!

How true that was! She'd felt that several times in her life. But once you knew something, or saw something, you couldn't un-know or un-see it.

'Excuse me,' Pete said, standing up and heading for the door.

'What's up with 'im?' Dave asked.

'He probably just needs the gents,' Eve said.

'Actually, it's the first Christmas since his wife died,' Olivia volunteered, then quickly realised she'd broken a confidence. 'Oh, please, don't let him know I've told you! I said I wouldn't say anything…But it might have upset him hearing about someone else dying.'

'Mum's the word!' Dave said, touching his finger to his lips.

'Do you have any medical training, Eve?' Janet asked.

'Not really. I've got a first-aid certificate, I mean I'd know what to do if one of you started choking, or fainted, but let's hope I won't need to practise any of it this afternoon!' she laughed. 'What do you do, Janet?'

'I've just retired after forty years of being a midwife,' she replied.

'Ehh! The emergency services are all well-represented here!' Penny joked.

'So if anyone goes into labour you'll be alright!' Dave said.

'That's something I've never had to deal with, thank God!' Eve said. 'Nobody's ever given birth on one of my trips. Perhaps I should add the little word *'yet'* to that and touch wood,' she said, tapping the back of the chair.

'Ain't you ever bin on a plane where someone's had a baby?' Dave asked.

'No, I haven't. And if I had, it would be nothing to do with me!' Eve said laughing. 'The cabin crew would have to deal with that.'

'Have you dealt with any multiple births?' Tall Sue asked Janet.

'On many occasions.'

'What's the most you've been at?'

'I've been present four or five times when triplets have been born, and two sets of quads but all those births were by Caesarean and only one set of triplets were conceived naturally, all the others were IVF. It's rare to have a natural conception with more than twins.'

'I've got twins,' Tall Sue said. 'Identical boys. Ricky and Robby. They're twenty-eight now. That was a natural birth, but Robby was breach. I had twelve stitches.'

"Err!' Dave said, looking queasy.

'I've never had any more kids after that!' she laughed.

'I don't blame you! A single birth was enough!' Frances said. 'Especially with the size of my Darren's head!'

'How many births have you seen over the years? It must be hundreds…' Kim asked.

'More than ten thousand.'

'What?' Everyone was open-mouthed.

'Forty years is a long time,' Janet said.

'And how many children have you got yourself?' Frances asked.

'I have never been married,' Janet replied, returning to her lunch.

There was a moment's silence and then everyone else followed suit.

'Lovely grub!' Dave said.

✦   ✦   ✦

ON THE ROUND table the atmosphere wasn't as pleasant as on the oblong one. John, who was already back on the beer, wasn't pleased to see his mate Don muscling in on the woman in the group he considered to be *with him*. The more he tried to edge into their conversation, the more Angela shut him out. At one point, she even put her cutlery down and ran her hand along Don's arm. Blonde Sue and Vince were also deep in conversation. Blonde Sue's son, Gav, had been scouted by West Brom and she was as pleased as punch about it.

'How old is he?' Mick asked, overhearing what they said.

'Fourteen.'

'You've got a fourteen-year-old son?' he asked.

'Yes,' Blonde Sue replied, blushing at the expected compliment. But Mick didn't tell her she looked too young to have a fourteen-year-old.

'So, how come you're not spending Christmas with him, then?'

'He's with his dad.'

'Well, obviously. But it's usually mothers that claim the kids for Christmas. I mean, why do you think the four of us are here?' he asked, looking round at the others.

'His dad lives in Cyprus and he asked if Gav wanted to spend Christmas in the sun for once. I could see he wanted to go and so I let him.'

'Fucking hell! I wish my ex was as understanding as you! All she sees me as is the one who foots the Christmas present bill. She thinks I'm fucking Father Christmas, she does!'

'How many kids have you got?' Blonde Sue asked.

'Five.'

'Well, it must be hard for her to pay for everything if she's looking after five children, mustn't it?'

'The miserable bitch should've stayed married to me, then, shouldn't she?' he snarled.

'I can't think why she wouldn't have,' Angela said, catching Blonde Sue's eye as she sipped her wine. Mick looked at her, unsure as to whether she'd paid him a compliment or not.

'Don't get him started on the ex,' Don said. 'I'm looking forward to the quiz this afternoon, aren't you? I like quizzes,' he said, to nobody in particular in an attempt to change the subject.

'I can't think of anything more boring!' Angela said. 'I certainly won't be taking part.'

'What you gonna do instead?' John asked.

'Go and have a siesta probably.'

'Oh, yes.' His eyes lit up at the prospect.

'Yes. I had a terrible night's sleep for all the wrong

reasons,' Angela said. 'An absolutely ghastly night! One of the worst of my life!'

'Well, we're looking forward to the quiz. Eve's going to set it up in the lounge for quarter past three, I think,' Blonde Sue said.

'Bully for bloody Eve! You know, I really don't see why the rep, or tour manager or whatever she calls herself, has to be with the group all the time. I mean, why does she even have to eat with us, for God's sake? When all's said and done, she's an employee, not a group member.'

'So where would you suggest she eats, then?' Blonde Sue asked her, truly amazed at Angel's attitude.

'With the hotel staff, of course! In the kitchen, or staff canteen or wherever.'

'This morning you were complaining we didn't have a tour manager, now you're complaining because we have.'

'Yes, some Essex woman they've brought in because they couldn't get anyone else!'

The two women's voices had become louder and those on the oblong table had quietened down and could hear what they were saying.

'All I'm saying,' Angela continued, 'is, that yes, we should have a tour manager because that's what we've paid for and so the company should provide one. And by not providing one for more than twenty-four hours, they were negligent. But now that they have sent one, I fail to see why she has to be with us twenty-four-seven, even eating at the table with us, because when all's said and done, she's an employee, she's working for us!'

'You're bang out of order!' Dave called from the oblong table. 'Who do you think you are, talking about Eve like that?'

'I'm having a private conversation over here, that I'd thank you not to butt into,' Angela said, defensively.

'You're having a very public, private conversation that we can all 'ear. An' you're being very rude about a lovely woman who's doing' 'er job and doin' 'er best so that someone like you, who probably ain't got no-one else to spend it with, can 'ave a nice Christmas. An' this ain't friggin' Upstairs Downstairs, just cos we're in an old 'ouse. Eve ain't no poor parlour maid who 'as to eat below stairs, you stuck-up cow!'

'Right! Well, desserts are on the trolleys over there,' Eve said, jumping in before Dave or Angela said anything else; something even worse that they might regret. 'And they'll bring coffee in just a moment. I'm going to get ready for the quiz. No obligation to take part, but I hope you will. I'll be ready to start in the lounge at quarter past three. Okay?'

And with that, she pushed her chair back, smiled polite-ly at everyone, on both tables, and strolled out of the restaurant with her head held high.

✦   ✦   ✦

PETER ROLLED OVER and out of the foetal position he'd been in for the last fifteen minutes. His body gave one final heaving sob and he looked at the clock on the bedside table, which showed *15:11*.

This has to stop!

He chided himself, yet he really didn't want to go down and join in the quiz, but knew that if he didn't he'd only stay up here in his room wallowing in his grief and feeling sorry for himself. And besides, if he didn't put in an appearance people would only wonder where he was and why he wasn't joining in and then he'd have to pretend he'd had a headache or a stomach upset and he didn't want to tell lies.

There have been too many lies and secrets!

He forced himself to get off the bed and go into the

bathroom and wash his face. He splashed on a bit of aftershave that Marilyn, his kindly, elderly neighbour had given him as a Christmas present when he'd dropped off his spare key to her so that she could go in and feed Jack and Jill, his two cats. He looked at his reflection in the mirror and sighed.

Smile, though your heart is aching!

He gave another sigh and then pulled his mouth into a beaming smile.

Fake it until you make it! Sometimes the grief-counsellors gave good advice!

He turned the key and opened the lock and stepped out of room three to face the world again.

✦   ✦   ✦

ANGELA HADN'T APPEARED for the quiz, which had suited everyone, not least of all Eve. Not because of Angela's earlier rudeness – after all, she'd dealt with ruder people than her over the years – but because it meant there were sixteen instead of seventeen, therefore four teams of four.

The Four Friends had insisted on being together.

'We're the A-Team, we are!' Mick had boasted. 'We always do the quizzes in our local. The rest of you haven't got a chance! Especially with the sport questions. That's why we don't want no women on our team. They never know fuck-all about sports.'

'And we all speak very highly of you!' Penny had called back at him, making the women, and a couple of the men, laugh.

The Three Sues and Geoff made up the second team; Dave, Penny, Frances and Kim the third and Pete, Colin, Janet and Olivia the final team.

'Right! There are seven categories; history, films, geography, Britain, science and sport. There is to be no arguing with the answers, okay? The answer that I've got here on the sheet is final. You can play your joker on any category, but would you please tell me now, which category you're going to play it on?'

'Sport!' Mick shouted out.

The other teams consulted with each other before making their decisions. Dave's team went for films, Geoff's history and Pete's also went for sport.

'Right, then! No looking anything up on your mobile phones. Anyone found cheating and their whole team will be disqualified,' Eve said.

'I like a bossy woman!' Mick called out.

'You'd have to be a bit sad to cheat at a little quiz like this, wouldn't you, now?' Pete said to his team-members.

'Some people are very competitive,' Janet replied.

'Okay. We're starting off with history. Here is your first question…'

✦   ✦   ✦

ANGELA HAD WORKED herself up into a bit of a temper. In fact, it was quite a paddy. She felt so very angry and her heels beat out a rapid tattoo to show it as she strode back down the lane towards Tolleshunt D'Arcy. It was already getting dark; the clouds had brought the dusk earlier than usual so that although it was only three-thirty it seemed much later.

Fucking Christmas break! Fucking group of people! Fucking tour rep!

Angela wanted to take her anger out on someone, anyone and everyone. She marched on through the gloom, muttering to herself as she went. She was furious that she'd been stupid enough to book a Christmas break in the country.

What is wrong with me? I LIVE in the country! Why didn't I go to some exotic city?

She didn't really have the answer to that. She'd only decided to go away for Christmas the previous week, once it became obvious that she wasn't going to be on the receiving end of any invitations to spend Christmas with anyone; not even one for Christmas Dinner. The thought of spending another Christmas Day by herself with a ready-meal, watching crap television and getting slowly drunker as the day went on made her shudder. That was how she'd spent it the last five years, since the most awful Christmas of her life. She squeezed her eyes, tightly, not allowing the memories to come flooding back in. She regretted not making plans sooner. That way she could have gone to somewhere like Barcelona, or Prague, or Rome. Or somewhere even further afield. She could have taken the whole Christmas period off and gone to a glorious beach, somewhere exotic, like Bali! That was what she would do next year!

And I don't give a toss if I have to go on my own. I'm AL-WAYS on my own!

Her last three affairs had been increasingly briefer, the third lasting only four dates. They had all been as equally disappointing and empty. Yet, she would never, ever, consider that perhaps she'd brought this state of affairs on herself. No. Angela was always the victim. She was always in the right and everyone else was in the wrong. It was Angela against the rest of the world. She hated her job and the people she worked with, treating them all with distain, never bothering to hide her contempt for them. In spite of marrying well, she'd always wanted her own career. She'd been a very successful senior marketing executive with the same company for fifteen years, being promoted to Director of Marketing four years ago. She'd considered leaving, but just the thought of starting out again somewhere else, that might prove to be even worse than Foster White didn't bear thinking about.

She hated her family. She hadn't had any contact with them for a number of years. She had nieces and nephews she might walk past in the street and never recognise. Her older brother had told her he wanted nothing more to do with her. And the younger one had gradually called less frequently, until their contact collapsed completely.

She hated her house. It was a cottage really, a rather sweet-looking semi in the Berkshire village of Bradfield, that had no mortgage. She sometimes thought of moving, but somewhere bigger would mean taking on a mortgage again, which she didn't want to do, and somewhere smaller than the two bedrooms, one bathroom she had at present wasn't to even be considered. She'd liked living there originally, but gradually, the neighbourhood had gone down. Chav families had moved in from Outer London; people who'd made their money with trades such as scrap iron became her neighbours. Their raucous voices, loud music and general lifestyles had all disturbed her peace and quiet. And in a village, everyone knew your business, which she didn't like at all. She'd brought in a local landscaping company to plant a six foot hedge all around her property to keep it safe from prying eyes. And then, travellers had appeared on some farm land not a mile away. The Council said there was nothing they could do about it and the local vicar, accompanied by one or two bleeding-heart liberals had actively encouraged them. Angela didn't know what was wrong with people sometimes.

Only two cars had passed her as she'd stomped her way on down the lane, each step crunching the head of the useless councillors who refused to act.

My whole life is a mess!

But that wasn't exactly true. The only time she was truly happy was when she was riding Butterscotch, her beautiful, pale cream horse. She'd had him for four years and loved him more than she'd ever loved anyone. She loved the weekends because she'd get up early and go to the stables, where Finn and Davina always had him ready and the two of them would set off together for a wonderful time. They'd gallop across the countryside, Angel, with her long, fair hair streaming behind her from beneath her hat, tits bobbing up and down was indeed a sight for sore eyes. She stifled a sob at the thought of him.

Why didn't I just stay home and got out riding with you, boy?

Yes, Butterscotch aside, her life was, indeed, a mess. She recognised that, but had no solutions. All that she knew was there was no way she was staying in the Blue Boar doing a quiz when there were decent men waiting to buy her drinks in the Golden Goose. And she wasn't going to waste another night with a loser like John. Just the thought of the previous night's debacle made her shudder.

By the time she got into the village it was already dark and she was feeling quite warm. Her anger had put a spring in her step that had got her there within forty-five minutes. She turned up the lane from North Street and saw the welcoming lights of the pub and smiled.

Good time: here I come!

✦   ✦   ✦

THE QUIZ HAD become a close-run thing and extremely tense. They were on the final category, sports, with Geoff's team in the lead with 98 points, but they had already played their joker, getting full marks on it as Tall Sue had a degree in history and worked in a museum. The Four Friends were lying second with 90 points and Pete's team and Dave's team were tied in third place with 85.

'Right! This is it! This is where we come right up on the outside and shoot straight over the winning-line!' Mick boasted.

But the questions had been about an eclectic mix of sports, which had upset the Four Friends.

'How we supposed to know that?' Mick shouted out when Eve had asked the final question; who holds the record for the most medals won for athletics in the history of the Olympic games?

Everyone went into a little huddle, suggesting names to each other.

'Do you want the man or the woman with the most?' Vince asked.

'The athlete,' Eve replied.

'She don't give fuck all away, does she?' Mick could be heard to complain.

'It's okay. We've got most of the others right, I'm sure we have,' Don said.

'Yes, but we didn't know who the royal brother and sister was…'

'Do you think anyone else did?' Don said, laughing.

'And even if we haven't got all of them right, we must know more than this bunch,' Vince added. 'I think it's someone like Carl Lewis or Michael Johnson. Put either one of them down. Carl Lewis! Yes, I think it's definitely him.'

Everyone swapped their answers with the table next to them and Eve prepared to read the answers. Things were going well, with the Four Friends cheering every correct answer, until they got to question fourteen.

'Which female tennis player holds the record for the most number of singles grand slam titles in the Open Era?' Eve asked.

'Martina Navratilova!' Mick shouted out, raising his fist.

'Steffi Graff!' Eve said in unison with Janet.

'No it's not! It's Navratilova. She equalled Billy-Jean King's record of nine.'

'That was Wimbledon titles,' Janet said. 'Graff holds the grand-slam record with twenty-two.'

'No! She can't do! Federer holds the record. He's won twenty. She hasn't won more than him. Nobody has!'

'Actually, she has. And the person who holds the most is Margaret Court, who won twenty-four, but she won before the Open Era,' Janet said, authoritatively.

'Anyway, we agreed, no arguing,' Frances said. 'If Steffi Graff is on Eve's answer sheet, then it's Steffi Graff.

'I'm gonna prove to you lot that it was Navratilova,' Mick said, taking out his phone and furiously attacking the keys. Then he looked at the screen in disbelief and put the phone back in his pocket.

'I can't get onto the internet,' he said.

Eve continued with the answers, all flowing smoothly until they reached question eighteen.

''Which royal brother and sister represented their country in sailing in the 1960 Olympics?'

The Four Friends kept quiet, not having known the answer to that one and they smiled to see that Geoff's group, whose paper they were marking hadn't know it either.

'It was Crown Prince Constantine and Princess Sofia of Greece.'

'Oh, well done!' Frances said, beaming at Pete's team.

'How did you know that?' Mick was aghast.

'It was Janet again. She certainly knows her sports,' Pete said.

'This is a fiddle,' Mick complained, aware that Pete's team were now only one point behind them.

Everyone got the answer to question nineteen right,

knowing that the team that had won the most UEFA Champion League titles was Real Madrid. The Four Friends were already high-fiving each other in celebration.

'And the final question; who holds the record for the most olympic medals ever won in athletics?'

'Carl Lewis!' Mick said, jumping up again.

'No. It's Pavlo Nurmi of Finland,' Eve said.

'Yes!' Pete, Colin, Janet and Olivia shouted out in unison, happy that they'd got the answer right, but even happier at knowing what it had meant.

'Never heard if him!' Mick said. 'You sure it's not Carl Lewis?'

'He's got twelve medals,' Janet said. 'Lewis has ten. He ran in the nineteen-twenties.'

'And we're really supposed to know that!'

'Well, Janet did!' Penny said.

'She must have seen the answer sheet,' Mick accused Janet.

'Oi! Don't be stupid!' Dave said to him.

'Well how would someone like her know that?' Mick asked. 'And watch who you're calling stupid!'

'I just love sports. I watch all sports and I like looking up facts and figures, especially when the Olympics are on, or the Commonwealth Games.'

'You don't have to justify yourself, love,' Frances said. 'Well done!'

'Just leave it, Mick,' Don said to him. 'It's only a poxy little quiz. What's the matter with you?'

'I don't like losing when it's not been fair…' he started to say, when Vince laid a hand on his shoulder.

'Like Don just said, leave it.'

'So, if I can just have your final scores, please?' Eve requested, inwardly jubilant as she did the mental arithmetic which showed that Pete's team had beaten the Four Friends by one point. She made a big thing of adding up the scores and then making her announcement. Before she could, Mick had got up and walked out muttering under his breath.

'So, in fourth place, we have Dave's Devils with ninety-five points!' She waited for the applause and cheering to die down. 'In third place, with a hundred and seven points; the Single Pringles!' There was more applause as the Three Sues and Geoff congratulated each other. 'In second place with one hundred and twenty-four points; the Bridgewater Brainboxes!' The applause and cheers were decidedly muted. 'And our winners by one point with one hundred and twenty-five are the Unusual Suspects.' Everyone cheered them and Don, Vince and John made a point of going over and shaking their hands, which everyone thought was nice.

'Sorry about Mick,' Vince said. 'He's very competitive, he hates losing.'

'Yes, he's a bit of a twat sometimes,' John said. 'Christmas isn't a very good time of year for him, not seeing his kids and that and not getting on with his ex.'

'It's not a very good time for a lot of us,' Pete said, 'but we mind our manners. But thanks for a good game. It couldn't have been closer,' he said, shaking Don's hand.

'And how come you really know so much about sport?' Vince asked Janet, unconvinced by her earlier answer.

'Like I said, I've always loved watching it. I spend the whole weekend watching football, rugby, motor-racing, tennis, whatever's on. My favourite is the cricket. Shame we didn't have any cricket questions, or I could have really showed off!' she said, as everyone laughed and applauded her again.

✦   ✦   ✦

EVE WAS GLAD to get back to the sanctuary of her room

once the quiz was over. She looked at the clock and saw she had a little over two hours before pre-dinner drinks. She kicked off her shoes, pulled her sweatshirt off and laid down on the bed. She grinned to herself at the outcome of the quiz. She'd loved the fact that Janet's team had won, not only because they had beaten the Four Friends – and try as she might she just couldn't warm to Mick – but it had shown the others that there could be more to someone than meets the eye. Not just with Janet, but Tall Sue, too. Her historical knowledge was amazing. She'd even known who'd allegedly entered into secret, bigamous nuptials with Elizabeth the First.

Eve suddenly remembered she still hadn't called her mother and turned to pick up the phone, but then a wave of tiredness swept over her.

A short siesta and then I'll ring.

She set the clock for six forty-five pm. She always did that, terrified that she would sleep through and not wake up. She laid back on the pillow, thinking she'd ring her mother after a short power nap.

✦　✦　✦

FRANCES HAD ALSO gone back to her room. She'd enjoyed the quiz and like everyone else had been pleased Pete's team, starring the Surprising Janet, had won, but she decided she wanted a bit of peace and quiet with her book for a couple of hours before meeting up for drinks. And besides, her phone had remained stubbornly silent throughout the quiz. She took it from her handbag and placed it on her bedside cabinet so that it would be close to hand if it should ring.

When! Not if!

Frances yawned. She hadn't slept much the previous night and the walk had been quite tiring, but a nice tiring.

She'd enjoyed getting the fresh air. And Milos had winked at her as he'd served coffee after lunch, whispering 'See you later,' as he'd leant forward to pour into her cup.

She yawned again. All this multi-orgasmic stuff was fine, but she hoped that by 'later' he'd meant tonight and not later this afternoon. She giggled to herself at the thought of being multi-orgasmic; it never failed to amuse her that she'd become so at almost fifty-one. Milos had been more than satisfactory last night, but without a doubt the King of the Orgasms had been Neville, the Jamaican she'd met in Antigua. They had had a real sex-fest. Neville had set her on the path of Cougars and Toy-boys but not only that, he'd taught her that she was a whole, earthy, sexual woman who deserved to be happy and have some fun. She'd certainly had that with him. And although she was saddened when she finally realised what he'd done to her, she regretted nothing about her time with him.

Je ne regrette rien!

She giggled, then checked her phone again; still no missed calls, texts or messages.

He's so bloody stubborn!

She sighed and picked up her book. She took a sip of the hot chocolate with brandy she'd brought up to the room, snuggled down under the duvet and started to read. She was asleep after two paragraphs.

✦   ✦   ✦

PENNY HAD DECIDED to stay on in the bar. She'd enjoyed her day so far; the walk had been pleasant and uplifting and had passed very quickly as she'd been lost in conversation with Dave. Then there had been a yummy lunch with more than a couple of glasses of wine. She'd loved the quiz and felt warm and mellow as she sank back into the comfy sofa and sipped her Rioja. Pete, Colin and Olivia had also stayed for a drink with her and Dave. Pete came back from the bar holding his pint and pocketing his change. He took the seat next to her. She liked Pete. And she liked Colin. And Dave. Especially Dave.

'I'm so sorry to hear you lost your wife,' she said to Pete as he made himself comfortable. 'My condolences. This Christmas must be very hard for you.'

'Penny!' Olivia screeched, going scarlet and looking at Pete. 'I'm really sorry, Pete, but I let it slip out when you left the table at lunch-time. I did ask those who heard me not to say anything.' She glared at Penny.

'Ehh! I'm sorry, pet. I didn't mean to shout my mouth off. I've had a couple of wines, like.'

'It's okay. It's not a secret,' Pete said, in some ways glad that the others knew. At least that way if he got tearful or sentimental again they would guess why.

'Sorry to hear that, mate,' Dave said. 'God, rest 'er!'

'Thank you,' Pete said, sipping his beer.

'Is that why you came away?' Penny asked him. 'To get away from the memories and such-like?'

'In a way,' Pete replied. 'So, didn't we do well?' he asked, beaming at Olivia and Colin, wanting to change the subject.

'Yes, indeed! Who would have thought Janet was such an authority on sports,' Colin said. 'Still, I suppose everyone has something that they're good at.'

'What are you good at then, Colin?' Penny asked, her cheeks rosy from the wine and the warmth of the open fire.

'Horticulture, I suppose. It was a shame there wasn't a section on gardening, or we'd have really stormed into the lead,' he beamed. 'And perhaps jazz. I do like jazz.'

'You need to 'ave a word with Kim,' Dave said. 'She's a musician. I think she said she plays the piano and the violin. She likes nocturnal things, or something like that.'

'Nocturnes, I think that'll be,' Colin said, smiling.

'Do you play yourself?' Penny asked him.

'Oh no! I'm just an avid listener and fan,' he said. 'I have quite a collection on vinyl and CD.'

'I like some jazz but not when they start doing all that made-up stuff, improvising, like. It sounds all out of time.'

'That's syncopation. The best part!' Colin said, smiling.

'What's your speciality then, Olivia?' Dave asked her.

'Well, I don't really know. I don't know much about a lot of things,' she joked.

'Pete?'

'Hmm. Well, probably golf. I was a bit disappointed there was only one golf question in the sport section, so I was.'

'I haven't got a speciality,' Penny said, sounding sad and upset with herself.

'Yes you 'ave! You must know all about the 'uman body and that, with your job.'

'Oh, I suppose so. Yes, I was able to answer the question about the biggest organ, wasn't I?'

'Yes, I was well disappointed with that. I thought my name might've bin mentioned somewhere in the answers,' Dave joked, making the others laugh.

'And I know quite a bit about soaps; I do like my soaps,' she concluded. 'What about you, Dave?'

'Well, motors. I know about motors, cos of me business. And I follow the football, although I ain't an authority.'

'Well, all in all, we're a right little bunch of know-alls!' Penny joked, finishing off her glass of wine.

'Want another one, Miss P?' Dave asked her. She blushed, delighted that he had a little pet name for her.

'I'd better not. I want to go and get myself ready for dinner in a minute,' she said, grinning at him.

Dave felt his heart flip. He really liked Penny. There was something so nice about her; she was lovely. He didn't care if she'd opened her mouth after a couple of wines. That was the sort of thing he'd often done himself and he found it quite endearing. And besides, Pete hadn't been upset by it. He looked at her out of the corner of his eye as she launched into a tale about something that had happened during one of her tap-dancing classes. He looked at the other three and saw they were all captivated by her, too. When he'd been on his previous Travel Together trip, everyone had mixed with each other well and Eve had been keen to impress on them all that it wasn't a dating agency. However, a few people had got together and he'd felt a couple of times that everyone had pulled except him. He'd been the only one not to get his leg over.

Even the really old dear had got off with someone.

Still, he'd got to meet Geri, and although they hadn't got together during the holiday, they had afterwards.

And look how that turned out!

He reminded himself that it hadn't exactly been a fairy-tale romance. But, looking at Penny, he felt something shift, and it wasn't just below the belt, but also in his heart. He wanted to spend time with her, getting to know her, not necessarily shagging her. Well, not immediately, anyway! He'd make sure that he sat next to her at dinner and that he'd dance with her at the disco. And perhaps suggest that they went for a walk on their own tomorrow. And he had an excellent excuse for keeping in touch with her once the break was over; she wanted a motor. And he would make sure he got her the best deal of anywhere in the whole country.

✦   ✦   ✦

CHRIS EDWARDS WALKED briskly through the kitchen and into the large preparation area. The extra staff they'd brought in for tonight and tomorrow were waiting for him and consisted mainly of local students looking for a way to bolster their incomes and two of Milos's friends. The local students, two girls and a boy, all knew each other and were introducing themselves to the other two.

'Right!' Chris said, clapping his hands to get their attention. 'We've got a group of eighteen who are residents and then another forty-two booked for the disco and buffet, so that's sixty all together. Not too many, but enough for us tonight. Kirsten and Alfie, I want you on the buffet. Make sure you keep it replenished, and that includes cutlery and crockery as well as platters of food. Chef will let you know when he gives you the last of anything, although there should be more than enough for sixty with plenty over. Alice, you can help Milos and Beniamin behind the bar and Stefano and Novak, you can collect the glasses and put them straight into the washer and also collect the dirty cutlery and crockery and bring it in for the kitchen staff to put into the dish-washers. I expect you all to help each other. I don't want to see anyone standing around while there's work to be done, okay? If the bar's busy, jump behind and give a hand and if the bar's quiet and the buffet needs replenishing then get yourself into the kitchen and start topping up. Any questions?'

Chris was pleased to see there were no questions and so he made his way back towards the reception desk where Tania stifled a yawn upon seeing him and leant forward to grab the phone, which had just started ringing.

✦   ✦   ✦

THE ALARM GOING off made Eve jump. She shot out her

hand and grabbed the clock and felt for the off-button. Not finding it she opened her eyes and saw that it was *18:20*. Not the alarm, then. The ringing continued and then she realised it was the phone. Not her mobile, the room phone. She reached out and lifted the receiver, coughing to clear her throat as she did so, in the hope of not sounding as if she'd only just been woken up.

'Eve speaking.'

'Hello. Are you the person in charge of the singles' group staying there?'

'Yes, I'm the Travel Together tour manager.'

'This is Jean, or Barbara as I'm usually called, from the Golden Goose, down in the village.'

'Oh, yes! Hi!' Eve sat up, remembering the tiny woman with the big blonde hairdo and ready smile. 'What can I do for you, Barbara? Jean!'

'It's alright I answer to both!' she laughed. 'Actually, it's about one of your group. Angela. A tall, slim sort of woman. Fair hair in a long plait. Talks a bit posh.'

'Oh yes, that's Angela. What's happened?' Eve was on the edge of the bed now, body alert.

'Well, can someone come and get her, please? She's had enough; been drinking for the last two and half hours solid. She seemed alright or I wouldn't have kept on serving her. I'm not one to turn away business, but she really needs to go home now. Nobody here can take her, cos they've all had a drink and I know it's not far, but you can't depend on the Old Bill not being about just because it's Boxing Day. And the local cab company won't take her in case she pukes in the back of the taxi. Well, you can't blame them, can you?'

'I'll come and get her myself,' Eve said, grateful that she'd only had her usual diet cola all the afternoon. 'I'll be about ten minutes or so.'

'Alright, love! Thanks. And you might want to bring a

couple of plastic bags with you, just in case.'

Oh, charming!

Eve's first reaction was that Angela should have to get herself back home, but then she couldn't leave her knowing she was drunk, even if it was of her own doing. She decided to have a quick shower and get into her dress and then she could fix her make-up and hair as soon as she got back. She needed to put her skates on or she'd be late for pre-dinner drinks at half-past seven.

✦   ✦   ✦

ANGELA'S AFTERNOON HADN'T gone to plan. Although she wasn't sure she'd had a plan, really, when she'd gone storming off to the Golden Goose. All she knew was she wanted to get back into conversation with Alec, the rather attractive older man she'd been talking to at the bar that morning. But when she went inside the pub there was no sign of him. She went to the bar and ordered herself a double gin and tonic and had slid onto an empty bar stool to drink it. The other stools had been taken by two couples, all deep in conversation who hardly seemed to notice her. She looked around. There were four elderly men playing dominoes at one of the tables, two young girls and a boy sitting in the armchairs at another.

Where were all the people who'd been in here earlier? Where was Alec?

She'd downed her drink in one go and signalled to the barman, a tall, spotty, rather gormless-looking man of about thirty, to bring her another one. He smiled as he placed it before her.

'Do you know Alec?' she asked him.

'Alec?' He said it as if he'd never ever heard the name before.

'Yes! Alec!' Angela could feel herself becoming irritated. *Why is everyone so thick? Alec! Alec! Alec!*

'He was in here this morning. Silver hair, beautiful dog.'

'Oh, that Alec! Alec Johnson!'

'Yes. Alec Johnson. Did he leave long ago? Is he coming back, do you know?'

'He's upstairs having a lie-down with the missus.'

Angela felt herself blanche at the barman's words. He hadn't told her he was the landlord.

'Is he coming back down to work?' she asked, choosing to avoid the mention of *missus*.

'He might be. But he don't work here. He's just Jean's boyfriend. They went upstairs for their dinner about an hour ago. She'll be down in a little while. She don't like to leave the business too long.'

That sort-of made sense to Angela. Alec had said he was an architect not a publican. What he'd failed to mention was that he was shagging the landlady.

Did I read too much into it?

She didn't think so. Angela knew a come-on when she saw one. He'd invited her back to the pub 'at any time'. That's why she'd come rushing back down. She felt a bit of an idiot now. The two couples at the bar finished their drinks and looked like they were making a move.

'Come on, you three!' one of the men had called to the three young people who were sitting in the bar. 'Look sharp if you want a lift to the Blue Boar.'

The youngsters got up and Angela could see they were dressed as waiting staff; the three in black trousers and white shirts. They pulled on their jackets and followed the two couples out.

'Bye, Adrian! See you tomorrow lunch probably!' one of the girls called to the barman.

'Righto! Have fun tonight!'

Fun? Fun? There's no fun to be had anywhere in the whole fucking county!

Angela looked round and saw she was alone in the pub apart from the grandfathers who were playing dominoes.

'Another double gin and tonic,' she snapped at Adrian. 'Haven't you got any music to liven this shit-hole up?' she asked as he brought her drink. Adrian went to a music deck and after a moment *muzak* started playing.

'Christ Almighty! I wasn't expecting jungle or hard rock, but haven't you got anything a bit livelier than this?'

'Well, what sort of music do you like?'

'Anything but this! It's the sort of stuff they play in lifts!'

Adrian headed back to the music deck just as the door opened and seven young men came in. Angela saw them from the corner of her eye and swivelled her head round to get a better look.

Well, hello!

She shifted a little on her stool and smiled as they came up to stand at the bar. They were speaking a language Angela didn't understand, but from their air and the way they dressed she assumed they were Eastern Europeans. She saw that they had noticed her and she returned their smiles.

'Seven pints please, Adrian' one of them said to the barman in almost accent-less English. 'And if she will allow it, please serve this lady with a drink from us to wish her the compliments of the season,' he continued.

'Well, thank you, very much. I'll have a double gin and tonic, please!' Angela said, pleased that the afternoon was suddenly looking up.

By the time that Jean and Alec came back into the bar an hour later, the whole place was shaking with the CD of Romanian folk songs that the men had produced and Angela, who had shed her jacket and sweater and was wearing just a very tight-fitting t-shirt that was soaked with sweat, was dancing round the bar with two of them trying to keep up with the intricate steps. The other five together with six local men and three women were all standing around clapping in time to the beat.

'Oi! Oi! Good evening, everyone!' Jean shouted, smiling and waving at her clients. 'Romania's finest are in again I see!' Several of the men stepped forward and kissed her on both cheeks, saying 'Merry Christmas!' as they did so.

'And Merry Christmas to you all, too, my darlings! Nice to see you back with us. Hello, Maria! Hello, Charlie! Hello, lovelies!' she called to her regulars. 'Come on then! Let's have a right good Boxing Day knees up!'

✦   ✦   ✦

EVE COULD HEAR the music as she turned into Goose Lane and pulled up in the pub's empty car park. Nobody was driving tonight, which made sense and she guessed rightly that most of the patrons of the Golden Goose lived within walking distance. She could hear the final strains of Abba's *Dancing Queen* as she opened the car door, which quickly morphed into something by Chas and Dave – *Chas and Dave?*— as she pushed the door of the pub and went inside.

Barbara/Jean waved at her from the middle of the bar, which seemed to have become a make-shift dance-floor. A group of people, their arms around each other, like football players during their national anthems were marching three steps forward and three steps back in time to the music.

'Here she is!' Barbara/Jean shouted. 'Hello, darling! She's through there. We've put her in the snug!'

Eve, picked her way around the dancers, jigging, smiling and joining in until she managed to get to the snug door. The silver-fox, who Eve had seen talking to Angela that morning was at the end of the bar. He smiled at Eve and held out his hand.

'Hello, I'm Alec. Can I get you a drink?'

'Oh, no thank you! I've only rushed down to pick Angela up. I've got the rest of the group waiting for me for pre-dinner drinks back at the Blue Boar. I'll just go through, shall I?'

'Yes. This way.'

Alec pushed the snug door open and stood aside to allow Eve to pass through. The snug was empty except for Angela, who was lying full-length along one of the benches. She was on her side, her mouth open and dribbling.

'We thought we'd better put her in the recovery position, just in case she threw up,' Alec said and Eve noticed a red bucket had been strategically placed on the floor in alignment with her head. 'One minute she was life and soul of the party, doing Romanian folk dances with that group of lads who are working on the new houses over towards Maldon. They're nice blokes, often come in here during the week for a drink or for a meal. They're never any trouble. And then, we looked round and she was on the floor; she'd passed out. Mind you,' he added, lowering his voice as if he were afraid Angela might hear him. 'I bet *she* could be trouble if she wanted. She was all over me like a rash at one point. I had to get behind the bar to pretend I was helping out while Adrian was on his break. The only way I could get rid of her!'

'Oh, dear!' Eve looked at Angela and and felt a wave of pity sweep over her.

What made someone drink themselves into oblivion?

'I mean, we all like a laugh; Jean more than anyone. She always flirts and has a drink and dances with the customers. I take it all in my stride. I'm an architect,' he said, 'I only spend time in the bar because Jean and I have been seeing each other for a little while,' he explained. 'But when Angela started twerking, even Jean called time on her! Good job she passed out when she did!'

'Right! Well, I'm going to need some help to get her into the car,' Eve said, going into professional mode. 'Come on, Angela! Time to go home!' she said, shaking her. Angela grunted and groaned something which sounded like 'Leave me alone!'

Eve bent down and got hold of Angela under the armpits and pulled her into a sitting position. Her head flopped back like a rag doll's and her eyes stayed tightly shut. Eve pulled her round so that Angela's face was towards her.

'Get her legs, please,' she said to Alec. 'No! Don't lift them up! Put them down so that her feet are on the ground. That's it!'

Alec did as he was told and then stood back. Eve looked at him in disbelief.

The words, chocolate fire guard, are coming to mind here!

'I can't manage her alone, so you are going to have to get to one side of her and put her arm round your neck. It's okay, I'll square it with Jean!' she couldn't help adding, feeling, perhaps irrationally, that Angela's being in the pub and being in this state was somehow down to Alec.

Alec stepped forward gingerly and reluctantly lifted Angela's arm round his neck as if she had some contagious disease. Eve got hold of the other side, Angela's left arm round her neck and her right arm round Angela's waist.

'Okay, Alec? On a count of three. One, two, three!' Eve and Alec flexed at the same time, in perfect synchronisation and managed to get Angela to standing, although her feet weren't holding her at all. She was a dead-weight around their necks. Eve gave a mental sigh. Fortunately, she'd thought to tell Chris Edwards where she'd gone and asked him to just check on the pre-dinner drinks and send her apologies if she was a few minutes late. At this rate she'd be lucky to be back before the disco was over!

Eve and Alec shuffled forward dragging their burden between them. Then they hit an obstacle in the form of the snug door, which opened inwards. This meant that one of them was going to have to let go of Angela to open the door.

'You keep a hold of her. She'll be too heavy for me on my own. You take her for a moment and I'll open the door,' Eve said to Alec. 'You got her?'

'Yes.'

Eve slid her arm from around Angela's waist and pulled Angela's arm over her head. She heard Alec grunt as he took the weight of Angela's unconscious body down his left side. Eve sprang forward and pulled the door open and grabbed a three legged-stool that was just inside the snug to wedge it open with. That done, she went back to help Alec, but before she could take hold of Angela again, she was swept aside by the youngest – and Eve had to add, the most handsome – of the Romanian builders who came across and effortlessly lifted Angela into his arms.

'You have car outside?' he asked Eve.

'Yes I do!' she said, walking ahead as everyone waved.

'Mind how you go, sweetheart!' Barbara/Jean called from the arms of an elderly bearded man. 'Come back and see us!'

'I will! Thank you!' Eve called back to her.

She walked ahead of Angela and her Knight in Shining Armour, clicking the car open with the remote as she did so, thinking what a shame it was that Angela was in no fit state to appreciate where she was and who she was with.

'Better she is in front of car,' the young Romanian said, standing by the front door. Eve pulled it open and adjusted the seat back as far as it would go. He then turned round and gently placed Angela in the front seat and then pulled the seat-belt over her and fastened it.

'There! She sleep and be safe until you reach hotel,' he said beaming.

'Thank you very much for you help…'

'Lucian' he said, offering his hand.

'Eve,' Eve replied, shaking it. 'Thank you, Lucian.'

She slammed the door and went round to the driver's side and got in. The dashboard clock was showing *7:40*.

Great! I'm already ten minutes late!

She reversed in a big semi-circle, waved at Lucian, who was standing by the door of the pub and then drove out of the Golden Goose car park at speed.

On the journey back to the Blue Boar Angela hadn't stirred. Eve knew that she couldn't get her inside and to her room without help, so she made straight for the reception area. Chris Edwards was behind the desk.

'Hi! I've got one of our group who's a little worse for wear outside in my car. Can someone give me a hand with her, please?'

'I'll come. Everyone else is busy in the ballroom.'

Chris followed her back outside and Eve could see that Angela was stirring inside the car. Eve opened the passenger door to hear Angela screaming.

'Help! Help! Get me out! Get me out!'

She was pulling on the seat-belt, not realising what it was or that she was even in a car. She looked at Eve without recognising her and continued to scream.

'Help! I've been abducted! Help!'

Eve leaned inside to undo the seat-belt as Angela struck out at her, landing a glancing blow on the side of her head with one hand and scratching Eve's hand with the other. Eve had had just about enough. She grabbed Angela's hands with her own and held them down, bringing her face to within two inches of Angela's.

'Now, pack it in! Do you hear me? Just calm down and behave yourself! We're trying to help you and get you inside safely. I'm trying to undo your seat-belt so that you can get out of the car. Okay? So just keep still for a minute.'

Eve could tell by the way Angela was looking at her through glazed eyes that she didn't know who Eve was and that she wasn't really taking in any of what she'd been saying. But she kept still and silent while Eve undid the seat-belt and then stood back, pulling the car door open wide for Angela to get out. She swung her left leg round in a very ungainly fashion and then seemed to have trouble bringing the right one to join it. As she managed it, she leant forward to stand up and toppled forward in an awkward somersault, vomiting as she did so, all down Chris Edward's immaculate trousers and over his shining, patent-leather shoes. He looked down at her in stunned disbelief, too shocked to speak or react.

Oh, Earth, swallow me!

Eve couldn't have been more embarrassed if she'd vomited herself. She looked at Angela who was still on her hands and knees and heaving and felt an outrageous urge to walk away and leave her there. But she knew she couldn't do that.

'I am so very sorry...' she started to say to Chris.

'It's not your fault, is it? Let's get her inside and then I'll sort myself out,' he said generously. He took hold of one of Angela's arms and pulled her to her feet.

'Come on! Let's get you inside,' he said as he walked off with her stumbling along at his side. Eve followed behind, admiringly, wishing she was that one-step away from the clients sometimes, so that she could stop being non-judgemental and treat them as they often deserved to be treated. When they reached the foyer, Chris sat Angela in a chair while he went and took her key from behind the front desk. He brought it round to her and placed it in her hand.

'Are you able to go to your room alright by yourself or do you need someone to go with you?' he asked.

'I can manage!' Angela hauled herself to her feet and staggered across the foyer, key dangling from one hand, which she then dropped. She realised she'd dropped it after a couple of steps, so she turned round and walked back and took three attempts before she could fish it up from the floor. She realised that Eve and Chris were watching her. She gave them a filthy look, pulled her jacket down, spun round, waited a moment for her eyes to slow down and stop whirling round in their sockets and then headed for the stairs, which she went up on all-fours. Eve and Chris watched her go and then turned to each other and burst out laughing.

'Just when you think you've seen it all!' Eve said. ''I'm just going to follow at a discreet distance to check she gets to her room okay. 'I'm really sorry about your trousers and shoes, though'

'I always keep spare everything in my room,' he said. 'I'll go and sort myself out before the aroma I'm giving off puts everyone off their meal.'

'Do you want me to stay here while you've gone?' Eve asked. She knew she should go and see how the group was, but she reasoned that they'd probably be doing fine without her. After all, they'd managed the whole of Christmas Day by themselves. 'Just let me check she's got back to her room okay and then I'll come down and hold the fort for you.'

Eve went up the stairs and turned into the corridor to see Angela sitting on the floor leaning against the wall opposite her room. She picked the key up from the floor next to her and opened the door. Angela's eyes opened as it creaked.

'There you are!' Eve indicated the open doorway. Angela struggled to her feet, which then immediately buckled under her again, sending her head-first into the room.

'Can I help you?' Eve said.

'Fuck off!'

So Eve went back down to the reception, where Chris was more than pleased to see her.

'Thanks, Eve, I'll be five minutes max!' he called, going through the staff door at the back of the reception desk.

Eve felt there was no need to actually stand behind the desk itself. She took a seat, thinking that she could leap forward if anyone needed any help. Just as she got comfortable her mobile phone rang. She took it from her bag and smiled to see that the call was from Melv.

'Hey, baby! You not at home? I've been calling you.'

'Hi! No I'm not. I got called to a job.'

'What? Where are you?'

'I'm in Essex, but the other side to me. A newbie tour manager did a disappearing act and left the group high and dry.'

'You're kidding!'

'I'm not! I got the call not long after talking to you yesterday.'

Yesterday? Was it only yesterday?

'So that's why you didn't pick up. I couldn't get back to you until real late last night and I wouldn't call in case I woke you. So I've been calling since, like eight am today. So how long are you there for?'

'Only tomorrow and the day after. I made sure it would all be over by the time you arrived before I agreed to take it.'

Well, that's good.'

'Oh, yes! Nothing is going to get in the way of your visit and Michael's wedding. So what happened yesterday, with the flood?'

'It was a burst pipe, which we were able to seal off

almost immediately. Fortunately, there was a maintenance man on standby. We had an empty suite we could move the people into. The room looked worse than it was. The housekeeping department have been working on it today, drying it out and such. All part of the running of a resort!' he concluded.

'And how was your Christmas?' Eve asked, imagining him sitting behind his desk in his office, swinging his chair back and forth, looking gorgeous and handsome.

'Much as I told you it was going to be. I had lunch with the kids, they then went to their mom's. I stayed here and last night a few local dignitaries and VIPs came and had dinner, so I ate with them and then we watched the cabaret for a while. Nothing special. How about you? What you up to?'

'Well, I'm in an old country-house style hotel, which is really nice, with a group of seventeen. And you know what Christmas can be like with a singles' group; most of them trying to escape it, not wanting to be reminded of bygone Christmases or of being alone, really. So I've got one or two horrors and several really nice ones. I've just been down to the village pub to bring back a woman who went off on her own and got horribly drunk. She was unconscious, out cold. And then when we got back here she threw up all over the duty manager.'

'Man! I don't know how you do it! I really take my hat off to you, Eve.'

'So now I'm manning the front desk while he's gone to change and then I'll be joining the group for a disco and buffet supper.'

'Well, you enjoy! Weather still okay?'

'Yes. It's cold, but dry. We had a lovely walk this morning and there's another one planned for tomorrow. But listen, I'd better go.' Eve had seen Chris re-appear, waved at him and headed for the stairs. 'I've got to tidy myself up and go and join the others.'

'I'm sure you look as beautiful as always,' he said.

'Oh dear! Mr Smooth or what?' she laughed.

'I mean every word!' he said. 'You know I do.'

'I'll ring you on the twenty-eighth, as soon as I'm home.'

'Okay, babe. Take care of yourself. Love you.'

'Love you, too,' she said, hanging up and smiling as she let herself into her room.

✦   ✦   ✦

WHEN SHE SCUTTLED into the ballroom ten minutes later, Eve was pleased to see that things were going well. Her group were sitting together on three tables except for John, Don and Mick, who were standing drinking at the bar. The tables were all beautifully adorned and set around the edge of the dance-floor and were taken with groups of lively people, all wearing their glad-rags and chatting and drinking. At the far end a deejay was busy at work and over to his right was a long table laden with food. As she was making her way over to her group the deejay brought the music to a stop.

'Ladies and gentlemen! I'm pleased to announce that the spectacular Boxing Day Buffet is now open! Please make your way over to this splendid table on my right-hand side and help yourselves. And while you're making the most of this feast, I'm going to slow the tempo down until you've all had your fill and are ready to work it all off on the dance-floor again!'

Eve saw there was a space between Kim and Vince and so she jumped in.

'Sorry I'm late, everyone! But I see you've all carried on without me,' she joked.

'Everything alright?' Kim asked her. 'You went to get Angela, didn't you?

'Yes, fine thanks. You know what it's like, Boxing Day, no cabs, nobody able to give her a lift back because they'd all been drinking.'

'Where is she now? Is she coming down?'

'I'm not sure. She's gone back to her room for the time being.' Eve had no intention of telling anyone about the state she'd found Angela in.

'Oh, I see!,' Kim said, cottoning on. 'Mum's the word! I love the way you're so discreet,' she added. 'And rightly so. I wouldn't have liked to think that you'd have discussed any of my business, you know, what went on in India.'

'My lips are always well and truly sealed. But it is nice to see that you've moved on in every single way,' Eve said.

'Well, no point in doing otherwise, is there? When I got back from India I made a complete change in the house. I rang my ex and asked him to come and get the rest of his stuff. He'd left a load of old junk in the garage and the spare bedroom and to be honest, I didn't see why I should be the one to sort it out. I surprised myself by being quite assertive about it. I think I surprised him, too, because I was assertive without whinging or whining at him. Anyway, within a week he'd come round and taken what he wanted and then ordered a skip to take the rest. And we were actually quite amicable with each other. Once his stuff had gone, I completely redecorated from top to bottom. I actually enjoyed doing it. I bought some new furniture and the house is now warm and comfortable and well-and-truly mine.'

'That's great to hear. You always feel better when you take control of your own life,' Eve said, thinking back to the time she'd left her family to return to England and then when she'd left her husband and had gone to live by herself.

'Exactly! And since then I think I've become a different

person. I'm no longer bitter about him or the woman he went off with. I've become very active in local politics. Oh, I'm not standing as a candidate or anything, but I help out with leafleting and such. And I've joined a book club and a group of singles who go out together once a fortnight. To the theatre, cinema, dinner, that sort of thing. No romance, but good company!'

'I'm really pleased for you, Kim.'

'But much of what's happened is down to you, Eve. You and that holiday. It's not being overly dramatic to say it was the catalyst that changed my life. Certainly my attitude and outlook on life. And Eileen. She was a lovely woman. We had a smashing afternoon together when you'd all gone off on that second safari. Talking to her helped, too. You know she's still seeing Murray?'

'Really? Well, that's a surprise. I'll be seeing him next week, he's going to Natalie and Michael's wedding.'

'Well, remember me to him. He turned out to be quite a nice bloke in the end, didn't he?'

'Yes, he did!'

'And give my best wishes to Natalie and Michael. I bet she'll be a beautiful bride.'

'I will. Shall we go and eat?' Eve said, indicating the buffet table where the queue was going down.

Kim and Eve went to the buffet as the rest of the group were returning to the tables. The food did, indeed, look delicious. Eve felt her tummy rumble as she looked at it. She hadn't realised she was hungry. As she was putting food onto her plate, she saw the *Vegetarian Dishes* sign and thought of Angela.

All this food and she's not here to eat it! I wonder if she's hungry?

Eve put her plate on the table and went out into the foyer. Chris was behind the desk, talking to two women. They took their leave of him and went back towards the ballroom as Eve approached.

'From what I've heard it's all going well in there, isn't it?'

'It's going great guns. It's a fabulous spread and the atmosphere's good. I just wanted to ring Angela and see if she wants me to take any food up to her. Can you put me through, please?'

'Sure. Pick up the phone in the booth over there, please,' Chris said.

Eve crossed the foyer and picked up the phone. Angela answered on the third ring.

'Yes!'

'Angela, it's Eve. I was wondering how you are and whether you want any food.'

'Good God, no! I'm not in the mood for any second-rate disco.'

'I didn't mean for you to come and join us. I was offering to send some up to your room. The vegetarian selection tonight does look good.'

'Are you being funny?'

'Not at all! I'm simply offering to send some food to your room if you don't feel like coming down to get some yourself. If you want me to, fine and if you don't that's fine, too!' Eve had just about had enough of this woman. The sudden, unexpected sharpness of her tone seemed to have an effect.

'Well, okay then. I will have something. And water! They didn't replenish the water in my mini-bar today.'

They did, but you're probably so dehydrated that you've drunk it all.

'Right! I'll get something send up to you. Is there anything you don't like.'

'Meat and fish.'

'Yes, I know that. You're a vegetarian. I'll just send a

selection, shall I?

'Yes.'

Would it kill you to say 'Thank you'?

Angela had hung up abruptly. Eve put the receiver down and went back to talk to Chris.

'Can a plate of vegetarian selection be taken up to Angela's room, please?'

'Hmm. We're a bit pushed to do room service at the moment,' he said.

'I understand. I'll grab a few bits and take them up myself,' Eve said. 'Once I've had my own dinner.'

'Yes, you make sure you eat first. I know she's a client, but she doesn't deserve the care and attention you've given her tonight,' he said ruefully, thinking of his soiled trousers and shoes. 'I just hope she appreciates it.'

Eve went back into the ballroom, where she found the others were now all digging into the desserts. She ate her food while listening to snatches of their conversations. She looked round and saw that they were all chatting and laughing as they ate, looking for the world like they were all life-long friends and not strangers who'd only met two days previously. Eve cleaned her plate, sighing in food-contentment as she did so. Thinking of the gorgeous, old-gold outfit she'd bought for the wedding, she decided, with regret, not to help herself to dessert. She picked up a plate and put a couple of pieces of everything that was on offer from the *Vegetarian Dishes* onto it. She took some cutlery and a napkin and then asked the young waitress for a tray. She then went to the bar and asked for a glass and a bottle of water, which she charged to Angela's room, and then made her way out of the ballroom to deliver it. Her knock was followed by the sounds of a crash. Angela must have tripped getting to the door. When she finally answered, she seemed taken aback that Eve herself was doing the room-service.

Her face was sallow and her eyes bloodshot.

'Oh! It's you!'

'Indeed it is! Here you are!' Eve offered the tray. Angela opened the door wider to allow her to pass through.

'You can put it on the dressing table,' she said, curtly.

Eve stepped inside the room and did as she'd been asked. She stood the bottle of water next to the tray. And then she turned to Angela.

'I've only spent today with you, but I have to say, that rarely have I met anyone so belligerent, aggressive, full of her own self-importance or downright rude!' Her tone was hushed and even, which meant it took a moment for Angela to register what was actually being said to her.

'You have gone out of your way to be obnoxious with everyone, myself included. I don't know what your problem is; perhaps it's just attention-seeking. And if it is, you need to grow up! Nobody is impressed by you and your antics. You've made yourself look foolish in front of the group, in front of a pub full of people and in front of the hotel manager. Getting drunk and vomiting over people might be your usual behaviour, but the rest of us are not impressed.'

'How dare you? Who do you think you are?' Her face had turned to a shade of puce that matched her eyes, which were bulging out of her head with fury.

'I'm the tour manager who's had the misfortune to have to deal with you. I know that you see me as just the hired help, from your insulting comments at lunch-time. I'm also the person who's just gone and rescued you from a pub where you were lying, blind-drunk, after making a complete and utter fool of yourself.'

'I'm going to report you! You'll never work again once I ring your company.'

'When you do ring ask to speak to Alan Dryden. He's the managing director. And he'll probably take great delight in telling you that after today's little episode you'll never be allowed on another Travel Together holiday again.'

'Good! Do you think I'd want to come again, with a bunch of losers?'

'I, more than anyone, understand that Christmas can be an upsetting, emotional time for some people…'

'Don't you fucking patronise me!'

'… But most don't go around taking out their upset and emotion on everyone else. That *'bunch of losers'* are some of the nicest people you could wish to meet. Not mixing with them, thinking yourself better than them is your loss, not theirs.'

'Get out!' Angela screeched at Eve, grabbing for the door knob and missing it. She grabbed again, successfully this time, and flung the door wide open.

'Enjoy your meal. Goodnight.' Eve turned and walked out of the room, quietly closing the door behind her. She gave a little grin to herself, then jumped out of her skin at the sound of the plate of food being hurled against the door and Angela's howl of rage.

✦   ✦   ✦

THE REST OF the Travel Together group were having a great time in the ballroom where the disco was in full swing. They had all been on the dance-floor, except Mick, who apparently didn't dance. He stood at the bar watching everyone else, including Don and John who were strutting their stuff with a couple of local women, Sandra and Janice. The music was due to finish at twelve. Eve looked at her watch and saw it was just after eleven and yawned and thought she'd probably go up to bed soon. It had been a very long day indeed.

Sitting across the table from her, Penny and Dave were

deep in conversation, talking about Angela and her lack of appearance at the disco.

'I reckon she got right drunk and Eve's 'ad to put 'er to bed,' Dave said. 'If no, she'd've bin 'ere. She'd've got 'erself all dressed up an' come down.'

'Unless she's got off with someone,' Penny said, mischievously.

'You reckon? What makes ya say that?'

'Ehh! I'll tell you a little secret!' She sat closer so that he could hear her over the music, but so that nobody else could. 'We've got intercommunicating rooms, her and me, like. It's locked, but you can hear through it.' She paused for dramatic effect and took a sip of her drink.

'And….?' Dave was well and truly hooked and reeled in. He knew it was a human failing, but he loved a bit of gossip!

'Last night she obviously had someone in with her. I think it was John but I can't be sure, like. But she was with him most of the evening.'

'Yeh, she was!'

'Well, I suddenly heard all this commotion, her coaxing him on. She was saying things like *Come on, big boy!* and screaming and making all sorts of noises, like. And so was the bed.'

'No!'

'Yes! And then suddenly, the bed slowed down to a stop and she got really annoyed with him. She was shouting and swearing at him and telling him to keep on going. And then it sounded like he threw up.'

'Bloody 'ell! Yet they ain't bin togevva today, 'ave they?'

'No! She's avoided him, I think. Deliberate, like. And if you think back to lunch, he was talking to her and she cut him dead. He said something about *Are you sure you didn't stab me?* I heard him! But she carried on talking to Don, or Vince, was it?'

'Well, I didn't 'ear 'im say that, but you're right. She 'as ignored 'im all day. Well, fuck me! Oh, sorry!'

'I'm dying to ask Eve what's happened to her but I don't think she'd appreciate that.'

'I'll ask her,' Dave said, grabbing their empty glasses and standing up and excusing himself as he pushed past Pete and Frances.

'Can I get you a drink. Eve?' he asked.

'I'm fine, thanks, Dave. I'm thinking of going up to bed in a minute.'

'Not stayin' 'til the end? That ain't very tour manager, is it? Still, I don't blame you.'

'Yes, I know, I'm failing in my duty of staying right until the national anthem,' she joked.

'Is Angela okay? Only me an' Pen was just sayin' we ain't seen 'er all night.'

'I'm sure she's fine. She decided not to come down tonight. She had some food in her room.'

'Bit of a cow, if you ask me,' Dave said, winking at Eve, 'I know you can't say nothing about 'er, cos she's one of your group an' all that. But she is.'

Eve smiled at Dave and refused to be drawn. Seeing that Eve's lips were well and truly sealed on the subject of Angela's absence, he shuffled over to the bar, doing a little dance round Kim who he passed on her way back to the table with a tray of drinks.

'Am I boring you, Frances?' Pete asked her suddenly.

'No! Of course not! Why do you say that? I'm having a lovely evening,' she replied truthfully and thinking about the rest of the night that awaited her with Milos in a little while.

'It's just that I can't help noticing you keep on looking at your phone to check the time.'

'No! I'm not checking the time!' she said, horrified that such a nice man as Pete might think her rude.

'You're expecting a call then?'

'No!'

'But you must have looked at it twenty times in the last ten minutes, so you have.'

'Well, I'm not *expecting* a call. Just thought I might have had one this evening.'

'From your man, is it?

'No! I haven't got a man! I'm a totally free agent!' she said, laughing and raising her glass. She tapped it against the side of his. 'To free agents!' she said, laughing.

'To free agents,' he responded.

'Oh, Christ! Pete I'm so sorry!' Frances froze with her glass halfway to her mouth. 'That was crassly insensitive of me. You've just lost your wife and here I am going on about being a free agent. I'm so sorry.' She took one of his hands in hers and squeezed it.

'Please, don't apologise,' he said, squeezing her hand back. 'The whole world hasn't stopped turning because I lost my wife. People have been tip-toeing around me for the last few months and it's one of the reasons why I wanted to be on my own at Christmas. Everyone would have been on edge, worrying they were going to upset me, you know? And I have to say you're someone that seems very happy to be single.'

'I am! I never thought I would be at first.'

'You're divorced?'

'Yes. I found out my ex had been having an affair at the time I was having chemo and surgery for breast cancer. It was a young girl he worked with. The office junior who he'd promised to go and live with as soon as our son was off at university.'

'Now I'm the one that's sorry,' Pete said.

'There's definitely no need to be! I mean, his timing stank, but it was almost like the cancer was symbolic. They cut the cancer out of my body and I cut the cancer out of my life. Oh, he pleaded to come back, but I'd never have trusted him again,'

'I can understand that,' Pete said, looking sad and faraway. 'Once the trust has gone, there's nothing left.'

'And since then, well, I've got on with my life and I haven't looked back!'

'I'm sorry you had cancer,' Pete said, 'You're obviously clear now, though?'

'Yes, thank God. I'm completely healthy now. What did your wife die of? If you don't mind me asking, that is.'

'She had an accident.' There was a moment's silence when it became obvious to Frances that Pete wasn't going to elaborate any further on what had happened.

'Oh dear. That must be awful when someone dies like that. It's all so sudden. No goodbyes.'

'Aye, it is that.' Pete downed the rest of his drink and put the glass back on the table. Frances thought she could see tears in his eyes and could have kicked herself for asking questions.

'Want to have a last dance?' she asked him, as some of the others stood up to go onto the floor as Pharrell Williams' *Happy* started up.

'I'll be off to my bed, thanks. I'm just about ready for it.

'Oh, Pete, I'm so sorry if I've upset you. I really didn't mean to.'

'I know you didn't. It's just that it's still early days for me. The first Christmas without her. But I've had a surprisingly pleasant evening. A good day, in all. Thank you for your company.'

'I understand.' She stood up and put her arms around Pete and was pleased to feel him respond for a moment, before he broke away, smiled sadly and made his way out of the ballroom.

Everyone needs a hug now and then!

Frances looked at her phone again; no missed calls, no texts and no messages. She threw it into her evening bag and sighed loudly.

Bugger him!

Then she burst out laughing and went to join the others on the dance-floor.

✦   ✦   ✦

ANGELA WAS FURIOUS with herself for having drunk so much, in spite of telling herself she had a right to enjoy herself however she chose. But it also meant that she was way over the limit to leave this God-forsaken shit-hole tonight and drive back home. Half of her was inclined to risk it; after all, surely the roads would be empty?

But what about the police?

She knew that it would be just her luck that two bored coppers who wanted to be anywhere but on duty on Boxing Night would be lying in wait to catch any poor motorist who might go anywhere near the speed limit. She thought about going cross-country and avoiding the M25, but she didn't have a clue which route to take. She got out her iPad and put her postcode into the AA's Route Planner, making sure she clicked the *avoid motorways* box.

Oh for fuck's sake!

The journey would take her right through London on the North Circular and would take more than three hours. And in London there would be police at every fucking junction! There was no way she was going to do that tonight. Her stomach rumbled. She looked at the food that was adorning the back of the door and the carpet and cursed Eve for making her throw it. She went over to the minibar and looked inside.

Yuk!

It was full of the stuff she usually wouldn't touch with a barge-pole. But she'd have to make an exception, she was starving. She also thought about ringing for room-service but then thought better of it. She didn't want any member of staff nosing around until she'd had time to throw the food and broken plate into the bin, and she had no plans to do that tonight! She reached into the minibar and pulled out a packet of six Jaffa Cakes and a Kit-Kat.

Some Boxing Night dinner!

She pulled off her clothes and dumped them in the corner. Her t-shirt smelt of booze, sick and sweat, making her shudder. She went through to the shower and let the hot water run over her. She washed her hair and conditioned it and then wrapped it in a towel while she soaped her body. Ten minutes later she was lying on the bed eating her chocolate while watching a repeat of the Christmas Day episode of Eastenders.

She didn't know how long she'd fallen asleep for, but she was suddenly woken up by laughing and talking coming from behind the locked door on the far wall. There was also the unmistakeable sound of bedsprings. She sat up, startled. Curiosity getting the better of her, she got out of bed and crossed until she was standing in front of the door. She could hear the couple next door quite clearly.

'I'm nearly there! Oh, yes, that's it!'

Dirty buggers!

She grinned and stood closer.

✦   ✦   ✦

IN THE ADJOINING room, Penny and Dave were having the time of their lives. They were sitting side by side on the bed, both bouncing up and down in unison. Penny was slapping her hand on the bedside table and shouting out in her *posh* voice.

'Come on, big boy! You can do it! That's it! Oh, yes! That's it!' She slapped the bedside table again in time to their bouncing. Dave was joining in with yelps and heavy sighs of his own.

'Oh don't stop now! No!' Penny screamed as their bouncing became slower and the bedsprings made a softer sound.

'Sorry! Brewer's droop!' Dave shouted at the top of his voice.

'Bastard!' Penny yelled as they stopped bouncing and sat like two naughty kids, doubled up with laughter, their hands over their mouths and tears running down their faces.

✦ ✦ ✦

ANGELA STOOD IN shocked silence. What had been a laugh at eavesdropping on a couple in the throws of sex had suddenly turned into a mortifying experience as she realised that whoever was in the room next door had heard every detail of her highly-embarrassing encounter with John the previous evening. Her first instinct had been to rush out into the corridor and hammer wildly on the door until whoever was in there opened up and then give them a piece of her mind. It even occurred to her that it might be John himself, who'd got off with someone else tonight.

Whoever she is, she's welcome to him!

But then she realised, that he probably wouldn't want another woman to know that he hadn't been able to perform because of the booze. She walked slowly over to the bed on tip-toe and got back inside, trying to pull up the duvet without making a sound, hoping that they didn't know she'd overheard.

Bastards! They think they're so funny and clever!

She turned up the TV set as loud as she could bear it. She'd make sure they were disturbed all night. She'd brought earplugs with her. She didn't care.

Let them laugh! I'll be out of here tomorrow!

✦   ✦   ✦

PENNY AND DAVE did, indeed, think they were funny and clever. As soon as Angela had turned the TV up they had taken their hands from their faces and both collapsed on the bed, shaking with laughter. Every time one of them tried to compose themselves, they started to laugh uncontrollably again.

'Ehh! What a…….' Penny was hysterical.

'I know! I know!' Dave sat up and grabbed a tissue from the box next to Penny's bed and blew his nose and wiped his eyes. It was a good ten minutes before they had fully composed themselves again.

'Dear, oh, Lord!' Dave said. 'I ain't laughed this much in years!'

'Don't start me off again!' Penny said, taking a deep breath and making a conscious effort not to laugh.

'Come on, Miss P! Let's have another drink!' Dave crossed to the bottle of cava he'd brought up from the bar and poured it into the two champagne glasses they'd also supplied, before placing it back in the ice-bucket.

'Cheers!'

'Cheers!'

'It ain't been a bad Christmas, 'as it?' he observed, stoically, as he sipped his drink, leaning back against the headboard and crossing his ankles.

'It's been much better than I thought it was going to turn out. I mean, the first person I met when I pulled up outside was Ms High-and-Mighty,' she nodded her head towards the intercommunicating door, 'and that was hardly a friendly, warming welcome.'

'Yeh, I know what you mean. The first night I did wonder if I'd done the right thing. You know, Christmas is a funny time of year, ain't it?'

'What, you thought people might be upset, like?'

'Well, yes, but I thought as well that they'd all be a bit… well, at a loose end. Know what I mean? People with no-one to pull a cracker with. Saddos.'

'Well, you must be a saddo, then, because you're here with us,' Penny said, logically.

'Yes. I suppose I must. Although you don't think of yourself like that, do ya?'

'Well, I certainly don't think of myself as a saddo, no. I think it takes courage to come on one of these, myself.'

'That's what Eve says. I remember 'er sayin' that to someone when we was in Antigua. *'It takes courage to come on a singles' 'oliday,'* she said.'

'And she's right! We can all sit at home and feel sorry for ourselves, at the way our lives have turned out. But when all's said and done, the only person responsible for your happiness is you yourself. Other people can't do it for you, pet.' She paused for breath and took a swig of her drink, spilling some down her cleavage. 'Whoops!' she said. Dave offered her a tissue. She grabbed it from his hand before he could mop it up himself.

'Well, I must say, that's very philosophical!' Dave said. 'Bet you never thought I could use a big word like that, did you?'

'And why would I think that?'

'Well, most people see me as a bit rough. I never 'ad much schoolin'. I was always playing truant so I missed out on a lot of things.'

'Yet you run your own business! And from what you've said, it's very successful! You have to be clever to be able to do that!'

'Hmm! I've never thought of meself like that!. Thanks!'

Dave put his arm round Penny's shoulder and pulled her towards him, kissing her on the top of the head as he did so.

'An' I've enjoyed Christmas with you. You've made it nice.'

'Thanks, Dave. I've enjoyed myself, too. But it's not over yet, man. We've got another walk in the morning and then the black-tie ball in the evening. That should be good. I can't wait to see you in a dickie-bow!'

'Ooh! I love it when you talk dirty!' Dave said, giving her a squeeze and making her laugh. They sat quietly together, enjoying the moment, until Dave coughed.

'Miss P?'

'Yes.'

'Can I ask you somethin'?'

'Yes.'

'Can we have a selfie tomorrow night when we're both dressed up? I'd like a reminder of me an' you and this Christmas.'

'Ehh! Of course, you can!' Penny said, slightly disappointed at the question.

'And…?'

'Yes.'

'Can we keep in touch? I meant it when I said I'd get a motor for ya.'

'I'd like that! But it's a long way for me to come down from Stanley to At Albans to look at a car.'

'I'll bring it up to ya! You don't 'ave to come down to me.'

'Well, I call that right good customer service!' Penny

said, laughing. 'And I can introduce you to Sam.'

'Who's Sam?'

'My boy.'

'You've got a kid?'

'A substitute kid, I suppose he is. He's my little dog. He's in kennels at the moment and I'm worrying all the time that he's okay, like.'

'I'm sure he is,' Dave said, somewhat relieved. It wouldn't have worried him if Penny had had a child, but he somehow thought the less baggage the better! 'They take well good care of 'em nowadays. 'Ave to be inspected and everythin', don't they?'

'I'll be glad to see him, though. Only one more night!'

'You sound glad about that.'

'Well, I am when it comes to seeing Sam…'

'But?'

'But?' she teased him.

'Nothin'. I just thought you was gonna say somethin' else, that's all.'

'What would I say? That I want to spend more time with you?' she said, looking up at him over the rim of her glass. Dave gulped.

'Do ya?'

'I wouldn't say no, like,' she said, turning to put her glass down and pulling his head down to hers. 'And we can't see you with nobody to pull your Christmas cracker now, can we?' She planted a long, lingering kiss on his lips.

'Turn the telly up,' he said, moving to unzip her dress.

✦   ✦   ✦

IN ROOM SIX Frances was lying on the bed fidgeting. She looked at the alarm clock: *01:20*. After an evening spent sharing secret nods and smiles, Milos hadn't shown up.

She'd assumed he'd be involved with clearing up but she thought he'd have been here by now. She'd showered and got into her special nightie and perfumed her cleavage again and sat on the bed and waited. And waited. She gave a deep sigh. And checked her phone again. No missed calls, no texts, no messages. She sighed again. Then she heard shuffling in the corridor. She braced herself waiting for the sharp knock. But the shuffler shuffled on by. She laid back against the pillow and closed her eyes.

I'm getting too bloody old for all this!

✦   ✦   ✦

IN ROOM SEVEN Janet placed her bookmark at the end of the chapter she'd just finished and then put the book on the bedside table. She always used a bookmark. She knew that some people would find that a little old-fashioned nowadays, but when she was eight-year-old one of her teachers had told her it was a crime to fold the corner of a page; a crime that was punishable by a whack across the hand with a ruler.

'That's what bookmarks are for!' Miss Glanville had said, sternly, her deep, loud voice reverberating around the classroom where the children sat upright and motionless, afraid to even blink.

Janet had never folder the corner of a page.

Leaning over she turned off the lamp and settled herself into the pillows.

It's a shame it wasn't a white Christmas. I'd love to have seen a bit of snow.

✦   ✦   ✦

IN ROOM FOURTEEN Pete lay in the darkness thinking back over his short conversation with Frances.

When the trust is gone there's nothing left.

Someone else's words that had made him sound wise; words that would haunt him for the rest of his days. He thought, too about Frances' comments on cutting out the cancer from her body and her life. And a tsunami of despair rose from the pit of his stomach and engulfed him. He turned and buried his head in the pillow, his fists flaying either side of it, his body heaving with sobs.

Why couldn't you just have cut me out, Maeve?

And then a second question he knew he could never answer:

Why couldn't I have deserved your trust?

✦   ✦   ✦

IN ROOM TWELVE Eve was already asleep. When she'd come back to the room she'd taken one look at the paperwork and shoved it back into her bag.

That can wait until tomorrow! Or when I get home!

She knew that the report on Angela would take a while to write. Eve found it difficult to believe that she'd only been with the group for one day.

Thank God it's not a fortnight!

Brushing her teeth rigorously, she thought she'd never understand people like Angela. They were selfish through and through and totally self-absorbed. She'd met lots of them over the years and had always wondered why they chose to go away with a group of strangers and then expect everyone else to do exactly what they wanted. On one level she felt sorry for Angela because for a woman of her age – or any age, come to that – to behave the way she did just demonstrated that she was extremely unhappy. But then again, she was a grown-up and had to take responsibility for her behaviour, which would have been appalling in a teenager. No, she'd leave the report on Angela for when she was home. She sat on the bed and set her alarm clock for seven o'clock to give herself plenty of time to have breakfast and be ready for the walk. As she turned off the light she suddenly realised she'd forgotten to ring Corfu. Again.

I'll ring tomorrow. And as a penance, I'll speak to Babas, too.

Although quite what she and her father would talk about she didn't have a clue. But she couldn't help thinking, as she drifted off to sleep, that it never seemed to occur to any of her family to ring her.

✦   ✦   ✦

IN ROOM SIXTEEN, Slim Sue came out of the bathroom naked and crossed over to the chest of drawers. She opened the top one and took out a matching purple satin bra and thong and slipped them both on. They went on easily. Slim Sue was proud of her figure. Oh, some women criticised her for being too thin but she knew that was wrong. Having once been twenty-eight stone she could never be too thin! The scars of the cosmetic surgery that had got rid of the excess skin had been expertly hidden by her consultant so that nobody would ever know. It had cost her a fortune, having meant remortgaging her house, first for the stomach stapling and then for the body-lift but it had been worth every penny. She stood in front of the full-length mirror and was pleased with what she saw. She'd redone her make-up and she quickly brushed her shoulder-length dark hair and was suddenly brought back into the moment by a knock on the door. She stood still for a second and pulled her stomach in and then went and opened the door. He stood there looking at her shyly and then pushed the door open and came in.

'Would you like a drink?' she asked, her hand indicating

the mini-bar, suddenly feeling a bit nervous.

'No, thanks.'

He stepped towards her and pulled her into his arms, kissing her hard, his tongue pushing between her lips as he hands swept frantically over her body.

Blimey! He's keen!

Slim Sue felt herself reacting immediately. She felt a warm surge between her thighs as his hands unclasped her bra and then caressed her breasts. He pulled off his own shirt and pulled her to him, his erection so hard she felt it through his trousers against her belly. He kissed her wildly and passionately as he undid his belt and let his trousers drop to the floor. Slim Sue stepped backwards and laid herself on the bed as he came towards her, kicking off his boxers. With one stride he was on the bed with her, his hands and lips covering her body, lightly massaging and caressing, making her tingle and glow with pleasure and anticipation. He pulled her panties from her, thrusting his fingers into her at the same time, making her gasp loudly.

'Do you like that?' he asked.

'Oh, yes! Oh, yes! I really like that, Milos!'

DAY FOUR

✦

FRANCES HAD WOKEN up at four-thirty-five to find her head at a strange angle half off the pillow and the light still on. She straightened up very slowly, her neck aching. She looked at the door, almost surprised not to see Milos standing there, and somewhat miffed that he hadn't let her know that he wouldn't be coming to visit.

But how would he do that?

He didn't have her mobile number and it was probably too risky for him to try to call her room from the hotel switchboard. Added to which, he was probably tired, not having slept much the previous night and he'd worked on and off from breakfast right through until midnight. Thinking of phones, she reached and checked hers in case it had been ringing and she'd been in such a deep sleep she hadn't heard it. No missed calls, no texts, no messages. She was a bit put out that nobody at all had called her, but then she remembered that she'd told everyone she was going away and had made all her *Merry Christmas* calls before she'd left home on Christmas Eve.

Oh well! Get back to sleep!

She got up and went to the bathroom and cleaned her teeth. It never bothered her going to sleep with her make-up on, but she hated not cleaning her teeth. She went back into the bedroom and got into bed. As she did she thought she heard shuffling in the corridor again. She listened but it had stopped.

Obviously nothing to do with me!

She reached over and turned off the lamp, hoping that it wouldn't be too long before she went back to sleep again, especially with the earlier start for the walk. She closed her eyes and tried to relax.

Outside her room Milos paused as he crept down the corridor from his visit to Slim Sue. He could see light under the door and thought about knocking, but then was unsure as to what excuse he could give for turning up at half-past four. Just then the light was extinguished. He continued tiptoeing back to the staff bedrooms. He'd sort out an excuse with Frances by the time he saw her at breakfast. And then he'd have to sort out his *modus operandi* for both women for that night. It was a good job he'd stressed the need for absolute discretion on both of them. He didn't need any added complications, like them finding out about each other. He might lose his job, and that would never do.

✦   ✦   ✦

ANGELA ROLLED OVER and drifted up into consciousness. She passed her tongue over her dry, parched lips, realising that she'd probably been dribbling or snoring. Possibly both. Her mouth felt as dry and stale as a gorilla's armpit. She reached out for her bottle of water, only to find it was empty except for a couple of drops.

Fuck!

She got out of bed and wandered into the bathroom and half-filled the bottle from the tap, reasoning that they were in Essex not some third-world outpost. Here, she assumed, the water was *potable*. The smell of the food, which was still stuck to the door and on the floor reached her nostrils and she wrinkled up her nose. She wasn't going to clear that up now, however vile it might smell. She got back into bed and looked at the clock and saw it was only just after seven, yet she felt wide awake. She'd made her mind up to leave this morning, but just the thought of throwing her things into her case was too much to even contemplate. Her thoughts wandered to her beloved Butterscotch. She couldn't wait to ride him again. She'd made arrangements to go to the stables early on 29th and take him for a long ride.

That's what I need! A ride!

She smiled ruefully to herself at the *double entendre* but it set her wondering if there were any stables nearby and whether or not they would be open today. She knew that all stables would be attended because horses needed care, irrespective of the time of year or what day it was. And there was no way she was going on another bloody walk! She grabbed her iPad again and googled *Stables Tolleshunt D'Arcy*. Hunter's Stables came up. She made a note of the phone number on the pad on the bedside table, next to the phone. She wondered for a minute if it was a bit too early to ring them, but then decided that any stable worth its salt would be up and working by seven. She dialled the number and waited while the call connected. A male voice answered on the fourth ring.

'Hunter's Stables. James Hunter speaking,' he said. If he was surprised that someone should ring at seven o'clock in the morning, the day after Boxing Day, he didn't sound it.

'Good morning. My name's Angela Carlson and I'm staying at the Blue Boar Inn.'

'Good morning. How may I help you?'

'I was wondering if you're open today. I'd like to book a ride if you are.'

'No, not really. We're here, but we're not open to the public.'

'Oh, what a shame!' Angela could do charming when she chose; when she wanted to get something or her own way. 'I'm a very experienced rider who's missing her beautiful boy, back in Berkshire. I just wanted to sweep the Christmas cobwebs away a little bit,' she simpered.

'When you say experienced, what do you mean, exactly?' James Hunter sounded as if he might be wavering.

'I've ridden since I was eight years old. My horse, Butterscotch is a palomino. Sixteen point two. He's stabled with Jonathan Fonseca,' she added, knowing that mentioning Jonathan's name would carry a lot of weight. And it certainly appeared to.

'Hmm. Look, we're not open today, as I said, but as you're an experienced rider you're welcome to come down and help me exercise a couple of the horses.'

'Really?'

'Yes. You'd actually be doing me a favour as one of the girls has phoned in sick. Do you know where we are? About three miles down the Maldon Road. On the right-hand side. You can't miss us.'

'Oh, that sounds fantastic. How soon do you want me?'

'How soon can you get here?'

'I'll be leaving in ten minutes,' she said.

'I'll have the coffee ready.'

✦   ✦   ✦

IN SPITE OF hardly sleeping, Penny found herself wide awake at half past seven. Wide awake and starving hungry.

Well, I worked up an appetite!

She chuckled as she turned over and found herself fact-to-face with Dave, who was gently snoring, his top lip quivering. She kissed him on the nose and he wrinkled it, without waking up. She gently backed herself out of his embrace and out of the bed, wanting to shower and clean her teeth before he woke up. She thought it would be less embarrassing for him to get up and leave if she was already dressed and drinking tea, rather than lying naked in bed. Although, quite why she thought that she didn't know. She laughed at herself and quietly slipped into the bathroom, locking the door behind her. They might have been intimate several times and in several different ways during the night, but she didn't want him walking in on her while she was sitting on the loo. Some things took time! She showered quickly, humming under her breath as she did so. She felt very happy today; very pleased with herself and the world. And that was all down to Dave.

Ehh! When I tell them I've been with a Cockney!

Penny had three close girlfriends, Caroline, Wendy and Madeline, who she'd been at school with. Caroline and Madeline were married with children and Wendy was divorced with a ten-year-old boy. She lived with her widowed mother who helped her with her son. The four of them met up every other Thursday night, usually at Penny's house. Her roster always seemed to fit around it. She'd confided in the girls about her Christmas break only after she'd booked it because she knew that if she hadn't they would all be fighting each other to invite her to theirs, and, as grateful as she was, she didn't want that. They'd laughed about her going to Essex, all being great TOWIE fans, and joked about her getting off with an Essex boy.

But he's not an Essex boy!

She giggled because she knew he was as good as. And she really liked him. He was kind and considerate and he had old-fashioned values and manners, which appealed to her. During their love-making he'd been gentle and had made sure that she was comfortable with everything they did and that she had at least as much pleasure as he did. She liked that. She'd had enough of oafs. She dried herself and then slipped back into the bedroom with the towel round her. Dave was still asleep. She got dressed and then made them both a cup of tea. She shook him gently when it was ready.

'Well, this is good room service, ain't it?' he said, laughing as he took the cup from her. 'I shall 'ave to come again! Oh, no pun intended,' he added, making her giggle. 'What time is it?'

'It's eight o'clock,' she said, opening one of the small complimentary packs of biscuits and dipping one in her tea. 'Do you want one? I'm starving!'

Dave took a biscuit and they sat in companionable silence sipping and dipping until Dave drained his cup.

'Well, I'd best get back to me room and sort meself out for this morning's walk,' he said, pulling back the covers.

Penny busied herself with the dirty cups and saucers, affording him a modicum of privacy to go into the bathroom and get dressed.

'I'll see ya at breakfast then,' he said five minutes later, planting a shy kiss on her forehead, before slowly opening the door and looking down the corridor. Satisfied it was empty in both directions, he blew Penny a kiss and then fled down the corridor towards his own room, with a smile as wide as the River Blackwater on his face.

✦   ✦   ✦

FRANCES WAS ONE of the first in the dining-room for breakfast. She was honest enough with herself to know that wanting to see Milos and find out what had been the reason for his non-appearance had a lot to do with this. She saw from the corner of her eye that he was at the breakfast buffet. Colin and Janet were already at a table, talking quietly together as she sashayed over to them as if she hadn't seen him.

'Morning!' she chirped at them, slightly louder than was necessary. 'How are you this morning? Did you sleep well? Are you looking forward to this morning's walk?'

Colin, who had just popped a forkful of bacon into his mouth looked at her helplessly, unsure of which question to answer first. It hardly mattered. Before Janet could say that, yes, she had slept very well, Frances charged on.

'I had a great night's sleep. Didn't stir from the moment my head hit the pillow. Went out like a light. Right through until half-past seven,' she said, turning a cup upright on the saucer and pouring herself some fresh coffee. 'Mmm! I'm melting into the aroma. I just love the smell of freshly-brewed coffee, don't you?' she asked the other two.

Milos, who had picked up his pen and pad, had heard most of what she said and smiled inwardly, realising it was for his effect that she was talking of sleeping well. Of course, she didn't know that he had seen her bedroom light on at four-thirty. How could she?

'Good morning, madam. What would you like for your hot breakfast?' he asked, beaming at her. Frances pretended she was looking at the menu. She took her time.

'I think I'd like a mushroom omelette. With some fried tomatoes, please.'

'Would you like toast?'

Yes. Thank you.'

'Please don't forget that there are pastries, cereals, yo-ghurt and fruit on the breakfast buffet,' he said, smiling as he took the menu from her and gesturing towards the breakfast buffet with his head. Frances glanced nervously at Janet and Colin, but they were completely oblivious to what was going on between Frances and Milos. He walked away into the kitchen to place the order. Frances waited until she saw him coming out again and then stood up.

'Well, I think I'll have some cereals or a yoghurt and some fruit. I seem to be very hungry this morning,' she said, leaving the table.

She picked up a bowl and started serving herself some muesli. Milos came and stood beside her, holding a cloth and pretending to wipe off some non-existence yoghurt that hadn't spilt on the bar.

'Frances, I am so very sorry. I could not come to you last night because we had a big problem,' he whispered, without looking at her.

'What problem?' she whispered back.

'At the end of the evening I was just leaving, thinking how good it will soon be to be with you again and then Mr Edwards is angry because the bar takings is wrong. He make us count three times but it still wrong. When we finish it is after two o'clock and I did not want to wake up you. I also very tired from night before. I hope you not angry and understand.'

'Of course, I understand! I thought something must have been wrong.'

'I cannot ring your room. Night porter will know I have sex with you.'

'Sshh!' Frances looked round nervously in case anyone had come over to the breakfast buffet without her seeing them.

'I am very sorry. And very sad. If you allow I come tonight and make up for you sleep alone last night.'

'Okay,' Frances said, feeling like a conspirator and jumping back from him as she saw the door open and Eve stride in. 'See you later.' And she scuttled back to the table.

Soon everyone, except Angela, of course, was in the dining-room and tucking into breakfast. Eve leant back in her chair, savouring her third cup of coffee and looked round the table, smiling at seeing everyone so relaxed. She knew she would have to ring Angela's room and enquire as to whether she would be coming on the walk with the rest of the group, but she'd do that a little nearer the off. Mick broke off from noisily munching on his full-English and turned to address Eve.

'I'm coming with you this morning,' he announced as if he were doing them all a favour by bestowing his presence upon them.

'Good! That's good,' Eve said, smiling at him. Although she found little to like in the man, she was glad he was joining in the activity with the others and not just sitting in the bar drinking his way through the day. She'd learned from her snatches of conversation with the Four Friends that they knew each other from their rugby club in Somerset and she couldn't help wondering why Mick hadn't just stayed there, in the club over Christmas as he'd hardly done anything different by coming to Essex. Still, everyone's break was their own! She couldn't help noticing, her tour manager radar on full power, that Penny and Dave were becoming very friendly.

That's nice!

People getting together was a common occurrence on a singles' holiday, although Eve would be annoyed when it was automatically assumed that anyone who was on one was looking for a dirty week or even weekend. Most people came away for the company and almost all of them left with new friends. But putting a group of single adults together, of course, meant there would doubtless be romances, some fleeting, some enduring. Whichever theirs would turn out to be, Eve was pleased for Penny and Dave. She'd really taken to Penny, with her sing-song accent, her bright smile and upbeat take on life and when she thought about it, she matched Dave really well. He was pouring Penny another cup of tea, looking happy and content at doing so. He must have sensed Eve's eyes on him as he looked up and smiled at her, his cheeks going red. Eve smiled back and gave him a little wink.

She looked further down the table on the other side and thought she sensed a bit of an atmosphere among the Three Sues and Geoff. Slim Sue looked decidedly worse for wear and seemed to be barely taking part in the up-beat, lively conversation that Blonde Sue and Vince were having. Tall Sue sitting on the other side of Vince was joining in and laughing with them while Geoff, who was on her right, was sitting there with a scowl across his face. Several times he started talking to Tall Sue while she was talking to Blonde Sue and Vince. Eve could see she was having a hard time trying to talk to Geoff while not losing the thread of her conversation at the same time. For a split second Eve thought of Geoff as a petulant child vying for his mother's attention.

Cockerel with his feathers ruffled!

He obviously didn't appreciate having another male muscling in on his little harem. Eve gave an inward chuckle. She'd also noticed that Frances had been checking her phone throughout the whole stay and a couple of times she'd seemed somewhat distracted. She hoped Frances was okay and that nothing was troubling her. Eve glanced at her watch and saw it was quarter past nine. She picked up her teaspoon and knocked it against her empty mug.

'Excuse me, everyone! Sorry to bellow at you at the breakfast table, but just to say it's now a quarter past nine and we have to be ready, outside by twenty to ten as Mr Harris wants to set off at a quarter-to-ten sharp. When we get back from the walk, which will be about two o'clock, lunch will be served and then there is another quiz planned.

Now, if you want to do the quiz let me know, but someone is going to have to be question master as I have to be ready in reception from three o'clock onwards to meet and greet the Travel Together clients who are coming to join us for the black-tie ball tonight. You'll get a chance to meet them at Afternoon Tea, which will be served in the bar from four-thirty, or at cocktails at seven-thirty in the ballroom.'

'I don't want tea, but there might be a bit of new talent!' Mick called out, winking his eye and laughing. 'I mean, this break's supposed to be for Over-25s. Where are all the twenty-five-year-old birds?' he asked, looking round and holding out his hands as if lost for an answer.

'With the twenty-five-year-old blokes probably,' Frances called back at him, making the whole table erupt into laughter. Mick looked furious.

'Mate, you drop yourself in it every time,' Vince said, shaking his head.

'Yes, well, it's alright for you, you're getting your leg over!' Mick retorted, nastily, causing Blonde Sue drop her gaze to her coffee cup and colour up.

'Anyway,' Eve said, retaking control of the situation, 'is everyone clear on today's programme?'

'Yes, Eve' the group chorused back.

'There will be a refreshment stop again this morning, which is, of course, at your own expense. So, I'll see you all at nine-forty just outside the door!' And with that she smiled, picked up her key and phone from the table and made her way out of the dining-room.

✦   ✦   ✦

MILOS STOOD BACK and observed the group of guests from afar. He was pleased to see that Frances and Slim Sue didn't sit near each other at the table and that there was no reason for them to engage each other in conversation. As soon as Eve had left some of the group started to follow suit, Frances being one of the first to leave. He congratulated himself at how well he'd handled her this morning. He was getting very experienced at *taking care of more mature ladies* as he liked to think of it. His friend Petar had put the idea into his head. Petar had worked as a steward on cruise ships for a number of years and had doubled his salary by *taking care of more mature ladies.* And in the seven months he'd been working at the Blue Boar Inn, Milos had done quite well, especially as Beniamin was gay and therefore offered no competition. There were events on most weeks and almost without exception these involved unaccompanied women who would be staying at least one or two nights in the hotel. Last night, the session with Slim Sue had been sudden and unexpected, after all, he had already told Frances that he would be returning to her room and her bed. But with an hour or so to go Slim Sue had come to the bar to order some drinks and they had got into conversation. She had been slightly tipsy, but not drunk; just enough to lower her inhibitions and make her receptive to his flattery and to flirt back. Before he knew it, she'd given him her room number and had agreed that he should go and visit her. Then the older man who was her friend had come to see what was taking her so long and she had gone off with him. He had had his doubts about whether or not he should go, but then, as she left the bar when the disco finished, she'd smiled at him and mouthed *'I'll be waiting for you'* as she passed by. His intention had been to visit her and then go onto Frances, but to his surprise he'd actually found Slim Sue very willing and very athletic and two condoms later he'd collapsed on the bed and fallen into a deep sleep, waking just after four to get dressed and slip out of her room.

He saw Slim Sue stand up from the table and he crossed

smoothly to her side. Her two friends were each talking to a man and didn't notice him.

'You are okay?' he asked her, smiling. 'You look unhappy today when I think you will be very happy.'

'Headache. I'm a bit hungover,' Slim Sue said, touching her forehead with her middle three fingers.

'I am very happy after we have nice time,' he said. 'You?'

'Yes, I'm happy,' Slim Sue said, laughing at his persistence. 'I'm happy but hungover.'

'I will come again tonight. When ball is finished. When work is over. I cannot let you leave without time with you tonight.' He brushed her hand with his as he leaned forward to pick up the crockery. 'Okay?'

'Okay,' Slim Sue agreed, smiling inwardly at the thought of another session with this young, hunky guy. She hadn't said anything to the other two Sues, but she could tell they knew something had happened to her. They just hadn't had the chance to ask her about it as Blonde Sue had Vince in tow and Geoff looked like he needed to be surgically removed from Tall Sue's side. She'd suggest they came to her room for tea or coffee sometime later that day and then she'd tell them all about her escapade with her toy-boy, and just how extraordinarily good the sex had been.

✦   ✦   ✦

AT ABOUT THE time Eve was in the booth in reception ringing her room, Angela was enjoying herself to the max, galloping across fields with James Hunter's sixteen-year-old daughter, Matilda. She was riding Dewdrop, a dark mare with a proud, haughty look, while Matilda, an exceptional horsewoman for her age, was on a grey pony called Slate. The whole morning had been somewhat of a surprise, not least of all, getting out of her car to meet James, who was in a wheelchair. Her surprise must have shown on her face.

'I was thrown when my horse refused a fence. I broke my back and was left with no movement or feeling in my legs,' he explained. 'I like to get that out of the way when I meet new people so that we can talk about other things,' he added, smiling.

James explained that he still ran the stables, did all the paperwork and administration, while his wife Annabelle and his daughter and one of his two sons did the physical work, with the help of two stable hands. Unfortunately, both sons had stayed over at a party they'd gone to near Colchester and one of the stable girls had phoned in sick.

'So, if you're happy to help us out for a bit with the graft, we'd then be delighted for you to help with exercising, too!' he'd said.

Angela had taken off her coat and set to work. She'd worked quickly and expertly, helping wherever they asked her to, finding physical activity to be very therapeutic. James had kept the coffee pot replenished and she'd found Annabelle and Matilda pleasant and professional.

This is where I belong! Not on some poxy singles' break.

Annabelle and James had be naturally curious about what Angela was doing in Tolleshunt D'Arcy and she'd just said that she'd been talked into taking a Christmas break at the Blue Boar Inn by a group of friends, but she'd found the whole stay quite tedious and the others boring and that she'd really needed to get away for a few hours.

'Oh dear! It must have been ghastly for you, being with people you have little in common with,' Annabelle had said, sympathetically. 'When do you leave.'

'Well, it's supposed to be tomorrow. There's a black-tie ball tonight to end up with but to be honest, I'm not sure I'm going to stay for that. I think I'll have lunch and then leave before it gets dark. I can be home in a couple of hours.'

'Yes, quite. There's no point in staying somewhere if you aren't enjoying yourself, is there?'

And now, here she was, doing what she loved. Matilda had set off on a back road from the stables, through narrow country lanes, that they'd taken at a walk, until they went through a small wood, with well-work pathways that the horses obviously took every day. As the wood petered out, open fields lay before them.

'We usually go right across and let them have their heads,' Matilda said, 'until we get near the copse on the far side. That's two miles away and then we slow down, walk through the copse and then take the lane on the far side and walk back. Does that sound alright?'

'Sounds perfect!'

They'd set off and sailed through the fields, both taking the low hedges easily until they approached the copse, both women slowing their horses at the same time.

'Good girl! Good girl!' Angela said, patting Dewdrop's neck.

'This is where Dad had his fall,' Matilda said, pointing to an old, worn, weather-beaten tree trunk that lay on its side. 'He came at it at a gallop and for some reason his horse refused and shied up. Dad was thrown and slammed back against that big tree,' she said, pointing at a very large oak.

'Poor man!' Angela was genuinely sorry about James's plight.

'Don't let him hear you say that!' Matilda said, sharply. 'He just hates having anyone's pity. He's living a full, useful life, one that he really enjoys. He even gets back into the saddle sometimes,' she added. 'That's when he really comes alive, when he trots round the ring. If it was up to him he'd be galloping again.'

As they walked the horses back towards the stables Angela marvelled at James's fortitude and strength. She wondered how she would react if – God forbid! – she ever ended up in a wheelchair.

I'd probably kill myself.

✦   ✦   ✦

EVE GOT NO answer from Angela's room. She whipped a pen from one of the many pockets in her weatherproof coat and turned to Tania.

'Can I have a sheet of paper, please?' she asked. 'Just to leave a note for one of the group.'

Tania gave her a sheet of the Blue Boar Inn's headed notepaper, which Eve thought was quite classy. Leaning on the reception desk she wrote a hasty note to Angela.

Good morning, Angela.

I have been unable to reach you and did not see you at break-fast. I hope you are feeling better this morning.

We are setting out now for this morning's walk and should be back just before two o'clock when lunch will be served. There is a quiz planned for three o'clock, should you wish to take part. Afternoon Tea, at which you can meet those joining us for tonight, will be at four-thirty in the bar and cocktails before the ball will be at seven-thirty in the ballroom.

Regards
Eve.

She folded the sheet into three and then tucked it into itself so that it formed its own envelope and handed it to Tania.

'Can you make sure someone takes this up to room

nine, please?'

Pocketing her pen, she headed outside where the others had gathered and Mr Harris was just getting out of his car.

'She ain't coming then?' Dave asked. 'Angela.'

'It doesn't seem so,' Eve said. 'I've left her a message to remind her what's happening today.'

'Her car's gone!' Penny said, pointing to an empty space in the car park, next to her Peugeot. 'She must have gone home!'

'Strange,' Eve mused, 'Tania said she hadn't checked out.' Eve though about Angela's disappearance. Of course, it was quite possible she'd gone home without checking out. Eve wouldn't put anything past Angela! Still, wherever she might be and whatever she might be doing, Eve knew that she couldn't have done any more for Angela. She gave a mental shrug and turned to greet Mr Harris, feeling protective of him, somehow, now that she knew his home circumstances.

'Good morning! That's better! Everyone here, ready for the off and not hanging about inside!' he said, as he strode towards them. 'Everyone is here, I take it?' he turned to Eve, raising his eyebrows as well as the inflection of his sentence.

Yes, indeed. Just one not coming today.'

'Oh, is that the woman who got drunk in the Golden Goose?' he asked, totally unaware that Eve was the only one who knew that. The group members all looked at each other, some grinning, some registering surprise. 'I heard it from someone who'd been there when I stopped at the petrol station just now. Made a right fool of herself, apparently. Passed out.'

'Right! Well, we're all ready when you are!' Eve said, pulling on her gloves and stepping forward.

'Yes, we'll be off! Just to say that we're going to take the back lane for about five hundred yards and then onto a series of footpaths that will take us all round beyond the eastern borders of the village. We'll be going in a clockwise direction, if that makes it easier for you to envisage. And we'll actually come into the village from the south side this time. We'll see the Hall and I'll tell you more about that when we're outside it. And we'll have the chance to have a look round St Nicholas's Church as well, before refreshments in the Golden Goose again, and then we'll walk northwards out of the village, taking the reverse walk from the way we went in yesterday to bring us back to the Blue Boar. Everyone clear?'

Nobody would have dared say the weren't even if that had been the case, so Mr Harris nodded his approval and they all set off down the drive. The subject of conversation in every sub-group was Angela and her behaviour in the Golden Goose the previous afternoon and evening that they'd all missed. Aware of this, and not being prepared to get into any gossip about her, partly because she couldn't trust herself not to be absolutely scathingly unprofessional about Angela, Eve kept a distance between herself and the walkers at the back of the crocodile as they reached the bottom of the driveway and turned right. Walking along, Eve cursed quietly to herself.

I didn't ring Corfu!

She decided there and then that as Christmas was over, she'd wait and ring on New Year's Eve or New Year's Day. That would be much better, although she did feel that she was chickening out, having promised herself to speak to her father when she made the call.

What will we talk about? He probably won't want to speak to me.

She gave a mental shrug. Her relationship with him had always been more than difficult. On her infrequent visits back to her native village she had spent all her time with her mother and sister, her father and brothers barely acknowledging her presence. But at least she would show willing when she rang on New Year's Eve. Or New Year's Day.

Towards the front of the line the Three Sues and Geoff walked with Vince, Don and John. The three of them weren't the type of men that Geoff would usually mix with in a million years, or indeed, had anything in common with. But the Three Sues seemed to find them pleasant company so he decided to make an effort even though he was miffed at what he felt was their barging in where they weren't wanted. Although Blonde Sue did seem to want Vince's company. The two of them had been practically inseparable since the previous day and he wondered if anything had gone on when he'd seen the two of them slip off together as the disco came to an end. Usually, when they were at Travel Together black-tie balls, or discos, the four of them would sit and have a nightcap together while the bar staff cleared up around them. But last night Blonde Sue had gone and then Slim Sue had disappeared, too, saying that she was tired. Tall Sue had said she wasn't bothered either way about a late night drink and so he'd gone off to his room on his own and not more than a little put out by their behaviour. And then this morning at breakfast he felt as if he was being completely ignored by them. Slim Sue was quiet to the point of silent, Blonde Sue was engrossed in conversation with Vince and Tall Sue seemed to prefer to talk to the two of them instead of to him. And now Vince and two of his mates were tagging along beside them on the walk.

Still, at least that ginger oaf wasn't with them!

If he had been, Geoff would have had to make a point of walking along by himself!

The ginger oaf was walking alongside Olivia in the middle of the group. She wasn't quite sure how she'd ended up next to him because she'd started off with Frances, who was slowly falling further and further behind. It seemed as if she was walking deliberately slowly. Up ahead Olivia could see Janet, Pete and Colin walking alongside Mr Harris, just like yesterday. If she put on a bit of a spurt she could catch up with them. Just as she was thinking of doing so, Mick decided to strike up a conversation with her.

'It's not bad round here, is it?'

'What do you mean? The scenery?'

'Yes. I mean, it's not Somerset, but it's nicer that I'd imagined. Where you from?'

'Surrey. Chertsey.'

'That's posh. isn't it?'

'Not really. I mean, it's a nice area and it's close to places like Weybridge and Ascot and Windsor, which I suppose can be posh. But I'm not posh, if that's what you're hinting.'

'Alright! Fuck! There's no need to bite my head off. I wasn't insinuating you were posh. And since when has calling someone posh been an insult?'

'Sorry! I didn't mean to snap. I suppose it's because we've been saying that Angela's posh…'

'Bit of a come-down that was, wasn't it? Hearing that she'd got so drunk she'd passed out,' Mick said. Olivia turned to look at him, expecting his face to register the tongue-in-cheek that was missing from his tone, but there was none. Mick, who'd been drunk more than he'd been sober since he arrived, was criticising Angela!

''Err… pot, kettle black?' she couldn't help saying.

'What do you mean? All 'cos I had a couple of bevvies and missed the walk? That's not the same as collapsing in a pub, is it? And besides, it's different for women, isn't it?'

'No. It's no different. Drunk is drunk. Getting so drunk you miss your breakfast and a walk is no different from passing out in a pub. And whether it's a man or a woman, it's still a loss of dignity and control.'

'Alright! Keep your fucking hair on! I was only making polite conversation!' Mick said, his tone turning nasty.

'Well don't bother, because nobody asked you to!' Olivia retorted, walking faster to catch up with the others, leaving Mick to continue the walk on his own.

It was all Dave could do not to take hold of Penny's hand as they walked along together. But he wouldn't because she'd asked him not to make their friendship public.

'It's not that I'm ashamed or anything. Of course I'm not! But they'll all be having a gossip about us if they think something's going on and it's not like it's their business, is it?'

'No, you're quite right, it ain't,' he'd agreed. But walking alongside her he wanted to take her in his arms and shout out to the whole wide world that this was the woman he'd been waiting all his life for. Penny Pomphrett from Stanley was the woman he wanted to spend the rest of his life with. The strength of his feelings surprised him. He'd known her for only three days and yet he was deeply and hopelessly in love. He'd been so lost in his thoughts of love for her that he'd lost the thread of what she'd been saying.

'Don't you think so?' she asked him.

'Yes,' he replied. She looked at him a little strangely.

'Is that it? Just *Yes*?' She looked at him a little longer. 'You weren't listening were you?'

'I was! But for just a second I was thinkin' about you an' I missed what you said.'

'Thinking about me? Ehh! I hope it was nice!'

'Oh, it was.' He looked behind them to check nobody could overhear. 'I was thinkin'' how strange it is that I can have such strong feelings for you after only knowin' you for three days.'

'Oh, well that's alright then!' she said, laughing.

'What? You takin' the piss?' he asked.

'Course I'm not! I'm flattered. And I can't believe it's only three days. It seems like ages since I left home.'

'Yes, it does, dunnit? And this time tomorrow we'll all be on our way 'ome.'

'Well, don't think about that today, pet! We've got the rest of the walk, all the afternoon and the ball tonight.'

'An' then the rest of the night!' he added, looking at her out of the corner of his eye, pleased to see she was smiling. 'I've bin thinkin' about something,' he said, giving a slight cough and clearing his throat. 'Shall we miss the quiz this afternoon and spend a bitta time togevva? On our own? I mean, we don't 'ave to be like right on our own in your room, or mine. We could sit in the bar. Well, unless you want to…'

'Well, let's see how we both feel after we've had our lunch. We might be in the mood for a little siesta, like.' She turned and gave him a beaming smile and he gulped as he felt the involuntary jerk inside his boxer shorts.

Frances had slowed right down until she was walking alongside Eve. Her hands were in her pockets where her phone was on vibrate, but so far she had felt nothing from the bloody thing.

Perhaps it's broken!

But every time she pressed the little green receiver she got a dialling tone. And when she'd gone back to her room to clean her teeth and get her coat after breakfast, she'd actually rung it from the room phone and had jumped out of her skin when the theme from her all-time favourite TV series had blasted out from the bedside table beside her. She just wished that she could stop checking the phone, stop waiting for a call or a text from him, stop being so needy and stop feeling so bloody upset about the whole situation. But she couldn't. She just couldn't. She heard Eve's footstep and half-turned as she heard her voice.

'You okay, Frances? Not striding ahead with the others?'

'I don't believe in over-doing it! Moderation in all things is my mottos. Well, in most things!' she laughed, making Eve giggle. 'I see you're not leading by example, either.'

'Well, you heard Mr Harris yesterday. I have strict instructions to bring up the rear while he leads from the front and the rest of you must stay between the two of us!'

'It's good though, isn't it? I mean, he doesn't go charging off, does he? He walks at a fair pace, but not so that we can't keep up.'

'That's true. Sometimes walking holidays – and I know that strictly speaking this isn't a walking holiday, just a break with two walks thrown in – but sometimes, they can get very, very competitive.'

'I can imagine. I bet you get everyone trying to walk faster than everyone else.'

'Yes, unfortunately it can be a bit like that. The last walking holiday I did was about six years ago along the north coast of Spain. The *Camino* from Santander to Santiago de Compostela. There were about twenty in the group and the majority of them belonged to rambling and walking groups at home, so there was a lot of one-upmanship. You know, *'I walk ten miles every Sunday.' 'I walk twelve miles every Sunday,'* that sort of thing.'

'Dick measuring is the term I believe.' Frances said, making Eve laugh again.

'Yes, dick measuring, indeed! We had a fabulous walking guide; experienced, full of great information, lovely with the group, and yet we had two men who didn't stop complaining the whole time that he was going too slowly.'

'Oh, you always get someone, and it's usually men!' Frances said, warming to the subject.

'He was doing a great job. He wasn't going slowly he was pacing us. Anyway, on the third or fourth day, we stopped for a mid-morning coffee and when we went to set off again these two men were missing. We waited. Both of us, the guide and I, walked round looking for them, until after almost half an hour we decided we would have to go on without them. Anyway, about twenty minutes further on into our walk we saw one of them rushing towards us, greatly agitated. They'd decided they didn't want to wait for us and so they'd gone on ahead of us…'

'What? Without telling you?' Frances couldn't believe what she was hearing.

'Yes, without telling us. And then they'd wanted to have a wee and so they'd gone into this little wooded area, up a sharp incline…'

'Bloody men! They always wee anywhere and everywhere! Do you know, though, it's the one thing I envy them.' Frances interrupted.

'I know what you mean! Many's the time I've wished I could just go up against a tree or something. Anyway, as they came back to join the road, one had twisted his ankle and lost his footing and tumbled down. They couldn't get signals on their mobiles, so the one that wasn't injured had come rushing back to find us and get help.'

'I'd have left them to it!' Frances declared, livid on Eve's behalf.

'The guide, Alberto his name was, now I think of it, had a signal and he phoned for an ambulance and then we went on to find the other man lying on the ground, in shock and shaking with what was obviously a broken ankle!'

'Well, I can't say I'm sorry. And I certainly won't be going on any walking holidays, the tennis was more than competitive for my liking.'

'I didn't know you played tennis,' Eve said.

'I don't really. I have a lesson over the park every Sunday morning and then we all go for coffee and a chat. It's social more than anything else. I've certainly got no wish to play competitively. I don't belong to our local tennis club and when I saw what the lot in Turkey were like, I'm glad I don't!'

They walked on in silence for a few yards, Frances frantically fingering her phone as they did so, desperate for it to vibrate.

'I'm ever so excited about Natalie and Michael's wedding, aren't you?' she asked Eve after a moment. 'I can't believe they invited me! It's so nice of them!'

'Yes, I am. It's always nice when we have a Travel Together wedding. I sort of feel as if I made it happen,' she said playing the tour manager, while trying hard not to give the game away about her real relationship with Michael.

'Our own Cilla Black! What are you going to wear?'

'I've got a nice dress and jacket in a sort of old-gold, with a black and gold fascinator.'

'Ooh! That sounds lovely. I bet you'll look nicer than the mothers of the bride and groom!'

Eve swallowed hard and tried to show no reaction to what Frances had said, although she couldn't help wondering if perhaps she should wear something a little less dressy if she was, indeed, just another guest.

'I haven't made my mind up yet what I'm going to wear. I'll have to wait and see what fits on the day, and what the weather's like, of course! Still, it'll be nice to see some of the others again. They were a nice bunch on that holiday on the whole, weren't they?'

'They were.'

'Dave said he's been invited. Do you know who else is going?'

'I'm not really sure,' Eve fibbed. 'It'll be a nice surprise when we get there to see who else is on the guest list.'

'Yes, it will.' Frances paused for another minute before

leading the conversation off on another tangent again. 'So what's happened to Angela?'

'I honestly don't know, Frances. I haven't seen her this morning; she didn't answer the phone in her room; the hotel say she hasn't checked out, yet according to Penny, her car had gone. So your guess is as good as mine!'

'Fancy showing herself up like that, though, in the pub,' Frances said.

'Can I just say *two legs in one in a swimsuit*?' Eve said, looking at her and smiling. Frances blushed and then burst out laughing.

'All right! All right! Point taken!' she giggled as they found they'd almost caught up the others who were gathered around Mr Harris.

'Right! Can everyone hear me?' Mr Harris called out. There were various shouts of *'Yes!'* and *'We can!'*

'Good! Now we'll soon be coming into the village from the south and you'll see the Hall on our right. It was built in the early sixteenth century by Anthony D'Arcy and his name and the date 1540 still remain carved on wood panelling inside the Hall itself. There is a bridge going over the moat, and that bridge is Elizabethan, as is the dovecote that remains in the garden.'

They came to the end of the footpath and turned right, walking in single file along the bendy road until they came to an open gateway and Mr Harris stopped again, ushering them off the road and onto the land inside it.

'Now, I told you about the Hall just a few minutes ago. We can walk along and take a look now. The moat is to our left and as you'll see goes around the house and we'll walk up to the Elizabethan bridge. Please don't cross it,' he added, officiously. 'Now, are any of you familiar with the D'Arcy Spice?' He looked round, suddenly surprised to see that Colin had put his hand up.

'You know what a D'Arcy Spice is, do you?'

'Yes. It's a Russet apple,' Colin replied, blushing to see that everyone was looking at him.

'Yes it is! How are you familiar with them?'

'I've got a gardening centre and a bit of an orchard of my own,' Colin said.

'Ah! Yes! Well, that would explain it,' Mr Harris said, nodding his head vigorously. 'Well, the first ever D'Arcy Spice apple tree was planted here, in these gardens in 1840,' he declared, waiting for the group's reaction. Led by Eve, they didn't disappoint, with a little chorus of *oohs* and *aahs*. They walked along the side of the moat and looked across at the house and the little bridge, taking photos as they did so.

'It's not as grand as I thought it was going to be,' Colin said to Janet, as they stood looking at the two-storey house with its oblong windows and white front door.

'I find they rarely are when they're this old,' she said. 'I'm rather glad they haven't built newer wings on it. Sometimes the results of that can be monstrous.' She shuddered as she spoke.

'Hmm, yes,' Colin pondered. 'I think the moat gives it any grandeur that it does have,' he observed.

Checking they'd all got their pictures, Mr Harris walked back to the road and turned to St Nicholas's Church, just a hundred yards or so from D'Arcy Hall. Mr Harris stopped and everyone gathered round him again.

'This is St Nicholas's and it's fourteenth century. It's built in the Perpendicular Style and has, as you can see, a rather splendid West Tower. And if you like to follow me, I arranged for it to be unlocked this morning so that we can take a look inside.'

The group moved towards the church door, Mick grumbling about losing good drinking time. It was impossible to tell whether Mr Harris had heard Mick or not.

If he had, he chose to ignore him completely.

'The nave ceiling,' he continued,' was beautifully decorated as you can see, by Ernest Geldart in 1897. The Chapel was the burial place for many of the D'Arcy family.' Mr Harris walked on and they followed him into the old, cold church.

'This memorial marks the demise of the D'Arcy name,' he said pointing at a cluster of figures. 'You can see the father, kneeling in a suit of armour with his wife and the figures of three sons and three daughters. If you care to read what's written underneath the figures of the sons, you will see it says *'whoe dyed all yonge'*. Obviously, if all the male heirs died, the name died with them,' he concluded. 'Some of the glass in the chapel windows is fourteenth century, unlike, this one before us,' he announced, opening his arms towards a beautiful stained-glass window. 'Yes, this is a very recent stained-glass. It was installed to mark the Millennium and was paid for entirely by local contributions. It was designed by Micheal Smee and produced and installed by local craftsmen. Please step closer and you will see how the local area and life are represented alongside the Christian Millennium symbol. You can see the D'Arcy Spice apple we were talking about; the blue line, which represents the River Blackwater; agriculture is represented and so are strawberry plants because let's not forget the importance of the soft fruit and jam industries to this area.'

The group moved forward to get a better look at the window, some of them taking photos.

'The leaves of the trees are for the healing of the nations' Frances read an inscription from the base of the window.

'Revelations twenty-two, verse two,' Janet said, coming alongside her. 'It's rather splendid, isn't it?' she added, looking up at the glass again.

'It certainly is,' Frances agreed.

Mr Harris let them wander through the church, to take photos, some to look at the brasses.

'The vestry was added in the sixteenth century,' Mr Harris said loudly, so that everyone could hear. 'And the West Tower holds six bells, the oldest of which dates from 1755.'

Gradually, having seen all they wanted to see inside the church, the group members made their way outside, passing two smaller stained-glass windows, one donated by Basil and Jessie Golding and the other by the Vicar and Mrs Dawson to commemorate their Silver Jubilee in 1967. Pete, Janet and Colin stood looking at the very old gravestones that stood either side of the path.

'Some are so old you can barely read them,' Pete said, 'This one's 1740. *'Here lies Alexander, son of Sir Thomas Smyth of Crow's Hall Suffolk','* he read.

'It must be nice to think that almost three hundred years later people can still read something about you, even if it's only your name and the date of your death,' Janet said, wistfully.

'And now, if we're all done,' Mr Harris said, pulling the latch on the church door to lock it behind him, 'we'll make our way along to the Golden Goose for some refreshments, before starting the second part of our walk back to the Blue Boar Inn. May I just remind you that, like yesterday, the refreshments are not included in the tour.'

Mr Harris, beaming broadly at the success of the visit to St Nicholas's Church, strode ahead of the group on his way to the Golden Goose. As they approached the pub Eve braced herself, knowing that she would probably face a barrage of questions as to the well-being, the whereabouts and the condition of Angela, especially given that she wasn't part of this morning's group.

Well, I've faced worse than this!

Once again, Alec was sitting at the bar, dog at his feet, talking to three men. Barbara/Jean welcomed them like old friends and invited them through to the snug.

'You alright today, darling?' she asked Eve, giving her a kiss on the cheek and then looking round at the group. 'I see our friend's not with you today. What? Sleeping it off, is she?'

'She's keeping a low profile,' Eve said. 'Can I have a black decaf coffee, please?'

'Of course you can, darling! I'll come through and take everyone's orders.'

Eve took a seat at one of the tables and after a moment Tall Sue came over.

'Do you mind if I sit here, Eve?' she asked.

'Of course not! Help yourself! Enjoyed the walk so far?'

'Well, yes and no.'

Something in Tall Sue's voice made Eve sit up and take note.

'Is something wrong, then?' she asked, as a young barmaid brought her coffee over.

'Jean says it's on the house,' the girl said.

'Oh, thank you very much.' Eve smiled at the girl.

'Could I have one of those please? But, I'll pay, obviously!' Tall Sue added, laughing.

'I'll be straight back,' the waitress said. Eve turned back to Tall Sue.

'Want to talk about it?'

'I want to talk to someone other than Geoff!' Tall Sue said, looking fraught. 'Sorry! No offence, Eve! I didn't mean it to sound like that. I'm more than happy to talk to you, of course I am. It's just that he's so possessive around us. He doesn't like us to talk to anyone, especially a man, who isn't him!'

'I sympathise with what's happening, but I think that's

probably because over the years I've seen evidence over and over again that it's not a good idea to go on a singles' trip with a group of friends.'

'Well, we weren't friends to start with. We didn't know each other. We met at a black-tie ball in Birmingham. We all live in and around the city; Blonde Sue and I live in Hall Green, Slim Sue lives in Edgbaston and Geoff lives in Solihull. We just sort of hit it off on that weekend and we all kept in touch and sort of fell into the pattern of doing a couple of balls a year together. Then, when it looked like we all might be going to be on our own for Christmas, we decided to take the bull by the horns and book this break.'

'One thing is a one-night ball, another thing is four or five days together?' Eve guessed.

'That's exactly what it is! Blonde Sue had a bit of a snog with Dave on the first night and Geoff couldn't stop running him down the next morning and now she's with Vince and he doesn't like that. Slim Sue's hungover. Between you and me,' Tall Sue lowered her voice, 'she had a one-night-stand last night but she doesn't want Geoff to know because he'll be a bit funny with her. Well, she hasn't even really told me and Blonde Sue any of the details. And he's spent the whole walk clinging to me like a limpet. Don and John walked alongside us and every time I started chatting to one of them, he just kept on butting in.'

'He obviously sees you as *'his'*.' Eve put her fingers up to show commas.

'It's pathetic! He's behaving as if we're in primary school! Sorry, Eve, I don't know why I'm telling you all this.'

'That's okay, that's what I'm here for. Where is he now?' Eve asked, looking round the snug unable to spot Geoff.

'He's gone outside for a ciggie with Slim Sue. I've never been so glad that I don't smoke!' she said. 'I've already said I don't fancy doing the quiz this afternoon. And it's simply because I know what'll happen; he'll go into a strop if the three of us don't want to be in his team.'

'Oh dear! Oops! He's just come back into the snug. He's gone over to join Blonde Sue and Vince.'

'Where's Slim Sue?'

'I don't know. She isn't with him.'

'She's probably made an excuse and gone to the loo.'

'Well, stay here with me. We'll put our heads together and make it look as if we're deep in a private conversation, and if he comes over... Oh! Here he comes!' Eve said as Geoff approached their table. She leant close to Tall Sue and started talking in almost a whisper. Geoff butted straight in.

'You having a drink, Sue?' he asked.

'I've already ordered one, thanks. The waitress said she'd bring it. Oh, here she is. Thank you.' Tall Sue took the coffee and placed it on the table, turning back towards Eve. Geoff didn't move.

'Can I have a beer, please?' he asked the girl, as he sat down next to Tall Sue.

'You have to go to the bar for anything other than coffee,' Eve said to him, defying the waitress to contradict her.

'Oh, I see,' he said, standing up somewhat reluctantly and going over to the bar.

'See what I mean?' Tall Sue asked. 'For a minute I thought he was going to say he'd have a coffee instead so that he could stay here!'

At that moment Slim Sue came into the snug and came over to join Tall Sue and Eve. She sat down and took a big swig from a bottle of water she was clutching.

'Perhaps a long walk after a heavy night isn't such a good idea,' she said. 'I'm really dehydrated. I've nearly finished this and it's my second one!'

'Still, you're doing the right thing by drinking water,'

Eve said.

'I've never been so thirsty.'

'I was just saying to Eve, that I don't fancy another quiz this afternoon.'

'Well, that's alright. Come back to mine after lunch and we can have a chat. I've got lots to tell you,' she smiled and winked at Tall Sue. 'Bring Blonde Sue if she's not doing the quiz or anything else with Vince,' she added.

'Just as long as you don't invite Geoff. He's driving me nuts, Sue.'

'Yes, he's been a bit clingy, hasn't he? I noticed that at breakfast. And just now, he kept on butting in the conversation. Not that I had much to say. It was as much as I could do to keep up with everyone and walk in a straight line.'

Just then Mr Harris popped his head in the snug and waved at Eve.

'Can we say five minutes, please?'

'Yes, of course. Five minutes, everyone, please,' Eve called out. Then it occurred to her that she hadn't organised a tip for Mr Harris. So she went round the group, asking them to give him as generous a tip as they could muster when the walk ended and they were back at the Blue Boar.

'Of course. He's a nice chap and he's been very informative, so he has,' Pete said.

'Well, he hasn't done much other than walk in front of us, has he?' Mick complained.

'Oi! Tight-arse!' Vince said to him. 'Put your hand in your pocket for the man!' He raised his eyebrows as he looked at Eve. 'How much do you suggest, Eve? Couple of quid each?'

'That'll be fine,' Eve said.

✦   ✦   ✦

WHEN ANGELA AND Matilda had got back from their ride, Angela rubbed Dewdrop down and took care of the horse, who had actually seemed to enjoy her little outing and being with Angela.

Why can't people be more like horses? It's so much easier to get on with them.

Once the stable duties were over, Annabelle came over and invited Angela to have some elevenses before she left.

'Oh, I'd love to, thank you.'

She followed Angela and Matilda through the offices and across a private yard, which led to a large, square, detached, brick house. They went round to the rear of the house and into a long, narrow porch where they left their boots and then through a door into a large, welcoming farmhouse-style kitchen, complete with Aga.

'Nice place!' Angela said, looking round, appreciatively, taking it all in.

'Thank you! Have a seat,' Annabelle said, indicating the large, oval distressed-wood table and chairs that sat to one side of the kitchen. 'Matty, go and ask Dad if he's going to join us here or if he wants me to take his coffee and mince pie through. He's in his den,' Annabelle explained to Angela. 'He's probably on the phone to the bookies. He loves a bet.'

Angela stood and walked over to take a closer look at the diplomas on the far wall. Annabelle was a qualified counsellor and psychotherapist.

'The kitchen doubles as my therapy room. I find it works rather well because it's warm and cosy.'

'I can imagine. It's a great set-up you've got here, with the stables and this lovely house,' Angela said, as Annabelle set a plate of rather large mince pies in the middle of the table and got the coffee percolating. 'Hmm! That smells great!'

'Well, we used some of the money that James got from

his settlement to extend the house and adapt it for him. Fortunately, he'd taken out a decent accident insurance policy a couple of years earlier. If not, I don't know how we'd have managed. It paid for a lot of his treatment and rehab, too. Originally the house was little more than a cottage really, with just two bedrooms. Now we've got five and three bathrooms, one is a wet-room for James.'

'Do you manage him all by yourself?' Angela asked. Then she saw the look on Annabelle's face.

'Manage him?'

'I'm sorry! That sounded insensitive, I didn't mean it to.'

'That's okay, I've become desensitised over the years. James has a fabulous nurse and companion, Bob, who helps him with bathing and dressing and also does some PA work for him. And when it's his day off we have agency carers helping us.'

'Dad said don't think him rude, but he's a bit tied up at the moment so he'll have his in the den,' Matilda said, coming back into the kitchen.

'Here! Take it through to him for me then, please,' Annabelle said, putting a large mug of black coffee and a pie onto a tray and handing it to Matilda.

'But tell me all about you,' Annabelle said. 'What you do and how you've ended up in our neck of the woods. I've a feeling there's a bit of a story here,' she added.

And to her complete and utter surprise Angela found herself telling Annabelle the whole story of her singles' Christmas break. Unsurprisingly, Annabelle was a good listener; she was interested, without being nosey, and for the first time in her life Angela felt as if she wasn't just being brushed off as nasty, posh woman who revelled in being vile to people, but rather she was being seen, non-judgementally as a human being with failings. Annabelle kept the coffee coming and replenished the mince pies.

'And what is it that makes you dislike Christmas so much,' Annabelle asked softly.

Angela took a gulp of her coffee and nibbled on her pie and considered a moment before she replied. She couldn't believe she was actually sharing this story with another person and a therapist, at that.

'I was married for fifteen years to a kind, older man, who ran his own manufacturing company. He treated me like a piece of fine porcelain. He bought me jewels, he took me on expensive, exotic holidays, I had a wardrobe full of designer clothes and shoes and we loved each other. He bought me a horse for my birthday and he loved watching me ride. Some people found it surprising that I worked, but at the time, I enjoyed my job and I didn't want to be one of these women who spent their whole day going from the gym to the masseuse to lunch and carrying out charitable works and only really being seen as *wife of.* Harry was happy with this and he encouraged me to have a life of my own. He would have done anything for me, anything at all.'

She paused to take another sip of her coffee and to gather her thoughts. Now that she was finally opening up about what had happened that Christmas five years ago she wanted to get it all clear in her head.

'But, sooner or later, the age gap began to make itself felt. Harry was fifty-nine and I was thirty-eight. He was looking towards retirement, playing golf and pottering in the garden, perhaps buying a boat and doing some sailing, and I was restless and looking for some excitement and a few thrills in my life. I wasn't ready for slippers and knitting. And I found excitement, or at least I thought I had, in the shape of Seb, a guy I met on a conference. He was everything that Harry wasn't. He was young, he was charming, he was up for anything and everything, he was virile and sexy and I couldn't spend enough time with him. I started inventing meetings that went on until late at night. I told Harry I'd been given a client's portfolio that meant I had to travel to Glasgow for a couple of days every week. Instead I worked from Seb's during the day, telling the office I was working from home and spent the night in his bed and Harry never suspected a thing.'

Angela paused and looked at Annabelle for the first time since she'd started talking. Annabelle barely recognised the vibrant, beautiful woman who'd sat down at the table. Now her face had taken on a sallow look; her eyes were pained and she looked sick, tired and old.

'Harry had been married before me and had a daughter and three grand-children. It was a family tradition that we'd all spend Christmas Eve together at our house. Melissa and her family would stay over and then my parents and some friends would join us for Christmas Day. But Seb had planned a surprise for me. He'd booked tickets for a matinee show in the West End and then a suite at a boutique hotel in Soho. I'd explained to him that I couldn't stay all night because the family would be coming. I told Harry that I might be home a little late because I had to finish my project before leaving the office. All the food and drink had been ordered and Miriam, the house-keeper was coming in on the morning of 24th to prepare everything, even lay the table, so that all I would have to do would be step in the front door and take off the cling-film and we would be ready to eat. The house was beautifully decorated, as it always was for Christmas and Harry was as excited as a little boy. He accepted what I told him without question because he loved me and he trusted me. When we got to the hotel I couldn't believe the trouble Seb had gone to. The suite was palatial, adorned with dozens and dozens of red roses and candles. The meal consisted of all my favourite foods, but we barely touched it. We only wanted to feed off each other. Before I knew it, I'd fallen asleep in his arms and when I woke up it was four o'clock. I went into a panic. I grabbed my phone and saw that I'd had thirty missed calls; from home, from Melissa's mobile and her husband Scott's. And I realised I hadn't heard them because I'd put my phone on silent in the theatre and hadn't switched it back on. All the way to Berkshire I invented a thousand stories, but none of them sounded plausible because I knew they were lies. Finally I decided to say I'd fallen asleep at the office and that my phone was on silent because I'd been in a meeting. I planned to slip into bed beside Harry and wake him up with a wonderful Christmas love-making session, convinced that that would diminish any doubts he might have had as to my whereabouts. But as I approached the house I knew something was wrong because the lights were on. Not just in our bedroom – I'd been expecting that – but all over the house.'

Angela stood up and walked over to the big, wide bay windows that gave out onto the large, well-kept garden behind. She looked out at the dull green grass and gloomy grey sky and continued her story with her back to Annabelle.

'As I pulled up the front door was wrenched open and Melissa came out. Her hair was a mess, her eyes were red and she hurled herself at me. 'Where the hell have you been?' She screamed. 'We've been trying to get you for fucking hours! Where were you?' Scott appeared behind her and pulled her back in, enveloping her in his arms and holding her tightly, making soothing noises as you would to a child. I went in and closed the door. I started to say I was sorry as I walked towards the drawing-room expecting to see Harry in his dressing-gown waiting for me, when Melissa screamed out 'He's dead!' I turned to jelly. I felt myself stumble forward and I sat on the bottom stair while Scott held and soothed Melissa and told me what had happened.

When they had turned up at seven o'clock they were surprised to see the house in darkness, even though Harry's cars were both on the drive. They rang the bell several times and rang the house phone, Harry's mobile and mine. In the end they called Miriam and she came round to let them in. They found him dead in the bath. And then, of course, they'd tried to get hold of me but they couldn't. The emergency services had come. And by the time I'd turned up he had already been lying cold and alone in the undertakers for several hours.

Angela turned to face Annabelle, gripping the back of a chair.

'While I was screwing around in a luxury suite, my husband was dying at home. If I had been there he'd still be alive.'

'You don't know that!' Annabelle said.

'I do. If I hadn't gone off with Seb I'd have been home by three o'clock in the afternoon. Thirteen hours earlier. According to the post mortem he'd died between four and six.'

'Heart attack?'

'Carbon monoxide poisoning. The water heater in his bathroom was faulty.'

'But perhaps if you'd been there you'd have died, too,' Annabelle said.

'I very much doubt it. I would have realised something was wrong if he was a long time in the bathroom and I'd have saved him. Then, of course, at the inquest the whole story about my affair with Seb came out and I was pilloried and ostracised by his family, my family and most of my friends. Even my work colleagues. I expect you think I'm such a bitch, a right…'

'I don't think anything, Angela, other than deep sympathy for your loss, the circumstances of your loss and the way it's scarred your life ever since.'

'Of course it scarred me! I hate myself! Who wouldn't? Who could possibly like someone like me?' She put her arms on the table and cradled her head on them and sobbed uncontrollably. Matilda came into the kitchen to find out what was wrong but was waved away by Annabelle, who sat with her arm around Angela's shoulder, waiting until she'd cried herself out.

It was a full half-hour before Angela raised her head. Annabelle was ready with a handful of tissues.

'I'm so sorry. What on earth must you think of me? I can't believe I just told you that,' Angela said, patting her face. 'I've never ever spoken to anyone about it. Ever.'

'Well, then I'm honoured you felt comfortable enough to open up to me. And I hope you'll find it's helped. Sometimes, we bottle things up and they eat away at us. Talking about them takes the lid off the jar and helps them to find their own way out. It's our secrets that do us the most harm. They fester inside us and eat away at our well-being.'

'You're a very good counsellor.'

'I hope so. Thank you. I do a lot of work with addicts, especially helping them through twelve-step programmes. And a big part of those, of course, is Step Five, which includes admitting to another human being the nature of your wrongs. I usually notice a huge improvement on the road to recovery after people take that step. And although you're not an addict...'

'No, I'm not!' Angela jumped in.

'...you've sort of gone through your own Step Five with me this morning.'

'I say I'm not an addict, but if I'm honest, it's almost as if I'm addicted to being an absolute cow. A real bitch. I shout at people, I bark orders, I criticise, I scream and shout to get my own way, I humiliate them. And yesterday I completely humiliated myself by getting so drunk I had to be taken back to the hotel and then I hurled abuse at the two people who'd tried to help me.'

'Then why not make a conscious effort from now on not to do that?' Annabelle suggested. 'Make friends with yourself. Like yourself, grow to love yourself. You can't love yourself at the moment because, from what you've just said, you're deliberately making yourself difficult to love. So change. Turn yourself around. Don't punish yourself forever because of what happened when Harry died.'

Angela paced up and down and then leant back against the sink, hugging herself, deep in thought. She exhaled noisily.

'That's what I've been doing, isn't it? Punishing myself and taking my grief and disgust and loathing at myself out on everyone else.'

'You hate yourself so you behave in a way that will make other people hate you, too. I know it won't be easy, but you've got nothing to lose. You made a mistake and it led to horrible consequences that you are convinced you could have stopped happening. Personally, I think that's debatable. But you've done your time. Now just ease up on the self-loathing. Change your attitude towards yourself and that will lead to a change in your attitude towards others and their attitude to you.'

The two women sat in silence for a moment until it was broken by the soft sound of James's wheelchair coming along the hallway and into the kitchen.

'What's for lunch? I'm starving. The mince pie is long gone,' he said, smiling at the two women.

'I was going to do some mushroom soup with bread and baked apples or cold Christmas pudding with cream,' Annabelle said, going over to him and kissing him on the forehead.

'Sounds like a feast! You'll join us, won't you, Angela,' he asked, smiling at her while squeezing his wife's hand.

'Yes! Do stay!' Annabelle said. 'You're more than welcome.'

Angela looked at this kind, wonderful couple and couldn't believe she'd only met them that morning. She suddenly felt very happy that they had come into her life.

'Thank you. I'd love to,' she heard herself reply.

✦   ✦   ✦

IT LOOKED LIKE the quiz was going to be a non-event. The Three Sues said they didn't want to take part and neither did Penny and Dave or Vince or Mick. Olivia said she wasn't bothered because she quite fancied a couple of hours to herself in her room before having to get ready for the ball. So that left Frances, Janet, Pete, Colin, Kim, Don, John and a very grumpy Geoff.

'Why don't we play as individuals or pairs?' Pete suggested.

'That's a good idea, but who's going to be question-master?' Frances asked.

'We don't need one. I'll ask Eve to get the hotel to photocopy the questions. We can write our answers on the question papers and then when we've done all the sections we can swap sheets and mark it all at once.'

'Yes, that makes sense,' Frances agreed. 'Everyone alright with that?'

The others were all in agreement so Pete went into the foyer where Eve was sitting nursing a hot chocolate and waiting for the ball-goers to arrive. She said it would be no problem and passed the questions over to Tania, asking her to take six photocopies.

'Are you sure you don't want the answers copied, too?' she asked.

'No, you're fine, thanks. Just the questions.'

Once Pete was on his way back into the lounge, Eve resumed her seat by the door. She was wearing her T2G badge and had her checklist in front of her. She ran her eye down the page and pulled up sharp at one name she recognised.

Well! I never thought I'd see him book with us again!

An hour later, all those who were staying at the Blue Boar Inn had checked in, except one, plus those who were staying in the nearby B&B. Everyone had seemed very pleasant, and quite a few of them already knew each other from other black-tie balls. Eve had gone through the spiel each time, telling them about afternoon tea and what time cocktails were, adding breakfast and check-out details for the following morning. She was just thinking about getting herself another hot chocolate when the main door swung open and a man carrying a large, leather holdall and a suit-bag over his shoulder swaggered in. Eve stood up to greet him. He saw her and did a double-take.

'Eve! Hello! I never thought I'd see you here.'

That's exactly what I thought about you!

'I thought you'd be off on some exotic trip not Essex,' he said dropping his bag, putting his suit over the back of a chair and giving Eve a kiss on the cheek.

'I was supposed to be having a Christmas off, but the tour manager doing this trip had to pull out. But how are you, Deano? You look well.'

'Mustn't grumble, you know. Mustn't grumble. Oh, yes, and before you ask: I am single.'

'Well, that's very reassuring, given that it's a singles' black-tie ball,' Eve said, smiling in spite of herself. 'Although, I take it that means you're now divorced?'

'Yes. Rachel wasn't very understanding about what happened. I thought she might've taken pity on me, you know, having a nasty accident, and that. It was ten months before I was sorted out and walking again on my own, you know,' he added.

Eve made a sympathetic sound. There was no doubt that his accident, caused when he'd tripped over a rock he hadn't seen at Devil's Bridge, had been a particularly nasty one. The fact that he was married, had been trying to get off with a very nice woman all holiday and his wife had thought he was at a trade fair in Madrid or somewhere had slightly diminished the degree of sympathy that Eve had felt for him.

'She filed for divorce as soon as we got back home. Still, I'm happy being single now,' he added, not too convincingly.

'And no more contact lenses,' Eve observed, looking at his hazel eyes.

'I was a right, vain tart, wasn't I?' he laughed, as they both remembered Deano's bright turquoise eyes which had caused so much comment but had, in fact, been due to lenses. And the loss of one of his lenses had meant he'd been wearing his sunglasses on a dull day resulting in him tripping over a rock because he hadn't seen it. If it hadn't been for the quick-thinking of the local guide, Larry, who'd dived into the Atlantic and pulled him out, he might well have drowned.

'There are a couple of people here you'll know. Dave and Frances,' Eve said.

'Dave! Oh, blimey! I got on well with Dave. It felt like we were mates, even though I'd only known him a couple of days. It'll be good to see him again! But who was Frances?'

'I am! Who wants to know?' Frances said, coming out of the bar where the quiz had finished.

'Oh yes! Frances! Remember me? Deano,' he said, turning to greet her.

'Oh, Deano! From Antigua!' she said, giving him a hug. 'How's your leg?'

'I was just telling Eve, it took more than ten months to heal up properly, with physio and that, but it's fine now. I can play football, dance, do anything really.'

'That's good! You were very lucky, then. Well, it's nice to see you. I'm just off to have a little siesta before getting ready for tonight. I won't be coming to afternoon tea, Eve. Don't think me rude. I'll meet the new people at cocktails.'

'Not at all!' Eve said.

'See you later!' Frances said, as she walked towards the stairs, her phone in hand.

'Right, well, if you want to go and check in with Tania. You're in room twenty,' Eve told him. There's afternoon tea in the bar being served now and cocktails are from seven-thirty in the ballroom.'

'Okay, thanks,' Deano said, picking up his stuff and crossing to the reception, a smile for Tania already on his lips. 'I'll take this up to my room once I've checked in and then go and meet everyone else.'

Eve collected her paperwork together and went through to the bar, pleased to see that most of the original group, except Penny, Dave and Frances, were having afternoon tea and mixing with the ball-goers. Geoff was standing to one side deep in conversation with a woman with dyed red hair and glasses. Denise, if Eve remembered rightly. She assumed from the level of intensity the conversation appeared to be at that they knew each other from a previous ball. Tall Sue and Slim Sue were talking to three men, whose names Eve couldn't remember and Kim and Pete were sitting at a table with two men and three women. Kim stood up and pulled two more chairs over so that Colin and Janet could join them. Another large group, which included the Four Friends and Blonde Sue and several more of the newcomers were standing in a ragged circle in the far corner next to the long table where afternoon tea had been laid out.

Eve helped herself to a cup of tea and a slice of Christmas cake and did the rounds, chatting and smiling to everyone, pleased to see that they were all mixing. She was happy that there was only the ball tonight to go and that they'd all be straight off after breakfast the following morning. She found the four who were staying in the B&B, Margaret, Tina, Joan and Barry and confirmed that a taxi would pick them up at seven-fifteen and be waiting to take them back at midnight when the ball ended. The B&B would be serving them a full breakfast so they wouldn't have to come back to the Blue Boar Inn.

'It was a shame we couldn't get booked in here,' Barry said.

'Still, we've been accommodated close by, haven't we?' Tina said, wiping the remains of her scone from her lips with a serviette.

'Yes, teach us to book earlier next time, Margaret said. 'I hesitated for weeks over this. I don't know why exactly because I knew I wanted to come. And looking round I'm glad I'm here. And the B&B's lovely!'

Eve smiled and moved on towards another group when she saw Deano come into the bar. She grinned to herself as she saw that most of the other women had also noticed him come in.

What is it about him? He hasn't even got the turquoise lenses in this time!

He certainly dressed well. Eve knew that his business took him abroad a lot and his oyster-coloured cashmere sweater, which showed off his suntanned skin and black hair to their full advantage, had surely been bought in a smart boutique in Madrid, Barcelona, Milan or Rome. And although the women liked him, Deano was also a man's man. Within minutes, he'd shaken hands with the Four Friends and three other men, kissed several women on the cheek and had already become one of the group. The door opened again and Eve did a double take.

Angela came in.

She took a few steps and then stopped, looking round until she saw Eve and came hurrying over to her. Eve could see she was holding the note she'd sent to her room earlier that morning and mentally braced herself for another confrontation. She put her cup onto a table ready to take Angela back out into the foyer as she had no intention of getting into any type of altercation with her in front of everyone, especially the new arrivals, who knew nothing of what had happened the previous evening.

'Good afternoon, Eve. Have you got a moment, please?' Angela said.

The polite tone was unexpected and took Eve back although she didn't show it. In spite of the words of truth she'd spoken to Angela when they'd been alone the previous evening, feeling that a few home-truths had been needed, she would be text-book professional in front of the rest of the group. Sometimes, saying what needed to be said to a client wasn't a bad thing.

'Of course, Angela. Are you going to have tea or would you like a private word outside? Or perhaps both?'

'I'd like a private word but I will have a cup of tea,' she said, going to the table and helping herself to a cup and saucer, her gaze averted, not making eye-contact with anyone. She quickly popped a teabag into a cup and covered it with boiling water from the urn. She stirred it vigorously, took the teabag out, added milk and turned back to Eve. The rest of the group were all aware that Angela was there and Eve could see several of them looking at her out of the corner of their eyes, while others weren't quite so discreet. Eve hoped that they wouldn't start telling the ball-goers what had happened the minute the two of them had left the bar. And Eve could see from the way she hung her head as she walked ahead of her that Angela also knew they were looking at her. Yet there was something in the way she walked; the arrogance was missing from her step. The two women sat in armchairs on the far side of the foyer where they could talk privately without being overheard.

As long as we don't raise our voices!

Angela coughed to clear her throat and took a sip of her tea.

'So, what can I do for you?' Eve said, to break the ice.

'Well, it's not that you can do anything really. First of all I'd like to say sorry. I really and truly am deeply sorry for my behaviour and attitude towards everyone, but especially you and the manager. I know that you were only doing your job. More than your job! After all, I'm sure that other people in your position would have left me to find my own way back from the pub, especially given the state I was in.'

'It was because of the state you were in that I went to get you,' Eve said. 'How could I leave you there like that?'

Angela lowered her head; her cheeks were scarlet, but this time not with anger, but shame and remorse.

'And then this morning, after all the shouting and insulting I'd done last night, you still tried to contact me and include me in the activities. And I don't deserve that, I really don't. Just as you didn't deserve me screaming at you and throwing food.' She paused and gulped. 'I'm so ashamed of myself. Please find out which maid cleaned up the room this morning, would you. I really owe her a huge tip,' she said.

'That's okay. Thank you for apologising and apology accepted,' Eve said. 'But what happened to you? I've been concerned. I thought you'd gone home when we saw that your car had gone.'

'I went riding.' She paused to take another sip of her tea. Eve sat quietly waiting for her to continue. She was curious to know just what Angela had been up to and how she'd spent her day, and whether or not this complete about-face was genuine and to be long-lived or not.

'You see, I have my own horse and some of the happiest moments of my life, the only happy moments of my life recently have been those I've spent riding him. I live in the country, Eve, in Berkshire, in a village not unlike Tolleshunt D'Arcy, so what on earth possessed me to come to another country village I don't really know. I realised early this morning that I was really missing Butterscotch and all I wanted to do was ride him and if I'd stayed at home I would have been able to. So I found a local stables and well, long story short, they're run by the loveliest family imaginable, who let me ride one of their horses in exchange for helping out. I know I was wrong! I should have at least had the manners to leave you a note, the way you did for me, to let you know where I'd gone.'

'Well, I'm just glad to know you're safe and it sounds like you had a really good time.'

'I did. As I say, the family, the Hunters, are so nice. James is in a wheelchair due to a riding accident and his wife Annabelle is a counsellor. And… Oh, you're going to think I'm some sort of nutter!'

'What? Why would I think that?'

'Well, with what I was going to say…although you probably can't think any worse of me than you already do! But, it almost feels as if I had some sort of…' she hesitated before taking a deep breath, '… spiritual experience. It was just like an awakening being there with them today. I know that sounds crazy and… dramatic… but I don't know how else to describe it.'

'Really?' Eve was taken aback. She wasn't laughing or thinking Angela was crazy, just wondering what on earth had gone on. 'What happened then?'

'Eve, I had the worst time ever at Christmas 2009. My husband died on Christmas Eve and I wasn't there when it happened.' Angela didn't see the need to give Eve all the details. 'Since then I've been blaming myself and taking it out on the rest of the world. I haven't been a very nice person.'

'When tragedies happen to us, we all react in different ways,' Eve said. 'Who's to say how the rest of us would have behaved, you know? Walk a mile in someone's shoes and all that.'

'Thank you. Anyway, after my stint in the stables and my ride I sat and had coffee with Annabelle, who's a psychotherapist as well as a counsellor and before I knew it I'd told her every single detail of the events leading up to Harry's death and what's happened since. I just blurted it all out! And she actually understood. I came away from there half an hour ago feeling that there's been a change, a sort of shift in me, my feelings, the way I have to go forward. And the first thing I saw when I came back here was your note. And so, I wanted to find you and say how sorry I am before I pack and leave tonight.'

'Aren't you going to stay for the ball?' Eve asked.

'I'd be too ashamed. I behaved appallingly in front of the group and I'd feel very awkward being back in their company.'

'There's no need to feel awkward. You can sit and dance with me all night if you want to. You'd be very welcome. And besides, there are twenty-one new people who don't know anything about yesterday or the day before who will be keen to meet you and be in your company.'

Angela looked at Eve, unsure of what to say.

'Look! It's entirely up to you, but the offer of sitting with me is there. And please don't take that wrong as if I'm saying that you need looking after or shielding from anything. Why don't you come along to cocktails and see how you feel? If you feel uncomfortable, you can go back upstairs, change your clothes and leave. But if you feel okay, you can stay and have a great evening and leave after breakfast in the morning.'

'Hmm! Yes, I understand what you're saying...'

'The choice is yours. Do whatever feels right for you.'

'You know what? I'm here! I might as well stay and see how it goes. And at cocktails I'll apologise to Frances for our little *contretemps* at lunch yesterday, too.'

'That's fine! I'll see you at half-past-seven, then.'

'Yes. And thank you, Eve.' Her eyes became moist. 'I really don't know how you do it, dealing with monsters like me all the time.'

✦   ✦   ✦

PENNY AND DAVE were lying locked in each other's arms on the bed in her room. They had had a blissful afternoon together. After lunch they'd brought drinks up and lain cuddling on the bed chatting about life in general before suddenly having smouldering sex, which had left them both exhausted. Penny was pleased to see that it was only five o'clock; that meant at least another hour and a half before she'd have to start getting ready for the ball. Her nails still looked fine – in spite of the assault they'd made on Dave's back a little earlier when they were in the throes of it – and her hair and make-up would only take half-an-hour max. She had a long black, one-sleeve dress, which she knew really looked good on her. She snuggled up against Dave and kissed his left nipple before placing her head closer up on his chest. He sighed with contentment.

'What I don't understand, is 'ow a girl like you ain't bin snatched up before now, Miss P. 'How come you've never bin married? Just bin lucky like me?' he quipped, using one of his favourite jokes.

'I lived with someone for a long time but I knew we'd never marry.'

'Why was that? Was 'e married or somethin'?

'No. I wouldn't live with another woman's husband!'

'Course you wouldn't! I didn't mean no offence…'

'He had OCD.'

'What?' Dave looked down at Penny, his eyes wide with disbelief. 'Poor bloke. Did it kill 'im?'

'You don't usually die from being OCD, Dave.'

'Well, some did! I remember seein' it on the telly. They kept on showin' them cows fallin' over…'

'That's CJD!' Penny said laughing. 'Ehh! What're you like?'

'What's OCD then?'

'Obsessive Compulsive Disorder.'

'What, like when you keep doing things? Washing your 'ands and that?'

'It can be. Wayne's was checking that he'd turned off the television and unplugged the iron and things like that.'

'So why did you know you'd nevva marry 'im then?'

'Because I couldn't live with his condition,' she said, turning from Dave. 'I know you're probably thinking that if I loved him I should have accepted him as he was, but it wasn't quite as straightforward as that.'

'I ain't sayin' nothin'. Only you knew what livin' with 'im was like.'

'It affected every aspect of our lives. We'd have to start getting ready to go out, and I don't mean having a shower and changing, like, I mean actually leaving the house, ages before. It got so bad that, say we were going out at seven, like, well, we'd start leaving at six because he'd have to keep on going round and checking the windows were closed and that the back-door was locked time and time again. It didn't matter how many times I told him that we'd checked it – I even used to go round with him saying *'Right, the bedroom window is closed and locked.'* – but it didn't matter. Before he could close the front door he'd have to go back upstairs and check one last time.'

'Blimey! Ain't there no cure for it?'

'He went into hospital for cognitive therapy treatment. His parents insisted that he had to. His behaviour was ruining their lives as well. And he was a hoarder, too. He hated throwing things away. He'd told me that when I first met him and I thought he kept perhaps old comics from when he was a kid like. But when I went round to his house… Ehh! I couldn't believe it. His dad couldn't get the car in the garage it was so full up with Wayne's stuff. An old bike with only one wheel, boxes and boxes of broken toys and lumps of wood, old string, newspapers piled up, three broken guitars, the plaster-cast from when he'd fractured his leg when he was ten … It's not funny, Dave!'

'I know! I ain't laughin' at 'is condition, I'm laughin' at the way you're tellin' it!' he said, holding her close again and kissing the top of her head. 'It musta bin terrible for ya.'

'It was.'

'But what 'appened then? Didn't the therapy work?'

'I don't know. We got to the stage where I had to put myself first. And all the worry about him and the aggrava- tion just took its toll on our relationship. It was hard for me; OCD is stress-related and I didn't want to cause him any more stress, like, by finishing with him, but in the end it was making me ill, too,'

'You poor thing.' He held her close in silence for a few minutes.

'So, tell me about your exes. Have you had any strange relationships.'

'Nah. Not really. Compared to what you've just told me, mine 'ave all bin more or less normal!' he laughed. Dave was a man who believed in keeping it simple. He thought there was nothing to be gained from telling a girl he'd just met and a girl he really liked about his married women, or Geri. He was a great believer in ignorance being bliss.

'Miss P, Miss P, Miss P, Look what you're doing to me!' he sang to a made-up melody as he took her hand and placed it on his groin.

'You're far too cheeky, you are!' she said, giggling as she felt him grow.

✦   ✦   ✦

THE BALLROOM LOOKED amazing when they began to arrive for cocktails. The staff had changed the decorations slightly from the previous evening, adding balloons in a large net suspended from the ceiling and putting poppers, crackers and gorgeous centrepieces on every table alongside the sparkling, elegant glasses and polished, silver cutlery. There were five tables of eight around the edge of the dance-floor and the idea at these balls was that the men moved around clockwise after the first course, main course and dessert. This meant that all the women would have met almost all the men and vice-versa by the end of coffee and cheese. The men and women sat alternately on each table. Eve, as the odd-one-out sat on a table for two in the far corner with Chris Edwards, who was co-hosting the evening with her. Once again, she'd been in the foyer to welcome the four from the B&B and to meet the other four who hadn't booked their accommodation in either place. They turned out to be two women, Vicky and Tracey, who were friends who lived in Maldon, and two men, who also knew each other, Eric and Terry, who lived in Clacton. Both pairs had come in taxis which they had booked to return and collect them at the end of the evening. Although Eve had worked for Travel Together for such a long time, she was unused to so many people knowing each other. What was unusual on a holiday, and often rocked the boat, seemed to be the norm at a black-tie ball.

Everybody looked extremely smart. Eve loved a man in a dinner jacket. Melv had told her he had one for the wedding and she couldn't wait to see him in it. She looked round and thought that even Mick, perhaps the most sartorially challenged of the group, looked good tonight. The women had all pushed the boat out, too, looking elegant and chic. Eve had fallen back on a little black dress she'd had for several years, but it still fitted her and nobody had seen her in it so she didn't care. She was very pleased to see Angela and that she was talking to Frances, who was smiling and nodding in response to whatever it was that Angela was saying. It must have taken a lot for Angela to come along tonight, just as it had for her to apologise to Eve earlier. There appeared to be more staff on duty, all of them moving among the clients offering trays of cava and canapés. Eve could see three or four faces that were new as well as those who had worked the previous evening.

She made her way round the group, paying special attention to the ball-goers as she wanted them to feel included. There was a piano in the corner of the ballroom, next to Eve and Chris's table, where a young man was quietly playing *Music from the Musicals*. He would continue to play until dessert had been served and then the Phil Austin Quintet would take over, providing dance music for the ball until midnight.

Suddenly, there was a commotion. Deano had found Dave. The two men hugged each other as if they were life-long friends forced apart by a terrible natural disaster only to find each other again some years later.

'Good to see you, Dave!'

'What a surprise! 'Ow you doin' you ol' rascal? 'How's ya leg?'

They shook hands again pulling each other close and patting each other on the back. Eve smiled.

Better a cuddle than a fight!

Chris hurried in, smiling at everyone as he did so, and came over to tell Eve that the first course would be ready to serve in five minutes. Eve crossed to the pianist, who, as luck would have it, was just coming to the end of his West Side Story medley.

'Can I borrow your microphone, please?' Eve asked. He turned it towards her and adjusted it.

'There you are!'

'Thanks. Ladies and gentlemen, if I could have your attention please? Thank you. Well, our food is almost ready so I'm going to invite you to take your seats in just a moment. Would the ladies please sit at the places where there are purple napkins and the men where the napkins are green. That way we should have alternate boy, girl, boy girl. Then, after each course, including dessert, you will hear a klaxon sound. That will be me! And that is the signal for the men to get up and move in a clockwise direction to the next table. Once the meal's over you can sit where you like and with whoever you like!' she added, laughing. 'And before you do take your seats, can I ask you to show your appreciation for our amazing pianist, Bernie Browne!'

There was a great cheer from the group and a round of applause.

'Right! Ladies and gentlemen! Please be seated and enjoy your meal and the evening!'

They made their way to the tables and Eve, who usually went out of her way to make sure nobody was left out or alone, felt that there really wasn't any need as almost everyone knew at least one other person. She was intrigued to see that Geoff hadn't gone to sit with the Three Sues. Instead he'd taken a seat next to Denise and because the Three Sues were sitting on the table next to him in an anti-clockwise direction, he wouldn't be sitting with them at all.

Oh dear!

Geoff might be a bit heavy-going but nobody had forced the Three Sues to come away with him and Eve didn't like there to be any ill-feeling within her groups. Still, he looked happy enough so perhaps it was all working out for the best. Olivia made up the fourth woman on the Three Sue's table. Frances and Angela were sitting with Margaret and Tina and Janet and Kim with Vicky and Tracey. Penny's female companions were three ball-goers, but she wasn't letting the fact that they'd just met stop her. She was chattering ten to the dozen and already making them laugh. Eve did like Penny.

Once everyone was sitting down, the waiters came and offered red or white wine, which, unlike on the walks, was most definitely included. And then, drinks having been served, the food was brought out. Eve and Chris went and took their seats at their special table for two.

'Oi! Oi! Be'ave yourselves!' Dave called out, seeing them sitting together.

It must be Deano's influence!

Dave had reverted to the Jack-the-Lad he'd been in Antigua.

Chris was a charming dining companion. His conversation was as articulate and intelligent as it was witty. He kept

SINGLE ALL THE WAY   213

her amused with his observations and anecdotes, all littered with acerbic comments that made her laugh out loud. She was so engrossed in talking to him that she almost missed sounding the klaxon after the main course. And as the meal had gone she'd realised that he was a gay man and that Beniamin was his boyfriend.

'Well, the job has to have some perks!' he said, explaining that they'd met when Beniamin had come for an interview six months earlier. 'I don't know if it'll last and I'm not sure if I want it to, but for the moment it works for both of us so why not?'

'Absolutely!' Eve agreed, clicking glasses with him. 'Good on you! Cheers!'

'I can't believe I'm toasting with someone who's drinking diet cola!' He said it much as he might have said *'Bleach'*. 'So tell me, anyone special in your life?' he said, thinking that his frankness deserved the same from her.

'I have someone….special, yes. But with the job it's difficult for us to be together permanently. So at the moment, a bit like you, we take it as it comes. I was so glad to see Angela back among us,' she said, not-too-subtly changing the subject.

'I was going to tell you a few minutes ago that she came up to me in the foyer on her way into cocktails and apologised. She said that her behaviour had been completely unacceptable and offered to pay for the cleaning of my suit and for replacement shoes. I said it was okay, which I thought was very gracious of me. I mean, those shoes cost me a fortune. Bloody Paul Smith! Still, it must have taken a lot for someone like her to say sorry. What's been the reason for her sudden character change, do we know?'

'Apparently she went riding this morning. Met some nice people at the stables, had a good day with them and realised she'd behaved like a bit of a prat.'

'Oh she probably went to Hunter's. They are a lovely family. He's in a wheelchair, James. Had a riding accident. That was years ago. Long before I came here.'

On the round tables the conversation was flowing along with the wine. Any awkward moments were few and far between as most of those present were seasoned ball-goers. Angela's companions for dessert were Deano on one side and Dave on the other. She'd braced herself when she'd seen Dave sit down but he'd been friendly and funny, making all of them laugh. Deano was very attentive, signalling for the waiter to fill her glass when it was almost empty, although she'd put her hand over it so that he couldn't.

'You're not driving home tonight, are you?' Deano asked. 'You can't be!'

'Why can't I be?'

'Well, I've only just met you and by the time the dancing finishes the night will still be young. I'd hate to think of you driving out of my life like some up-market Cinderella on the stroke on midnight.'

Angela laughed at him. She felt relaxed and was enjoying herself. She'd decided to take the bull by the horns as soon as she'd come into the ballroom and had gone straight over to Frances, who had accepted her apology without a second's hesitation.

'Don't worry about me! I'm no-one to talk. I made a right idiot of myself when I was on my first Travel Together holiday in Antigua. I had a right falling out with a woman called Deborah. We'd got on really well for the first couple of days and then one morning round the pool, she told me all about her twenty-something year affair with her boss. Yes! She'd been his bit on the side for all those years and then – listen to this! – when he'd retired a couple of years earlier, he hadn't told his wife. He pretended he was doing a couple of days a week and on those days he went round Deborah's and spent the day. For a couple of years! Well, I was fresh from my divorce then. I'd been traded in for a younger model, although it never worked out for them and he begged me to take him back, but it was too late. Anyway, this Deborah got right up my nose bragging about true love with this married bloke that I really laid into her and then I went off and got myself well-and-truly pissed.' She screamed out laughing as she remembered and Angela couldn't help but laugh along.

'And I went into the ladies and I came out and bumped into Eve and she had to take me back to my room. I could barely walk, but it wasn't all the drink! No! I was so drunk I'd put two legs in one leg-hole. I was lurching along with a lump of swimsuit hanging from one side!' The two women had screeched with laughter and Angela had relaxed then and had known that it was going to be a good evening. And now, with Deano sitting next to her she felt even more sure that it was. Not that she had any plans of ending up in bed with him! She wasn't going to repeat the mistake she'd made with John of going for a drunken fumble. From now on she was going to start valuing herself. But there was something rather charming about him and a chat and a dance and perhaps even a bit of a snog would do nicely, thank you!

Milos was tired. He'd served breakfasts and then gone to his room to sleep until four o'clock when he'd had to go and help decorate the ballroom and lay the tables. He'd eaten in the staffroom at six o'clock and since then he'd been rushed off his feet. He was seriously worried he wouldn't be able to visit even one of the women that night, let alone both of them. All evening he'd made sure they'd seen he was paying attention to them. Fortunately, yet again, they were on separate tables and with their backs to each other so he didn't have to worry that one might see him being flirty with the other one. As the meal drew to an end he raced round collecting crockery and cutlery and clearing the tables and began to think he would have to chose just one of them and that would be a wasted opportunity. Then, he hit upon a plan.

The pianist had finished and the Phil Austin Quintet had started up and people were gathering on the dance-floor. He saw that Slim Sue had gone outside to have a cigarette. So he went over to Frances, who at that moment, was, fortunately, alone at the table. Her pashmina had fallen to the floor, so scooped it up and handed it back to her, taking the opportunity to talk quietly to her.

'I have some bad news. I have just been told we must do bar inventory after close tonight. But I badly want come see you. I can get away for half-hour at half-past ten o'clock. I can come your room. Okay?'

'Oh, alright then.' Frances looked at her watch and saw it was already ten o'clock. She was a little disappointed but then again thought that half-an-hour of orgasms was better than no orgasms at all.

'I knock on your door at ten-thirty.' he said to confirm their *date*. And then he was gone.

He congratulated himself on his timing, which was perfect. He slipped out of the ballroom and walked through the lounge towards the bar just as Slim Sue was coming back in. She was alone. He took her arm and pulled her into a small conference room that led from the lounge, closing the door behind them. It was dark and deserted. He knew nobody would come in and he hoped that nobody would notice he was missing. It was a chance he would have to take and he knew he could make something up if anyone asked. He pulled Slim Sue into his arms, kissing her face and moving his hands all over her body. He could feel her responding to him already. He'd made sure that he'd kept her glass filled all through the meal and he could see that the alcohol was having an effect. Her hands moved swiftly down his body, too, grabbing at his crotch and rubbing until she could feel him start growing, sighing and groaning as he did. This is what he liked about older women, they were always so hungry for it.

'I cannot come your room tonight,' he said, without slowing down. 'I have inventory in bar.'

'Oh, no!' Slim Sue said.

'But I make love to you now.'

'Here? But someone might come in,' she said, undoing his belt and sliding her hand inside his zip.

'Nobody come here.'

He pushed her against a table, laying her down on it, lifting her evening dress to her waist and pulling down her tights and panties. Then he lowered his head and heard her squeal in pleasure as he used his tongue, frantically working it to bring her to a fast, loud orgasm. She grabbed his head and thrust it hard against her groin, knocking his nose on her pubic bone, which brought tears to his eyes, but he didn't stop. She was squealing and thrashing around and within a very short time gave out a loud groan and her whole body shuddered. She straightened her fingers, gradually releasing her grip on his head and her breathing, which had been a loud, fast pant, slowly returned to normal. He waited a brief moment, then stood up and tucked his shirt back into his trousers and tightened his belt. She sat up and pulled him to her, holding him tightly round the waist as if she didn't want their time together to end; that she didn't want to let him go. He smiled in the darkness. That was just what he wanted. Tomorrow morning he'd make a quick very early call to her room. He'd tell her how fabulous she was, how he felt about her, how much he'd enjoyed her company. He would be deliberately quiet, with just a slight air of sadness, causing her to ask him what was wrong. He would say that he was very sad they were saying goodbye, but, that he'd also just taken a phone call from Serbia, from his mother, who had three jobs trying to earn enough to take care of his four younger siblings, telling him that his father, who was terminally ill had taken a turn for the worse. He was afraid his father might die before he could gather enough for a ticket back to Belgrade to see him for what was probably the last time. She would then say that he must let her help. She'd open her purse and insist he took the money she was offering him. He, of course, would protest, and say that wasn't what he meant, and she would then be contrite and say she hadn't meant to offend him. And then, with some more coaxing, he would, reluctantly take the money. He would kiss her and tell her she was a good woman. There might even be time to give her another quick orgasm and then he would be gone; out of the room and out of her life. It never failed. His savings account was growing nicely. But for now he had to get back to work.

'I must to go. If I can, I come see you in the morning before I start work on breakfast. Okay?'

'Oh, yes, okay!' she said, sighing. She slid off the table, pulled up her tights and panties and straightened her dress. He took her hand and led her through the tables and chairs in the dark room as far as the door to the lounge. He opened it slightly and looked out. The lounge was empty, the coast was clear.

'I go. You count twenty and then you come,' he said. And then he had disappeared.

The whole episode had taken nine and a half minutes.

Back in the ballroom everyone was having a great time. The Phil Austin Quintet was proving to be a great band, playing dance music for everyone's taste. Eve was in the middle of the floor, doing her best dance steps, actually enjoying herself at seeing the sea of happy faces dancing around her. Forty wasn't a large number of people for a black-tie ball, which often ran to two hundred, or for the size of the ballroom, but Chris, in his wisdom, had pulled the long, rich diving-curtains halfway down, so that the venue was, in fact, cut in half. This made it feel intimate and atmospheric, which was just right for the group. Few people sat at the tables, and those that did, Eve could see, were deep in conversation. Nobody was on their own. She was pleased to see Angela looked as if she was enjoying herself as she danced with Deano and Kim and Janet were shuffling around the floor in the arms of two of the ball-goers.

As the number finished, Frances checked her watch and saw it was twenty-past ten, so she made her way back to her table and picked up her bag and then walked out of the ballroom, looking to all the world as if she was going to the Ladies. She passed Milos on her way, who was carrying a tray of drinks over to the Four Friends and their new best friends, who had also just come off the dance floor. He nodded at Frances as their paths crossed.

✦   ✦   ✦

ONCE SHE WAS out of the ballroom Frances quickened her pace, wanting to get herself ready before he came. He'd said he had half an hour and she didn't want to waste a second of it. She went into the bathroom and had a little freshen up and had barely finished when she heard the knock. She opened it and Milos tumbled in. She pulled him to her, kissing him hard on the lips, her hands in his hair as his worked their way over her breasts and her hips. Frances pulled away from him and licked her own lips.

'Hmm! You've had some of the taramasalata,' she said. He said nothing; just kissed her harder thinking back to his little episode in the conference room fifteen minutes earlier.

They moved straight over to the bed, eager to get started, each taking off their own clothes, too aware that they were going against the clock for any seduction to take place. Milos quickly got to work, doing his best to make Frances enjoy herself. And she was enjoying herself, in spite of the rush. She was thrashing around, warm, wet feelings taking hold of her body, giving little gasps of pleasure as they became more intense. But when the unexpected knock on the door came they both suddenly froze.

✦   ✦   ✦

CHRIS CAME BACK into the ballroom from the front desk looking for Eve, who he found talking to Pete.

'I'm sorry to interrupt,' he said, 'but who's Frances Dawson?'

Eve looked around the ballroom but couldn't see her.

'I think I saw her walk out about ten minutes ago,' Pete said. She looked as if she was going to the ladies.'

'What's up? Is there a problem?' Eve asked.

'No. Just that there's someone at the front desk asking for her.' His expert eyes ran all over the ballroom, taking in every single detail as they spoke. He couldn't see Milos anywhere and some of the tables were covered in empty glasses. The rest of the staff seemed to have their hands full. 'You couldn't go and see what he wants, or find Frances, could you, please, Eve? I think the staff need my help.'

'Of course! Please excuse me, Pete.'

Eve went out into the foyer and Chris set to work in the ballroom. As Eve entered the foyer, Slim Sue came shivering in from having a cigarette outside, her hair flecked with white.

'It's snowing!' she shouted. 'It's snowing!'

Eve looked out through the main door and she could see the snow falling quickly, lit up by the lights on the Christmas tree. She approached the reception desk where a handsome, young man in jeans and a heavy reefer-style jacket was standing chatting to Derek, the night receptionist.

'Can I help you?' Eve asked, approaching the desk.

'This young man is asking for Frances Dawson,' Derek said.

✦   ✦   ✦

FRANCES AND MILOS remained totally still, like two stone statues, her hand cupping his balls, his fingers on her clitoris. Frances realised she wasn't even breathing.

'Keep still and quiet and they'll go away,' she whispered in Milos's ear.

There was a second knock, this time followed by a voice.

'Hello! Christmas surprise!'

Recognising the voice Frances dropped Milos's balls, causing him to yelp in pain. She leapt off the bed in a mixture of panic and joy. She grabbed Milos's clothes from the floor and shoved them into his arms.

'Quick! Outside!' she said.

'Bathroom?' he said, heading towards it.

'No! Not there!' she said, pushing him towards the French doors which opened out onto a small balcony. The doors obviously hadn't been opened in a while as it took her a moment to open them.

'Just coming!' she shouted back into the room as the French door gave way and she pushed a stark-naked Milos out onto the balcony where the snow was falling fast.

'My shoes!' he said, spluttering as the snow went into his mouth. Frances rushed back into the room and grabbed his shoes.

'It'll only be a moment,' she said, thrusting them at him before slamming the door shut and pulling the curtain across. She grabbed her dress and pulled it over her head, kicking her underwear under the bed out of sight. She patted her hair into place, took a deep breath and opened the door.

'Well, you're a sight for sore eyes,' she said, holding out her arms towards the young man.

'I'm so sorry, Mum,' he said, stepping into them.

✦   ✦   ✦

WORD OF THE snow had spread throughout the ballroom causing the group to respond gleefully, like children. Several of them had run out to the foyer or to the windows, pulling back the heavy curtains to watch the snowflakes fall. The sight of the snow seemed to spark a need in everyone for a warm, soothing drink and most of those who had been drinking wine or cava now switched to cognac or whiskey, some preferring theirs to be taken in a hot chocolate or coffee. Chris was working behind the bar, brewing coffee as fast as he could, while Beniamin took care of the chocolates. As manager, his deal included a small percentage on bar-takings, so he was please to see the sudden upsurge in consumption.

'Where the bloody hell is Milos?' he asked Beniamin for the third time in as many minutes.

'I don't know,' Beniamin shrugged. He turned to Kirsten, who was serving further along the bar and Alice who was frantically washing glasses. 'Have you seen Milos?' he asked them.

'Not for a while,' Alice said, without looking up from her task. 'He might be in the kitchen, perhaps. Have you rung his mobile?'

'Chris says he has but there is no reply.'

'Last time I saw him he was collecting glasses,' Kirsten said, shrugging, then turning and smiling at Dave whose drinks she was serving.

'Thanks, doll. One for yourself,' Dave said, as he handed her his money and picked up the tray. He made his way back to the table where Deano, Penny, Angela, Olivia, Don, Pete, Colin, Janet and Kim were all sitting together. He handed out the drinks, pausing to be extra nice to Angela as he put her cognac down in front of her.

'There you are, babe. One cognac, served with luv!' he said, winking at her. Half-an-hour earlier Penny had said how awful she now felt about the trick they'd played on Angela the previous evening.

'It was funny at the time, wasn't it? But we thought she was a bit of a cow then. But tonight she's been nice, almost like she's a different person.'

'Yes. P'raps she's got that multi-personality disorder thing. What d'you call it?'

'What? Schizophrenia? Ehh! You are funny!' Penny had shrieked and Dave had laughed along, although he wasn't really sure why.

'I just feel, we were a bit, you know, nasty, like,' Penny added. 'So I think we should be extra nice to her tonight because she's being nice and friendly to us,' she declared. And for Dave, Penny's word was law.

'I wonder what happened to Frances,' Pete said to Colin, noticing that she still hadn't come back into the ballroom.

'Perhaps she was tired and has already gone to bed,' Colin said, unconvincingly.

'I'd be surprised if she had, so I would,' Pete said. He felt there was something that Frances was uneasy about; the way she kept on looking at her phone and tonight he'd noticed that she looked at her watch a couple of times.

I recognise another troubled soul when I see one.

Perhaps the phone call she'd been waiting for had finally come through. If that was the case, he hoped it brought her some happiness and peace. He liked Frances and he hoped he could have a chat to her before they left. Not that he thought of himself as any sort of counsellor, but he thought that perhaps a chat to someone with a sympathetic ear might help ease her situation, whatever that might be. And helping someone else, might be like an act of penance for himself.

As there was now just over half-an-hour to go, the Phil Austin Quintet raised their performance another notch and everyone surged back onto the dance-floor, strutting their stuff and dancing their socks off.

✦   ✦   ✦

FRANCES DID NOT have words to describe the sheer, blissful, happiness and joy she felt holding her son in her arms again. She loved the feel of him, the smell of him, and every single hair on his head.

'Don't you apologise! It's me who should be doing that,' she'd said. pulling him into the room and sitting down next to him on the bed. 'How could I have been so insensitive?'

Darren smiled at his mother, taking her hands in one of his and pushing a lock of hair out of her eyes with the other. He felt a stab of pain at the hurt he knew he'd caused her by his stubborn ignoring her and he felt particularly ashamed that after all his father had put her through and the trauma of the breast cancer and the ensuing operation, that he had added to it by expecting her to just accept everything he'd thrown at her and carry on regardless and take it all in her stride.

'You have been a brick; my rock,' he said, suddenly

feeling a lump in his throat. 'I've got friends whose parents threw them out when they first came out, even in this day and age. But you didn't. You just took it in your stride.'

'Of course I didn't throw you out! You're my son and I love you with all my heart. When I told you that I loved you unconditionally, gay or straight, I meant every single word. When you set up home with Gary I was happy, because he's one of the nicest, kindest men I have ever met and I was genuinely happy that you had found each other…'

'But…'

'Look! I'm in my fifties. I was born into a world that is so different from today's. Bear in mind that homosexuality was still illegal until I was eight or nine. I grew up in a world where men married women and had a family together. I had nothing to do with anyone gay, well, apart from Ginger, my old hairdresser, until you told me about yourself,' she said, smiling. 'And as I've told you time and again, I love you unconditionally. Being gay is not an issue,'

'And yet you know from your own experience with Dad that hetero marriages don't always work out. Men can be right bastards!' he added, camping up his tone in an attempt to make her smile.

'Of course they can! And so can women! And as I've just said, it's not being gay that I have the problem with. I would much rather you were in a stable relationship with a man like Gary than with a woman who made your life impossible. There's no doubt about that whatsoever. It's having a baby I have the problem with.'

'Don't you want to be a grandmother?'

'Of course I do! Although I'm not altogether sure I'm old enough,' she added, laughing at her vanity. 'But there are lots of issues here. The child has to be taken into account.'

'I know! And I want to explain all of that to you. Look, I'm sorry I've just come barging in here like this, but I think we've both behaved a bit silly and I wanted to talk to you face to face.'

'So have you driven all the way from Edinburgh tonight just to see me?'

'Well, we're on our way to some friends but we've done a detour. Gary's with me. We've booked into a B&B just a mile or so away because there was no room at the inn here. I was going to wait and come early in the morning and invite you to brunch with the two of us, but knowing you were so close by I had to see you tonight and talk, Mum. We have to clear the air. And I'm sorry for butting in on your evening. But why aren't you downstairs enjoying yourself?' he asked, suddenly aware that his mother wasn't taking part in the fun that was going on in the ballroom.

'I am enjoying myself,' she said.

'Well, come on! Let's go down to the bar. I'll have a drink and wait for you while you spend the time left with your friends if you want to, or we can find a quiet corner, have a drink together to toast Christmas belatedly and talk to each other,' he said standing up and offering her his hand.

Frances stood up and slipped her feet into her shoes and grabbed her bag and key. She took her son's hand and left the room with him, the shivering, snow-covered Serb on the balcony totally forgotten.

✦   ✦   ✦

'AND NOW, LADIES and gentlemen, our final medley of the evening. "We hope you've enjoyed yourselves as much as we've enjoyed playing for you. This is Phil Austin wishing you the compliments of the season from the Phil Austin Quintet and saying GOOD NIGHT! GOOD LUCK! AND A HAPPY NEW YEARRRRRRRR!'

The quintet went into a medley of slow dances starting

with *The Last Waltz*, followed by *The Party's Over*, most of the group grabbing the person they most fancied to have the final dance with, before getting into a big group circle for *New York, New York*. Cameras flashed and phones videoed as people enjoyed the final moments of what had been a great evening. Weaved into the circle, between Eric and Terry, Eve looked round and gave herself a mental pat on the back, taking much of the credit for the way the evening had gone.

'These little town shoes, are longing to stray,' she sang at the top of her voice while feeling happy inside that everyone was smiling, singing and looking as if they really had enjoyed themselves. Opposite her in the circle, Janet kicked her legs high alongside Kim and Colin. Further round, Penny and Dave were singing their lungs out. Next to them, Deano and Angela were having a contest to see whose kicks were highest. Geoff was gripping onto Denise as if his life depended on it; Blonde Sue was between Vince and Don, Tall Sue between Mick and Barry and Slim Sue between Barry and John and Geoff didn't seem to mind a bit! Only Pete looked a bit subdued, Eve, thought, although he was a quiet sort of man, not a party-animal and it must be difficult for him to get into the swing of things when partying was probably the last thing he felt like doing.

'It's up to you…New York………………NEW YORK!' everyone sang out the closing bars as Eve realised that Frances wasn't there. A few moments later she caught sight of her sitting in the far corner of the bar, deep in conversation with the young man who'd asked for her at the bar. Eve smiled to herself. She loved the way that Frances wasn't afraid to flaunt her penchant for younger men.

'You see, I have so many questions,' Frances was saying, sipping her rum and cola.

'Well, ask away, Ma!' Darren said. 'This is why I'm here,

for us to talk.'

'It's things like…' she coloured a little at what she was about to discuss with her son. 'Who will be the father? I mean the biological father? Because if it's you, say, won't Gary feel left out? That the baby's not his?'

'We will both be the father,' Gary said. 'For the insemination sperm is taken from both of us and mixed together so that the egg could be fertilised by me or by Gary. We won't know whose it is, but it won't matter.'

Wow! Too much information!

Frances ticked herself off for her thoughts. Darren was right; he was here to answer all her questions, and she had asked, after all!

'Oh, so you don't both…you know…?'

'What, have intercourse?' Darren burst out laughing. Frances looked around to check that nobody was near enough to overhear them. 'Oh, Mum, you're priceless,' he said. 'We are both gay men. Not bi-sexual. Gay. We don't have sex with women.'

'But you used to!'

'Yes, I did, because I thought it was what I wanted and what was expected of me. I've already told you, that all through university I knew that it was men that did it for me, not women. So, Gary and I aren't going to take it in turns to shag a woman! What do you take us for?'

'And, who is …the woman…the mother going to be?' Frances asked, taking another sip of her drink, trying for all she was worth to look like a cool, understanding, woman-of-the-world kind of mother.

'A lesbian friend of ours.'

'Three gay parents!' Frances had said it before she could stop herself.

'Mum, listen to me!' Darren's tone was stern, although there was a smile in his eye. 'Are you and Dad both straight?'

'Yes,' Frances nodded.

'And yet, I'm gay. Gary's parents are both straight and yet he's gay. So there is no evidence whatsoever that a person's sexuality is passed onto their offspring. And even if they were, so what? Didn't you tell me ten minutes ago that you loved me unconditionally?' Frances nodded. 'So we will love our child, unconditionally, too. Even if it turns out straight,' he joked.

'But what if it's a girl?'

'It won't matter, will it? If I was a straight man you wouldn't be mentioning things like that, would you? Yet look at how many straight men, fathers, interfere with girls.'

'Yes. Sorry. I wasn't suggesting anything like that! Of course I wasn't!' Frances bit her lip. 'I mean, how will you do the whole period thing and....'

'Mum! Stop! You're getting way ahead of yourself. If we have a daughter we'll cross that bridge when we come to it.'

'I just can't help worrying that the child, my grandchild will be teased at school or bullied. Children can be very cruel, you know.'

'Of course they can! But the more that couples like us are accepted as the norm, the more same-gender families there are, the easier it becomes.'

Frances sat and thought for a moment. Darren had been open and honest with her and she was grateful for that. He'd come all the way from Edinburgh to see her and to offer the olive branch. She loved him so much!

'Well, I'd better start looking at baby clothes, because I can't wait to welcome my first grandchild!' she said.

'Oh, Mum! I love you,' Darren said, reaching for her hand and kissing her fingers. 'And so does Gary. He loves you as much as his own.'

''Erm, I'm sorry to interrupt.' Derek had appeared by

their side. 'But we need to go into your room, Ms Dawson. With your permission, of course. I can't think how it's happened, but a member of staff appears to be stuck on your balcony!'

'What?' Darren said, looking from Derek to his mother and back again.

'Oh! No!' Frances let out a screech and jumped to her feet. 'Darren, your mother has a few secrets of her own she needs to talk to you about,' she called, ruefully, over her shoulder as she skittered across the reception towards the stairs.

✦   ✦   ✦

MILOS'S PLIGHT HAD come to light when the taxi that had come to pick up Vicky and Tracey had, fortunately, arrived a little early. The weather seemed to be closing in and the driver, Reg Brookes, wanted to collect the women and head back to Maldon before it got much worse. He came to the top of the drive and saw that all the parking spaces were taken, so he drove along the side of the building, swooping into a big circle to turn the cab around and park as close to the front door as possible, when through the teeming snowflakes he saw movement on the first floor. He stopped the car and put the headlights on. He could see a man on one of the balconies waving his arms and shouting out at him. Reg opened the car door and got out, pulling his warm, weatherproof coat around him.

'You alright, mate?' he called, barely able to look up at the man due to the ferocity of the snowflakes that were whipping against his face. The man shouted something back that Reg couldn't make out, but what was clear from his demeanour and the weather, was that he was probably freezing to death.

'Hang on, mate!' he shouted, getting back into the car and driving to the front of the hotel. He pulled up alongside the Christmas tree and ran inside. The night receptionist looked startled to see him as he stumbled into the foyer bringing snow and cold with him.

'Can I help you, sir?' Derek asked.

'There's a bloke in shirtsleeves, looks like he's freezing, on one of the first-floor balconies. Looks like he's been there a while.'

Milos couldn't believe his eyes when he saw Reg get back into the car and drive off. He cursed the man, he cursed himself and he cursed Frances for forcing him onto the balcony in the first place. He'd only stepped outside because she'd said it would be just for a couple of minutes. It was difficult to see his watch through the falling snowflakes, but it felt as if he'd been there for hours. After about ten minutes he had really begun to feel the cold. He'd managed to get dressed, although doing so in the wind and the snow hadn't been easy and by the time he'd got his shirt and trousers on he was soaking wet, having put wet clothes onto a wet body. His socks had been reasonably dry as they were tucked inside his shoes, but once again, as soon as they went over wet feet, they, too, became sodden and cold. Frances had pulled the heavy, velvet curtains across the French doors so that whoever the visitor was couldn't see him, but that also meant that he couldn't see in, either. The snow began to fall faster and thicker and his plight became more miserable. Frances must open the door to him soon, surely? After another ten minutes he was frantic. He knocked on the door. She would hear him and she would have to let him in. He knocked again and again, kicking the door in his anger and frustration, but Frances didn't pull back the curtain or open the door. He strained his eyes and thought that the chink of light he'd seen earlier had disappeared. There was nothing for it! He would have to ring the reception or Beniamin and tell them where he was so they could come and rescue him. He knew it would mean dismissal, but that was a small price to pay when compared with freezing to death. The memory of Serbian winters in the mountains paled into insignificance when compared to the cold he was now feeling. Or rather, wasn't feeling. His hands were numb and as he pulled his phone from his pocket, his frozen fingers fumbled and it slipped from his grasp, falling alongside the fat snowflakes to the ground below. He stood as close to the doors as he could, his arms around himself, desperately trying to keep himself warm. Under his breath he prayed. He begged God to spare him, to send help before he froze to death. He offered all kinds of promises in exchange for God's mercy; he would stop being a gigolo; he would stop lying about his father, who was a fit and healthy Geography teacher in Loznica and about his mother who only worked as a part-time librarian, three days a week, and about his siblings, who were non-existent as he was an only child.

Please, God! Please, God! Please, God!

He repeated the prayer over and over, not wanting to think about what the consequence would be if God chose not to answer his prayers soon. He wriggled his toes inside his shoes, at least he hoped they were wriggling as he couldn't feel them any more. And then, when all hope was fading, he'd seen the headlights swooping round the side of the building. From deep inside him, he'd found the strength to wave his arms and shout out, although he knew the man would never hear him from inside the vehicle. But he had seen him! And he had got out of the car! But now, he'd driven away! Driven away and left him there, to his freezing fate on a small balcony on the first floor of a sixteenth century English hotel.

Then, he was aware of movement on the other side of the French doors. The curtain was pulled back and the door was thrust open to reveal Mr Edwards, Derek and Frances. He couldn't move. His face was a frozen mask, covering chattering teeth. Mr Edwards reached forward, took hold of his arm and pulled him inside. Frances was hovering and holding the duvet, which she passed to Mr Edwards, who wrapped it round his shoulders.

'Take him to the staff quarters and make sure he has a warm bath, not too hot!' Mr Edwards said to Derek. 'He has to warm up gradually. Put him in dry clothes and give him a hot drink, like milk or chocolate and put him into bed. And you'd better see if an emergency doctor can come and check him over.'

'Yes, of course,' Derek said, putting an arm round Milos to steady him.

'I don't know quite what's been going on here, but we'll discuss it in the morning. Let's get you warmed up, tonight,' Mr Edwards said to Milos, who nodded, his teeth sounding like hyperactive castanets as he slowly edged his way forward with Derek, leaving puddles of water behind on the carpet.

'I can't begin to apologise,' Frances said. 'I was just so happy to see my son, that I forgot he was there. God! I could have killed him!'

'Well, you didn't. But you were very foolish in allowing him to come to your room and he was foolish for coming as he knows that it is a sackable offence.'

'Oh, dear!' Frances felt dreadful. She didn't want Milos to get the sack and she didn't want him to freeze to death either.

'Well, I'll speak to you in the morning before you leave. I will need to take a statement from you, I hope you understand.'

Frances nodded, miserably. She followed Mr Edwards

out of the room and went back down to the bar to tell Darren what had happened, certain that for him, this would definitely be *too much information*!

✦　　✦　　✦

ALTHOUGH THE BAR had closed, most of the group sat around in groups, chatting, the topic of conversation being the snow and the mystery man on the balcony. Word had got around that a taxi-driver had seen someone on a balcony and the rumour mill had changed that into *A burglar got stuck on a balcony in the snow while trying to rob a room.* Even Eve was unsure as to what had really happened and she saw that Chris looked a bit too stressed to ask as he came through the bar and went on into the ballroom. She'd find out before she left, and anyway, as long as all her group were safe and unaffected by whatever it was, she would leave the gossip to someone else. Another topic of conversation between a couple of the group was the young man who was sitting with Frances.

'She's pulled a young bloke again,' Dave said, nudging Deano and nodding towards her.

'What do you mean, *again*?'

'Oh, blimey! Didn't you know? It musta bin after you 'ad your accident, then. Yes, she got off with some young local in Antigua. Spent all 'er time with 'im. I think it might've bin one of them off the boat,' he said.

'Well, well, well! Sly horse!' Deano said, turning back to Angela and taking her hand.

'Would you be reacting that way if it was an older man with a younger girl?' Angela asked. 'No! Of course you wouldn't!' she answered her own question before he could. 'So butt out and let her enjoy herself!'

'I was just thinking that myself!' Penny said, laughing.

She had had such a good night. And although she wanted to go upstairs and spend the rest of it with Dave again, she didn't want what she was enjoying downstairs to end. Knowing that the bar would close as soon as the music stopped, Dave and Deano had got in several rounds of drinks and now the two couples were sitting enjoying each others' company. Penny was surprised at how much she actually liked Angela. This evening they had got on like a house on fire. And she didn't want to go up to bed at the same time that Angela did, because once she saw Penny was next-door Angela would realise who it had been that had taken the mickey out of her the night before. And looking round, it seemed to Penny that most people had the same idea; they were all chatting and laughing and drinking, wanting the night to last as long as was possible.

'Ehh! I'm so glad I came on this break,' she said to the others. 'I wasn't sure, like, if it would be for me, but I've had a cracking Christmas,' she said.

'I'm just sorry I only joined you all tonight,' Deano said, thinking of what might have been with Angela if he'd turned up four days earlier.

'Did you spend Christmas on your own?' Penny asked.

'More or less. Went to my parents on Christmas Day, It was nice to have Christmas dinner with them, but then they both ended up snoozing in the chair for a couple of hours, so I was practically on my own anyway!' he said, making the others laugh.

'You drivin' 'ome tomorrow?' Dave asked Angela and Deano. ''Cos if you are an' you ain't gotta rush off, we could 'ave a bit a lunch somewhere all togevva before we 'ave to go our separate ways.'

'That sounds good,' Deano said.

'Hmm, fine by me, as long as it's not too late. I said I'd go to the stables tomorrow as soon as I was home,' Angela said.

'Well! We might not be going anywhere if this snow keeps up!' Penny said, voicing what everyone else was thinking.

✦   ✦   ✦

DARREN HAD LISTENED to what his mother had had to tell him in stunned silence, his brain unable to take in exactly what it was that she was saying.

'And so all I could think of when I heard your voice, was to get him out of sight. I couldn't hide him in the bathroom in case you wanted to use it, so I pushed him out onto the balcony. Well, I didn't realise it was snowing until he was out there and then there was nothing I could do! I thought it would only be for a couple of minutes.'

'And you forgot he was there?' Darren asked, incredulous.

'I'm turning into one of these right dotty old birds, aren't I?' Frances said. *When I am an old woman I shall wear purple with a red hat which doesn't go and doesn't suit me,'* she quoted.

'And shag blokes younger than my son!' Darren said, causing them both the burst out laughing. 'Mother! Tonight has been a real eye-opener!' he said, leaning forward and kissing her on the forehead. 'I'd better go, before I get snowed in and then you and I will end up sharing a bed and I'm not sure how I'd feel about that, given that I'm no longer six. The B&B's only five minutes away.'

'Well, come for breakfast in the morning!' Frances said.

'We've got breakfast included. Why don't you ring me when you're ready to leave and then Gary and I'll meet you in the pub. We can do a pub lunch. You haven't got to rush off, have you?'

'No, not at all.'

'And our friends aren't expecting us until early evening.' Darren had said. 'It's not too far to south-east London from here.'

'I thought you'd have spent it in Scotland.'

'New Year's Eve's what you make it. We'll enjoy being with our friends and each other, wherever we are,' Darren had said.

Frances had walked to the front door of the hotel with him, mindful as she did that she wasn't wearing underwear and that her right breast, the full one, was swaying around like a sexy pendulum, all of its own accord. She quite liked the feel of her silky dress against her bare backside. She chose not to share that with Darren. He turned and gave her a hug.

'See you tomorrow for lunch,' he said and then pushed the front door open, disappearing into a wall of white.

✦ ✦ ✦

THE BAR GRADUALLY emptied out. As drinks were finished, yawning started and slowly and reluctantly the clients of the Travel Together Black-Tie Ball took leave of their new friends and went up to their rooms. Once there, without exception, they pulled back the curtains and looked out on the beautiful blue-white spectacle of moonlight on the snow-covered grounds of the hotel. The wind had dropped and so the blizzard-like conditions that Tracey, Vickie, Eric, Terry, Barry, Tina, Margaret and Joan had all left in had died down to a soft, steady snowfall. As Eve dropped the curtain and turned back into her room she hoped they had all had a safe journey and she double-hoped that the snow would have disappeared enough by morning to allow them all to leave. The click of the kettle as it reached boiling point brought her out of her thoughts. She emptied the sachet of chocolate powder into a mug and added the water, putting it on the bedside table to cool down a bit while she got ready for bed. As always, she held a mental post-mortem of the evening and smiled with satisfaction, knowing that it had gone well. Even the incident with Milos hadn't ruined it.

Well, perhaps it had for him!

She thought about Frances' son turning up. He seemed like a really nice young man; Eve had liked him. She hadn't asked why he'd found the need to seek out his mother on the last night of her Christmas break and Frances hadn't offered to tell her. She'd also been mortified that she'd forgotten about Milos on the balcony.

'I honestly don't know how I did that, Eve' was one of the only things she'd said about the incident. 'Poor bugger could have frozen to death.'

Eve knew she'd get the whole story this morning as Chris had told Frances she'd have to make a statement and Eve would also need to talk to her to find out exactly what had happened for her report. She couldn't help chuckling to herself, though.

In bed with someone younger than your son when he walks in on you!

She thought of her own son who she'd be seeing in just a couple more days. She had planned a lovely, cosy New Year's Eve at home for the four of them and she couldn't wait! The next time she saw Natalie and Michael after that would be at the church. The thought sent her off to bed with a huge smile of satisfaction on her face.

✦   ✦   ✦

PENNY WAS CUDDLED up to Dave feeling warm and fuzzy and happy. He was humming *'Let it snow!'* under his breath.

They had just made love and were both lying quietly with their own thoughts about tomorrow and the future. Occasionally they had heard muffled footsteps along the corridor and whispered and not-so-whispered voices calling *'Good-night'* to each other or laughing. But the moments of quiet produced a silence that was almost tangible. The silence of snow had penetrated the walls and enveloped the building. They both heard whispers and footsteps, which stopped at Angela's room and then more whispers followed by the turn of the large, key in the lock and the almost-creak of the door opening and then the dull, metallic thud of the door closing.

'We're gonna 'ave to put the telly on again, I think,' Dave said.

'I think they'll be quiet. After all, she knows we heard her. I feel so mean about that,' Penny whispered.

'Look, it was a laugh. We didn't mean no 'arm by it. An' if they start gettin' too loud we'll just 'ave to 'ave anuvver round ourselves.'

'Anuvver round?' Penny mimicked him. 'Ehh! Who could resist you, Mr Romantic?' she teased him.

'Sorry!' he said, leaning over to kiss her.

'You're going to have to persuade me that you really do fancy me all over again now!'

'Oh no! That'll be terrible. What an 'ardship!' he said, as she pushed the duvet away and pulled herself on top of him.

✦   ✦   ✦

ANGELA WAS ALONE in room ten although that wasn't through any lack of trying on Deano's part. He'd made it clear the whole evening that he wanted to spend the night with her. She'd enjoyed his company; he was witty, intelligent, amusing, entertaining, attentive and she'd found him quite charming. A bit too charming, though. She'd stayed behind in the bar talking to him until everyone else had gone. They were sitting closely together on a sofa, his arm around her back, gently caressing her arm and occasionally flexing his fingers in an attempt to touch her breast, and her head against his shoulder. They had talked about themselves, or rather she had let him talk. How could she talk about herself when she was only just now finding out who the real Angela was? She had finally made it clear that she was sleeping alone.

'Well, how about the bit before sleeping? I'm quite happy to go back to my own room if you don't want me to hear you snoring,' he'd quipped.

'Not even the bit before sleeping,' she'd said, firmly, standing up and picking up her bag from the table.

They'd strolled arm-in-arm out into the foyer and up the stairs, making a very handsome couple, and looking, to all intents and purposes, as if they were just on their way to a smouldering session. At her door he'd had one last try.

'You're sure now? I don't want to just get comfortable with my winceyette pyjamas on and my teeth out when you come hammering on the door, begging me to let you in,' he said. She'd roared out laughing.

'I promise you I will do everything to resist the urge, should it suddenly come upon me. You can take your teeth out, put your jim-jams on and put your light out without fear of intrusion.' She gave him a final kiss, pulling gently away as she felt him start to get more intense. 'Good-night, Deano,' she said and turned and unlocked the door and slipped inside.

She kicked her shoes off and pulled her dress over her head, dropping it on the back of the chair and made herself comfortable on the bed in her ivory, silk underwear set. It wasn't that she hadn't been tempted by Deano, because she had, but she knew that a one-night-stand with him would muddy the waters of her thought process, just as they'd suddenly started to run clearly. She needed time to herself.

What a day it's been!

She thought back over it and the huge range of emotions she'd gone through. The anger and loathing of the early-morning – and she couldn't believe it had only been that morning – had completely disappeared. Her thoughts took her back to the Hunters' kitchen. In her mind's eye she was there again, sitting at the solid, oval table, drinking good, strong coffee from a brightly-patterned orange and green mug, looking through the window at the garden, feeling the warmth from the Aga and the even greater warmth of Annabelle Hunter. She still didn't understand why she'd suddenly opened up to Annabelle and told her the truth about Harry's death. She had honestly thought she could never, ever talk about it to another living soul. Her shame and embarrassment when she'd been discovered had been so deep and all-encompassing; the words that Melissa had spat at her would ring in her ears for ever; her own family's disappointment and distancing themselves from her had cut her like deep sabre slashes and her own self-loathing had eaten her through.

Is Annabelle a witch? An angel? How else would I have told her all that?

Angela didn't know. All she knew was that she was beyond glad that she'd gone for a ride that morning and met her. And now, her shame and embarrassment were less. She would never forget it, but now she could live with it. She had made a mistake. If the heater hadn't been faulty Harry would still be alive and her affair with Seb would have died a natural death and nobody would have been any the wiser. And she knew that she had to start to let go of the self-hatred. She knew there was much to love about herself and that's what she was going to set about doing.

'You have to remember, the faulty heater was the cause of his death, not you,' Annabelle had said.

Angela had nodded her head in agreement. His death had been a terrible tragedy made worse by occurring on perhaps the most emotional day of the year, Christmas Eve, and compounded by her infidelity. But her infidelity hadn't been the cause of it. And there had been so many factors and reasons behind her infidelity, she saw that now. Today. Something special had happened and inside her something enormous had shifted.

The Angela of yesterday would have dragged Deano up to her room and ripped his clothes off before the main course had been served. Spending the night with him now would have served no purpose other than momentary gratification.

He's just a guy and the world is full of them. I have to concentrate on this girl now, on Angela.

She was suddenly aware of sounds coming from the other side of the intercommunicating door. She found herself smiling, and also laughing at the memory of what the occupants of the next room had done to her the previous evening. She slid off the bed and padded across to the door. Raising her fist she banged on it.

'Keep it down, Penny! Or should I say, keep it up, Dave!' she called out. There was a beat of silence before she heard them both giggling loudly. Smiling to herself, she went to the bathroom to clean her teeth, take of her make-up and have, what she already knew would be, a great night's sleep.

✦   ✦   ✦

FRANCES COULDN'T SLEEP. The evening's events kept on whirring round in her head. Being in the throes of it with

Milos, the knock on the door, the joy of hearing Darren's voice and holding him close, sitting and talking things through with him, the night-receptionist's face as he asked permission to go to her room, the sight of Milos freezing on the balcony, Darren knowing she was a cougar. Over and over and over, her thoughts went round. But she was so very glad that she and Darren had thrashed things through. She still wasn't one hundred per cent convinced about her future grandchild being conceived by means of a turkey baster.

Too, too, too much information!

But, it was the way of the world. A modern, forward-thinking woman such as herself should accept it for what it was and for what it meant.

I'll be a grandma someday soon. I might have to give up these toy-boys.

She gulped at the thought, unsure if she was quite read for that, yet. She'd spent too much of her life being Frances the Mouse. She quite enjoyed being Frances the Cougar.

✦　✦　✦

AND IN HIS bed in the staff quarters, cocooned in a heavy duvet that he'd wrapped round every part of his body and head Milos slept soundly. Not even the dressing down from Mr Edwards; not even thought of losing his job the following morning; not even the humiliation of everyone knowing what had happened and what he'd been up to disturbed him. He was warm again and that was all that mattered.

DAY FIVE

J ANET WOKE UP and realised that it was the last morning; the Christmas break she had awaited with trepidation, at times, almost bordering dread, was over and, to her surprise it hadn't been too bad at all. Most of the group were very pleasant, professional people and she had felt comfortable in their company, slightly regretting having gone to bed early on Christmas Eve. She'd eaten more than her fill of Christmas Dinner; her short walk with Kim and Pete, who had been agreeable walking companions, had blown away the cobwebs, and the Christmas Night Dance, the Boxing Day Disco and last night's black-tie ball had all been unexpectedly good, apart from the unfortunate incident with the drunken members of the group and a member of staff being locked out in the snow. She had danced with the others and had a few drinks and…yes…enjoyed herself. The walks had been pleasant and informative, although not terribly challenging and she had really enjoyed the quiz, having been on the winning team on Boxing Day and in the winning pair with Colin the day after. Who would have ever thought she'd spend such an important Christmas in Essex? Yet from what she'd seen from the train on the journey from Liverpool Street, and from their morning walks, it was a pretty, picturesque county. The Blue Boar Inn had been splendid; it was very comfortable and the food had been exceptionally good. She'd put ten pounds in an envelope to give to Eve who was collecting a tip for the staff.

She gave a contented sigh.

All in all, it's worked out very well!

Several years ago the thought of spending such a time with people she'd never met would have seemed strange and wrong, but not now. So much of the last year had been strange and wrong that this had all seemed normal. Now, it just felt right.

She had wished it could have been Trinidad, but that had proved impossible for a myriad of reasons. But, as she'd told Kim and Dave at dinner, she would be going there in the summer; making one last trip to see the beautiful island of her birth. A one-way trip. She rolled over and pulled the duvet back and got out of bed and opened the heavy, blue velvet curtains. Pale, winter light poured into the room. She looked around it. It was a very pleasant room, with its oak beams and period furniture. She smiled to herself as she wondered what stories it could tell of the things and people and events it had witnessed through the last four hundred years. She was sure it could tell some ripe old tales. She touched the beams. Much of the hotel had been renovated but an original beam ran through the rooms on the first floor the manager had told them over cocktails. She reached and touched it, liking the feel of security and continuity it gave her, feeling its deep sense of history.

I wish I could leave something as impressive and durable behind.

She turned to look out of the window and gasped at what she saw. The snow was so deep it reached the roofs of the cars in the car park. She looked passed them to the grounds and gardens of the hotel and then the open fields beyonds. They had all merged into one enormous spread of white.

Oh, thank you! Thank you for allowing me to see such beauty!

She clapped her hands gleefully, like a small child. Her beautiful dark eyes were huge with joy and delight at the glorious spectacle before her. Snow had always fascinated her, from the very first time she'd seen it when she'd arrived in England on a freezing February day when she was ten years old. She knew exactly what she wanted to do. She moved towards the bathroom, running her hand over her head, touching the short fluff that covered it. She stopped next to her wig which stood on its stand on the dressing-table. Taking up her brush, she worked it rigorously a few minutes until the wig gleamed. Several people had remarked on her beautiful shiny hair. That had made her feel good. Appearances had always been important to Janet. She put the brush down and continued into the bathroom, giving a little skip as she went.

✦   ✦   ✦

THE PHONE RINGING at seven o'clock was a bad sign. It was always a bad sign, but Eve knew she had to answer it nonetheless.

'Good morning, Eve, it's Chris.'

'Morning, Chris.'

'We're snowed in. Right up to the door. We've got a snowplough that fits on the front of our jeep, but at the moment, we're waiting for backup so that we can make a start on shovelling the snow away from the groundsman's lodge so that we can get at it.'

'Oh, no! Is it just the hotel? I mean, are the roads clear?'

'No, they aren't. The snow is three feet deep in the village, I understand and there's ice on some of it. Even roads like the A12 are closed because they're full of abandoned vehicles. Nobody will be able to leave this morning. Perhaps not even for the rest of the day.'

'What do you want me to tell the group? Presumably everyone will have to vacate their room?'

'To be honest, at the moment they can stay where they are. We haven't got anyone coming in until tomorrow when guests start arriving for our New Year's Eve do. And even if we did have reservations for today, we can't get out, which also means nobody else can get in.'

'Okay. Breakfast is going on as normal, is it?'

'Yes. Enough staff live in for us to provide breakfast, fortunately. The maids all come from out-lying villages, so I'm not expecting them in yet. So, we'll just let everyone carry on until we hear that they can get at least part-way home.'

'That's good of you, Chris. Okay, I'll come down now and start spreading the word.'

Eve showered and got dressed in five minutes flat and made her way down to the dining-room. Nobody was there, just Beniamin and a waitress laying out the breakfast buffet. Eve helped herself to a cup of coffee and wandered back towards the foyer where she saw Janet, dressed in her outdoor clothes talking to Pete, Frances, Olivia, Don, Tall Sue and Deano. She was excited and animated.

'Morning!' Eve called to them. 'Erm, you can't leave, Janet, we're completely snowed in. We can't get out of the hotel grounds, and even if we could the lane and the village are impassable at the moment.'

'Oh, I'm not going home!' Janet said. 'I'm going outside to play in the snow! I'm going to make a snowman and I'm up for a snowball fight if I can persuade any of these to join me!'

'That's a great idea!' Eve, who was a big kid herself, said. 'Nobody can leave, you can hold onto your rooms for the time being and breakfast is served until ten, so you might as well go and play snowballs and then come in and dry off and have a warm breakfast.'

'Well, if you put it like that,' Pete said, 'I'll go and get my coat.'

'Me, too!' Frances said, following him.

'I'm not missing out!' Deano took the stairs two at a time with Don close on his heels.

'I don't do cold, I'm afraid,' Olivia said, turning to walk through to breakfast.

'Neither do I usually,' said Tall Sue. 'But when will I get another chance to behave like a big kid?'

✦   ✦   ✦

HALF-AN-HOUR LATER ALMOST the entire group had joined Janet and her crew in the grounds of the hotel. Janet had been the first one out, taking great delight in the giant steps she took through the virgin snow, that came several inches above her knees. As the others arrived, they slipped and pushed each other over in the deep snow. They pelted each other with snowballs and then had made a crazy-looking snowman with his head to one side next to the Christmas tree by the entrance.

'Looks like 'e's got a crick in 'is neck,' Dave laughed. 'Or as if 'is 'ead's falling off!'

'He's probably hung over,' Penny said, pulling her wooly hat down over her head. Her cheeks were bright pink, her gloves were soaking and her feet felt damp, but she didn't care. Dave couldn't stop thinking how pretty she looked. 'Ehh! I haven't enjoyed myself so much in a long time,' she said, taking Dave's arm and then, just as he thought she was going to give him a kiss, smacking a snowball in his face.

'Thanks very much! And there I was, finking you'd

enjoyed yerself with me!' he said, turning his head away just a second too late and spitting the snow out of his mouth as he spoke.

'Dave! Come on, mate! It's the blokes against the girls!' Deano called out to him. Dave, not wanting anyone to think his friendship with Penny might lead to him being a traitor to his own sex, dropped her arm as if it were a hot coal and made his way over to where the men were gathering.

'Right! Come on, girls!' Not to be outdone Penny went and joined the women. They armed themselves with as many snowballs as they possibly could, each cradling them along one arm while forming them with the other hand.

'They're going to be so sorry!' Angela said, having the time of her life. The moment she'd seen the others go outside she knew she had no option but to join in. This was what enjoying life was all about: the little, unplanned moments of happiness.

'Ready? Charge!' Deano led the men with all the fervour of Lord Cardigan leading the Six Hundred into the Battle of Balaclava.

'No! Not fair! We're not ready!' The women's protests were lost as the men pelted them without mercy. Eve, who'd taken her place alongside her sisters, had run out of snowballs and was now aiming armfuls of snow at Mick and Colin who were both giving as good as they got. Frances found herself on the floor and being rolled along by Pete and two of the ball-goers.

'Help! Help!' she screamed, loving every moment.

They played on for ten more minutes, each of them enjoying the freedom, the joy and the bliss of being like children again, until, almost as one, they slowly wandered back inside, to dry off and have their full-English breakfasts washed down with steaming mugs of tea and coffee.

✦   ✦   ✦

AN HOUR LATER most of the group were sitting in the
lounge chatting, playing cards, reading or watching TV. They
had all been able to contact relatives and cat-sitters and
kennels to let them know of their plight. Nobody was
surprised; the whole country was under a deep, unexpected
blanket of snow.

'I don't know why the bloody weathermen don't just
give up,' Deano said to Pete at breakfast. 'They never seem
to get it right, do they?'

'They don't. God knows when I'll get back to Belfast. A
lot of the flights are cancelled and I can't get to the airport
even if they weren't.'

'Where you flying from?'

'Stansted. I'll just wait until I can get out of here and
then go to the airport and wait.'

'That's a bit of a bugger, isn't it? I'm lucky, just. Couple
of hours drive for me. But if you want a lift I'm happy to
drop you at Stansted. I go right past it on the A120.'

'That's good of you, thanks. If the trains aren't running
and if you don't mind…'

'Even if they are, mate, it'll be quicker for you. Well, as
long as we can get out!' Deano added, laughing.

Olivia and four of the ball-goers were missing, all deciding to take coffees back to their rooms and relax there.
Blonde Sue and Vince hadn't put in an appearance for
breakfast. Don had phoned Vince and told him they were
snowed in for at least the next couple of hours and so he
and Blonde Sue had decided to make the most of it. After
all, who knew when or if they'd ever see each other again?

Chris Edwards appeared in the lounge and looked
around. He spied Frances, who was sitting with Kim, Janet

and Angela, and was actually in the middle of telling them an edited and heavily censored version of what had happened the previous evening. She saw no reason to explain why Darren had wanted to see her. Chris crossed the lounge, heading towards her. She coloured slightly when she saw him approaching from the corner of her eye.

'Good morning, Ms Dawson. I'm sorry to interrupt, but may I have a word?' he said, smiling at her and the others.

'Of course,' Frances said, getting up and following him out through the bar and into the foyer, behind the reception desk and into a short corridor, which led to three offices. He opened the first door and went in, holding it for her to follow.

'Please have a seat,' he said, going round behind the desk and sitting down. He drew a large notepad towards himself and picked up a pen, which he clicked on and off nervously.

'Before you start,' Frances said, wanting to jump in before her nerve failed her, 'I don't want to get Milos into any trouble.'

'I'm afraid he is already in a lot of trouble.'

'But it's not as if he'd broken into my room! I invited him in there of my own free will. And it wasn't the first time, either.'

'Can I just stop you there, Ms Dawson, and say that by telling me that it wasn't the first time, makes it far more serious, not better. Whether or not you invited him, Milos knows our company rules. Staff are not allowed into guests' rooms under any circumstances. Any circumstances. And that includes, specific invitation.'

'But I feel so awful! I was more than happy for him to come to my room and then I shut him out, forgot about him and left him to almost freeze to death! How is he? I haven't seen him this morning…'

'He is fine. We were unable to get a doctor here last night but we spoke on the phone and carried out the instructions we were given and he spent a comfortable night and appears fully recovered this morning but is spending the day in bed just to be sure.' Chris Edwards did everything by the book and he didn't want Milos to try and say he hadn't been given due care and attention. 'And the reason you haven't seen him,' he continued, 'is because he's suspended pending my investigation into his behaviour.'

'Don't you honestly think he was punished enough last night?'

'And do you honestly think that you are the first guest whose room he's gone to?'

Frances looked at him, taken aback. The frequency or not of Milos's visits to rooms hadn't entered her head.

'From what I understand, he'd been in someone else's room the previous night.'

'No, it was the night before that. Christmas Night.'

'To your room, perhaps. He'd been in someone else's on Boxing Night.'

'No!' Frances sat with her mouth wide open letting Mr Edwards' words sink in, her mind immediately racing, wondering who it could possibly be. Mr Edwards waited a moment before continuing.

'He decided to come clean this morning. He appears to have been a frequent visitor to the rooms of female guests throughout his time here. I think he was under the misguided impression that by admitting everything before I found out would mean we were easier on him. It makes no difference whatsoever. His employment contract states quite clearly that he may not go into guests' rooms. He's broken that contract and that means he's fired.'

'Well, you won't need me to make a statement then, will you? If you've already made your mind up that he's fired, then my statement is neither here nor there and at least I won't have it on my conscience that I've helped to get him sacked as well as causing him severe hypothermia!' Frances grabbed her bag and stood up.

'The choice is yours, Ms Dawson. You are under no obligation to make a statement. But might I suggest that next time you decide to accept the services of the hotel's resident gigolo that you take extra care? You are very fortunate that you still have your credit card and you money in your handbag.'

Frances involuntarily clasped her bag tighter to her body, hoping upon hope that her card and purse were, indeed, still both safe inside her bag. Even after the episodes with Neville, it hadn't occurred to her to check. But she wasn't going to let Mr Edwards speak to her like that!

'And may I suggest, that next time you interview staff, you vet them properly so that no apprentice gigolos are taken on?'

And with that she turned on her heel and swept from the office, letting the door swing shut behind her.

✦   ✦   ✦

EVE WAS IN the phone booth in the foyer talking to Alan Dryden, who was still in Gloucestershire.

'It's not too bad down here,' he said, 'but we weren't planning to leave until tomorrow, anyway. And I understand that further east is where it's heaviest, so we might have to stay put, anyway.'

Do you think I've phoned you to ask about your travel arrangements?

'Of course, we had quite a few groups going out last night and today who can't take off and a couple due back today and tomorrow who'll probably end up having an extra night or two's holiday. Apparently the office staff have been fielding phone calls all morning.'

'Well, that's why I'm calling. We're snowed in.'

'What? In Essex?'

'Yes, Alan, in Essex. Essex is in the east of England and you've just said yourself that the snow's worst furthest east.'

'Hmm! I hadn't thought about you lot.'

'Obviously! Well, in spite of that, let me reassure you that us lot are all fine. The hotel manager's agreed that everyone can stay in their rooms for the time being, and he's happy to provide some sort of lunch and dinner tonight, because it looks as if it's going to be at least tomorrow before the roads are clear enough for us to leave. And that totally messes up my plans!'

'Wrong kind of snow, eh?'

'Too much of it! If we need to stay over, and as I said, that seems increasingly likely, then he'll charge for the room for tonight. I've told everyone they'll have to pay that themselves and then sort it out with their insurance company. He's not going to charge for lunch as they're all in the bar spending money so he's quite happy with that.'

'Oh, well that's good. I know that you'll keep them all happy until they leave and you'll get an extra day's pay.'

'Ooh! Lucky me!' Eve suddenly realised she'd spoken out loud.

'Or two days, however long it takes. Keep me posted, then, will you?'

'Yes, I'll let you know as soon as we leave. As I say, I'm hoping it will be tomorrow morning, unless there's more snow tonight.'

'Great. And, thanks, Eve. I really appreciate all you're doing.'

Blimey! Wonders will never cease!

Eve put the receiver down and sighed. If Melv's flight

did come in on time she wouldn't be able to get to Gatwick to pick him up. At least it didn't look that way. He was due to land at six am. That meant she'd have to leave the hotel at four am, and that was going to be impossible, not least of all, because she knew the roads wouldn't have been cleared by then, even if there was no further snow. She came out of the booth and turned to head back to the lounge when her mobile rang. She saw it was Michael.

'Hello, love! You alright?'

'Hi, Eve. We're okay. We've had two days of snow here, but I'm just ringing to see how you are. We saw on the news that Essex took a heavy beating last night. Did you get home okay?'

'I'm still at the hotel. And it looks like I'll be here until tomorrow. The snow's three feet deep and the lanes around the hotel are impassable. So are the major roads, apparently. We saw on the local news that they're trying to get snowploughs out, but it's proving difficult. There are lots of abandoned vehicles on the road.'

'Do you think Melv's flight will be affected?'

'I think it's sure to be. I was just talking to our MD and apparently lots of flights are cancelled. I just hope he gets here, even if it's a bit late. What about your travel plans?'

'No change, really. It's snowed heavily here but the roads are all passable so we'll be setting off for Nat's parents tomorrow morning. And all being well, we'll see you on New Year's Eve.'

'Fingers crossed! I just hope there's no more snow to interfere with the wedding.'

'We're getting married even if it's just the two of us in wellington boots and puffa jackets,' he joked. 'Listen, keep in touch and let me know your whereabouts. I'll ring Melv a bit later and see what the news is about his flight. It's about ten o'clock tonight our time he's due to take off, isn't it?'

'Yes. I can't see it happening, though. I mean, the flight going out to Antigua is probably still sitting at Gatwick, unless, of course, it couldn't land coming back from its previous trip, in which case, it could be anywhere!'

'Oh well, there's nothing much we can do about it. Let us know how you are and I'll ring you later after I've spoken to Melv.'

'Alright, Michael. Thanks for calling.'

'Love you!'

Ooh! She always got a tingle when she heard her son say that!

'Love you, too.'

✦   ✦   ✦

SLIM SUE PICKED up her coffee from the bar, smiled her thanks at Beniamin and went to rejoin the Other Two Sues, Vince, Mick and Don at the table. But before she'd gone a couple of steps she saw that Frances was making her way over.

'No, I'll get these!' she called out to Colin, Kim and Pete, who she'd been sitting with. 'It's my turn.' She smiled at Slim Sue as she passed her.

'Warmed up, yet?' she asked, pleasantly. 'It was fun this morning, wasn't it?'

'Yes, it was,' Slim Sue agreed. 'Frances, have you got a minute?'

'Me? Yes. Can I just order the drinks, first, as they're for the others?'

Slim Sue nodded and then sat down at an empty table nearby.

'Two hot chocolates, a latte and a beer, please,' she said. 'It's for the table over there, but I'm paying.'

Beniamin looked worried. Pillow talk with Chris had given him the whole story of Milos's sex life and a visit to

Milos to see how he was early that morning had confirmed it. Although Milos hadn't admitted to anyone the little stories about his moribund father and family's dire straits. He let them just believe that sex with older women was his particular fetish. Beniamin mentally shook his head, wondering how Milos had got away with it for so long.

'So…' Frances sat down next to Slim Sue, unable to hide her curiosity.

'I heard that it was Milos who was caught in the snow on your balcony last night.'

'And?'

'Well, he'd been with me earlier that evening and the night before,' Slim Sue said. 'I'm not telling you to shit-stir, just so that we both know that perhaps we've been a bit silly. Well, at least that's how I feel. I don't know about you…'

'Jesus! The manager told me this morning that he'd been in someone else's room but I just thought he'd got confused. You know, because Milos had been with me on Christmas Night, too.'

'So, he was with you on Christmas Night, me on Boxing Night, me again early yesterday evening and then you later on?' Slim Sue asked, her eyes wide in disbelief. Frances burst out laughing.

'Well! It looks like it! Little liar! He told me he hadn't been able to come to me on Boxing Night because he'd finished really late.

'And that he'd had to come early in the evening yesterday because he had to do an inventory in the bar at the end of the night?'

'Yes!'

The two women looked at each other in silence, each shaking their heads and then both giggling.

'Well! He's got some stamina I'll say that!' Frances said. 'Does the manager know it was you?'

'No. Only the Other Two Sues know about it. But when I heard the rumours this morning and then I saw you go off with the manager I put two and two together.'

'I think Milos told him there were two of us, because he knows, but perhaps he didn't tell the manager who you were.'

'I've gone red every time I've seen him today,' Slim Sue said.

'He expected me to make a statement! I refused. After all, I think I've done him enough damage with leaving him on the balcony in the snow.'

'How come you forgot he was there?' Slim Sue's blue eyes twinkled over the rim of her coffee cup.

'My son popped in to see me. He knocked on the door just after Milos had arrived in my room. I was so shocked at it being my son, I mean, I wasn't expecting him at all. So I grabbed Milos's clothes and shoved him out on the balcony.'

'What? Naked?'

'Yes. I hadn't realised it was snowing and anyway I thought it'd only be a couple of minutes. But then we came down to the bar and got talking about some family business and I completely forgot he was there!'

'Ha! Ha! Serve him right!' Slim Sue screamed.

'Well, yes, he'll probably think twice before seducing a mature woman again! Menopause makes you forgetful!' The two women squealed with laughter.

'So do we know how he is today?'

'Apparently, he's resting in bed with no ill-effects, but he is suspended from work, pending an enquiry. Although, from what the manager said, it's a sackable offence so he's on his way out enquiry or not.'

'Oh, dear! Still, he massaged my ego a bit,' Slim Sue said. 'I can't dislike him.'

'Neither can I! Even when I'm sitting here listening to

you telling me that he had the two of us on the go at once! After all, it's only what my ex-husband did and I'd been married to him for twenty-five years,' she added.

✦ ✦ ✦

BACK IN THE lounge Eve told everyone that lunch would be served at one o'clock in the dining-room.

'How much will it be?' Angela asked.

'I understand it's on the house.'

'Oh, that's very generous. We'll all have to leave an extra-large tip.'

'Apparently it's mushroom soup with crusty bread, various cooked meats, fruit salad and cream and a cheese board with crackers.'

'That's not much of a lunch,' Mick grumbled.

''Er, gift horse, mouth?' Angela said, voicing what most people were thinking.

'And this afternoon there are several films on TV that we can watch, either here in the lounge or in our rooms. It looks as though we're going to be here until at least tomorrow.'

'It's really that bad, is it?' Geoff asked.

'Yes. All the roads are closed.'

'I couldn't even get down the drive to turn into the lane,' Colin said. 'And I've got a four by four.'

'Well, we could be stuck in worse places,' Geoff said, beaming at Denise. Tall Sue and Slim Sue looked at each other and raised their eyebrows.

'We'll get something going entertainment-wise for this evening. I'll let you know later.'

'We could do karaoke,' Penny suggested.

'I was just going to say that,' Deano said. 'Or the Blue Boar's Got Talent! Anyone sing, dance, tell jokes?'

'Kim plays the piano,' Dave said, causing her to blush.

'Yes, I play, but I'm no concert pianist!' she said, quickly.

'Well, we'll see. I'm sure we can sort something out,' Eve said.

'Let's play charades! I love that!' Blonde Sue said. 'It always makes me laugh.'

'Two words, one syllable each,' Mick said to Don, holding up two fingers and then putting one finger against his forearm. He pointed at Don and then made a large circle in the air using both hands.

'Your round!' Janet called across the lounge, guessing correctly and everyone laughed.

✦   ✦   ✦

IN SPITE OF Mick's trepidation, lunch had been delicious. They'd devoured the hot, tasty soup with the thickly buttered bread, except Slim Sue, who didn't eat carbohydrates. Afterwards, some went to their rooms to have a siesta while others wandered back into the lounge to watch a film together. Pete stood looking out through the large, ornate French doors at the garden when Frances came and stood beside him.

'Well, at least it hasn't snowed any more.'

'No, it hasn't. And it looks like it's maybe starting to melt a little bit,' he said.

'To be honest, I haven't minded staying here a bit longer. I've really enjoyed this morning.'

'I see from the way that you no longer keep on checking your phone that the call you weren't waiting for from the man who didn't exist must have taken place.'

'Not exactly. As I was telling you earlier, my son came to see me last night, but he hadn't just called in as he was passing. He'd made a special journey. You see, we had a stupid argument just before Christmas and I kept on hoping he'd ring to apologise. Or not even apologise! Just that he would ring!'

'And you couldn't have phoned him?'

'Unfortunately, my son gets his stubbornness from his mother,' she said. 'Actually, that's not really true. I didn't ring him because I was afraid he'd either hang up on me or not answer when he saw it was me.'

'Well, we're all afraid of rejection at some time or another. But, as it was, you needn't have worried!'

'No. It's all sorted out now. We had a long talk and, well, everything's fine.'

'I'm glad to hear it. I didn't like to see you looking troubled.'

'Troubled? Did I? I thought I was putting on a good act of being life and soul of the party.'

'I think I probably recognised another troubled soul,' he said. Frances looked at him, but before she could say anything Kim and Colin had come to join them to give their take on the weather situation.

✦   ✦   ✦

JANET HAD GONE back to her room to rest for an hour or so. Part of her wanted to stay downstairs with the others; she'd discovered the joy of being with others in the last couple of days but she also knew the power of sleep and an hour's nap would leave her feeling like new. She took off her wig and emptied her medication into the palm of her hand, downing the pills with a big swig of water. Her hand went involuntarily to her cross and chain as she offered up a silent prayer of thanks for such a wonderful morning. She couldn't think when she'd last enjoyed herself so much and what was especially heart-warming was that the others all joined in. That had made it even more fun! They had been like a class of kids in the school playground. Her hooded, weatherproof coat had ensured that she hadn't got too wet, although that wouldn't have mattered, but more importantly it had made sure that her wig stayed put. She would have been mortified if it had slipped or worked itself loose.

But it didn't! So that was the waste of a worry!

She slipped under the duvet in her underwear and lay back on the pillows and closed her eyes. She felt absolutely wonderful.

✦   ✦   ✦

'SO WHAT YOU doing, Ang?' Deano asked as they were leaving the dining-room after lunch.

'Angela. It's Angela, not Ang. I've never worked behind the bar at the Queen Vic.'

'Sorry, Angela!' Deano exaggerated her name and gave a flowery, almost Shakespearian bow.

'Was your mother Italian?' Penny asked, overhearing their exchange.

'No, she was from Swansea.'

'Oh! I just thought perhaps Deano was an Italian name. You look a bit sort of Mediterranean.'

'My first name's Robert, but I got called Deano at school from my surname, Dean. And it just sort of stuck. My parents are the only ones that call me Robert and I often don't even answer because I don't realise they're talking to me.'

'That's like me. I only ever get called Penelope by my mam, and then only when I'm in trouble.'

'So, anyway, what are you doing, Angela?' Deano asked again.

'I'll probably go and have a short siesta.'

'Are you sure you want to sleep alone? You don't want to sleep in the arms of a sex-god?'

'It ain't the sleepin' it's the stayin' awake you 'ave to worry about!' Dave said to her.

'I don't have to worry about anything!' she said, laughing. 'Yes, I am sure I want to sleep alone. I'll see you all a bit later.' And she went off through the bar and headed for the stairs. Deano shrugged.

'Oh, well. She doesn't know what she's missing! Beer?' he asked Dave.

''Erm I'm not sure what we're doing' he said, looking at Penny.

'We?' Deano said. 'Oh, come on, Dave, don't you blow me out as well. Penny gives you permission to have a beer, don't you, Penny?'

'It's not down to me. He can have as many beers as he likes,' she said, only sounding very slightly miffed.

'Can I? I mean, do you mind?'

'Of course not!' She did mind. They had already talked about having a siesta, but Penny wasn't the sort of girl to throw a tantrum. And she laughed to herself when she thought about it. She'd had more sex in the last two days than she'd had in the last six months. As much as she liked it, it was all quite tiring. She could wait a little longer for the next session. 'I'm going to sit in the lounge and watch the film. You have your beer. Or two. I'll see you in a bit!'

'I'll bring you a drink through,' Dave said, giving her a kiss on the cheek as she walked off.

'Is this all getting a bit serious?' Deano asked him as they turned and went to the bar.

'I dunno, mate. I'd like it to, but we live two 'undred an' fifty miles away from each uvver. Although, she 'as made noises about seein' me.'

'Oh well, that's good. Nice to keep your motor ticking over even if you have to go a couple of hours drive to get it MOTed!' Deano laughed.

'D'you evva see that vicar again? The one from Antigua? Judy, was it?'

'Joanne. No. I never saw or heard from her again. I was too busy getting over my accident. She came and saw me in the hospital before you all left. Gave me her e-mail address and phone number, told me to keep in touch but I didn't follow it up,' Deano lied. Jo had been visiting him when his wife had arrived at the hospital straight off a flight from England. She was understandably furious with Deano, who'd told her he was going to a trade fair in Madrid. She'd accepted the fact that Jo was a priest who was ministering, although she had been exceptionally rude to her, taking out her anger at her husband on other people. When he'd got back home and Rachel had immediately kicked him out, Deano had tried all means possible to contact Jo, finally tracking her down through the church. But she had told him in no uncertain terms that she wanted nothing to do with him and he'd never heard from her again.

Women could be so unreasonable!

'No, mate. Like I say, I was too busy recovering from the accident. And anyway, I hadn't been that bothered,' he said. Dave nodded wisely and empathetically.

✦   ✦   ✦

EVE HAD LOOKED on the internet to see what was happening at Gatwick Airport. She could see that the out-going flight to Antigua was one of hundreds that had been cancelled due to the inclement weather. She rang Melv.

'Babe, I was just going to call you,' he said. 'I've heard that my flight's not operational. Yesterday's flight didn't take off because the airports in UK were closed so it's still sitting here on the tarmac. I've been talking to a friend who thinks he might be able to get me on that when it does leave because there were spare seats, but even so, that's probably not going to be today.'

'I thought they might take off and get as near as they could.'

'So did I, but apparently it wasn't just the weather. Last night's flight had a tech problem and by the time it was fixed they knew it was pointless taking off as every airport in the south of England was closed and the crew were dangerously close to being out of hours.'

'A lot of very unhappy people I imagine,' Eve said, glad she wasn't dealing with any of them.

'Where are you? Did you make it home?'

'No. We're still in the hotel all snowed up. So, it's just as well you've got a delay as I couldn't get to pick you up tomorrow morning. That said, I'd rather know you were in a hotel at Gatwick waiting for me. At least then you'd be on the right side of the Atlantic!'

'Well, it is what it is! And you can be sure I'll do whatever it takes to get to you,' he said. 'How is your group?'

'They're fine. Well, why shouldn't they be? They're in a warm, comfortable hotel and they can see what conditions outside are like. Even two guys who have four by fours haven't been able to leave. Michael said they've had a lot of snow where they are but apparently the roads out are fine, so they don't think their plans will be affected.'

'Okay. That's good. Well, look, I'll ring you in a while and let you know if anything's changed. And you take care and stay safe.'

'I will.'

✦   ✦   ✦

As the afternoon wore on there was no more snow. Everyone watched the local News and Weather at six o'clock, either in their bedrooms or in the lounge to see what the latest update on the situation was. The Essex Police and AA Spokesperson both agreed that most major roads should be passable *if motorists proceeded with caution* sometime the following day.

'If that's the case, then I'll have to ask everyone to vacate by ten tomorrow morning so that we can start getting the rooms ready for our expected arrivals,' Chris said to Eve. 'And we're going to serve dinner at six-thirty tonight. I assume that will meet with everyone's approval?'

'Well, if it doesn't it will just be too bad. The needs of the staff have to be taken into account in a situation like this, too.'

'Thanks for your understanding.'

''Erm, can I ask… What's happened to Milos?'

'He's suspended. Bit of a pain, really with this big New Year's Eve do we've got coming up. The hotel's almost full tomorrow night and completely full for New Year's Eve and New Year's Day. Plus a hundred non-residents for the do itself. So, I could really have done with his help.'

'Can't you call a truce for a few days? Deal with him after New Year?'

'If only!' Chris laughed. 'But that wouldn't be ethical. I'll get an extra pair of local hands or from the agency. He'll be on his way as soon as I've got half-an-hour to hold a meeting with him. You know what it's like, Eve. We have to do everything by the book.'

'And do you think it's been a regular thing, this going to women's rooms?'

'Most certainly! By his own admission he's been with two of your women…'

'Two? Who was the other one?'

'Robson. Sue Robson.'

'Slim Sue!' Eve was very surprised. 'Fancy having two on the go!'

'Quite! He's admitted that these aren't the first two, and I am absolutely certain that there's something else going on.'

'You mean, he's light-fingered?'

'I'm not sure. I think that if he'd stolen from any of them we would have heard about it. Somebody would have reported a theft or something lost.'

'Perhaps they were too embarrassed to report it.'

'Could be. I think he's done something more along the lines of spinning them a line about needing money for family back home. So, really Ms Robson and Ms Dawson have had a lucky escape! And I do hope it won't reflect badly on us where Travel Together are concerned. We've done quite a few walking and activity weekends for you. It's lovely here during the summer and we go canoeing or rowing. It'd be a shame if we lost your business just because of a bloody waiter who can't keep it zipped up.'

'You'll get nothing but a good report from me,' Eve reassured him. 'I'm impressed at the way you've handled us having to stay on and I know the group appreciated the free lunch. My report will be all good!'

'Well, that's reassuring. It's good to work with a tour manager who knows the ropes. Jade was a bit of a dopey bird.'

'So I've been told! I have to admit, I came here kicking and screaming because I'd asked for Christmas off, but it's been fine, really. It's the first Christmas trip where I haven't sat with someone and a box of tissues while they sob their heart out over their own particular Christmas pain or memory.'

'Well, hopefully by this time tomorrow you'll all be safely home and I'll be welcoming the next group of guests. Are you working New Year's Eve?'

'No! And I really do mean it! I've got guests coming and coming from a long way; I've got a special evening planned and nothing or no-one is going to keep me from them!'

✦   ✦   ✦

OLIVIA WAS IN a foul mood. She was lying under the duvet, eating chocolate from the minibar with one eye on a film. She was pissed off at Frances, who had all but ignored her during this break. She huffed and puffed to herself as she thought about it. After all, Frances had said she was happy to have her along, if not she wouldn't have come. They'd got on so well in Turkey and Olivia had enjoyed the nights she'd spent with Frances and Umit and a group of his friends visiting Bar Street, while the rest of the tennis group went out and about together. She'd even listened to Frances' advice – and taken it! – about David and ending it with him. He had almost talked her round, but she had taken on board what Frances had said and she'd given him his marching orders. But ever since they'd been here it was as if Frances didn't want to spend time with her; didn't want to sit with her. She'd noticed that at every meal Frances had deliberately, or so it seemed, sat on the other end of the table from her. When the group was together in the bar or lounge Frances seemed to go and talk to the others.

She hadn't minded too much as the others were very nice, on the whole. She hadn't liked Mick very much, but since she'd put him in his place on the walk he'd been pleasant enough to her. And last night she'd ended up sitting next to Burt after the men had changed places for the last time. He'd seemed pleasant enough and was quite a good dancer but he was totally wrapped up in himself. His whole conversation had been about his car, his job, his holiday, his social life and never once had he asked Olivia anything about herself at all. And then, at the end of the evening he'd made a pass at her.

'Your room or mine?' he'd said, as the music had come to an end.

'Pardon?'

'Your room or mine? Mine's got a queen-size bed. I requested it especially. So perhaps we'd be better off there. Plenty of room for when I've got you thrashing round.'

''Er, I don't think so,' she'd said, cringing at his insensitivity and his conceit. 'I've no intention of thrashing round with anyone.'

'Oh, come on! You know you want to!' he said, taking her hand only for her to snatch it away. He gave her a serious look. 'What are you doing at a black-tie ball if you're not looking for a bloke to sleep with?'

'I couldn't possibly begin to explain because an ignorant cretin like you couldn't possibly understand,' she'd said, and turned on her heel and walked away.

Her first instinct was to tell Frances all about it, but she was busy talking to a young man, who it turned out was her son, and then there was a bit of a to-do over the young waiter being in her room.

How does she do it?

Olivia hated to admit it, but she was jealous of Frances, who seemed to have no trouble in finding young men to dance attendance on her. Yet Olivia, who was almost twenty years younger than her never pulled anyone other than the boring self-absorbed twat of the previous evening. She's hoped that if she went off to her room Frances might ring her or come and see if she was alright. But she hadn't.

Oh, well, she can fuck off!

Olivia decided to ignore her completely at dinner and during the evening and when they left tomorrow – *if they left tomorrow!* – she'd leave without saying goodbye and she wouldn't contact her again. Feeling better at that thought, Olivia stuffed another chocolate in her mouth, grabbed the remote and started sifting through the channels.

✦   ✦   ✦

PENNY HAD FINISHED watching the film with Pete, Colin, Frances, Kim and four of the ball-goers. She loved Roger Moore and as far as she was concerned he was the best James Bond by far. She stretched and looked at her watch and was surprised to see it was already after five. She looked round to see where Dave was, as his *one beer* had obviously turned into a session. She didn't really mind. She'd enjoyed the film and her initial upset as what's she'd interpreted as a slight by Dave had soon evaporated. She'd never been the jealous type and she couldn't understand those that were.

And after all, he's know Deano for a long time, much longer than he's known me.

'I don't suppose they'll do afternoon tea, will they? I mean, as dinner's going to be at half-past six,' Kim said.

'Well, we can always have a cup of tea,' Colin reasoned. 'Even if there aren't any sandwiches or cakes to go with it. I'll go and see.'

'I'll give you a hand,' Pete said, getting up to follow him through to the bar, where they saw Deano, Dave, John, Mick and two of the ball-goers sitting having a blokes-session.

'And the nun said, not with tiger I haven't!' Deano said as the men all roared with laughter.

'Wan' a beer yous two?' Dave called out, catching sight

of Pete and Colin, the amount of alcohol he'd consumed making him unaware of just how loud he was being.

'We're fine, thanks. Just getting some teas sorted for the ladies,' Pete said.

'Oh, fuck! 'How's Miss P? She alrigh'?' he asked, as he suddenly remembered she was in the lounge.

'She's fine. The film's just finished.'

'Tell 'er I'll be through in a bit,' he said.

'In a bit or for a bit?' Mick asked, causing them all to laugh again.

Pete and Colin ordered the teas from Benjamin, who said he'd have a look in the kitchen to see if there was any cake.

'I think we have Christmas cake, because Chef made many,' he said, smiling at them.

'I'm not sorry we've had an extra day,' Pete observed as they stood together waiting at the bar.

'No, neither am I. I've enjoyed myself, surprisingly. Especially playing in the snow this morning. But I hope we can get out tomorrow because I really do need to get back to work. If the snow starts to melt a bit I should be able to get through in the four by four.'

'Won't the business carry on without you?'

'It will, but with long faces and tuts and sighs. If the weather's bad we won't have any customers, so it won't matter if we open one day or another, but the family won't see it like that. All they'll see is that there was work to be done and I wasn't there to help do it.' He grimaced at the thought.

'You need to get away more often, so you do. That way they'll learn to do without you.'

'Believe me, it's not worth the aggravation,' Colin said, seeing his sister Avril's sour face in his mind's eye and hearing her grating voice going on in his ear. He sometimes thought that he could understand how someone just suddenly snapped and committed murder! God knew, she'd pushed him enough times.

Beniamin appeared with a large plate holding a pile of mince pies and iced-fruit cake.

'Is not enough for everyone,' he said, apologetically.

'It's okay, those in the bar won't want cake,' Pete said, hoping sincerely that they wouldn't. 'Here, you take them and I'll take the tray of teas,' he said to Colin, and the two of them made their way back to the lounge where the tea and cakes were very well-received.

✦   ✦   ✦

DINNER WAS A fairly casual affair. Nobody really dressed up for it, everyone enjoying the relaxed atmosphere after that of the more formal black-tie ball. There was a choice of vegetable soup, pate, or melon and ham for starters and then macaroni cheese pie, roast chicken or scampi for the main course eaten with chips, roast potatoes, sprouts, carrots and peas. Eve was sitting next to Olivia, who seemed a bit sulky, and Angela who was telling her that she'd spent an hour that afternoon making her *Action Plan* for the forthcoming year.

'I'm going to decide exactly what I want from life and I'm going to get myself a vision board. I've realised that I haven't been happy for such a long time and the only person who can do something about that is me.'

'Good girl!' Eve said, genuinely pleased for Angela.

'And, I'm going to set myself the challenge of doing something nice for someone every day, without them knowing.'

'Oh that's great! You mean like a *pay-it-forward*?'

'Sort of. I was thinking more along the lines of leaving some groceries on the front step of this elderly lady who lives near me. I've heard that her house is falling down and she really struggles financially because she hasn't got one living relative.'

'Oh, poor woman! That would be nice to do something like that for…' Eve stopped what she was saying and looked at Angela. Angela, aware she'd stopped mid-sentence, looked up from her plate at Eve. Eve looked from Angela's face to her plate and back up to her face again. Realising what Eve had noticed, Angela blushed.

'Chicken, Angela?' Eve said, looking at her in amazement. 'Chicken?'

'Oh, Eve! I do, very rarely, once in a while eat a little bit of white meat.'

'But I thought you were an orthodox vegetarian.'

Angela put her knife and fork down and touched her fingertips together as she turned to Eve.

'Please, please forgive me. I am a vegetarian, but as I say, once in a while I eat white meat. I know I was vile about the vegetarian food the other day, but that was…well… I don't know why that was! It was all part of Horrible Angela, who liked being nasty and causing a fuss. I really am so sorry, Eve. I just saw the chicken and fancied it.'

Eve sighed inwardly.

How many times have I had this with so-called vegetarians?

'Well, you're not the first! I've had people in my groups call themselves vegetarians and what they really mean is that they don't eat beef. Or they they will eat fish, so don't worry!'

'You are so lovely!' Angela kissed her on the cheek. 'Thank you for being nice to me when I really don't deserve it.'

'Perhaps you didn't deserve it the other day, but you do now,' Eve said, seeing that Deano was looking at them.

'Oh, it all falls into place now,' Deano called across the

table. 'I've been trying to pull someone who bats for the other side.'

'Just a little sisterly kiss of gratitude,' Angela said, smiling sweetly at him and then getting on with her meal.

'Did you have a nice afternoon, Olivia?' Eve asked, turning to her other side.

'Nothing special. Rather boring, really. I can't wait to get home now,' she replied petulantly.

'Me, too,' Eve said, smiling at her.

'Yes, but you're getting paid to be here,' Olivia sniffed.

And if you knew just how little that is!

'That doesn't necessarily mean I wouldn't rather be somewhere else,' Eve said. 'I'm sure there must be times when you're at work and you wish you weren't.' Olivia thought about that for a moment.

'Well, yes, perhaps. It's the not-knowing, isn't it? The uncertainty of how long we're going to have to stay here.'

The not-knowing? It's waiting for a bit of snow to clear not for the results of a colonoscopy!

Eve thought, not for the first time in her long career in travel, how different people were. Something that might really upset one person, someone else wouldn't even notice. Thirty people could accept the weather was bad and be thankful they were in a comfortable, warm hotel with food, drink and entertainment laid on, and one person would act as if they were in a stinking flea-pit. She gave a mental shrug; if Olivia chose to behave like a child there was nothing she could do about it.

The meal over, everyone left the tables and gathered in small groups throughout the lounge and the bar. Chris Edwards came into the lounge and looked around at everyone smiling and then clapped his hands for their attention.

'Excuse me, ladies and gentlemen, but I am very pleased

to announce that we have a special treat for you.'

Everyone sat up and took notice, eager to hear what he had to say.

'Beniamin, one of our bar staff who has been looking after you since you arrived on Christmas Eve is an accomplished musician. I have persuaded him to give you a little ten-minute concert this evening. I hope you will enjoy what he plays. Please welcome…Beniamin!'

Blushing, Beniamin came forward, clutching his violin and stood in the centre of the lounge. He cleared his throat and turned to look at his audience, smiling shyly, not realising that his coyness gave him an air of innocence which made most of the women in the room think on the old adage: all the handsome men are gay.

'Good evening. I will play for you a selection of Christmas songs,' he said, simply, before raising his violin to his chin and starting to play. It was evident after just a few bars that Beniamin was an extremely talented player. He went through a medley of carols, O, Little Town of Bethlehem, Once in Royal David's City, While Shepherds Watched, We Three Kings, Little Donkey, Silent Night and then O, Holy Night. In spite of the alcohol consumed, everyone listened and most sang along, Mick surprising everyone with his rich baritone, to the extent that they left him to sing the final carol as a solo, his voice and the violin giving everyone, religious or irreligious, a special tingle. There was a huge cheer at the end. Most of the group jumped to their feet cheering and applauding Beniamin, whose blush was now the colour of Santa's cloak.

'More!' Deano shouted.

'Oh, dear! That brought a little tear to my eye,' Janet said as Angela nodded in agreement, patting away a drop that threatened to roll down her cheek.

''Ere! Kim! Play the piano with 'im!' Dave said. 'Go on!'

'You play piano?' Beniamin asked her. She nodded. 'Then, please, we play together. And our friend can sing,' Beniamin said, turning to Mick, who had the grace to blush himself as he remembered how insulting he'd been to Beniamin on the first night.

'Ehh! Come on, Kim! Come and play for us!' Penny said.

Kim looked around at the group and saw, much to her surprise and delight, that they did seem to genuinely want her to play. Beniamin and Mick were both extraordinary performers and she thought it would be a slight to them and quite rude of her not to do as she was being asked, although she usually disliked playing in public. She hesitated slightly.

'Please,' she heard Pete say from the seat next to her. And so she got up and went and took her place at the piano.

'So, what we play?' Beniamin asked the other two. They spoke together for a moment and found a few songs that all three knew and soon the concert was in full swing. They played a Rat Pack medley; Strangers in the Night, Mack the Knife, Me and My Shadow, Chicago, I've Got You Under My Skin, Fly Me to the Moon, You Make Me Feel So Young, King of the Road and Everybody Loves Somebody Sometime. Members of the group stood up and danced along to the music, alone or in couples or, like Don, Vince and John, in a threesome, as proud as punch of their mate Mick; everyone was having a smashing time.

'I've got to have a beer! Carry on without me for a few numbers, I'm parched,' Mick said, going over to pick up his drink.

'Play one of them nocturnal things you told me about,' Dave called to Kim.

'You play a nocturne while I help behind bar for a minute,' Beniamin said to her.

Kim had surprised herself by how much she'd enjoyed

being part of the musical trio with Beniamin and Mick. She wasn't sure she suddenly liked being a soloist, but she knew she couldn't refuse. She flexed her fingers and paused for a moment and then, the sweet, soft, melodic notes of Chopin's Nocturne Opus 9 Number 2 in E-Flat Major began to fill the room. Eve was aware of a stillness, a quiet that enveloped them. Everyone was mesmerised by Kim's playing. The Four Friends sat together in silence, looking towards Kim. Many of the group were leaning back in their seats, their eyes closed, letting the music flow over them.

Music to calm the savage breast.

When she finished it was to a standing ovation; the whole group was on its feet for their own, lovely, talented Kim. Then Beniamin came back and spoke to her. She nodded her head and the two of them played the haunting duet Memory, from Cats, before Mick came back to join them and they started taking requests. For the next hour the lounge was rocking.

'I s'pose this is 'ow people entertained themselves in the olden days, eh, Miss P? Dave said, philosophically. 'You know, before we 'ad the telly an' all that.'

'Don't look at me, you cheeky thing!' Penny said, giving him a playful slap.

'Nah, I nevva meant you, did I?' he said, laughing. 'Christ! Look at them two!' he said, pointing at Janet and Pete, who were jiving as Kim killed the keys with Rock Around the Clock. 'And them!' he said, indicating Angela and Deano, who were doing a much simpler, gentler routine.

I love Janet!

Eve really did love her. She loved her intelligence, her sense of humour, her good manners, her beautiful eyes and hair and the way she was entirely her own person. She found herself beaming as she watched her on the dance-floor with Pete, who for once, seemed to have shed the cloak of sadness that Eve felt he always wore.

'You not dancing?' she said to Frances who was sitting next to her.

'I'm watching and listening. And thoroughly enjoying myself at the same time, I might add,' she said, smiling at Eve. 'To be honest, I thought I'd better keep a low profile tonight. You know, after last nights' little er…episode.'

'What? You're doing penance by not dancing?' Eve asked her, laughing.

'No. I'm just being reflective. There's a time to be centre of attention and a time to sit back. And tonight I'm sitting back reflecting.'

'As long as you're enjoying yourself…'

'Oh, I am! I'm having a really lovely evening. I mean, who'd have thought that Mick could sing like that? Or Kim play the piano so beautifully? And Ben on the violin! Well! Amazing. I think that sometimes these sort of unplanned, improvised evenings turn out to be the best,' she concluded.

'I couldn't agree more!' Eve said. 'Is your son still in the B&B?' she asked.

'Yes. He's phoned me twice today. They're over the far side of the village but still snowed in, although he said it looked like it was melting fast.'

'I take it you weren't expecting him?' Eve said.

'Not at all! We'd had a stupid row and we hadn't spoken all over Christmas. He didn't ring me and I didn't ring him, you know how it goes. And then, when I saw him last night, I was so happy.'

'Well, I'm glad you made it up.'

'I was just being really stupid. You see, Eve,' she said, the fifth glass of cava loosening her tongue, 'Darren's gay. I never really had a problem with that, although it was a bit of a surprise because he's not one of those camp gays, if you know what I mean. I never really had any suspicions.' Eve knew exactly what she meant. 'He's with a really nice man who I like and I haven't got a problem with any of it, but now they're talking about starting a family and I wasn't all right with that, I'm afraid!'

'But you're sorted now?'

'Yes.'

Eve sighed, wistfully. She'd never had the chance to be there for Michael, to talk things through with him, to guide him and give her opinion and interfere, just like Frances had always done with her son. A wonderful woman called Alice had been the one who'd listened to all Michael's trials and tribulations while he was growing up; she was the one he called 'Mum'. But, thankfully, Eve had him in her life now. Thinking of Michael brought her thoughts back round to Melv. She'd finish her drink and then go and give him a call.

✦   ✦   ✦

PETE WAS SLURRING his words a bit and he was only slightly aware of it. He'd lost count of how much he'd had to drink and quite frankly, he didn't give a damn. He was singing along with everyone else, mumbling when he didn't know the words, to Kim, Mick and Beniamin's final number, Louis Armstrong's Wonderful World, even though his heart was breaking with the weight of the memories. As the song reached its climax everyone's arms were in the air, although nobody quite knew why. From the air it was a logical step to put them around the person standing next to you and give them a hug. Pete found himself with tears running down his face and locked in an embrace with Colin, who was a nice enough bloke.

'Thanks for your company, Colin. I've enjoyed it, so I have,' Pete said as both men patted each other on the back. 'That song, just makes me a bit emotional.'

'Yes. Me, too. Thanks for yours,' Colin said, stepping back and beaming at Pete.

'Will you have a drink?' Pete passed his handkerchief over his face and put it back in his trouser pocket.

'Actually, I think I'm going to make my way up. It's after ten and I'm hoping to make a very early start in the morning. If it's clear I'll be on my way by six, six-thirty. So I'll say *'Goodbye'* now. I hope you get home safely to Belfast.' He shook Pete's hand. 'I'll just go over and thank Eve and take my leave of some of the others.'

A little lump appeared in Pete's throat as he watched Colin across the lounge through a light mist. Kim, flushed and happy from the success of the evening came and sat next to him, beaming from ear to ear.

'Let me get you a very large drink!' Pete said delighted to see her. 'A glass of champagne?'

'Oh, go on, then! Why not?' Kim beamed. Tonight she was as happy as if she'd won a Grammy.

'You deserve it, so you do!' Pete went to the bar and returned with a bottle and two glasses. 'Sure I've never heard playing like that. The two of you should be on the stage. Cheers!'

'Cheers! Oh, no thank you, Vince, I've got one at the moment.' Everyone was vying with everyone else to buy the pianist a drink. 'You okay, Pete? You look a bit upset…'

'It's that song. It… it was special to my wife and me. We had our first ever dance to it at the youth club disco in 1968.' His face was awash with tears, which he quickly wiped away again. 'I'm so sorry, Kim. I sometimes think I'll never get over her dying…'

'Of course you will! You feel like that now because it's recent. Raw. But as time goes by it will get easier. Think of the last time you saw her, and carry that memory with you.'

Pete closed his eyes tightly. Thinking of the last time he

saw her was what he'd been trying to avoid for the last year. It was what haunted him night and day, waking and sleeping.

He opened them again to see Mick and Beniamin were posing together so that the other Four Friends and the Three Sues and several others could take their picture. Then they came and stood behind Kim while more pictures were taken. Pete busied himself capturing the three of them.

I need to pull myself together and get through tonight.

'I haven't got a mobile,' Kim said, taking a big sip of her cava, 'so I can't take any photos on my phone and I didn't bring my camera with me.'

'Do you have e-mail?'

'Yes. At work.'

'Well, give me that before you leave and I'll send you the pics,'

'Oh, that'll be nice. And I'd like one of us two,' she said.

'Here!' Pete knelt down beside her and raised his mobile phone somewhat shakily above their heads. 'Ready? Cheese!' and the photo was eventually taken.

'I always use my camera for photos. I took some fabulous ones of our holiday in India. Got them all on my computer.'

'Did you take photos of everyone?'

'That's a funny question.'

Pete downed his drink and refilled his glass. Kim put her hand over hers.

'Not for the minute,' she said, realising that he really had had a few.

'Tell me about the holiday.'

'What do you want to know?'

'About the people. Who were the people on it?'

'Well, there were three older women, friends, who were a bit of a nightmare. They were seasoned travellers, had been on lots of Travel Together holidays, mainly to places where they could pick up young men. Then there was a lovely woman called Eileen... we became quite good friends, and she got together with a Scot called Murray, who'd started off as a bit of a pain but ended up being quite nice.'

'What about the man who died?'

'That was poor Jim. But I thought I'd told you that.' She had some more of her drink and allowed Pete to top it up and then he filled his empty glass again.

'What a brilliant night! What a lovely time I've had!' she sang, waving her glass around in the air, the cava working its magic.

'You said he'd died on the dance-floor?'

'Yes. We'd just been roped in to show the locals some British folk music and Eve had got us all doing the Hokey Cokey and when we turned round he'd died. But, he'd had a lovely holiday and at least he went happy. Let's talk about nice things!' She was so busy smiling and waving at Penny and Dave who raised their glasses to her that she didn't see Pete leave the table or stagger out through the door. By the time she'd turned round to talk to him again, all she was faced with was an empty seat.

✦   ✦   ✦

EVE BARELY RECOGNISED the man who was lurching towards her. Tears streamed down his face as he babbled incoherently.

'Pete! What's wrong?' She grabbed his jerking arm and pulled him to a halt. Unseeing, unrecognising, unfocused eyes looked back at her. His nose was running and his shoulders heaved. 'Let me help you back to your room.'

He offered no resistance as she tucked his arm into hers and then made for the lift. Eve helped him in and then out again once they got to the first floor.

'Fourteen,' Pete whispered. 'Room fourteen.'

He took the key from his pocket and opened the door making Eve realise that in spite of his slightly-slurred speech, he wasn't as drunk as she'd first thought, rather he was distressed. He went in, leaving the door open, so Eve took that as an invitation and followed him in, closing it gently behind her. Pete tumbled into the arm-chair.

'Can I get you anything?'

'A new life,' he said, leaning forward, his elbows on his knees, his head in his hands, sobbing. Eve went over to the jug and poured him a glass of water, then grabbed a handful of tissues from the box. She placed the drink on the coffee table next to him and pressed the tissues into his hands. His fingers curled around them as he continued to cry. Eve sat down quietly on the bed and waited. His voice, when it came from his bowed head, made her jump.

'Do you ever get the feeling that life's punishing you?'

'I have once or twice, yes. But looking back I can see that it wasn't really like that at all, but I was so wound up in sadness, or despair that I didn't recognise it at the time.'

'How many of you reps work for Travel Together?'

'There are about fifty on the books, I think…'

'Fifty! And I get you!'

He raised his head and looked straight at her. She met his gaze, somewhat stung by his words.

'Have I done something to upset you? Or offend you?'

'And how many people travel with your company every year?'

'I don't know exactly. A lot.'

'Yes, a lot! And I end up with a woman who was on the India trip you did!' He blew his nose, noisily and tossed the tissues into the nearby bin.

'Pete, I don't know what you're talking about and I

don't understand why you're so upset. Why don't you explain to me why someone being here from the India trip and my presence are distressing you.'

'I knew Jim.'

'Jim who died in India?' Eve asked slowly making the connection.

'Yes. How well did you know him?'

'He was my client, I knew him for nine or ten days…'

'But you knew about his little secret? Our little secret?'

Eve could feel the cogs in her brain clicking round and connecting with each other, gradually turning the wheel of realisation. Never before had she found such a need to choose her words carefully. Pete was teetering on the brink and she didn't want to be the one to send him crashing over into the abyss.

'It was me who packed up his things, so I knew what was in his suitcase,' she said, remembering the sari, the women's underwear, the make-up and wig. 'It was me who'd helped him choose the sari the previous day. He'd told me it was for his friend's girl-friend. I also saw that he'd filmed himself wearing it on his iPad. And I saw the pathologist's report that noted he had been wearing matching silk knickers and bra underneath his shirt and trousers.'

'The video he'd made was for me. I'd been talking to him on Skype and watching him dancing for me, undressing for me and…. Oh, God! How must all this sound? You must think I'm some sort of fucking pervert!'

Eve said nothing, she just let him take his time until he was ready to continue telling her his story again. He ran his hands over his hair and took a deep breath.

'I've gradually realised over the last ten years or so that I might be bi-sexual, certainly a transvestite. I've never actually been with a man. I'm just turned on by women's clothes and other transvestites. I was a fire-fighter for fuck's sake! Can you imagine what I'd have gone through if that had got out? And besides, I loved my wife. Loved her from the first day I set eyes on her.' He stood up and opened the minibar, grabbing a beer. 'Do you want something?' he asked Eve. She shook her head. He opened it and took a noisy gulp, before sitting down in the armchair again.

'We had a long, successful marriage, but as time went on the feelings I'd had, for wearing women's clothes became stronger, until every time she went to work I'd be in her wardrobe trying on her dresses. I took to buying her expensive lingerie so that I could enjoy feeling the touch of it against my skin. Eventually, about three years ago, I knew that I was going to go a step further and I started surfing the net looking for websites for men like me. It's a terrible thing, you know, when you can't be yourself, who you really are, because it would destroy those you love most in the world…'

'Perhaps your wife would have understood…?'

'There was never any chance of that!' He threw the empty beer can into the bin and helped himself to another. Eve thought that drinking even more probably wasn't helping but she knew she had to keep her mouth well and truly shut.

'And one night, when Maeve had gone over to her sisters and I was locked in the bedroom wearing her clothes, I met Jim. We clicked right from the very first moment, so we did. And our dates became more and more frequent. I found I was living for the time I could be with him online and because I worked shifts and he was self-employed we could spend hours at a time together on the net.'

'Did you never meet in person?'

'No. We planned to when he came back from that trip. I was going to travel across to Cumbria to meet him on the pretence of going to a pre-retirement conference. I couldn't understand what had happened when he just stopped coming online. Days went by. I'd sit and watch the video of him in the sari, alternating between wanting to talk to him or punch him for abandoning me. Finally, I went to see him. He'd told me where he was from, Askam-in-Furness. It's a small place and it wasn't hard to find out what had happened to him. A neighbour said he'd died suddenly on holiday. I was heartbroken. My wife and family knew something was wrong. Even the guys at work did, but they kidded me that I was depressed because I was dreading retiring. All I could do was sit and watch the videos of Jim over and over again. I wasn't sleeping, I was… I don't know! I just don't know how I could feel so much grief for someone I'd never met.' He finished the second beer. 'And then, last Christmas I got careless, I suppose. It was the day after Boxing Day and I was watching Jim stripping out of the sari for the millionth time when I fell asleep. Only for about five minutes, but in that time Maeve had come home from our neighbours where she'd gone for a drink and a chat and she'd come into the bedroom, which I'd forgotten to lock. I don't know how long she'd stood there, looking over my shoulder at the screen, before she let out a long scream and then ran into the bathroom to be sick. I went after her, but she wouldn't let me near her. She came out of the bathroom like a mad-woman. She flew at me, slapping me, scratching me, kicking me. Then she went downstairs and grabbed her coat. *Just tell me how long this has been going on for?'* she screamed. I ran down the stairs to try to talk to her. I told her that I'd come upon the site by accident, but she knew I was lying. I said that he was dead, that it was over and done with, that it was her I loved. *'Wasn't I woman enough for you?'* she said. Then she stopped by the front door and made me tell her how long I'd had these feelings and how long I'd know Jim. *'I hope you can live with yourself, because I certainly can't live with you. You've just turned the last forty years into one big lie.'* And then she went out and slammed the door.'

Tears were rolling down his face again and Eve's emotions were a moving kaleidoscope; pity, anger, disbelief all took their turn to go round and round in her head.

'I was working that night and she hadn't come home by the time I left about two hours later. I thought that was probably for the best as I hadn't wanted a row and I hadn't wanted to try to explain things to her rushing against the clock. The following day we could sit down and I would talk to her honestly and sincerely and let her know that whatever I might have done or felt with Jim, she was the love of my life.' He gave a huge, gulping sob. 'I calmed myself down and went to work. About two hours into the shift we got a call to the railway line. Someone had jumped in front of a train and it was Maeve.'

Eve's heart thumped so loudly that she thought Pete must have heard it. The kaleidoscope turned yet again. She felt physically sick.

'She'd known that the brigade would be called. She'd known that as the Leading Fire-fighter on the watch I would be on the scene. And that scene, the sight of her, the state she was in, knowing I'd caused it…' He buried his head in his hands again. Involuntarily, Eve put her fingers in her ears, trying to blot out what she'd just been told, fighting against the mental images of Maeve, lying mangled under the train and Pete arriving on the scene.

'You can't imagine how a body looks that's been hit by a train. The driver said she just stood there on the line, staring at him, waiting for it to hit her.'

They sat in silence for a long time.

No wonder he was finding Christmas hard!

Eve knew there was nothing at all she could say to Pete to make him feel any better about himself. Her words would be like putting a sticking plaster over the wound made by a sawn-off shotgun. She mentally kicked herself for boasting about not having had to spend Christmas mopping up tears. She slowly rose to her feet.

'I'm sorry for sharing that with you, Eve. I have a pretty good idea what you must be thinking of me...'

'I'm really only feeling terribly sorry and sad for all that you've been through and for your wife's death, especially as she took her own life. How could you have foreseen that? You couldn't!'

'But I should have. She left no note, so nobody knew the reasons why. I've saved face and my kids are living with the pain of not understanding why their mother would kill herself. And I thought I'd run away and spend Christmas with people who knew nothing about me. I could escape from myself for a while. But I ran into you and Kim.'

'And until you get some professional help, you'll always be running into yourself, Pete,' Eve said, gently. She walked to the door.

'Good-night, Pete.' She couldn't even be sure he'd heard her. He sat motionless in the chair as she slipped, silently from the room.

DAY SIX

✦

COLIN HAD SET his alarm clock for five-thirty. He made himself a cup of tea as he looked at the weather forecast on his phone. He was pleased to see that the main roads through Essex were now passable and he knew that the four by four would get him through the sludge in the country lanes. He peered out through the window but couldn't see much as it was still dark, but it looked like there was still a lot of snow in the hotel grounds. It hadn't all melted yet. He washed and dressed quickly, had a second cup of tea, eating a pack of complimentary custard creams with it. He'd stop for breakfast in a couple of hours, once he'd broken the back of his journey. He picked up his suitcase and looked round the room, checking that he wasn't leaving anything behind, smiling as he did so. It had been a nice room and a very pleasant few days and he was glad he'd got away for Christmas again.

He let himself out of his room, taking care to close the door quietly so that he didn't disturb anyone and made for the stairs. He'd settled his bill before he'd gone to bed the previous evening so he just walked to the reception desk to leave the key.

'Got far to go, sir?' Derek, the night receptionist asked

him.

'North Devon.'

'Well, I hope the roads are going to be open for you. Apparently the snow moved through the West Country during the night, so I just heard on the radio.'

'Well, I'll get as far as I can. At least the roads for the first half of my journey are passable.'

'I hope you enjoyed your stay with us, sir,' Derek said, putting the key on the board behind him.

'Oh, I did! Very much.'

'Well, have a safe journey!'

'Thank you!'

Colin squelched across the driveway and through the car park as he dodged the deep puddles in the semi-darkness. He felt his trousers wet round his ankles and he tutted to himself as he put is case in the rear of his vehicle.

I'll have to turn the heater right up!

✦   ✦   ✦

EVE WAS VERY business-like at breakfast. She was keen to see everyone off as quickly as possible so that she could then leave, too. She'd spoken to Melv last night and had been relieved to hear that his friend had been able to get him on the flight which was due to take off from Antigua at ten pm GMT. It was due to land at Gatwick at five-thirty the following morning. She gave a huge grin and felt a little thrill at the thought of seeing him again. He was already a whole day late, which meant she'd lost a whole day of his company, but at least he would be here.

She had come down at seven-thirty, settled her personal bill and the company's bill with the reception desk and put her case into her car. She was glad she was wearing boots when she saw the mess the melting snow was making of the pathway and that her case wasn't heavy as she carried it rather than pulled it through the slush. She had only been alone in the dining-room for five minutes when everyone else started pouring in.

'Well, I've had a good time, but when you've got to go, you've got to go, haven't you?' Kim said. 'And I don't like to drive fast, especially in this weather, the roads will be full of idiots.'

'I hope the trains are running. I suppose it's best to go to the station and wait,' Janet said, buttering her toast.

'Don't you drive?' Kim asked.

'I passed my test years ago, but to be honest, I like travelling by train. I like to watch from the window. You see such interesting things that you'd miss if you were driving and I inevitably get into conversations with fellow passengers. And besides, with my senior card it works out really quite reasonable.'

'I'll drop you at the station if you like,' Kim offered. 'Save you getting a taxi.'

'Oh, how kind of you! Thank you!'

'I'm not going to stay and have brunch with you all. Please don't think me rude!' Angela said, to Deano, Penny and Dave. 'I know we'd talked about it but I really do have to get back as quickly as I can.'

'Ehh! I know what you mean. I can't wait to see my little Sam. I bet he's missed his mam. I told him I'd be back yesterday.'

'It's 'er dog,' Dave explained to Deano, seeing his quizzical look.

Frances came to the table and poured herself a coffee, before ordering scrambled egg and bacon from a waitress they hadn't seen before.

'You haven't seen Olivia have you, Eve?' she asked, looking round.

'No, I haven't. I haven't seen Geoff or Denise or Pete, either.'

'That's funny because I rang her room and there was no reply. I sort of lost the run of her yesterday.'

'Hmm. She seemed a bit put out by the weather when I spoke to her. She wasn't happy at not being able to leave. Was wanting to go home.'

'She's a funny girl! I got quite fond of her in Turkey but to be honest, I found her a bit of a lame duck this time. I mean, Turkey was six months ago, no need to keep on going on about it. I've heard the story of the tennis-playing-love-rat-boyfriend fifty times! She acted as if we were joined at the hip, too. I had to deliberately sit with other people in the hope she'd mix a bit.'

'Well, she hasn't come into breakfast since I've been here and I came in just as they opened at half-past seven.'

Frances got up and walked out, returning a couple of minutes later, just as her scrambled eggs were being delivered to the table.

'She's gone! The receptionist said she checked-out early. Well, that's nice, isn't it? Not even good-bye, kiss my arse or nothing!' Frances sat down and flicked her napkin open and put it across her lap. 'Oh, well! Some you win, some you lose!'

The door to the dining-room swung open to reveal Geoff and Denise, hand-in-hand. They looked around and decided to sit on a table for two on the far side rather than take the two empty seats on the round table, which were between Tall Sue and John. Eve hoped they wouldn't all end up bad friends. Although Geoff looked extremely happy this morning, like the cat who'd got a very large dollop of full-fat cream. She had been surprised to hear that Olivia had left without saying good-bye to her or to Frances, though. Still, why something like that should surprise her after all the things she'd seen and heard she didn't know. She poured herself another coffee and took it out to the foyer so that she could check everyone off her list as they went and wish them *bon voyage*. She hoped to be away by half past ten. That way, she would hopefully be home in Horndon-on-the Hill by lunch-time.

✦   ✦   ✦

UPSTAIRS IN ROOM nine Dave and his Miss P were having a little private moment before going their separate ways. They stood in an embrace in the middle of the room, he talking to the top of her head, she talking to his fresh-smelling right armpit.

'So ring me when you get 'ome, so as I know you're safe. I'll be worried about you driving in these conditions.'

'Well, you've no need to be, I've been driving since I was eighteen and I drive ambulances, don't forget. If I can drive them I can drive anything!'

'An' I'll keep me eyes peeled for a motor for you. Soon as I've got something in mind I'll let you know. An' if I 'aven't I'd still like to come up and see you. In a few weeks, like.'

'I hope you will,' Penny said, turning to look into his face. She reached up and kissed him. 'I've had a smashing Christmas break and most of that's down to you. Thank you.'

'Nah, it's me what should be thankin' you. You've made it for me.'

They gave each other a long, sweet kiss, neither wanting to be the one that pulled away first. A brisk knock on the door meant they pulled apart at the same time.

'Housekeeping!' came the cry from the other side of the door.

'Five minutes, please!' Dave called back, even though it wasn't his room.

'Well, they'll be wanting to clean and get ready for their next guests,' Penny said, kissing the end of his nose and then turning to pick up her handbag. Dave sprung forward and picked up her case.

'Now, you've got me mobile number in case you 'ave a problem on the road, ain't you? And I've got yours. I should be 'ome in under two hours so you can give us a ring if you stop for a meal, or petrol,' he said as they walked through the foyer together.

'Course I will. Well, we're off,' Penny said to Eve as they walked over to her. 'Thanks very much for all you did for us. You've been great,' she said, leaning forward and giving her a kiss on the cheek.

'It's been my pleasure! Lovely to meet you, Penny, and lovely to see you again, Dave,' she said, as he, too, gave her a kiss on the cheek.

'Likewise. An' I'll see you at the *Wedding of the Year* next week!' he added. 'I can't wait for that.'

'Of course, yes, I'll see you there. Safe journey, both of you!'

Eve smiled at them as the Four Friends got out of the lift and rushed over to shake hands with Dave and kiss Penny, wishing them both a Happy New year and a safe journey home.

'Don't forget, if you're ever in Somerset!' Mick called to them as they walked out the door. 'And the same goes for you, Eve,' he added, giving her a peck on the cheek. The other three did the same.

'Thanks for all you did, Eve. We enjoyed ourselves,' Don said and they, too, moved off towards the doors, carrying holdalls and suit-bags, stopping to take their leave of Kim and Janet, who were at the reception desk settling their bills.

'Don't forget, if you change your mind about Britain's Got Talent, give us a ring,' Mick said to Kim, giving her a kiss. 'We could be the next Carpenters,' he said.

'Kim could, but you sing like Les Dawson used to play!' Vince ribbed him.

'Bye, Miss Mastermind,' Mick said to Janet, giving her a little peck while shaking her hand. 'No hard feelings about the quiz.'

'Well, I should hope not,' she said, her smile taking the sting from her words. 'We should all strive to be good losers.'

Angela whizzed through next, pausing to air-kiss Eve.

'I'm racing off just in case the weather closes in again, heaven forbid! Can't wait to get back and see Butterscotch. I'm hoping I'll be able to take him out for a ride this afternoon.'

'I wish you all the best, for the future, for your plans,' Eve said.

'Thank you.' Angela took Eve's hand. 'I've already started working on my vision board. Thank you very much, for your understanding and your patience with me. I'm going to write to Travel Together to complain about the first girl dumping us, but I shall sing your praises to the hilt. You've been fab! Oops! Nearly went without saying goodbye to you!' she said to Deano, who'd just appeared.

'Nice meeting you, Angela. Take care of yourself, yeh?'

'You too!' She air-kissed Deano and was gone.

'Thanks, Eve. All the best for the New Year.'

'Yes, and to you, too.' Eve said.

'Might see you again, who knows? I quite fancy another long haul holiday. I might go back to Antigua, without falling in the sea this time! I liked the Mango Tree Resort.'

Eve watched Deano strut across the foyer and out the

door just as Frances fell out of the lift, yanking a huge suitcase behind her, with a flight-bag over her shoulder and a handbag over her arm.

'I obviously thought it was five weeks and not five days,' she said, in self-deprecation to Eve, before dropping all three of them and enveloping her in a huge embrace.

'Thank you so much for giving me another fabulous time and I'm sorry to have been the cause of aggravation for you, yet again,' she said.

'No problem. I'm just glad you enjoyed yourself.'

'Yes, I did! Looking back it was a good few days. I enjoyed the walks, the food, the evenings, everything! Just a shame about Milos…'

'Who? Never heard of him!' Eve said.

'See you on Friday at the wedding! Just got time to get home, do the washing, sing *Auld Lang's Syne* and then glad-rags on again for another do. Fabulous!'

'Yes, see you there! Go safely!' Eve called to Frances' retreating figure, smiling to herself at the woman's energy and joie de vivre.

The Three Sues came next, in a gaggle, giggling girlishly over something or other.

'Thanks, Eve. Nice, meeting you,' Blonde Sue said.

'Yes, all the best, love,' Tall Sue called. 'Nice couple of days.'

'And to you, too. Take care. Nice meeting you!' Eve replied. Slim Sue just waved at her without saying anything. She was unsure how much Eve knew about her and Milos and didn't want to become engaged in conversation with her in case she started to question her about him, even at this late stage.

'We seem to have lost the run of Geoff,' Blonde Sue said. 'We did knock on his door on the way down but there was no reply. 'Can you tell him we've gone if you see him please?'

'Yes, of course, I will. And I'll tell him you were looking for him, shall I?'

'Yes, please. I'll ring him next week. He'll be okay with us, he just gets a bit possessive, that's all. Thinks we're his harem!'

'Still, looks like he pulled so he'll be happy!' Tall Sue said.

Eve checked her list. Everyone except Colin, Geoff, Denise and Pete had passed through the foyer and left. Colin had said goodbye to her last night saying that he'd be on the road as early as possible, so she wasn't expecting to see him this morning. She knew Geoff and Denise were well because she'd seen them at breakfast. But she hadn't seen Pete. She went over to the front desk.

'Has Mr Sullivan checked out this morning?' she asked Tania, who ran her pen down her list.

'Yes. It seems like he left very early. He checked out before I came onto duty,' Tania said. 'Only two people left.'

'Yes, I know about them.' Eve understood why Pete had checked out early, because he probably hadn't wanted to see her this morning. She didn't blame him and she actually felt relief as she was still reeling from what he'd told her the previous evening. If she'd seen him this morning she was unsure what she might have said.

She took her coffee cup back into the bar and saw Geoff and Denise sitting talking over two mugs in the corner, their heads together. She waved across at them and when they acknowledged her she went over.

'I'm on my way now,' she said. 'I hope you both get home safely. And the Three Sues said to tell you they've gone and they'll be in touch,' she added, delivering the message.

'Oh, I'm sure they will,' he said assuredly, gripping

Denise's hand in his as if so much female attention was his birthright. Eve shook hands with both of them and went back to the foyer to take her leave of Chris Edwards.

'Eve, it's been a real pleasure working with you,' he said, pumping her hand. 'I'm so glad you were Jade's replacement.'

'I'm just pleased it all worked out so well. Thank you for your co-operation.'

'Do you want a picnic box for the journey?' he asked, kindly.

'No, thanks. It's really nice of you to offer but hopefully I'll be home in an hour and a half. Say goodbye to the others for me and thank Benjamin again for the fabulous concert.'

'I will!'

'Bye, Tania!' she called, waving at the young receptionist before striding through the door into the chilly wind.

Ladies and Gentlemen, Eve Mitchell has now left the building!

✦   ✦   ✦

COLIN HAD JUMPED out of his skin after shutting his case in the rear of his vehicle that morning. He raised his arms, moving his keys to use as a weapon against the man who rushed at him from the gloom.

'Aaargggh! Stand back! I haven't got any money and I'm armed!' he shouted at his assailant.

'Colin! It's me, Pete. It's me.'

'Jesus! You gave me a fright. I didn't see you.'

'Could I get a lift with you, please?'

'Where are you going?' Colin's heart was still pounding, his nerves on edge.

'I have to get to Stansted, but you can drop me anywhere. Colchester, Chelmsford, wherever. I can get a train from there.'

'I thought Deano had offered to take you?'

'Yes, but I wanted an early start,' he said. 'He won't be leaving until about ten and I need to get my flight sorted out so the sooner I'm there the better.'

And besides, I don't want to see anyone, especially not Kim or Eve.

'I'll put your stuff in the back' Colin said, opening up the rear door again to let Pete put his case inside and slamming it shut.

'God! You did give me a fright!' he said, chuckling now at the thought while clicking his safety belt in place. 'I'm going down the A12, so I can drop you at Chelmsford. Will that have trains to Stansted?'

'Not directly, but I can get one to Liverpool Street and connect to Stansted from there. I don't want to take you out of your way.'

'Not at all. It'll just be a short diversion off the A12 into the town,' Colin said, setting the satnav.

'Fine. That'll do fine, so it will.'

As the vehicle swept past the front of the hotel and made its way down the drive Colin caught sight of Pete's drawn features under the lights. His eyes were bloodshot and baggy, his skin sallow, his hair standing on end, where he'd pulled his fingers through it repeatedly.

'Are you alright?' Colin asked him once they were going through the village.

'As fine as I'll ever be, I suppose.'

'We'll get a cup of coffee, shall we? As soon as we see somewhere open? I could murder one myself.'

'If you like.'

Pete's whole demeanour had changed from the pleasant, assertive, intelligent, sociable man of the last six days. He was now morose, silent, scruffy and somewhat scary. Colin felt as if he was in the presence of a stranger, and one that left him feeling very uneasy.

'I expect trains will run a normal service today.' Colin attempted to make conversation as he drove north-east on the B1026 toward Tiptree, following the satnav's instructions. Pete sat in silence staring through the windscreen. Colin always obeyed the speed restrictions but he allowed himself to drive at the limit in the hope that the eighteen miles to Chelmsford would pass as quickly as possible. Not another word was spoken between them until Colin pulled off the A12 and onto the A138 and Springfield Road which led into the town centre and to the slip road which led into the station itself.

'Nearly there,' Colin said. 'Didn't take us long, did it?'

'Thank you, Colin. I appreciate this,' Pete said as they pulled up and Colin leapt to the back of the four by four to get Pete's suitcase out. He stood there for a moment alone with the case and he was just about to go and open the car door when Pete slowly emerged from it. He looked at Colin and then looked around as if unsure of where he was.

'Are you sure you're feeling okay? Would you like me to stay with you for a while? Or come down and see you onto the train?'

'Train?'

'The train into London. So that you can get to Stansted.'

'Oh, yes. No. I'm fine. Thank you, Colin.' Pete shook his hand, picked up his case and walked towards the station entrance. Watching his solitary figure Colin felt a wave of pity and pain without knowing or understanding why. He got back in his car and sat with the engine off for a moment, unsure of what to do.

What can I do? He'd already said it was his first Christmas without his wife…

Colin gave a shrug and exhaled noisily. He turned the key in the ignition and the engine came to life.

Petrol, coffee and foot down!

✦   ✦   ✦

OLIVIA WAS BEGINNING to wish she hadn't rushed off in such a petulant manner. Because when she stopped and thought about it she realised she had behaved very childishly. After all, it was hardly Frances' fault that she'd got off with someone while Olivia hadn't found a man. She liked Frances, too, and she probably wouldn't want anything to do with her now.

Why was I jealous of Frances and Milos? I didn't even fancy him!

She realised, of course, that her jealousy stemmed back to David's infidelity, although she wasn't really even sure if that was what you could call it. After all, he'd been having an affair with Sally for almost a year before he'd started going out with her, using her as a smokescreen so that Sally's husband wouldn't suspect anything was going on between his wife and her doubles partner.

*If anything **I** was **the other woman**!*

And it was hard to believe that she'd been so hurt by David when they'd actually only gone out together for just over a month before she found out that he was holidaying with Sally while she was on her tennis week in Turkey.

Do other women get so deeply involved with men so quickly or is it just me?

Her thoughts wandered back to Frances as she strained to see where she was going as the snow pounded her windscreen. She was only at Junction 3 of the M25. She hated motorway driving, especially this one. The snow was settling and it was difficult to see where the lanes stopped and the hard shoulder started. Lorries and van sped past her, heaving more snow and sleet over her in their wake.

You bastards! Why can't you slow down a bit? They must be

mad!

She decided she'd ring Frances as soon as she got home and pretend she'd suddenly decided to leave early. No! She'd tell Frances the truth; that she'd been pissed off and angry because Frances had pulled and she hadn't. Knowing Frances she'd probably laugh. At least she hoped she would. She put the windscreen wipers on full speed, but that seemed to make very little difference. In fact, it felt worse, as if she was being hypnotised. Her back and shoulders were aching where she was clutching the wheel so tightly. She thought about stopping at Clacket Lane Services but realised that she might end up snowed in there. All she wanted was to get home safely to Surrey and that looked like it was becoming increasingly difficult. A weather update came on the car radio, talking of *heavy snowfalls throughout Kent, Surrey and Sussex.* And she could see they were right, looking in disbelief at the snow, already at least six inches thick, which was settling on the motorway. Even the lorries were slowing down now, almost driving in slow motion in the surreal world of white that was fast developing all around them. The rear wheels of a van in the outside lane veered to one side. Brake lights behind and beside him all flashed on as drivers seemed to suddenly wake up to the severity of the driving conditions. Olivia kept as far to the left as she could, praying that she wouldn't end up in a ditch. She looked at the speedometer and saw she was only driving at twenty miles an hour. Which was just as well as she slammed into a snow-covered barrier two minutes later.

✦   ✦   ✦

PENNY WAS SAD to see Dave's car drive off to the left down the ramp to join the A414 at Junction 3 of the A1(M). He'd made a slight diversion so that he could drive along with her as far as possible.

'Gotta keep you safe Miss P, just in case the snow comes back,' he'd said as they'd stopped for a coffee at South Mimms. 'We coulda come all the way on the A414, but I thought it might be rough,' he'd added, eager to prove his concern for her well-being was genuine. Penny knew that they were both trying to put off leaving each other for as long as possible. But she also knew, and so did Dave, that she couldn't hang around for too long as she had a long journey ahead of her. Part of her wished she'd taken the train, but she liked driving herself. She liked the freedom it gave her to stop when she wanted and to get out and stretch her legs. And besides, with the dodgy weather who knew what the trains were up to? She waved at the disappearing Audi, giggling to herself as she knew he couldn't see her. Still, that didn't matter, she felt better for waving. She was so happy about meeting Dave! She didn't want to run before she could walk, especially with a long-distance relationship, but she had a sort of good feeling about him.

I can always get a transfer from work.

Where had that thought come from? What happened to not running before you could walk? Penny giggled again. She knew in her heart of hearts that she'd just taken the first steps on the long road to her happy future.

As long as Sam likes him!

✦   ✦   ✦

DAVE FELT HIMSELF choke up as he drove onto the A414.

Get a grip, you silly sod!

He'd wanted to invite Penny to stay at his for a day or two, in case the weather got worse, but he didn't suggest it in case she thought he was being too forward. And besides, he knew she had to get home to her dog and her job. She was, apparently, going back to work tomorrow morning on an early shift. His sweaty hands slid off the steering wheel and he wiped them on his trousers one at a time, recognising that he was fearful that she was driving out of his life. He had one final glance in the rear view mirror and he could have sworn he saw her wave.

Is that a fond-farewell wave or a goodbye-and-good-riddance wave?

He spent the rest of the journey trying to puzzle it out.

✦   ✦   ✦

JANET'S JOURNEY HADN'T gone to plan at all.

'It's about forty minutes, more or less, from Chelmsford to Liverpool Street and then I get the 26 or 388 bus home. So as long as the snow's not holding things up, I should be home in time for lunch,' she said to Kim.

'Lucky you! Although the forecast says that the snow's falling heavily south of London and won't be moving further north until late this afternoon, so I should get in ahead of it.'

'Where is it you live?'

'Luton. Not too far.'

But when Janet had got out of Kim's car and waved her goodbye, she'd gone into the station to find that for the time being there were no London-bound trains. People were milling around reading the placard placed just inside the station. Janet couldn't help thinking it would be wiser for the staff to place it outside where people could see it before they were dropped off. She was sure that if Kim had known there were no trains she would have offered to take her to Romford, or at least somewhere further down the line which wouldn't have been out of her way.

'Excuse me, can you tell me what's going on?' she asked a station employee who was standing next to the placard.

'Yes. There are no trains, madame. For at least two or three hours,' he said, pushing his glasses back up his nose.

'Is it because of the weather?'

'No. Unfortunately, someone decided to walk along the track and throw themselves under the 7:42.'

'Oh, dear me!'

'We are running a replacement bus service to Shenfield, which will be in approximately half an hour.'

'Is the station buffet open?'

'Not today, but there's a caff just up the road.'

'Will there be room on the bus for everyone? I don't want to go off and get myself a coffee only to find I'm left behind.'

'There'll be more than one bus, madam. You'll easily get a place.'

Janet trudged along to the *caff* and bought a coffee and a Danish pastry to take away and then went back to the station to have them. As she sat and drank and ate, before taking her medication, she offered up a silent prayer for the soul of the poor person who had been so low and in such despair they had taken their own life. She thought about her own final months that lay ahead and knew she would be given the strength to accept whatever they might bring.

At least I'll be among the sights, the colours, the sounds, the smells and the warmth of Trinidad.

She had decided, when the time came, that she would ask to be taken into the garden of her family's lemon stucco house, so that she could take her final breaths on Earth among the palm trees and flowers in the open air and not in a sterile hospital bed. She felt blessed that she could make these choices.

Perhaps the poor soul under the train had felt all choices had been taken from them.

✦   ✦   ✦

'YES!'

Eve punched the air and gave a shout of glee as she closed the front door behind her and stepped through the small hallway into her open-plan lounge and kitchen. Looking round the little house that she so loved, smelling the fresh pine of the beautiful Christmas tree in the far corner, putting on the multi-coloured fairly lights that adorned it, she dropped her case and bag and gave a little dance of joy on the spot. She was so glad to be home! She flopped onto the big, comfortable, black, leather sofa, hugged a gold and cream cushion to her and ran her mind back over the events of the past few days, realising that it really hadn't been too bad – they never were once they were over! – and even the weather had behaved itself allowing them to leave this morning. She'd had the car radio on and had heard about the heavy snow coming in from across Kent and Surrey. More snowfalls were expected for Essex but not until that evening. She hoped she'd be able to drive to Gatwick; the thought of the slushy, wet roads freezing over with snow on top of ice wasn't a prospect she relished.

Please just let me get there! As long as I'm with him it won't matter what happens!

She hugged herself at the thought, but then added another term and condition to the prayer.

But let Michael and Natalie get here safely, too. For New Year's Eve!

The red light on her answer machine was flicking, indicating five messages, three from Melv and one from Michael, all left when they hadn't been able to reach her on Boxing Day. She leaned over and pushed the button and played each of them twice, revelling in hearing their voices.

The fifth was from Andrea at Travel Together asking her if she would do a Lanzarote that was leaving on New Year's Eve.

*Which part of **I'm having Christmas and New Year off** is giving the problem here? Talk about left hand and right hand.*

Alan obviously hadn't let the tour managers' dept know that she wasn't at home because she'd been snowed in in Essex doing a job because Jade had abandoned ship. She picked up the phone and rang the office, getting Andrea's voicemail.

'Hi, Andrea, it's Eve. I've just got your request to do Lanzarote. I'm not available, I'm afraid. I've only just this minute got back from doing a break in Essex because Jade walked out. I'll try and get the report to you some time later today, but if I don't you'll have to bear with me as I had requested not to work, as you'll remember, purely because I have lots of other plans at this time. I'm sure you'll understand and excuse me if, for once, I'm a little late getting the paperwork in. Oh, and by the way, Alan promised me triple-time for this job and double-time for the next three. I'll adjust the paperwork to reflect that. Happy New Year, Andrea! Bye!'

She hung up smiling; that was just nicely assertive! She dragged her case through to the kitchen and put the dirty clothes straight into the washing machine, added washing powder and started a wash. She wanted everything to be done so that nothing would get in the way of the next few days. She made herself a cup of coffee and put two slices of bread from the freezer into the toaster, deciding to have a quick snack and then get everything ready for Melv's arrival. As she buttered her toast her thoughts wandered to her little group and she hoped they had all got home safely, or were at least on their way.

✦   ✦   ✦

ANGELA HAD CRIED when she'd seen Butterscotch. She'd
hardly brought the car to a stop when she opened the door
and was out, striding across the stable yard towards the
block where she knew she'd find him. He neighed when he
saw her and she threw her arms around his neck and hugged
him.

Maisie, the stable-hand rushed in to see what all the fuss
was about.

'I've missed him so much!' Angela said, her arms around
Butterscotch's neck. 'Can you saddle him up, please? We're
going for a ride.'

'Of course, Mrs Carlson.'

'I'll go and help myself to a coffee and put my boots on
while you get him ready. Shall I bring you one?'

'Oh, erm…yes…please. Thank you,' Maisie stuttered as
Angela went over towards the stables' office. 'She must have
been on the sherry, mustn't she, boy?' she muttered to
Butterscotch, as she took his blanket off. 'It's not like her to
be happy.'

✦   ✦   ✦

JANET WAS FINALLY home after a journey that hadn't been
too bad. The replacement bus had, indeed, come along in
just under half-an-hour, as the railway employee had said
and she had managed to get a seat downstairs where she
could keep an eye on her suitcase. She'd quite enjoyed the
drive along the roads from Chelmsford, through snow-
covered villages toward Shenfield. And there had been a
train waiting for them, which had actually pulled out as soon
as everyone from the bus was on board. She'd found herself

drifting off to sleep on the train, coming round every time the next stop was announced, and before she knew it they were approaching Liverpool Street. She was surprised to see just how much snow had settled on the buildings around the station; that was unusual for the city, but the pavements were clear which enabled her to wheel her case easily along to the bus stop.

She was happy to see a note from her friend Doris had been pushed under the door welcoming her home and inviting her round to tea that afternoon before their usual Bible-study meeting. She gave a beaming smile because she'd had a good final Christmas on Earth and she had wonderful friends like Doris to come home to and to spend the next few months with before her final trip to Trinidad.

I am so well and truly blessed!

✦   ✦   ✦

OLIVIA WAS ON a trolley in A & E of Darent Valley Hospital, waiting to be seen. Wrapped in a blanket she finally felt warm. Her crash had happened two hours earlier; fortunately a camera had recorded what had happened and a vehicle was on the scene within about ten minutes, but it had taken more than an hour for the ambulance to get to her due to the weather conditions. As Mike the police officer had told her, she was so lucky only to have been going at twenty miles an hour. Her airbag hadn't deployed, even though she'd come to an abrupt stop. Her face had smacked against the steering wheel, which had also dug into her stomach. Her right knee felt gashed and her back and shoulders hurt.

'Probably whiplash,' Eddie the paramedic had said. 'Let's get you into a collar. No real damage, but we'd better get you to A & E so they can give you the once-over just to make sure.'

They'd taken good care of her and kept on apologising for the time it had taken to get to the hospital, even though it wasn't their fault. Mike had taken her details and said he'd get in touch with her neighbour Lucy, who was feeding her two cats, Bonnie and Clyde. He offered to ring her mother, but she said she'd do it herself once she was on her way home, knowing that if her mother received a phone call from the police telling her that her daughter had been in a car crash in the snow she'd probably have an attack of the vapours. Mike had said that he didn't live far from Chertsey. She sort of hoped he might call to see how she was tomorrow. She'd made sure he'd got her mobile number.

✦   ✦   ✦

DAVE FELT AS if he was at a loose end, which was rather strange as he'd always lived alone and had, until now, always enjoyed his own company. He sat by the window with a cup of tea that was going cold, looking out on the snowy, picture postcard scene that was his garden. His eyes looked at the snowflakes falling, the branches of the magnolia tree in the centre of the lawn gradually bowing down with the weight of the snow yet all he could see was a pretty, round face with a heartwarming smile that went right up to the clear blue eyes above it; all he could hear was the sweet, sing-song voice and the cheeky giggle that belonged to the beautiful Miss P.

For the tenth time in five minutes he wondered where she was and hoped and prayed she was safe. She'd promised him that she'd drive slowly and carefully, but the roads were full of other idiots. He'd never forgive himself if something happened to her for not persuading her to stay over at his. But then, she'd made it clear she had to be home tonight to see Sam and go to work tomorrow. He wanted to do something for her; something nice. He didn't know her address but she'd told him which ambulance station she worked from. He left the cold tea and picked up his phone, Googling to find the information he wanted.

✦   ✦   ✦

FRANCES HAD A long, hot shower. She was usually a bath kind of girl, but she was afraid that if she got into the bath this evening she'd never get out of it. Her back and shoulders ached from the drive and so did her left knee, which having a touch of arthritis often gave her a twinge. Warm water pounded down on her head, giving her scalp a massage, before sweeping down over her body.

That feels soooo good!

The thick, turquoise hand towel soaked up the water from her hair as she made it into a turban. A matching bath sheet did the same to her body. She wiped her bare feet on the bath mat and went through into the bedroom, dried herself and put on her pyjamas. Five minutes later, her hair dry but unstyled, she made herself a mug of cocoa, splashed some brandy in it and climbed into bed. Before turning out the light she saw her suitcase standing in the corner, untouched and unopened.

That can wait until tomorrow!

Darren had phoned to say he and Gary had got to their friends' place so that was a weight off her mind. She sipped her drink and snuggled the duvet up round her neck. She wanted to sleep for days.

Perhaps I really am getting too old for all this toy-boy stuff. Or perhaps I'll feel better in the morning!

She fell into a deep sleep and dreamt she was on a catamaran in Antigua with Neville, who was trying to seduce her on the nets, while lots of other people stood around knocking tennis balls to each other. Suddenly there was a lot of noise and shouting from the passengers as an iceberg appeared in front of the cat, with Milos hanging stark naked from the top of it with the biggest erection Frances had ever seen. She woke with a start, looked round the pink and lavender bedroom and chuckled to realise it had been a dream.

Dear, God! I worry myself sometimes.

She turned over and stretched before snuggling back into the pillows and within two minutes she was soundly asleep.

DAY SEVEN

✦

E VE'S ALARM CLOCK went off at 3:30am. She wanted to give herself plenty of time to get to Gatwick given that the forecast on the Ten O'Clock News had been of more inclement weather. Most of the southern section of the M25 was under snow and hundreds of people had got as far as Clacket Lane and been unable to get any further, sleeping inside on the floors when all the seats were taken. She'd decided to go through Central London, where she assumed the roads would be clearer and then down the A23 and onto the M23, keeping her fingers crossed that it would be open. She switched the alarm off and jumped out of bed, pulling open the bedroom curtain to see that some snow had fallen during the night. Her car had a thin cover of snow on it, but the windscreen would be clear as she'd invested in a shield two winters ago but had never needed it until now. The road was shiny and reflective under the street lamps and Eve hoped that it wasn't covered in ice.

She put the kettle on while she went to the bathroom, deciding to take a flask of coffee with her and drink it as she drove rather than waste precious time in the house before she left. She'd spoken to Melv late last night. He'd called her from the departure lounge at VC Bird International Airport just as the flight was boarding.

'Well, finally, we're off! I've been so damned lucky to get on this flight, you know? People were fighting for seats. I'm in Premium,' he added, 'because I thought I deserved a treat and besides, Economy was full.'

'Don't have to justify yourself to me. You could come in a spaceship, as long as you get here! Ooh! I can't wait to see you!'

'Same here, baby, same here.'

'I'm getting up early to make sure I'm there in plenty of time to meet the flight.'

'Just take your time and don't hurry. I can sit and wait all the time necessary so don't you go taking any chances in the bad weather. Drive slowly and carefully.'

'I will!' she promised him.

She crept out the front door, closing it quietly and crunched down the path to her car.

Bugger! It's icy!

She got in the Fiesta, closing the door quietly so as not to wake up her elderly neighbours, Cyril and Sheila Peyton, and turned the heater right up, letting it run while she got back out again to remove the windscreen shield. Then she slipped the clutch and reversed off the driveway, skidding as she did so, missing Cyril's Volkswagen by the width of the paintwork.

Shit!

She hadn't been expecting that and it had shaken her up a little. She steadied herself and pulled forward slowly, hoping that the ice would be less as she got onto the A13. She lurched through the village, grateful to see as she drove onto the A128 that the gritters had been out, which would make the journey easier. She glanced at the dashboard clock and saw it was already 4:15. Still, she still had two hours before the plane was due, although she knew from experience that often the west to east flight across the Atlantic was much shorter than the other way. She drove slowly along the A13, glad she'd chosen to drive through London as the road had been reasonably clear so far, just a bit dirty from the grit and sludge being thrown up by larger and faster vehicles swooping by. She was driving past the Asda store at Dagenham when her mobile rang. She glanced at it and saw the call was from Melv. She pulled over onto the hard shoulder – unsure as to whether or not she was breaking the law but not really caring if she was – and picked up the phone.

'Are you here already?' she asked.

'Well, I'm somewhere, but it's not Gatwick.'

'Oh, no! What's happened? Have you diverted to Heathrow?' her mind immediately thinking on the route through London to the airport that was situated to the west.

'We've diverted to Charles De Gaulle.'

'What? But that's…'

'In Paris. Yes, Eve, I know! Apparently Gatwick is closed again for in-going aircraft and so is Heathrow.'

'Well what about Birmingham? Or Manchester?'

'Eve, why are you asking me that? I don't know! The captain made an announcement as the crew were serving breakfast. He said we couldn't get into anywhere in the south of England so we were diverting to Paris. We're on the tarmac at the moment waiting to be told what's going to happen to us. Where are you?'

'On my way to Gatwick. I was going through Central London because the M25 is closed at the moment.'

'Are you far from home?'

'No, about half an hour.'

'Then turn back and go home. As soon as I know something I'll call you. I mean, I may not even be into London today.'

Eve was beyond disappointed but she hadn't spent a lifetime working in the travel and tourism industries without learning that there was nothing you could do about it. Her mood suddenly felt as grey as the morning that surrounded her.

'Okay. I'll turn round and go home and wait to hear from you, then.'

'Good girl! And as soon as I know what's happening you'll know, too. I promise. I love you.'

'Love you, too.'

✦   ✦   ✦

ABOUT THE SAME time that Eve was turning back along the A13, but some three hundred miles away, Penny was huffing and puffing to herself as she set off for work. Usually she loved her job, but she could have done with just one more day off to get over the long journey she'd had the previous day. She'd already made her mind up that when she went to see Dave – *if she went to see Dave!* – that she would definitely go on the train.

Let the train take the strain, as they say!

She stretched her arms up above her head in an attempt to pull the knots out of her shoulders. The only solace she could find in doing an early shift was that by three o'clock she could be back home in bed.

The morning started off quietly. She and Dan, her partner for the shift, were called to a road traffic accident half an hour in which involved two cars and a lorry. Both car drivers had been in a bad way, while the lorry driver, who'd been the cause of it, had walked away with a couple of scratches. Next they'd gone to the home of an elderly man who had slipped on some ice and fallen as he'd put his milk bottles on the step and had broken his arm, followed by an elderly woman who'd been taken ill in a supermarket. Once they'd taken off her coat, jacket, two cardigans and polo neck sweater, leaving her in just a blouse and thermal vest, she felt much recovered. The two of them were having a cup of tea and some toast and Penny was telling him all about Christmas at the Blue Boar Inn when her radio crackled into life.

'Penny we need you to come to the control room now, please.' Victor, the controller said, sounding serious.

'Me?'

'This call is for Miss Penelope Pomphrett. Control to Penelope Pomphrett! If you are Miss Pomphrett would you please come to the control room,' he said.

'Ehh, I'm just finishing my toast, man,' she replied.

'Look! Just get here quickly, before another call comes in! Over and Out!'

Curious, Penny, with an even more curious Dan, left the canteen and followed the corridor that curved round to the ambulance control centre.

'This better not be some bloody wind up!' she said as they pushed open the swing door. Then she stopped in her tracks. A huge splash of red and green on Victor's counter had caught her eye. She looked at the crimson buds, her mouth open.

'Wye aye! So who's the secret admirer, then?' he asked.

'Are they for me?' She stepped closer and touched the velvety softness of the leaves, leaning forward to breath in their sweet perfume before reading the name on the card.

Miss Penny Pomphrett

She took it from the holder just as Dan took a call.

'Come on! We're wanted,' he said. Penny slipped the card into her pocket.

'Can I leave them here until the end of the shift?' she asked Victor.

'Course you can, pet.' I'll make sure no harm comes to them. They're beautiful, they are.'

'Yes, and you can tell me all about him, and I want every single detail,' Dan said as they rushed outside to get to the next call, a teenager with an asthma attack.

All morning Penny kept reaching into her trouser pocket to make sure the card was still there. She told Dan that she'd met a nice man over Christmas – *and yes, he was a Southerner!* – but that it was very early days, yet. They were just taking it as it came.

'Well, I have to say I'm pleased for you, pet,' he'd said. He'd worked alongside Penny for three years and had become very fond of her. Sometimes he thought it was just as well he was married to Marjie, who would have his balls in a meat pie if he so much as looked at someone else. 'If anyone deserves a nice man it's you! Although from the size of the bouquet I'd say he's more than keen, like.'

She was touched by his comments as she considered him to be one of her closest friends. But she kept the card in her pocket because she wanted to be completely alone when she opened it. At ten past three she put the floral display on the centre of her dining-table. It looked absolutely stunning against the polished, dark wood.

Like something you see in a big posh hotel, or in a magazine.

She'd counted the roses and there were four dozen, which she thought must have cost Dave a fortune. She sipped her cup of tea and walked across the room to sit in the arm-chair by the conservatory door, not taking her eyes from the flowers. Breathing deeply, she slit open the small white envelope, revealing the white card edged with tiny red hearts that was inside.

I never thought I could miss anyone this much, Miss P! I think I'm in love. Dave xxxxxxxxxxxxxx

Tears sprang up in her eyes. She kissed his name on the card. She looked at the flowers again. Nobody had ever sent her a bouquet like that. And then, she picked up the phone.

'Dave Wright's Motors.'

'Hello. It's Miss P. I do know that I'm in love,' she said.

✦   ✦   ✦

EVE SPENT THE rest of the morning alternating between checking her phone for a call from Melv and checking on the internet to see if Gatwick had re-opened. She watched daytime TV, much of which dealt with the closed airports and featured spokesmen from the airport explaining why, yet again, the airport had been caught out by bad weather and why it didn't seem to be able to operate in any snowfall, and irate passengers calling from the airport itself to demand answers as to why airports in Reykjavik and Siberia were open when Gatwick was closed. She went all over the house, checking that everything was clean and tidy, although she knew it was because she'd cleaned thoroughly the previous day. She phoned Michael.

'Oh, no! What bad luck! Still, it's only the thirtieth today, as long as he's here by tomorrow, I suppose. Any idea when they might take off again?'

'None. Gatwick's closed so there's nothing he can do really. Anyway, where are you?

'We're on our way to Nat's parents. We left about an hour ago and we should be there late afternoon.'

'Well, drive carefully, won't you?'

'Yes. It's not snowing. The roads are fairly clear although the fields and sides of the main roads are all covered.

I'll ring you when we arrive, but ring me if you hear from Melv, won't you?

'Bye, Eve!' she heard Natalie shout out.

'Bye, Natalie! Bye Michael!' she called back and then hung up.

By lunchtime Eve was getting on her own nerves. She'd run Melv twice and had the same conversation both times.

'We can't leave for Gatwick because it's still closed and anyway, the crew is now out of hours.'

'Where are you?'

'We're inside the terminal. They've given us vouchers for food and drink and they've told us to listen out for announcements.'

She felt like a caged lioness. She decided to go for a walk to kill some time and just to get out of the house. She'd thought that by now she'd be spending a glorious day with Melv, instead she was pacing up and down alone. She put her boots on, slipped into her coat and pulled her hat down over her forehead. She sent a text to Melv and Michael.

Going out for a short while. Ring mobile if you need me not landline xx

She crunched her way down the drive and then slid towards the kerb. She thought she'd better walk in the road, which appeared less icy. The last thing she wanted now was a broken ankle. Well, not now or at any time, really. A thud on the back of her head came as a surprise from nowhere. Spinning round she saw three boys grinning and bouncing snowballs in their hands, daring her to retaliate. One of them was Tom, who lived next-door-but-one.

'Want to earn a couple of pounds, Tom?' she called.

'Doing what?' came the suspicious reply.

'Stop throwing snowballs at me and clear my path when

I get back in about half an hour.'

Tom and his two mates looked at each other, weighing up losing the enjoyment of bombarding her with snowballs against getting some money.

'How much?' Tom threw a snowball up in the air as if he were Flintoff eyeing up an Australian batsman.

'Six quid. That's two pounds each.' The three boys whispered to each other.

'That ain't much.'

'Alright. Three quid each.' They held another board meeting.

'Yeh. We'll do it. See you in 'alf-hour.'

The village was empty of cars but seemed full of happy pedestrians, calling to each other, commenting on the terrible weather, but agreeing it added to the Festive Season. Eve walked at a brisk pace and within ten minutes her cheeks were glowing and she felt quite warm inside her quilted jacket. She took her sweaty hands out of her pockets and swung her arms as she walked. The mobile ringing as she turned into her road made her jump.

'Hi, it's me!' Michael.

'Hello. What's happened?'

'Don't sound so worried! Why should anything have happened?'

'Because you said you'd ring me when you got to Natalie's parents and you can't possibly be there yet.'

'Well, it comes to something when I can't ring my birth mother to check she's okay!' he joked. 'But thank you for caring!'

'I'm just arriving home after a half-hour walk around the village to clear my head and work up an appetite for some lunch. Three of the local lads are going to clear my pathway for me, too.'

'That's good. It's nice to see they take care of the elderly,' he joked. It took a moment before she fell in.

'You cheeky thing!'

'Just joking! Well, keep in touch and we'll ring when we're at Nat's parents. We're going to stop for a bit of lunch now.'

'Drive carefully. Love you!'

Tom and his two mates made a good job of clearing the path and Eve was happy to give them their money. She spent the afternoon checking her phone and her body, making sure it was hair-free where it was supposed to be. It never failed to amaze her how she checked for facial hair every day and yet she'd suddenly find a hair that was about three inches long growing in the middle of her chin. How had that sprung up overnight? Tweezers in one hand and mirror in the other she checked her eyebrows, which would be one huge monobrow if she let them, her top lip, her cheeks by her hairline and her chin.

Don't we go through enough with menopause without turning hairy, too?

Not only did her eyebrows grow like grass, they were like wire. Yet the hair on her legs and under her arms was less.

Why is that? Why should older women be less hairy than younger ones on the body, yet turn into Hagrid in the face?

She sighed, supposing that Mother Nature must have her reasons. She thought about pubic hair and how that greyed, too. She wondered why that was and if some women dyed it, just like she often wondered why your sexual organs started shrinking just when you were having the best sex of your life. She read articles regularly about the trials and tribulations of older sex. The internet was flooded with them, many relating to problems like dryness. As far as Eve was concerned that had an easy solution; sex with the right man. She smiled smugly and self-congratulatory knowing that she'd found him.

She went to her desk and fired up her laptop, pulling out her notepad and printed lists from her work bag. To kill some time she'd do her report; at least it would be out of the way. She wrote objectively, reporting in neutral language about the incident with Angela at the pub – including Angela's apology and change of attitude towards the group, and about Frances locking Milos out in the snow. Part of her felt it was none of Travel Together's business, but then again, if Milos decided to take the Blue Boar Inn to an employment tribunal for unfair dismissal the company might get dragged in anyway, so it was better that they knew something had gone on. Twenty minutes minutes later she clicked on *send* and her expenses and report were on their way.

She made herself a coffee and ate it with a slice of the Christmas cake she hadn't got round to eating due to the interruption to her plans. She decided to give Melv another call but it went straight to his voicemail.

He's probably trying to ring me.

She rang Michael, who told her he wasn't far from Natalie's parents and that he'd ring as soon as they got there. He said he hadn't heard from Melv either.

'Don't worry. His battery might be flat. Perhaps he's saving it to ring you as soon as he knows what's happening.'

She watched a Celebrity Pointless, her mind only half on it as she went online at the same time to see what was happening at Gatwick. She jumped up and punched the air, sending cake crumbs all over the carpet when she saw that it was due to re-open at any time. She got the carpet-sweeper from the cupboard under the stairs and was just putting it back when the bell rang.

✦   ✦   ✦

'DADDY, WE'VE MISSED you!' Aisling ran forward and hugged her father. 'I understand why you wanted to be on your own but Christmas wasn't the same without you. Well, without either of you,' she added. 'So how was your break in Essex?'

'It was pleasant. The other people were nice, easy to get on with on the whole and we went on a couple of walks and had a couple of quizzes and in the evening there was dancing with a deejay or a showband.'

'Sounds like it was grand.'

'And speaking of grand, you look like you've grown a lot in a week.'

Aisling's husband Aidan leant across and ran his hands over her round belly, laughing as he did so.

'That's what I'm telling her, too. I want her to ask them to make sure there's only one wee one inside there. If there's more than one I want to be prepared.'

'Sure they've told us and shown us the scan. You know there's only one.'

'Will you have tea with us, Aisling?' Saoirse asked. 'I've plenty of stuff and I'm making for Daddy and me.'

'Yes, please! I want to hear all about his adventure being snowed in.'

'It wasn't much of an adventure. The hotel was very old but very well conserved and very comfortable. So, when the snow came in and we couldn't leave we just stayed on in our rooms, had breakfast, lunch and dinner, watched TV, played cards and read.' He stopped to take a sip of the tea that Saoirse had given him and to catch himself before talking any more about the last night. 'And it so happened that one of the young waiters played the violin, but he played it absolutely beautifully, so he did. It'd bring tears to your eyes. And then Kim one of our group joined him on the piano and we sang along and Mick, who had a voice like Pavarotti sang solos and we had ourselves a wonderful impromptu concert.'

'And did the snow lift yesterday?'

'Aye. I managed to get a lift to Chelmsford early with one of the lads, Colin who had a four by four. So, as soon as the roads started to clear he was away and he took me with him. From Chelmsford I got a train to Liverpool Street and from there to Stansted.'

'So how come you didn't get back yesterday?' Aisling asked.

'It was chaos inside the airport, so it was. Hundreds of people had camped out there, been stranded because it had closed. Anyway, I queued but there was no room on any flight to Belfast and because I hadn't shown up for my flight I'd no recompense, it was my fault. There was a seat to Dublin that was leaving at nine-thirty last night, so I booked myself on that and then went and took a room at one of the airport hotels for a few hours and had a meal and a long sleep and then did the same when I got to Dublin. I went to an airport hotel and got up this morning, awake and refreshed and took the train back home.'

'It's good to see you looking so good. A break away from us is what you maybe needed,' Saoirse joked.

'No. The one thing I learned by spending Christmas without you is that I never want to do it again.'

'We knew the first one without Mammy wouldn't be easy and it certainly wasn't. I spent the whole of Christmas Eve crying until Niall suggested we came home if I was having such a bad time,' Saoirse said. 'He understood that I'd be low. But I realised I was being selfish and self-indulgent. I accepted his family's kind invitation to spend

Christmas with them and now I was spoiling it for everyone.'

'This year will have been the hardest,' Aidan said. 'And sure, there's none of you will forget Mrs Sullivan. But it'll get easier to get through it as time goes on.'

'I hope so,' Pete said. 'So, what's for tea, Saoirse? Did I hear you say it was special?'

And as his daughters prepared the food and his son-in-law chatted about everything and nothing, Pete pondered the last day and a half of his trip. He'd boarded the train to London but instead of taking the Stansted train at Liverpool Street, he'd found himself wandering around Soho. He'd taken a seat at a pavement table outside a coffee shop, the weather not seeming so cold and wet in the centre of the city. He'd ordered a drink and found himself people watching; there was definitely a coming and going of all types. The person on the table next to him asked for their bill, their long, chestnut hair falling down over the embroidered pashmina covering their wide shoulders. Dark, kohl-rimmed eyes met Pete's; coral painted lips smiled at him before standing up and sashaying across the road, bangles jangling, above-the-knee-boots beating a rhythm on the cobbles into the neon-lit doorway opposite and then disappearing. His whole body trembled with the resurgence of feelings he'd hidden away for a twelvemonth. He ordered another coffee, his eyes watching the premises across the street and the people entering and leaving, his pulse racing, his heart beating fast, yearning and belonging sweeping over him.

The street had become busier with people coming out for lunch and theatre-goers wanting to grab a bite to eat before going to their chosen matinees. Still he sat there.

'Would you like to see the lunch menu?' A waitress with pink hair and a sleeve of tattoos pushed a card towards him.

Taking the hint he looked at it, the rumbling in his belly making him suddenly aware that he was ravenous.

'Liver and bacon, please.'

'With mash or chips?'

'Mash, please. Can I get a beer?'

'We're not licensed, I'm afraid. Soft drinks only.'

'Well, I'll have a lemonade or some such.'

Never had a humble dish tasted so good. Pete ate it with relish, clearing his plate.

'Is this seat taken?' He heard the jangle of bracelets and a wisp of a musky perfume floated before him. He looked up to see the same chestnut hair, kohl-rimmed eyes and coral mouth he'd noticed earlier.

'No. Help yourself.'

'I couldn't help noticing you've been sitting here a long time. Are you waiting for someone?' Pete put his knife and fork together on the empty plate and smiled.

'Do you know, I think that perhaps I am.'

And just over twenty-four hours later, sitting in the comfort of his own living-room he knew that he had punished himself enough. Maeve had chosen not to listen to him, not to wait for him to explain; she had chosen to take her own life rather than hear what her husband of more than forty years had had to say. Perhaps she'd had her own issues that he'd known nothing about? There could have been a dozen other factors that pushed her to do what she did. Now he owed it to himself to live his life the way he wanted. After all, who knew how much time he had left? He decided not to disclose to his daughters what had happened between himself and their mother. The time for telling them had long past. And. after all, he wouldn't be the first guy in history to be living a double-life and if he were to be discovered then he would face them and tell the truth. But not about Maeve. He knew he couldn't live with their hatred and hate him they surely would if they found out what might have pushed their mother over the edge. Better to say nothing at all!

And he was sure they'd be glad to see their Daddy begin to make regular trips back to England to spend time with some of his new found single friends.

✦   ✦   ✦

EVE'S FACE AS she opened the front door was a picture. Michael wished he'd had his phone ready to capture it.

'Ho! Ho! Ho! I bring tidings of comfort and joy!' he'd boomed, stepping aside to reveal Melv standing behind him.

'Waaaaaaa!' Eve screamed. 'You're here!'

She stepped forward and threw herself into the arms of the man she'd loved to distraction since she was eighteen-year-old, smothering his face with kisses, between squeals of delight and disbelief.

"Erm, Eve, could we come in, please? The neighbours are beginning to look,' Michael said, picking up Melv's case and brushing past them into the hallway. Clutching Melv's arm, Eve gently pulled him into the house and closed the door behind them.

'No kiss or greeting for your favourite son?' Michael said.

'Of course!' Now it was Michael's turn to be smothered in kisses. 'But how come you're here?' she asked as they went through to the living-room and sat down.

'As we were driving down Nat had a look online and saw Luton airport was open and there are direct flights into there from Paris. She rang Melv and told him and he got himself on a flight that landed at half past three. We did a little detour to pick him up, then I dropped Nat at her parents and here we are!'

'But you've got to come all the way back tomorrow…'

'That doesn't matter. The roads are clear between here and Hertfordshire. I'll have a quick coffee and use your toilet and then I'll set back off.'

✦   ✦   ✦

IT WAS COMPLETELY dark when Penny finally hung up the phone. By the twinkling lights of her Christmas tree she could see that it was five to six.

Almost three hours!

Her plans to get back into bed had disappeared along with any tiredness she might had felt the minute she'd heard his voice. She couldn't have told anyone on pain of death much of what they'd talked about, only that they'd agreed they were both in love and that they would, somehow, get together and make it work for them within the coming year. That was all she needed to remember. Her head was full of plans and perfect possibilities for their future together. But first on the agenda was to see each other again.

'I've got this weddin' Friday, an' I've booked to stay over in the 'otel they suggested so I can 'ave a drink. I could drive up straight from there Saturday?'

'I'm off Saturday, so that works,' she said, thrilled at the prospect of seeing him again and taking her roster as an auspicious omen for their relationship.

She sat in the cosy twilight of the Christmas lights, her mind whirling with what she would wear and where she would take him and what they would do and how many hours it would be until she saw him again. She worked it out at about ninety-six.

Far too many!

Sam padded over and put his head on her knee, feeling he'd taken second place long enough. He was hungry and it was time for his tea. She fondled his ears and scratched under his chin, which she knew he loved.

'Ehh, Sam! I've got someone wonderful I want you to meet,' she said.

Sam rubbed his head against her knee again his deep, dark eyes looking longingly at her face.

Never mind meeting someone wonderful, where's my dinner?

✦   ✦   ✦

EVE ARCHED HER back as the waves of orgasm rippled in all directions from her clit to the rest of her body; there wasn't a cell that wasn't vibrating and tingling. As the sensations gradually faded and her breathing slowly returned to normal she opened her eyes to see his beautiful face looking into hers, his hand gently pushing her hair from her forehead, his lips barely touching hers with the sweetest of kisses.

'So, tell me you haven't missed me,' he whispered in her ear.

'I haven't missed you.'

'You lie!' He looked at her in feigned shock, making her laugh into his chest. 'And even if you haven't missed me, I've missed you more than you could ever imagine. More than you could ever imagine.'

They lay as one, legs and arms entwined, each simply enjoying the other's presence; their pleasure in each other, the familiar feel and the familiar scent enhanced rather than weakened by that same familiarity. They were comfortable together but never bored or complacent. They could have spent the rest of their lives lying like this, content and happy. If she ever thought about it, which she sometimes did, Eve recognised that if she'd followed Melv to Barbados at nineteen and they'd got married, they might no longer have the spark that ignited into such a burning passion every time they met. And she worried that if she decided to go and live with Melv at some point in the future, as he never stopped asking her to do, that the spark might be extinguished or simply burn itself out. She chided herself for thinking about extinguishing sparks when, as she'd just seen, the blaze was roaring. Out of nowhere she recalled that they'd met in a club called Blazes. That was prophetic, surely?

After a while they got up and shared a pizza in front of the TV, watching a repeat of Midsomer Murders by the light of the Christmas tree. If felt cosy and warm, natural and right.

'So, what plans do you have for tomorrow? Michael and Natalie are coming by?'

'Yes. They're going to get here for seven. I'm cooking a meal for the four of us. I thought it would be nice and they agreed, to have their last dinner as singles with us. Especially given that Alice and Bertram will be to the forefront at the wedding as Michael's parents,' she added. Sometimes it still hurt for her to say that. He knew how she felt and he lifted her hand to his lips and kissed it.

'And what are you cooking?'

'I'm doing roast lamb with all the trimmings.'

'Oh, yes! Baby, you surely know the route to a man's heart!' he said, slapping his rounded stomach.

'Too much Wadadli beer!' she laughed.

'Beer? You saying I've got a beer belly? Woman! It's a fuel tank for a love machine!'

They laughed and kissed, both tasting of pizza and licking their lips.

'So are Natalie and Michael staying over?'

'Of course! That way they can both have a drink and not have to face driving back. They're leaving after breakfast on Thursday. Natalie will go to her parents to spend her last night as a single woman with them and Michael will check into the hotel where the reception is being held with Josh.'

'Hmm.'

'Hmm, what?'

'I'm just wondering if we'll be able to make love with such wild abandon as we usually do with our son and daughter-in-law in the next bedroom.'

'Well, perhaps not with such wild abandon as this evening. But I'm sure we can do it quietly so they won't hear us. And besides, parents all over the world do it with their children in the next bedroom, don't they?'

'Yes, but they're kind of used to it. This is a first for us.'

'Are you trying to get out of having sex with me?' she asked in mock horror.

'Not at all, I'm just saying let's turn the volume down. But we're all alone now, so let's take advantage of that, shall we?'

He took the plate from her hands and placed it on the coffee table then gently pushed her back against the cushions. He stood up and took off his own dressing-gown before slipping hers from her shoulders. She felt herself start to throb and then become wet as she looked at the fairy lights that reflected on his gleaming skin as he stood tall and dark and naked before her. She loved everything, every single thing, about this man. She loved the way he stood, the way he walked, the way he talked, the way he listened, the way he held her hand, the way he loved her. She just adored the feel of his skin, and she never tired of looking at every feature of his handsome face. She moved her fingertips over his broad nose and wide lips, touching him slowly, loving every single millimetre of him, finding him as gorgeous, as sexy and as exciting as the first time she'd ever seen him across the dance-floor at Blazes thirty-four years earlier.

✦   ✦   ✦

'WAS IT A total surprise, do you think? She didn't suspect anything?' Natalie asked Michael as they shared a bath.

'Not a thing! I'm surprised you didn't hear her shriek from here.'

'Oh, that's nice. I'd love for them to get together properly, they're just so good together.'

'Well, it's up to them. Melv's divorce is final so that's no longer an obstacle. I know Eve didn't want to think about anything longterm while he was still married. But it's up to them whether they have a happy-ever-after or not. Nobody would like it more than me.'

'They're obviously in love…'

'No doubt about that! It's electric between them. I grabbed a quick coffee and left before they started ripping each others' clothes off.'

'They're the same age as my mum and dad yet I can't imagine they still have sex.' Natalie observed.

'Don't be daft! They must do!'

'I don't know. I suppose I don't want to think about it,' she giggled. 'But with Eve and Melv it just seems…well…normal! I hope they won't be up to anything tomorrow night,' she added.

'We'll have to take our earplugs,' he joked. 'And we'll have to be quiet, too, because there's no way I'm not making love on our last night sleeping together before the wedding.'

'I wish you hadn't said that! I'll be aware of them in the next room, now!' she laughed. 'Silly really, because we sleep together here with my parents just down the hall.' She leaned back, her head wedged between the taps.

'Do you think we'll still be doing it in thirty years time?' she asked, wiggling her toes against his groin.

'No chance! You'll be fat and wrinkly and I won't fancy you.'

'That's alright! I'll find some young toy-boy who will!' she retorted, splashing water down at him. He got out of the bath, dripping all over the mat. He picked up the bath gel and rubbed some into the palms of his hands. 'Stand up,' he said, 'while I do still fancy you.' He gently covered her in lather, massaging her body slowly, slipping his fingers deep inside her as he did so, then teasing her by pulling them slowly out and then pushing slowly in again. He stepped back into the tub and stood behind her, still massaging the front of her body while gathering her against him.

'I'll never stop fancying you,' he whispered.

'I think we should add that line to the vows on Friday. To have and to hold, to never stop fancying,' she sighed, leaning back and surrendering to the love of the man she couldn't wait to marry.

DAY EIGHT

✦

E VE AND MELV enjoyed a long lie-in, both needing sleep, Melv from the jet-lag and journey, Eve from the nervous tension she'd gone through worrying over when or even if he would get to her. She'd woken up at just after seven, taking a second or two to realise she was in the arms of the man she was in love and in lust with. She turned and snuggled against him, pushing her knee between his thighs. He didn't wake up, just drew her nearer to him in his sleep. It was eight-thirty before she woke again, needing to use the loo and wanting a coffee. She brought two steaming mugs back into the bedroom, leaving Melv's on the side, not wanting to wake him. But he'd felt her absence from the bed and opened his eyes as he heard her come back into the room.

'Coffee?'

'Yes please.' He pushed himself to a sitting position in the bed and she took off her dressing gown and climbed back in beside him. They lay side by side in companionable silence, sipping their coffee, each with their own thoughts for a moment or two.

'Did you sleep well?' she asked him.

'Like a new-born. And besides I was next to you, wasn't

I?'

'What do you want to do today? Anything special?'

'Not really. Perhaps we can go out for a while a bit later on.'

'We could go to Lakeside for a spot of lunch. Not too much, obviously because of tonight's dinner. Tapas or something?'

'Hmm, yes! That sounds good. I'm wondering if I need a suit for the wedding?'

'Haven't you brought one?'

'Yes, but it's lightweight, Eve, made for the Caribbean. I'm afraid I'll freeze my arse off if I wear it to the wedding. And besides, I want to look the best I possibly can, you know, for Michael…' He trailed off.

'I know exactly what you mean. I've bought an outfit that's really more fitting for the mother-of-the-groom, which I know, biologically speaking I am, but to all intents and purposes, I'm not.'

'You'll look beautiful whatever you wear,' he said, planting a kiss on her cheeks.

'There are a couple of places you could get a nice suit. We'll go as soon as we've had breakfast, shall we? About ten?'

'Whenever. There's no rush. Got a couple of things to do before breakfast, though,' he said, taking her mug and then biting her nipple as he rolled on top of her.

✦ ✦ ✦

MURRAY WAS FEELING very pleased with himself. Catching sight of his reflection in a shop window, he pulled his stomach in and put his shoulders back.

That's more like it!

He felt he was a fine figure of a man, given his age and

his occupation. He liked to walk, feeling it combatted sitting down in the cab all day. Since he had bought Eileen a puppy, Lulu, last Christmas, they'd enjoyed walking her together as often as they could, which was most days as Murray was practically living with her now, much to her son, Luke's chagrin.

'It's not that he doesn't like you, as a person,' she'd said to Murray after Luke had been brusque to the point of rude to him early on in their relationship, 'because he does. He'd be just the same with anyone. He's a bit possessive about me.'

'Aye, well, there's no excuse for rudeness or lack of manners. I wasnae rude to him, I was just trying to make conversation and ask him where he was going.'

'Well, it can't be easy for him at his age,' Eileen had said, making excuses for him in Murray's opinion. 'He's a teenager and probably hates to think of his mother having a sexual relationship.'

'I suppose you're right,' Murray had conceded. 'Most teenagers think they invented sex.'

Fortunately, Luke had started at Loughborough University the previous September, so Murray now had Eileen all to himself during term time, as her elder son lived in Spain with his father. Luke had come home to spend Christmas with his mum and had actually been quite pleasant to Murray, who'd spent some time back at his own place to give the mother and son some time and space together. And now he'd flown out to Spain that morning to spend New Year with his brother and father, so Murray and Eileen would be all alone for New Year's Eve. They weren't going to do anything special, just some drinks and a takeaway, but at least they would be alone. And that was when Murray would spring his wee surprise. He thought about the contents of the bag he was carrying and gave a satisfied smile as he strode on through Romford Market.

✦   ✦   ✦

THE SHOPPING TRIP to Lakeside had been a great success.
Melv had found an off-the-peg dark grey suit that fitted him
perfectly and had teamed it with a light blue shirt and striped
grey tie. Eve had never seen him look more handsome. She
held his hand tightly with pride as they shopped in Marks
and Spencer for some bits and pieces of food to serve as
canapés that evening and for their lunch the following day.
They'd enjoyed some tapas, sitting inside the restaurant as
opposed to outside on the terrace. Even with the patio
heaters going full blast Melv knew he'd feel the cold.

'I sometimes wonder how I managed to live here for a
whole year,' he said as they took their seats.

'You were young and strong then,' Eve teased.

It was a pleasant lunch and by two-thirty they found
themselves back at home. Melv took his suit upstairs to hang
the creases out while Eve put the shopping away.

'You've got messages,' Melv said, coming into the kitch-
en. 'The light's flashing on your machine.'

'It's probably nothing important,' she said, not over-
keen to listen. 'If it's Travel Together again I'll scream. Do
you know, they hadn't even realised I'd gone and done the
Christmas break?'

They both went through to the living-room. Melv made
himself comfortable on the sofa and switched on the TV.
Eve pushed the button to listen to her message, never
expecting in a million years to hear the voice that boomed
around the living-room.

'Paraskevi, kalimera. O Spyros ime.'

'Problem?' Melv asked, seeing her turn white and realising the caller was speaking in a language he didn't

understand.

'My eldest brother. He wants me to ring him in Corfu as soon as I get this message.'

She pulled the phone towards her and dialled the number, praying as she did so that her mother was well. She waited five or six seconds and then heard the long, single sound of the Greek ringing tone. It was picked up after three rings.

'*Legete.*'

'Spyros, it's me, Evi. I've just got your message. Is everything okay?'

'No. I'm afraid it isn't. I rang you to tell you that *O Babas* died this morning.'

Eve almost dropped the phone. At first she was so grateful that it wasn't her mother, then a clammy coldness enveloped her as she registered what her brother had said.

'How?'

'He had a heart-attack, they think. A massive one to have taken him like that. He wouldn't have suffered. He had just eaten his breakfast and *I Mana mas* heard him call to her. By the time she went through he was on the floor. The doctor said he would have died instantly.'

'How is she?'

'How do you think? He was her husband for fifty-eight years. She is grief-stricken, broken.'

Eve couldn't help thinking differently; that perhaps it would have been a release, a long-awaited escape from the claustrophobic, restrictive, tight yoke of marriage for her mother.

'I was going to ring tonight, to wish you all a Happy New Year…'

'In the same way that you rang to wish us a Merry Christmas?' His tone was scathing.

'I was going to ring! I got called out on a job on Christmas Day…'

'Oh, yes! A job! The job that has kept you away from your family and your home for so long. The job that has made you a woman of the world!'

'Don't! I swear to you it was my intention to ring tonight.'

'Well, now your call would be too late. You saw our father how many times in the last twenty years? And now you will never see him again!'

'When did he or any of you ever phone me? Eh? Tell me that? When have you, or Lefteris or Iannis, or our father, ever picked up the phone to find out if I was dead or alive?'

'You chose to leave Corfu, Paraskevi. You left us, your family, and your home. Why should we ring a sister or a daughter who thinks so little of us? Why should our father ring a daughter who calls and only speaks to her mother or her sister, who never asks to speak to him?'

'He never wanted to speak to me!' she protested. 'Never! He was the one who told me never to go back to Corfu…'

'Because you left a good husband. You made a good marriage and yet life here wasn't good enough for you. Your husband wasn't good enough for you and neither was your family.'

'That's not true, Spyros! That's not true.' They were both silent for a beat. 'I want to speak to my mother.'

'She is too distraught to come to the telephone. She is lying down and Maria, Alexia and Eugenia are with her,' he said, naming his sister, his wife and his sister-in-law. 'You will have time enough to see her when you come.'

Eve's blood ran cold. As soon as her brain had registered her father's death, her mind had been racing ahead, knowing that the question of the funeral would soon be raised.

'When is the funeral?' she heard herself ask.

'January second. Friday.'

'Friday?' she echoed, the word sounding strange and foreign on her tongue, even though it was her first name. Paraskevi was the Greek for Friday. It had been shortened to Evi, which had then been anglicised to Eve.

'Call as soon as you have your flight details and one of us will pick you up from the airport. I have already spoken to Brian. He, too, is in England. Perhaps you can travel together.' It was a statement rather than a suggestion. 'You have his number?'

'I think so.'

'*Endaxi*. You can call at any time. I think none of us will sleep tonight.'

Although he didn't understand a word of Greek, Melv had known that something serious had happened from the moment Eve had started to speak. He jumped up from the sofa, taking the receiver from her hand, leading her back to sit down before he spoke.

'What's up?'

'My father died of a heart-attack this morning.'

'Oh, baby! I'm so sorry!' he took her in his arms and pulled her to him, unaware that her eyes were dry.

'I was going to call tonight. I've been going to call since Christmas Day, but then getting called out for the job got in the way and the moment was never right, so I decided to leave it and phone to wish my mother a Happy New Year. And now I can't.'

She sat up, manoeuvring herself from Melv's embrace in an attempt to stop the sudden claustrophobia, the feeling that her world was imploding.

'Have you got any brandy? You need something for the shock.'

'No, I'm fine. Really.' She took a couple of deep breaths

and found that she did feel better. 'I'm just sorry I hadn't spoken to my mother but to be honest, even if I had phoned tonight, I wouldn't have spoken to him, even though I'd told myself I would. And if I had asked for him mother would probably have said he was sleeping.

'But why?'

'Because we just…didn't speak to each other on the phone.' She ran her hands over her face. 'He was mad at me when I divorced Brian. He liked Brian, even though he wasn't Greek. *He is an honorary Greek, an honorary Corfiot*' he used to say. But he liked him because he was a good businessman and he thought that if his daughter was married to him it would be a great step along the road to prosperity for the Stefanou Family.'

'Well, I can understand that, I suppose.'

'But my happiness wasn't taken into account at all. I married Brian totally on the rebound from you, to tell you the truth. Within a couple of weeks of going home to Corfu, the Easter after Michael was born, I realised I'd made a mistake. In Brian I saw a way to leave again. Oh, don't get me wrong, I liked him. He was a good man. Is a good man. But I loved him like a brother.'

'Oh, baby! You must have been so unhappy. Why did you go through with it?'

'Because I was being a good, dutiful daughter. But also because I knew that Brian was crazy about me and I could wrap him around my finger.' She sighed and ran her fingers through her hair. 'I'm not proud of that,' she added, lifting her eyes slowly to meet Melv's gaze. 'Although he was building apartments in Corfu and his tour operator worked with our taverna and lots more all over the island, I persuaded him to move us to London and run the operation from here, the two of us together. My father could have no objections because to the world it seemed that my husband had made a decision and I, like a good wife, was following his wishes. But scarcely more than a year later, while he'd gone on a short trip to Corfu to see how the businesses were doing, I moved out. My father thought I'd gone mad. He shouted and screamed at me on the phone. He told me I was stupid, ignorant, ungrateful, a disgrace, even a whore because he was so sure I was having an affair. I mean, why else would I want to leave my husband? Every insult he could think of was poured down on my head.'

In spite of saying she was fine, her face looked drawn. Melv thought she suddenly looked exhausted.

'Well, now I can certainly see why you could never have gone back home with a black baby.'

'They said I was always the rebel. But could you blame me if I was? Night after night I used to look at my mother and my brother's fiancé, and squirm at their humiliation and their acceptance of it for the good of the business. I was horrified at the future that was sure to be ahead of me. And I refuse to accept that my mother has been happy. Well, certainly not during all the years of hard work in the taverna, made worse by having to sit watching her husband dance and flirt with tourists with no conscience, while she waited on them, smiling, being polite, never knowing which of them was her husband's current lover. And that would have been my life if I'd married a local man, if I hadn't made things happen to get out.'

She stood up and went over to the window and looked out, not turning to face him as she continued talking.

'I expect you think I was cold and calculating. I know that it looks like I used Brian, but I swear that I really tried to make a huge success of our marriage. After all, in Corfu I'd seen many marriages arranged by the families that had turned out happy and loving. That was my side of the silent bargain I made with myself. But it soon became obvious that it was never going to work in a million years.'

'Hey! I'm not judging you! Come here!' She turned and he crossed the room and took her into his arms.

'But you haven't heard the worst of it. The funeral is on Friday.'

'So soon?'

'It's the Greek custom. Burial is always one or two days after death.'

'But then you'll miss…'

'Oh, there's no way that I'm going.'

'But, it's your father's funeral.'

'And it's Michael's wedding. I've missed too much of Michael's life I'm not missing that!'

'Won't you be expected to go?'

'Oh, yes. Spyros just told me to let him know my flight details and someone will collect me at the airport. And that's just typical of him! Of them! They beckon and I am just expected to drop everything and run.'

'Probably because he was your father…'

'No, Melv! For years I've been all but dead to my father. My place is with the living not with the dead, don't you think? And we're not going to tell Michael any of this.'

'What? The man was his grandfather.'

'A grandfather he never knew. A grandfather who, I know, would never have accepted or acknowledged him. I've been foolish enough to think from time to time of taking Michael to Lefkimmi to meet them all, but it would have been a hideous, embarrassing trip if I had. My father would probably have had the heart-attack there and then when he found out I'd had a child more than thirty years ago. I must have been mad to ever have contemplated it and to have mentioned it to Michael.'

'But you know he's been so keen to find out about your side of the family. Especially since he's met some of mine.'

'I don't care!'

'Shall I call them and cancel tonight? You won't feel like an intimate family dinner…'

'No! Nothing is going to spoil tonight with Natalie and Michael. Nothing is going to cast a shadow over their wedding, either. Nothing! Tonight we carry on as planned. And when they're back from their honeymoon I'll invite them over and I'll tell him. And he'll understand why I kept quiet tonight. And if he doesn't Natalie will and she'll convince him. She's a bright girl!' she quipped. 'But not now, Melv. Please.'

'It's your choice, baby. I just don't want you to put yourself under any unnecessary strain or stress. What did your brother say, when you told him you weren't going to the funeral?'

'I didn't tell him.'

'What? You just going to not show up?'

'No. I'll ring him tomorrow, after Michael and Natalie have left. And I'll tell him I'm not going. I'll probably make an excuse about flight seats…'

'But he can check up on that.'

'Melv, please! Can we just drop it? Please?'

'Okay. It's your call.'

'Come on! Come and help me peel and chop vegetables and we can talk about anything but Corfu and fathers,' she said, taking his hand and leading him towards the kitchen.

✦   ✦   ✦

ANGELA HAD TAKEN Butterscotch for a long ride that afternoon. They'd gone alone and had galloped through the crisp, chilly countryside at full pelt both enjoying their freedom to the maximum.

True freedom is living with other people's disapproval.

She wasn't sure why that thought had come into her head. Perhaps it had been one of Annabelle's pearls of wisdom. Wherever she 'd heard it didn't matter, its source was unimportant, but Angela knew it would be the new mantra by which she lived her life. It wouldn't be other people's disapproval at her being such a bitch, which she had been, and which she'd revelled in in a perverse sort of way. Being a bitch had been how she'd coped with her guilt over her affair with Seb and the circumstances of Harry's death. But now, she would live her life with kindness and thoughtfulness towards others but she would make sure she did whatever it took to make herself happy, too. She knew that wasn't selfish, it was just doing what people had been put on earth to do. She'd spent a long time on the internet following leads and suggestions that Annabelle had given her for books and articles and it had all made fascinating reading. She was overjoyed at this gift she'd been given of a completely new way of life.

And now, on New Year's Eve, she sat crossed legged on the sofa, wearing her pyjamas, a glass of wine at her elbow and balancing her laptop so that she could continue reading. She made notes as she went and added and adjusted her *Life List*, on which she'd written out her life as she wanted it to be from now on. She took a sip of her Rioja and smiled approvingly. *I only drink good, vintage wine* was one of the details about her life that she'd written. Another was *I help someone every day without them knowing it's me.* And she'd already started that, leaving a box of groceries on her elderly neighbour's doorstep and posting twenty pounds through the letter box of a young, single-mum two streets away, whose purse had been snatched while she was out shopping. She wasn't doing this with rose coloured glasses on. She knew more than anyone that she wasn't going to be a born-again Mother Teresa. But she also knew that she was going to do her best to be the best possible version of Angela that she could. She saw her reflection in the blank 52" TV screen mounted on the living room wall and raised her glass to herself.

To a really Happy New Year, Angela!

✦   ✦   ✦

EILEEN WAS HAVING a lovely evening. She loved Luke to distraction and she would never let anyone come between her and her sons, either of them, although she sometimes wasn't convinced that Jason really deserved her unconditional love, but she was glad he'd gone off to spent New Year in Spain so that she could be alone with Murray again. After all, she might be a mother but she was also a woman who deserved to have a life of her own. And she was a woman with needs, which had been met within half an hour of Murray arriving. He'd been so glad to see her and had spent the whole evening smiling and making her laugh. Sometimes he really was Grumpy Old Man, but basically he was good and decent and she thought she loved him. Since September and Luke's departure to university, they'd been practically living together, which surprised her, as after her husband she thought she'd had enough of men. But she'd got unexpectedly close to Murray on a Travel Together holiday to India and they'd been together ever since. And now she was looking forward to going to Natalie and Michael's wedding with him on Friday.

'Another glass of wine, Eileen?' Murray filled her glass before topping up his own. 'It's quite good stuff, isn't it?'

'Lovely!' Eileen said, taking a big sip, aware that she might already be slightly tipsy. The TV was turned on but the sound was down as they waited for the countdown to the New Year, which was now less than half an hour away.

'I've got a wee something for you,' Murray said, smiling at her.

'Again?' she said, startled that he'd want sex twice in five hours.

'Oh, no, not that! Well, later perhaps. Tae see in the New Year. No, I've got something else I want tae give you. It's a special surprise. I'll just get it,' he said as he left the room.

Oh My God! He's got a ring! He's got a ring! He is going to propose!

Eileen made herself breath slowly and regularly. She felt really excited, giddy, girlie; she wanted to remember every second of the proposal and not have it pass in a blur of puffing, panting and hyperventilation.

'Close your eyes!' he called from the hallway. Eileen put her glass down on the coffee table and closed her eyes, her ear to ear grin showing her delight. She heard him come into the room and the rustle of plastic and paper. She forced herself to squeeze her eyelids tightly together to keep them shut as she was desperate to take a look.

'Open wide! Surprise!' Murray shouted.

Eileen's eyes sprung wide open. There was a loud pop as Murray, who instead of being down on one knee, was standing in the middle of the room, aimed a popper towards her. On the coffee table were toy bugles, blowers, streamers, two Chinese wishing lanterns and more poppers.

'We're going tae have our own private party!' he beamed. And just didn't understand why Eileen burst into tears.

✦   ✦   ✦

'WE'LL TAKE A cup of kindness yet for the sake of Auld Lang's Syne!'

Eve, Natalie and Michael sang out the words loudly and clearly, while Melv hummed along as the four of them stood in a circle, arms crossed in the familiar pose as Big Ben struck midnight on the TV set.

'Happy New Year!' Michael kissed his birth parents, they then kissed Natalie and then each couple took a moment to kiss and wish each other their own special private greetings.

Eve had worked hard and the evening had been a great success. As he held her Melv thought that nobody would believe the news she'd received that afternoon. Irrespective of her thoughts and feelings about her father, he was still her father and he had died. But she looked to all intents and purposes as if she was having a great time. It was probably the training and experience of her job that enabled her to do that.

But it was no act, Eve was enjoying herself. She was with the three people she loved most in the world, sharing a special meal as Michael and Natalie counted down the hours until they would marry. She had put the news of her father's death out of her mind, along with having to call Spyros back tomorrow and tell him she wasn't going. She would deal with all that in the morning; tonight was about joy and celebration.

'I feel quite pleasantly pissed,' Natalie said, leaning against Michael's arm and kissing it. 'But I'd better not have any more. I've got a big day tomorrow, not to mention the day after and I don't want to do it all with a headache and bags under my eyes.'

'You will look delightful, I'm sure,' Melv said, smiling at her, fully understanding and appreciating his son's choice of bride. 'To Natalie!' he said, raising his glass as Eve and Michael joined him, 'and to Michael!' he added and Eve and Natalie joined in.

'So, that's it! A New Year just beginning the old one well and truly over and done with!' Eve said.

'I hate all the maudlin stuff that goes with New Year, you know, all the resolutions and looking forward and all of that,' Michael said.

'Well, that's nice!' Natalie looked at him in mock-horror. 'This year, more than any other, is about looking forward and all of that, isn't it?'

'Yes it is. This year is special. I'm just speaking generally,' he said. 'I've almost always gone out on New Year's Eve. You know, you feel like some sort of social misfit if you're not at a wild party or at least in a pub, but I can honestly say that I've never really enjoyed myself. There's always an atmosphere of false bonhomie. This has been so much better, just being here the four of us. Thank you for organising it, Eve,' he said, leaning across and kissing her. She beamed with pleasure. It had been a very successful evening and she was really glad she hadn't spoilt it by telling Michael about her father and her family's expectation that she would be there for his funeral. It would have ruined what had been a really perfect evening.

The two couples slowly wound the dinner-party to a close. They stacked the dirty plates in the dishwasher, put cling-film over the leftovers before putting them in the fridge and then they said their goodnights and each went to their own bedroom, where they made love to each other, passionately, yet quietly enough so that the couple in the next room could only guess at what they might be doing.

DAY NINE

✦

I WILL NEVER *understand bloody women!*
Murray ate his breakfast in silence as Eileen banged crockery at the sink. He chewed on his toast and for the twentieth time went over what had happened the previous evening, when all he'd been trying to do was make the evening more enjoyable for them. Yet she'd got upset and started crying over a few poppers and a couple of Chinese lanterns. When he'd asked her what was wrong she'd just stormed off to bed saying that he just didn't have a clue as far as women were concerned. He'd followed her but she asked him to leave her alone. She said she had a headache and wanted to sleep. So he left her and went back downstairs and finished the wine and the rest of the takeaway and watched the Hogmanay party from Edinburgh with Lulu sitting beside him, her head in his lap, where Eileen's should have been. And by the time the programme had finished and he'd gone up to bed she was sound asleep. Then, this morning he'd tried to make conversation with her about their plans for the rest of the day and Natalie and Michael's wedding tomorrow and all he'd got was one-word answers or grunts.

Perhaps it's her age.

Although she wasn't yet fifty, Murray knew that some women started the menopause in their forties. And he'd noticed a little whisker on her chin the other day, which was quite possibly a sign that she was going through The Change. Perhaps he should approach the subject with her.

Perhaps not!

He was already getting his head bitten off for nothing as it was.

As she bashed pots and plates at the sink, Eileen's thoughts ran from thinking she may have over-reacted last night and feeling foolish to think he might have been about to propose, to rage at how he'd left her alone when she'd asked him to.

On New Year's Eve!

The stupid man hadn't realised that when she'd said she wanted to be left alone that he was supposed to have said that it was New Year's Eve and he wouldn't dream of it and to have taken her hand in an assertive, macho manner and led her back downstairs. Instead he'd gone out of the bedroom and back downstairs to watch TV. And he hadn't come back up until almost half-past one when she'd pretended to be asleep. And then this morning, he'd acted as if nothing had happened last night, talking about going out for a walk later and what time they'd have to set off for the wedding the following day. It had almost made her eat another couple of slices of toast and jam. And he was talking as if it was just another day. He hadn't even wished her a Happy New Year!

But you didn't wish him one, either…

The Voice of Reason in her head was seriously pissing her off. She'd already made her mind up that if he *should* try to get it out of her why she'd been upset that she would just say she'd been overcome by not being with her sons. There was no way she was going to admit she thought he was going to ask her to marry him. She put the last of the serving dishes away in the cupboard, industriously wiped the draining board down and dropped the tea towel into the washing machine to be bleached with the others later.

'Well, if you'll move over Lulu I'll come and stay in the dog house with you, will I? he asked the dog, patting her head as she impatiently sat beside him waiting for her morning walk.

'Are you being funny?' Eileen was not amused.

'I'm just trying tae break the ice between us. I dinae have a clue as tae what I said or did to upset you last night, Eileen, but I think you're carrying this silent treatment a bit far. Whatever it was, I didnae do it on purpose and I'm sorry.'

Eileen grabbed his dirty breakfast plate and mug, tutting loudly, as she'd been so wrapped up in her thoughts she'd forgotten the washing up wasn't finished. She banged them into the sink, sloshed washing up liquid over them and turned the tap on so much that water splashed back over the newly-dried draining-board.

'Eileen, I'm getting a wee bit tired of all this. I'm going tae get myself dressed and take Lulu for a walk. You're welcome tae join us, in fact, we'd both like that very much, wouldn't we Lu? But if you'd rather stay here then that's up tae you. But when I come back, unless you're prepared tae talk and tell me what the hell it is I'm supposed tae have done then I'll be taking myself back off tae Purfleet where I'll nae be bothering you.' He stood up and walked out of the kitchen, Lulu dancing at his heels.

'I thought you were going to ask me to marry you!'

✦   ✦   ✦

IT WAS ALMOST eleven o'clock before Michael and Natalie

had left. He was driving her back to her parents' where a manicurist was coming at one o'clock to do her nails and then going to meet up with his best man.

'Don't get drunk, will you?' Eve said, picking an imaginary cotton off his sweater as they crowded together in the small hallway to say their goodbyes.

'I've already warned him of the dire consequences if he does!' Natalie said. 'Believe me, he'll wish he hadn't!'

'Well, have a lovely last day as singles,' Eve said. 'In just over twenty-four hours you'll be Mr and Mrs Brown!' Her voice showed her delight at the idea.

'Thanks again, Eve, for such a fabulous meal last night. I bet I won't fit in my wedding dress now, and it'll be all your fault!' Natalie teased, bending forward to give Eve a huge hug. 'Bye, biological mother-in-law,' she said. 'Bye, biological father-in-law,' she said to Melv, hugging and kissing him, too. They both laughed at her name for them.

'I suppose that's what we are, technically speaking. But I wonder if there is an actual term for it?' Melv asked.

'It doesn't matter even if there is. Eve and Melv will do nicely,' Eve said.

She and Melv stood arm-in-arm on the front doorstep watching as Natalie and Michael got into the BMW, having put their overnight bags into the spacious boot. Michael turned the key and they both wound down the windows, in spite of the cold, and waved their arms at Eve and Melv until the car had turned at the t-junction and was out of sight. They both gave involuntary sighs and went back inside, Melv shivering as they did so.

'Do you think it might snow again?' he asked. 'It feels cold enough to.'

'They said no more snow, just to be careful of the ice as it might turn colder before all the slush had melted away. I hope he drives carefully,' she added.

'Of course he will.'

'And I think the idea of some snow at the wedding is quite appealing. Well, as long as it's only a smattering and not a bloody great avalanche that traps us in or out of Hertfordshire.'

They went into the living-room and sat down. Melv said nothing, wanting to let her decide to call her brother in her own time, when she was ready. In spite of her wonderful show for Natalie and Michael, Melv could see that now they'd gone her expression had changed.

'Right! I'm going to make a coffee and then I'm going to call Spyros.'

'Would you like me to make it?' he offered. She thought about it for a second.

'Yes, please. No point in procrastinating. Let's do it!'

Melv went into the kitchen to give her some privacy, even though he wouldn't have understood what she was saying. He didn't want to see her upset but he didn't want to leave her either, in case she felt alone and unsupported. So he made the coffee as quickly as he could and went back into the living-room with it.

Spyros had picked up the phone as if he had been sitting beside it waiting for her call.

'*Legete.*'

'It's me, Spyro,' she said. 'How is Mum today?'

'Much as she was yesterday,' was his curt reply. 'So, are you flying Olympic to Athens and then onto Corfu or taking the Ryanair direct with Brian?' he asked.

'Neither.'

'What do you mean.'

'I mean, I won't be at the funeral.'

'But there is room on the plane. On both routes. I checked. Brian offered to book your ticket for you…'

'I can't be at the funeral because I have already made

plans to do something else.'

'What? What?' He shouted so loudly that Eve feared he, too, might have a heart-attack. 'It is your father's funeral. You have to be here!'

Eve wasn't going to let him bully her. She'd made her decision and nothing would make her change it.

'I don't have to be there. I've just told you that I have other plans, plans that I can't cancel.'

'What kind of woman, what kind of daughter, would miss her own father's funeral because she has *other plans?*' he mocked.

'The sort of daughter who's been treated as an outcast and an embarrassment to the family for most of her adult life.'

'So it is our fault that you behaved like a madwoman? It is our fault that you ran off and left a good man, humiliating our family, blackening our name in front of everyone.'

'Don't talk to me about humiliation, Spyro! You wouldn't know what humiliation was if it jumped up and bit you on the arse. Humiliation, *pedimou*, is what you've done to Alexia since you first met her. It's what our father, our wonderful father did to our mother all their married life.'

'You really have taken leave of your senses. I don't know what you're talking about. I don't know what any of this… this…nonsense you're spouting has to do with not coming to the funeral.'

'You just don't get it, do you?' she said. She spoke icily, yet quietly, refusing to raise her voice to match his. 'It has everything to do with it. It has everything to do with why I left. I wasn't going to be the little Corfiot wife who sat meekly by while her husband cheated on her with a cheap tourist every night. I wasn't going to put up with all of that. That's why I left! That's why I couldn't stay. Because of what I saw with my own eyes, because of the example you and Lefteris and our father set. When it suited him he sent me away to England and then when I wanted to go of my own accord he refused to hear of it. He treated me like his property instead of his daughter. He only ever saw me in terms of what I could do for him and his taverna…'

'Our taverna! Ours! It was as much yours as it was his or mine. It belongs to our family and that's what it's always been about – the family pulling together and prospering.'

'But at what price? Eh? And when I did leave, he treated me as if I was a pariah. He called me every insult he could think of, including whore!'

'That was because he was angry. He didn't mean it.'

'Didn't he? He managed to stay angry for almost thirty years. When I came back he barely acknowledged me; wouldn't speak to me…'

'Because you came back with anger, too, and attitude! You came to visit like a foreign dignitary instead of a member of our family. You acted as if we should be grateful to see you. If you had come to him and asked for forgiveness you would have seen him behave differently.'

'I just love the way you've turned this all around on me!' She jumped up from the sofa. Her coffee splashed a large, brown stain over the oatmeal carpet. Melv rushed into the kitchen for a cloth. 'But I refuse to feel guilty about it. He chose to ignore me; he chose to treat me like an exile. So don't even try to make me feel bad for staying away from his funeral, because you'd be wasting your time. Let me speak to Mum.'

'She doesn't want to speak to you.'

'Don't tell me that! I want to tell her myself that I won't be there…'

'I will tell her. I will tell her how her daughter disrespects her and the family name and also how she disrespects the memory of her father by refusing to come to his funeral.

'You can tell her what you like. I'll write to her. I'll come and see her next week or the week after and tell her face to face why I could't be at the funeral.'

'Why you didn't want to be at the funeral!'

'Yes! That's true, I won't deny it. I don't want to be there.'

'And what is it that is so important that it keeps you away? A job? Where are you taking this bunch of tourists? The sewers of Paris? The whore-houses of Athens?'

'I'm going to my son's wedding!'

Melv knew what Eve must have said by the look on her face and the moments of silence from the tinny voice booming from the earpiece.

'What son?'

'My son. The one I had when I was studying in England when I was eighteen. The one I gave up for adoption. The one whose life I missed out on until three years ago. And all because I was too afraid to bring him back to Corfu with me. And because of the colour of his skin.' The sharp intake of breath was loud in her ear.

'I don't believe you!'

'Then don't! You asked me why and I've told you the truth. Whether you choose to believe me or not is up to you. But I have a son; a fine, good, kind, honest, honourable man of whom I am immensely proud. And tomorrow he's getting married. And I have every intention of being there.'

'You are a disgrace to this family!'

'Good! I'm glad, Because the feeling is absolutely mutu-al. My son has asked about his Greek grandparents, aunts and uncles and cousins. But I would be too ashamed to take him to meet you. Not because of him. He was born out of a loving relationship and his adoptive parents have done a wonderful job raising him. I could not wish for a finer son. No, I would be ashamed of all of you and your bitter, twisted, narrow-mindedness.'

'You are no longer a Stefanou! You are no longer welcome here!'

'I haven't been a Stefanou for a very long time. And if you recall, I was never welcome there. Tell Mum I love her and that I'll see her soon.' And she put down the phone. The silence in the room was almost tangible. Then Eve collapsed onto the sofa and cried her eyes out. Knowing there was nothing he could say, Melv held her in his arms until she became calm and silent.

✦   ✦   ✦

WHY DIDN'T I keep my big mouth shut?

Waves of embarrassment kept flooding over Eileen every time she thought about what she'd blurted out and Murray's reaction to it. She didn't even know where it had come from. If she actually thought about it in the cold light of day, she had absolutely no wish or desire to get married. And Murray had made it perfectly clear that the thought hadn't even crossed his mind.

'What?' he'd said, striding back into the kitchen. 'You thought I was going tae ask you tae marry me? What gave you that idea?'

'It was New Year's Eve… You said you had a surprise…we've done nothing but talk about Natalie and Michael's wedding for the last three months…'

'But they're kids! They're getting wed for the first time. We've both been married before, and I dinnae have the slightest inclination tae do it again.'

'Well, that's settled that then, hasn't it?' Eileen said, stung by his words. 'I don't know what came over me. I must have been drunk to think that you would do anything as romantic as propose on New Year's Eve. No! Your idea of a romantic night in is a couple of poppers and a plastic trumpet. Whoopee-doo! Murray really pushed the boat out!'

'I cannae win with you. I thought I was giving us a nice evening as we were alone…'

'What? A bottle of cheap wine and a quick visit from the Domino's man? Other women are being taken to smart restaurants and chic parties. I've got a bottle of Pinot Plonkio and a ham and pineapple stuffed crust! Be still my beating heart!'

'But you never said you wanted us tae go out…'

'I shouldn't have to say! You're a Scot, for God's sake! You boast about New Year's Eve. We English are rubbish at it. Just like we're rubbish at so much according to you! *Nobody's as welcoming as the Scots! Nobody does Hogmanay like us!*' She mimicked him. 'All I hear from you is English-bashing. Well, you really pushed the boat out, didn't you?'.

'I dinnae know what you're talking about. I dinnae English-bash! I live in England. I voted 'NO' for God's sake!'

'And then you've got the cheek to say you've got no inclination to marry me! Well, I wouldn't now if you begged me.'

'You're taking it wrong. I didnae mean tae say it like that! It came out wrong…'

'Go on! Get out! Get out!' She'd thrown the dishcloth at him and gone and locked herself in the bathroom until she'd heard him leave. She sat on the edge of the bathtub with tears of anger and embarrassment rolling down her cheeks. His words had been so hurtful; she had felt completely and utterly rejected by them, leading to this morning's reaction. It hurt her deeply to think that he would never marry her, even though she wasn't sure she even wanted him to. But he had been adamant: *'I dinnae have the slightest inclination to do it again.'* His words caused fresh tears to spring into her eyes as they spun round and round in her head. She chided herself angrily as she stood up and washed her face, then she opened the bathroom door and went into the bedroom to get dressed. She went downstairs and opened the fridge. She picked up a chunk of Cheddar to make herself Welsh Rarebit. But then she opened it up again and slammed the cheese back inside deciding he wasn't worth comfort eating over.

'Come on, Lulu! Let's go for a long walk it'll make us both feel better,' she said, going to get her lead from the kitchen cupboard. There was a note on the table.

Ring me about what time I should pick you up tomorrow. I'd suggest about 12 o'clock. Murray

She screwed it into a tight ball and tossed it into the pedal bin.

Very short and sweet! No sign of being sorry.

Eileen and Lulu walked for two hours. When they got home Eileen gave Lulu food and water and made herself a cup of tea. Then she picked up her mobile phone. He hadn't called while she'd been out; nobody had. She went into *text*.

I've decided not to go to the wedding. I'll ring and make my own excuses. I'll drop your stuff at yours and leave it in the garage while you're out tomorrow. Shame it's ended like this, but I don't want to ever see you again. We aren't right for each other.

Then she phoned her *Compulsive Eaters* sponsor, Chris, told her what had happened and discussed her own feelings and reaction for more than half an hour. She knew she still had issues with rejection as evidenced by her actions earlier that day. But what she found startling, were the feelings of anger and resentment she'd obviously been harbouring against Murray. The ferocity and speed with which she'd spat insults at him had shocked her. She didn't understand just where they had come from and that had upset her. Too much of her compulsive overeating was rooted in resentments. But, she also accepted that although her time with Murray had been fun and in her own way she loved him – and she really did believe that he loved her – they weren't soul mates.

I settled for second-best once, I'm not going to settle for it again because I deserve better.

She took out her special journal, the book where she noted down all her innermost thoughts, hopes, dreams and confessions and started to write. She knew that she had to finish with Murray because she would feel awkward in his company in future and if one day he should suggest marriage, she would never know if he was doing so simply out of pity or because she 'd given him a bollocking. Although it really wouldn't matter; she wasn't ready to marry him, or anyone. And she certainly didn't want his pity. As her pen flowed, she thanked Murray for the good times, forgave him for his insensitivity and released him. She recognised her own part in their split up and apologised. And then she wrote about being on her own again and was amazed and pleased to see she wasn't afraid. In fact, she felt quite relieved; relieved that she wouldn't have to choose between her boyfriend and her son. Relieved that she could do exactly as she pleased.

I enjoy my own company. I am my own best friend… I only deserve to be in the best of relationships. No more second best. Perhaps I am destined to be single all the way through the rest of my life, and if I am, that's okay. It's more than okay. My life is happy and fulfilled.

And then she unwrapped the first of the six bars of chocolate she'd bought during her walk with Lulu and began to eat it.

✦ ✦ ✦

EVEN THOUGH HE'D been expecting it for the last three hours, Murray jumped as his mobile beeped out the message alarm. He grabbed it from the coffee table, a smile on his face.

So! She's seen sense. Silly woman!

The smile fell from his lips as he opened and read the message.

✦ ✦ ✦

'NO MORE FOR me, mate,' Michael said, shaking his head. 'I've already had a skinful and I don't want to wake up wasted in the morning.'

'Oh, come on! Just one more!' Josh, his best man said. 'This time tomorrow you'll be well and truly handcuffed.'

'No, mate. We did all our celebrating on the stag do,' Michael said, wincing at the memory of a long weekend in Dublin in early December with a dozen of his mates. 'I'm ready for bed.'

Josh shook his head in disbelief, but he was secretly proud of his mate for being sensible. He loved Michael, who'd been his best friend since the day they'd started senior school together and was proud and honoured to have been asked to be his best man. He liked Natalie, too, and could see just what Michael saw in her and how they were so right for each other; she bubbly, out-going, gobby; he quietly mature, sensible and sensitive. They made a great couple and everyone loved them.

'I'm going up. I want to talk to Natalie one more time tonight and I don't want to wake her up.'

The two friends left the bar, went up to their adjoining

rooms, shook hands, shared a man-hug and then both went inside. Michael had barely closed the door when he dialled her number. She answered sleepily on the first ring.

'Hello.'

'Did I wake you up? Sorry.'

'S'alright. I've only just got into bed. I was waiting for you to ring. Nice evening?'

'We just sat in the bar and had a few beers. Getting into bed now because I want to be fresh and clear-headed for tomorrow.'

'Good! I was dreading you saying you were naked and chained to a lamp-post.'

'Who told you?'

'Ha! Ha!' she said sarcastically. He grimaced guiltily at the thought of how that very nearly happened in Dublin. But he had been chained to the stripper instead.

'So, this time tomorrow, I'll be calling you Mrs Brown. That is…erm…if you turn up. You are going to turn up, aren't you?'

'Has a rag doll got cloth tits?' she asked, laughing. 'I'll be there. Just make sure you are. I don't want any of this having to keep on riding round the block because there's no sign of the groom.'

'You won't have to. I'll be there early. I love you, Nat.'

'Love you, too, Michael. And I'm so glad it's you I'm marrying!'

DAY TEN

✦

FRIDAY THE SECOND of January was bright and crisp, with the forecast suggesting the possibility of light snow later in the day. Natalie had been awake since seven o'clock, finding it impossible to sleep with such excitement ahead of her. She lay in bed and looked round her bedroom at the photo-covered wall; from gappy-toothed seven-year-old schoolgirl with her hair escaping from her ponytail, to adolescent actress, to teenage tap-dancer, to beach-babe. There were photos alone, with her parents, with her sister, with her nieces as newborns and more recently with Michael, the photo of him proposing to her from the back of a kneeling elephant at the Taj Mahal taking pride of place. It was a wall that was full with such memories and that told the story of her life up until today. And today was the start of a new chapter as Mrs Michael Brown.

✦　✦　✦

IT SEEMED AS if it was only a few weeks since they had all been together and not almost three years. Suzanne, Stewart, Murray, Jo, Dave, Frances, Grace and Trevor all stood beaming, delighted to be in each other's company again.

'Well, you dinnae get any thinner, do you?' Murray said to Suzanne, releasing her from a hug and looking at her ample bosom which appeared to have a life of its own under the long, flowing, brown, velvet kaftan she was wearing with a mustard jacket.

'Well she's not normal weight, is she?' Stewart immediately jumped in to defend his beloved.

She certainly isn't!

Murray didn't really understand why the others were giving him dirty looks; he'd only said what the rest of them must surely be thinking.

'I'm pregnant!' Suzanne sang out. 'Expecting the second week in March.'

'Oh sorry. I didnae know. Congratulations.'

'Yes, and we're sorry we couldn't invite you all to our wedding, but it was a small, quiet affair that we organised as soon as we knew we were going to be parents,' Stewart beamed. 'Just a registry office, but nice.'

'Sorry, Stew, I can't hear you over that jacket,' Dave roared with laughter at his old joke, and at Stewart's green, tartan dinner jacket.

'There goes another rib!' Stewart gave his usual reply. But it felt good to be together and poking good-natured fun at each other.

'I've got some photos on my phone.' Suzanne pulled it out of her bag and started fiddling with the buttons and swiping the screen to find them to show to Frances, Jo and Grace.

'So, 'ow you bin? Thought you was with a woman,' Dave said to Murray.

'Aye. So did I.'

'What 'appened then?'

'It all got a bit too intense. Turns out she wanted a ring

on her finger and I didnae want tae put one on it, so we've called it a day.' Murray had decided that was going to be his story. After he'd got Eileen's text the previous day he'd phoned her to talk but she wouldn't pick up any of his twenty or so calls. He sat alone in the darkness of his house in Purfleet for several hours, more upset than he would ever admit to being. He'd really thought that with Eileen he'd found his future. His comments about not wanting to get married had been said with bravado and to hide his vulnerability because he wasn't sure if she'd been serious or not and his ego could not have taken the rejection if she'd been joking. And it had all gone horribly wrong. Now there was no future; now there was no Eileen. He gulped.

Pull yourself together, for God's sake!

'So, apart from yous two,' he said, pointing at Suzanne and Stewart, 'the rest of us are all still single, then!' Dave observed.

'Well, I am,' Grace said, putting her hand up, 'and very happy to be so, too.'

'Still working, Detective Chief Superintendent?' Dave asked her.

'The Guv's retired!' she said. 'Hoo-bloody-ray!'

'Got lots of plans for your retirement, Grace?' Jo asked.

'Yes, indeed. I'm going to Australia mid-January to spend three months touring. Driving, all over. And later in the year I'm going on a cruise to Hawaii and Alaska.'

'Blimey! Sounds fabulous,' Dave said.

'Well, why not? I've certainly worked hard enough for it.'

'Don't blame you at all, Grace,' Frances said. 'I want to do something like that.'

'Yeh, but you wanna do it with some young bloke!' Dave teased, shutting up the moment he saw the warning glare she gave him. He knew he'd better keep his mouth shut about Milos.

'I've heard from Olivia,' Frances said. 'She had a car-crash in the snow on her way home from the Blue Boar.'

'Nevva!'

'Yes. Apparently the snow started coming down very heavily and she couldn't see and smashed into a crash barrier.'

'Was she 'urt?'

'Broken collar bone, twisted knee, black eyes, but nothing too bad. And apparently, she's met a very nice young constable who was in the police patrol car that found her.'

'Well, every cloud and all that!' Grace said. 'Was she someone you met over Christmas, then?'

'Yes. Nice girl. I met her in Turkey during the summer,' Frances said. 'We were both on a Travel Together tennis holiday. Don't ask!' she added quickly, seeing Suzanne's expression. 'And when I said I was going on a Christmas break she booked it, too.' She 'd asked Olivia during their phone call why she'd just run off at the end of the break and she'd said she just wanted to get away early. Frances thought it might be more than that, but she decided not to push it. Besides, in spite of her injuries, Olivia seemed very happy, especially when she talked about her new beau.

Murray tried to put on his best beaming smile as he and Frances turned to Trevor while Dave turned to Jo and Grace.

'I was on the same Travel Togevva Christmas break as Frances and guess who turned up to the black-tie ball on the last night?' Jo shook her head. 'Only Deano! Remember 'im?'

Oh, yes! I remember him all right!

'Of course I do,' she smiled and said, as she thought of the dark, handsome, married man with the bright turquoise eyes, which turned out to be lenses. He had been quite a charmer and Jo was sure that if he hadn't had his accident then their holiday friendship would have turned into a holiday romance. After all, she'd guessed he was married long before the accident and the arrival of his wife, but as such he was probably the only member of the group who wouldn't have wanted to carry on seeing her when they got back home. But, they had never had the chance to find out.

Divine intervention!

'And how is he?' she asked.

'Yeh! Good! On 'is own, no girl-friend or nothin'. He was tryin' to get off with a righ' posh bird called Angela, but she weren't 'aving none of it.'

'You still got the ladies of the parish fighting over you, Trevor?' Frances teased him. He coloured.

'I rarely go to church now. Only once in a while. And when I do go I don't stay behind for tea and biscuits. But I do still do my Spanish classes. I'm taking an exam in the Spring,' he beamed.

'Oh, good for you! Good luck!'

'Well, looks like we'll all have tae book another Travel Together holiday,' Murray said, trying to look on the positive side, gaining an irrational pleasure and consolation from the fact that the others were still all single. Dave had decided not to say anything about Miss P, not wanting to put the mockers on himself and his wonderful, new relationship. He'd have to form a pact with Frances; he'd keep quiet about her locking out the waiter if she kept quiet about Penny. He'd find a moment to get her on her own.

'Oh, here he comes!' Stewart had caught sight of Michael and Josh coming into the bar, with his parents. Everyone crowded round to hug, kiss or shake his hand as he showed genuine pleasure at seeing them.

'My parents, Alice and Bertram,' he said, introducing them as the group stepped forward to shake hands with them, 'And this is my best man, Josh.'

They chatted together, sipping champagne, eager to catch up with each other's news and wondering what had happened to other members of the Antigua holiday group.

'Celestyna! Will you come and join us?' Murray called to a slim, girl with purple hair, dressed in a black and cream mini-dress, carrying a black maxi-coat over her arm who stood a little unsurely by the door. 'This is Celestyna, everyone! She was with us on the India trip. The one where Michael proposed.' The group introduced themselves to Celestyna and Michael gave her a kiss before looking at his watch.

'There's plenty of time yet,' Bertram said to him. 'If we leave at two-thirty we will be at the church in less than five minutes. In plenty of time for a three o'clock wedding.'

'I don't want to be late,' Michael said.

'Have you listened to a word I've just said?' his father rebuked him gently. 'Josh! Your job as best man is to quieten the bridegroom's nerves, I believe.'

'Yes it is. I'll get him another beer!'

'So, no Graham?' Murray asked Celestyna.

'No. No Graham. We have not been in touch since the India trip ended.'

'Really? I thought you two were making plans…'

'No. We said goodbye on the train and it was the end of the holiday and the end of the holiday romance, too.' She gave a smile and a shrug. 'And Eileen? She is not here today?'

'Apparently not.' Murray looked around as if checking she wasn't there.

'So it was just a holiday romance for you, too?'

'Indeed! Now, can I get you another wee drink?' he asked, lightly taking her elbow and guiding her back towards the bar, thinking the day suddenly looked much brighter.

'Wow! You look stunning, Eve.'

Eve blushed but took the compliment from Michael, followed by his wolf-whistle as she and Melv walked into the bar. A group of familiar faces turned to look at them, each breaking into broad smiles at seeing her and Melv. She walked forward with her arms out wide to greet her son. The suit felt comfortable on her and she knew that it had been worth every penny of the almost two hundred pounds that it had cost. The short-sleeved, old-gold, lace dress was long and fitted her curves beautifully. The matching, peplum-jacket was classy and unusual, and her gold and black fascinator complemented the outfit beautifully. She actually did feel attractive. She kissed Alice, who looked like an exotic bird in her turquoise and fuchsia dress and pashmina and large fuchsia hat with frilly bow. She kissed Bertram who, like his son and the best man, was dressed in a dark navy-blue suit with mauve shirt and purple striped tie. The best man gave her a pink and purple button hole, the same as Alice's and gave Melv his, a single purple rose the same as Michael, Bertram and himself.

Eve turned to greet the others who were queuing up to kiss her, genuinely delighted to see them all again.

'Long time no see, innit?' Dave joked, loudly as he kissed her on the cheek and then shook hands with Melv. After chatting to Jo, Grace and Trevor, who she hadn't seen since Antigua, she congratulated Suzanne and Stewart on their wedding and pending parenthood, looking at the photos on Suzanne's phone and making encouraging sounds about their bohemian wedding outfits; a white suit with a long skirt covered in pink roses for Suzanne and blue trousers with a turquoise Hawaiian shirt for Stewart.

'We wanted something non-traditional,' Suzanne explained.

It had been that, all right!

Eve chided herself for her bitchy thought. Suzanne and Stewart were two of the nicest people that had ever been on a Travel Together holiday. Both were wide-eyed innocents with no malice and that was a lot more than she could say for a lot of the people she'd met over the years. Alice took her arm, while sipping her sherry. She drank little, but as today was her son's wedding day she was going to make an exception.

It was a strange moment, Eve thought afterwards when she relived it. It was almost as if the world had slowed right down and almost stopped. The muzak that had been playing in the bar was silent for about ten seconds, before the loop restarted and every single conversation between them had gone quiet when Alice dropped her bombshell.

'I think that as Michael's birth parents you two should be sitting on the top table with us,' she said to Eve. 'I've told Michael to make sure he mentions you in his speech. We are so thrilled that the two of you are here to share in our special day.' She kissed Eve on the cheek, totally unaware of the nine Travel Together heads that whipped round to look at her, each wondering if they had heard correctly, their minds racing as they tried to digest this unbelievable piece of information, their desire to know the full story rampant.

'Did she say Eve was Michael's mother?' Murray asked out loud, causing Frances to dig him sharply in the ribs.

'I think we'd better drink up,' Josh said, looking at his watch, grateful to see that it was twenty-eight minutes past two and very eager to change the subject.

Michael mouthed, *'Sorry. You okay?'* to Eve. She nodded back and smiled. In one way it felt like a bit of a relief that the truth had come out. And she suspected that none of them would ask her about it; that would probably be left to Natalie and Michael to explain when they came back from honeymoon. Doubtless   discreet   and   not-so-discreet messages and text would be sent. She really didn't care. Telling Spyros the truth had given her such a lift; a boulder she'd been unaware she'd been carrying had been removed from her back. She would take handling the story of her son, as it inevitably rippled through the Travel Together community, in her stride. People would be curious; that was human nature. But quite honestly, it was nobody's business but hers, Melv's and Michael's.

And NOTHING is going to spoil this afternoon and this evening!

She walked out, one arm linked with Alice, who was still totally unaware of how she'd just put her foot in it, and her other with Melv, as the wedding party made its way through the chilly afternoon following Michael's wide strides to walk the five hundred yards to the quaint, old, picturesque church of St Mary's. The Travel Together friends followed at a discreet distance, whispering and wondering over what they had just learned. All agreeing on one thing; Eve and Melv made a very handsome couple.

✦   ✦   ✦

MICHAEL THOUGHT HIS heart would burst with love and happiness as he turned to greet his beautiful bride who came down the aisle of the packed, candle-lit church on her father's arm, a vision of loveliness in a shimmering silver and pure white wedding dress, a slim, silver angora cape round her shoulders against the cold and a delicate crystal tiara on her head, fixed to a long silver train. She looked like a Disney Princess or the Ice Queen from a children's storybook. Violet, Daisy and Rose toddled behind her in shiny, white dresses, with purple sashes, carrying little sprays of lilac roses and Leanne, classy and chic in a purple dress with purple and white bouquet brought up the rear. Michael could barely catch his breath and he couldn't take his eyes off Natalie; his love, adoration and devotion etched on his face, so obvious to all those present that many of them were already wiping tears from their eyes.

The ceremony was starkly beautiful in its simplicity; the vows tender and traditional. Within twenty minutes the newly-married couple were making their way back down the aisle to the obvious delight of the congregation, who were smiling, cheering, wiping their eyes and clapping loudly. They all piled out of the church then stopped in their tracks as the unmistakable opening notes of One, from A Chorus Line, took over from the Wedding March. From round both corners of the church building, Natalie's senior dancers, dressed in gold tailcoats, top hats and tap shoes, defying the cold weather went into their song and dance routine across the Church's courtyard and pathway. Phones flew from bags, flashes lit up the grey afternoon and everyone, without exception sang along. As the number reached its climax, the dancers formed a guard of honour for Natalie and her handsome new husband to walk down on their way to the church gate.

'I love you sooooo much!' Natalie said, grabbing her groom and planting a huge kiss on his lips, knowing, just knowing without being told that organising the number had been his doing. Tears welled up in her eyes as she looked round at all the people she loved, sharing in the celebrations on the happiest day of her life, including these talented young women who had danced at her school for the last twelve years, since she'd first opened the doors and they had been just primary-school kids. Michael held her close, their heads together, his black braids a stunning contrast against her shimmering silver and delicate crystals.

Eve thought they were the most dazzling, striking couple she had ever seen. She swelled with pride at the sight of her handsome son and Natalie who was beyond radiant. Tears of happiness rolled unchecked down her cheeks as she watched them.

Please let them always be as happy as they are today!

Melv squeezed her hand before raising it to his lips. She smiled at him and saw he was fighting to keep his emotions in check. All the wedding guests, being led, of course, by the singles' group of friends, linked arms, kicked their legs and sang at the tops of their voices as snowflakes began to fall upon them like gentle, white confetti. The scene would remain for ever in Eve's memory as a snapshot which defined and captured pure happiness.

Plenty of people would continue to book with Travel Together, hoping that just maybe, this time, the man or woman of their dreams would be there, on this holiday, waiting for them. Eve always told people not to expect to find the love of their life on a singles' holiday, but today her son and his bride were proof that sometimes a miracle happened. Michael had booked to seek out and find his biological father, and he had been exceptionally lucky, not just because he'd found his biological mother, too.

But, because he had found his own, very special, singular sensation: Natalie.

The One.

THE END

Printed in Great Britain
by Amazon